THE SHADOW PARADOX

THE SHADOW ENFORCER SERIES BOOK THREE

N. M. THORN

The Shadow Paradox

By N.M. Thorn

Copyright © 2021 by N.M. Thorn. All rights reserved.

nmthornauthor@gmail.com

This is a work of fiction. Any resemblance to actual persons living or dead, businesses, events, or locales is purely coincidental. Reproduction in whole or part of this publication without express written consent is strictly prohibited.

Cover art design by Original Book Cover Designs

Edited by Spirit Editorial

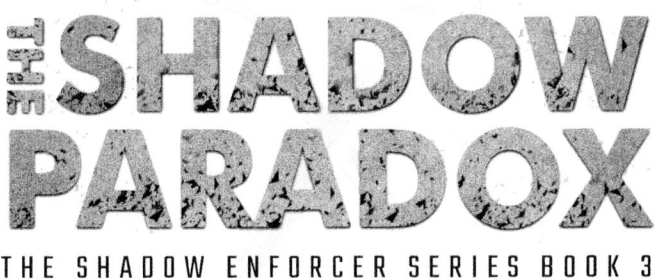

THE SHADOW ENFORCER SERIES BOOK 3

N.M. THORN

PROLOGUE

* * *

***Selo Preobrazhenskoye, Russia.
August 1689***

A SOFT VEIL of clouds stretched across the midnight sky, and the silvery light of the full moon barely broke through it, giving a mystical glimmer to their fluffy edges. The door of a large, wooden palace opened with a light squeak, and the figure of a woman dressed all in black rushed along the dark pathway and down the hill toward the river Yauza.

She didn't stop and didn't look back until she reached the narrow strip of a beach well-hidden between the thick shrubbery and tall trees. For a brief moment, she froze in place, checking the area around to make sure no one had followed her from the palace and was watching her now. As a light wind rushed across the beach, rippling the dark waters of the river, the earthy smell of fresh greenery and moss touched her nostrils, and she sucked in a deep breath, visibly relaxing.

Lifting the heavy folds of her black dress, she lowered herself to the cold sand and raised the dark veil, exposing her face. She looked up at the sky, and her large eyes flooded with darkness, widening. Reaching toward the invisible moon, she started to chant, her body moving from side to side, following the rhythm of her incantation.

As her voice grew stronger and deeper, her appearance began to change. Her soft features became sharper, dark shadows lying beneath her sinister eyes and cheekbones. Her lips turned black and stretched wider across her face, exposing hideous fangs protruding from her mouth. Two dark, webbed wings sprouted from her back, and her delicate fingers morphed into terrifying talons. A dark, purple mist surrounded her, its tendrils wrapping around her like poisonous serpents.

She reached into the folds of her dress and pulled out a strange mask. Made of black silk and lace, its entire surface was covered with tiny pieces of mirror. The woman placed the mask over her grotesquely misshapen face and continued her chant. A thin ray of light broke through the veil of clouds and fell on her mask.

The shards of the mirror reflected the silvery moonlight, shattering it into thousands of blinding flares and tiny beams, and the woman cackled, her voice as ghastly as her appearance. She stopped chanting and stilled in place, listening intently to something only she could hear. After a few endless minutes, she exhaled and let go of her magic. Her wings dissipated, and her face and hands returned to their normal appearance.

She took her mask off, placed it back into the pocket hidden in the thick folds of her dress and lowered her lacy, black veil. Then she hopped to her feet and took off running. Dark and silent, she flew across the entrance into the palace and rushed through the countless passages and halls until she reached a tall, oak door. She glanced around warily and pushed the door open without knocking.

A large, semi-dark chamber was illuminated by the flickering light of a few candles. The smell of smoke mixed in with the delicate scent of perfume permeated the air, making it seem stuffy after the freshness of the night outside the palace walls. A woman dressed in a richly embroidered dress sat by the table with a small book in her hand. As the door into her chamber opened, she put the book away, and her unyielding eyes stopped on the newcomer. She frowned and pressed her lips into a straight line, displeasure reflected on her hard features.

The woman in black lowered into a graceful curtsey and lifted her veil, exposing her face. "My lady," she whispered, her musical voice soft and insinuating, "Tsarevna Sophia Alekseyevna…"

"What brought you here at this late hour, Donna Luna?" The regent of Russia got up, her posture straight and regal like that of a true tsarina. Her eyes darted from Donna Luna to the book on the table, and a shadow of regret crossed her features. "It better be important. I'm not in the mood for social gossips and theater plays."

"It is, my lady." Donna Luna straightened, readjusting the folds on her dress. "The news I brought is of extreme importance. As a matter of fact, it's so important, I couldn't wait until morning."

Tsarevna Sophia sighed and gestured at an empty chair across from her, her movements projecting a vibe of fatigue. "Tell me what's going on."

With a mysterious look on her face, Donna Luna sashayed to the chair and sat down. "It's time, my lady," she said softly. "It's time for you to claim your birthright and become the true Tsarina of all Russia."

Sophia Alekseyevna sighed, tilting her head. "And how do you propose we do it? I don't have enough supporters to take the throne from my half-brother."

"But you know what you need to do, my lady," whispered

Donna Luna. Leaning forward slightly, she took Sophia's hand, giving it a reassuring squeeze. "People who are loyal to you and want to see you on the throne are ready. All they are waiting for is your signal. Tomorrow, the theater—*Choromina Comedy*—will be full of guests, many of whom are Peter's supporters." A sinister glimmer ignited in her eyes as she gave Sophia a pointed stare. "All you have to do is let the show commence…"

Sophia Alekseyevna rose to her feet, staring down at the woman in black, a chain of emotions crossing her face. "If I agree, how are you planning to give a signal?"

A mysterious smile crossed Donna Luna's face. "Magic, my lady," she whispered, inclining her head. "I will use a Hyperborean mirror to channel my magic and set the theater on fire. Fire and smoke will be visible from far away, and that will be the signal to your loyal warriors—*Streltsy*—to start the revolt."

Tsarevna pressed her hand to her mouth, staring down at her mysterious friend with a mix of awe and horror. "But where are you going to get this"—she twirled her wrist—"Hyperborean mirror?"

"But I've always had it, my lady." Donna Luna chuckled and showed Sophia her mask, the pieces of the mirror reflecting the candlelight, throwing sinister flares on the walls of the chamber. "The question is, are you ready to take what's rightfully yours?"

Tsarevna Sophia frowned and turned away, staring out the window. Her position had been weakened by two unsuccessful campaigns against the Crimean Khanate, and she had to think hard before agreeing to something so dangerous.

"It's your last chance, my lady. Peter is seventeen, and his influence is growing. If you don't do something now, he'll take power," said Donna Luna. "It's now or never."

Sophia turned around sharply and squared her shoulders, her eyes lingering on the mirrored mask. "But how are you planning to leave the theater after you start the fire?" she asked at length.

A cold sneer stretched Donna Luna's lips, and Sophia cringed inwardly at how malicious her trusted friend looked at this moment.

"Don't worry about me, my lady," replied Donna Luna, rising. "Fire can't kill me." She headed toward the exit but halted by the door, looking back at Tsarevna Sophia, darkness rising around her. "Be ready. It all starts with fire."

She opened the door and walked out of the chamber.

* * *

Same night.
Preobrazhenskiy Palace

A DARK SHADOW separated from the wall, blocking Peter's way into his chamber. The young man came to an abrupt halt and sucked in a sharp breath, wrinkling his nose as the heavy odor of alcohol assailed his nostrils.

"Petrukha," he grumbled, grabbing the man's shirt and yanking him out of the shadows. "Stop sneaking around like a thief in the night."

"Not a thief, my Tsar, just a fool." Petrukha giggled, alcohol fumes getting heavier around him. "But I think sometimes fools are smarter than those sitting on the thrones."

Young Peter sighed, raking his hand through the thick mane of his black hair. "What do you want, Petrukha? It's late, and I want to get some sleep. Tomorrow—"

"Tomorrow is going to be a new day," the fool said, shaking his head. Suddenly, he sobered up, the wandering, drunken grin disappearing from his face, and even though he barely reached Peter's chest, somehow, he seemed to become taller. "We need to speak, Tsar Peter. If you want to survive tomorrow, that is."

Peter pushed the door open and motioned for the fool to get in. Throwing a quick glance around, the young tsar followed him and closed the door with a soft thud. Then he crossed the room and sat down on a wide armchair by the window, crossing his long legs at the knee.

"I'm all ears," he said, his fingers tapping impatiently on the armrest. "Make it quick, Petrukha, and be on your merry way."

"I'll make it quick and to the point," promised Petrukha, folding his arms over his skinny chest. "The darkness is coming, the kind of force you can't fight with your toy army." A deep frown settled on his face, his blue eyes blazing. "It's coming for you, Peter. Rising from the moonlight, surrounded by fire, the demoness will rise. She will open her wings, as black as the void, and bring the fiery Hell upon Earth. She already enthralled your half-sister Sophia, and if the tsarevna gives in to her malignant plans of lies and betrayal, the darkness will swallow everything you hold dear to your heart."

Peter's eyes widened, his fingers clutching the armrests of his wide chair. But he took a deep breath and relaxed his tensed shoulders.

"Sophia wants to be the Tsarina of all Russia. I know that." He shrugged indifferently. "But she's still my sister." He waved his hand. "And all these stories about magic and demons... I don't believe any of it. I believe in science, my friend."

"As you wish, Tsar, but can you do me a favor?" A drunk grin appeared on Petrukha's face, and he swayed a little. "Tomorrow night, please stay in your chamber and be ready to leave at any moment. Don't open your door to anyone until I come back for you. Can you do that for me, Tsar Peter the Great?"

Peter laughed at the words of the drunken fool but waved his hand, dismissing the matter. "Fine. I'll do as you ask." He tapped his fingers against the thick book lying on a small table by his side. "I need time to read and think things through, anyway."

Petrukha bowed, brushing the floor with his fingers. "I'll see you tomorrow night, Tsar." He turned around and made his way to the door but stopped there with his hand on the handle. "Just remember—it all ends with fire."

He opened the door and slipped outside, quiet and soundless like a shadow.

* * *

Twenty Hours Later

No one in their right mind would allow a drunken fool inside the theater, so Petrukha crouched in the shadows just outside the main entrance, all his senses stretched to the maximum. The play had started already, and the occasional words of actors reached his heightened hearing through the cracked door.

He closed his eyes and channeled his magic, gently probing inside the building and the surrounding area. At first, he didn't notice anything out of the ordinary, but soon after, he sensed a slight fluctuation in the magical energy field. Weak and faint in the beginning, the spikes became stronger and stronger, and now he could detect the constant flow of magic originating somewhere at the far end of the theater.

Petrukha shivered in his thin shirt as if the hot August night had suddenly become too chilly, goosebumps rising on his arms from the sheer darkness and malignancy of the magical energy. Moving as stealthily as he could, he walked around the guard unnoticed and pushed his skinny body through the tiny opening.

The spacious room of the theater was filled with guests—not a seat unoccupied. Candlelight danced on the walls upholstered in red, throwing long, slithering shadows on the floor covered by a thick green carpet. The play was in progress, and everything seemed to be absolutely normal and peaceful, yet

Petrukha knew better. Pressing his back against the wall, he tiptoed his way toward the stage.

Unseen, he sneaked behind the curtain and stilled, blood running cold in his veins. Donna Luna stood at the edge of the stage. Protected by her spell, she was invisible to anyone who wasn't touched by the World of Magic. Her body slithered and moved in the unsteady candlelight like that of a giant serpent, surrounded by a dark veil of demonic essence. As she progressed with her spell work, her appearance continued to change further, and a few seconds later, a demoness in her full glory stood before Petrukha.

Fear the likes of which he had never felt before squeezed his heart, but he took a deep breath and channeled his magic, extending his arm. A bright energy orb materialized in the palm of his hand, rotating and crackling with electrical discharges. Donna Luna noticed him, and her black eyes angled up, turning into furious blazing slits. Her brows snapped together, and a predatory hunger reflected on her face. Petrukha pulled his arm back and propelled the energy orb at her while conjuring the next one. The demoness screeched and had no choice but to break her enchantment to protect herself. With her demonic essence spinning around her like a funnel cloud, she held out her hands, and two dark rays of magical energy escaped her palms.

"*Procedia Amnia*," muttered Petrukha. A soft glow of his magic surrounded him just in time to deflect the assault of demonic energy. Without skipping a beat, he rushed forward, propelling one energy orb after another, forcing her to retreat toward the back of the building.

The demoness howled and hissed, fury distorting her malformed face. Her webbed wings expanded behind her back, throwing terrifying shadows at the red upholstery. Pushed into the corner, she muttered a spell, and a thick wall of magic rose around her, pulsating with purple flares of light. She reached into the folds of her dress and produced a black mask. Small shards of mirror reflected the light of the candles and the purple glimmer of her magic.

Black flames ignited in the bottom of her eyes as she placed the mask over her face and started to chant again. With horror, Petrukha recognized the shards of the Hyperborean mirror embedded into the mask, and he knew if he didn't do something now, a moment later, it would be too late.

Channeling all the magical energy he could gather, he extended his arm toward her and yelled, *"Exitius!"*

The magic of his spell impacted the wall the demoness had erected around herself, and it shattered into tiny pieces, falling to her feet in dirty gray flakes. Slightly disoriented by the impact of his spell, Donna Luna froze in place, glowering at him with malice. Petrukha covered the distance between them in one long stride and ripped the mask off her face, crushing it in his fist.

The mask broke in two, a thin stream of blood running down his fingers where pieces of the mirror cut his palm. She squealed and reached for him, but it was too late. In one swift motion, he jumped back, manifested a powerful energy orb and threw it at her. The orb impacted her straight in the chest, propelling her backward.

She hit a small backdoor and flew through it, falling to the ground outside the theater. Petrukha shoved both pieces of the mask into his pocket and followed her through the door, only to find that she recovered a lot faster than he had expected. Hopping to her feet, Donna Luna spun in place and spread her wings. Flying low above the ground, she circled the building, disappearing around the corner.

"No, you don't!" Petrukha shouted desperately, bolting after her. As he turned the corner, he saw the demoness taking her human form and climbing into a carriage.

"You won a battle, but you will lose this war, wizard!" she

yelled, thrusting her fist in the air. "I'll find you, if not in this world than in the Dark Nav." She cackled, a maniacal glimmer in her black eyes. "This isn't over, fool, for I always get what I want."

She pulled back into the carriage, closing the door, and the horses took off, running away from the theater.

"Igneous Orbus Amplio!" Petrukha shouted and a massive fireball materialized in his hand. Touching it with his finger he added, *"Illucious"*, infusing it with the purifying energy of creation and propelled it at the carriage with all the strength he had, immediately casting another spell to lock Donna Luna inside it.

The magically conjured fire, amplified by the purifying energy, engulfed it, turning it into a giant torch in a heartbeat. The demoness tried to break his spell but to no avail, and her screams and curses reached his ears, echoing through the empty street. A few minutes later, there was nothing left of the monster.

"It all ends with fire…" Petrukha whispered. But as he watched the dark swirls of smoke rise high into the midnight sky, he cursed quietly and took off running, realizing that even though he got rid of the demoness, the signal to the uprising was still sent.

With his heart beating desperately against his ribcage, he burst through the doors into a stable and kept running until he reached the last stall, a neighing of spooked horses accompanying his progress. Although the stall stood dark and empty, he walked inside, muttering a summoning spell. The air before him lit up with a brilliant white light and when it dwindled, a beautiful horse stood before him, its white coat in stark contrast with its black mane and tail.

Petrukha approached the horse and wrapped his arms around its neck, pressing his cheek to its warm coat.

"Thank you for coming, my friend," he whispered, pulling away. "I need you to do me one last favor…"

The horse neighed, nodding its head. He mounted it, easily rising on its back, and it took off, galloping at full speed toward the palace. As they reached the tall building of the palace, Petrukha jumped off the horse and ran without slowing down until he reached Peter's chamber. Taking a deep breath, he knocked on the heavy oak door and opened it without waiting for an invitation.

The room was dark. The light of a single candle was too weak to fight the gathering darkness. Peter sat behind his desk, a thick book in heavy leather binding opened before him. He raised his head, staring at Petrukha puzzled. The fool bowed low, brushing the floor with his fingers.

"It's time, great Tsar." He crossed the room and picked up a small, silver box sitting on Peter's desk. Opening the lid, he looked inside, and the corners of his mouth lifted just a touch. A single silver ring with a black stone embedded into it lay on the cushion of red silk. He took the ring out, placing it on the desk, and then put the pieces of the broken mask inside and closed the box, whispering a short spell. For a heartbeat, the box lit up with the barely noticeable glimmer of his magic. Then he gave it to Peter, gesturing at the door. "No matter what you do, keep this box safe. Your horse is waiting for you by the door, my lord. Ride like the wind, gather your army and fight for what is rightfully yours!"

Peter walked around the desk and placed his hand on Petrukha's shoulder. "Thank you, my friend," he said softly, taking the box. "I will never forget."

Petrukha lowered to one knee and pressed his fist to his chest, inclining his head. "I'm yours to command, great Tsar."

He rose to his feet after the young Tsar left the room and shook his head, his features turning hard.

"The demoness was right. It isn't over," he whispered, staring at the closed door. "For as long as the forces of Darkness fight the army of Light, it'll never be over. But at least I can make sure she'll never find what she was looking for. Neither here nor in the Dark Nav…"

Petrukha snapped his fingers and vanished from the room.

CHAPTER 1

~ DAMIAN BLAKE ~

Blue Creek, Arizona

The large, orange disk of the moon hung low over the horizon, bathing the dark suburban neighborhood in its soft light. Despite the late hour, it was still too hot to be comfortable, and the asphalt road emitting additional waves of heat didn't improve the situation. The wind-deprived air felt stuffy, and the silence of the scorching evening seemed to be too heavy to be natural.

Damian halted in front of a dark intersection and raised his arm to stop Jamie. The young wizard halted by his side and pointed at a dark house on the south-east corner, across the road. Damian nodded and sharpened his senses, quickly scanning the area. A barely noticeable spike in the magical energy field attracted his attention, and he channeled his magic, opening his other sight.

"Dammit," he cursed, frowning.

The magical energy flowed around the house in unsteady waves, spiking up and dropping to nearly nothing like some crazy EKG of a monstrous heart. Some of it was basic protective magic—a turn-away spell cast to keep humans as far away as possible. Besides that, he detected a strange, dark energy he couldn't identify right away. It was pulsing in short, continuous bursts, dark-purple flares accentuating each spike, aligning with the overall uneven flow of magical energy around the building.

What bothered him the most, however, was that this unusual pulsating magic completely blocked his second sight, and he couldn't see what was going on inside of the building. The idea that someone was powerful enough to block his other sight made his skin crawl with the expectation of trouble, and he tensed, channeling more of his magical energy toward his eyes to enhance his vision.

"What do you see?" Jamie asked, shifting closer to him.

"River was right," Damian replied in a soft whisper, wishing with all his heart that she wasn't. "I have no idea how she does it, but whenever she tells me that her case is supernatural, she's always right."

"Do you know what we're dealing with?" Jamie shivered, rubbing his arms with his hands as if he were cold in this unusually steamy ninety-five degrees evening. "I can't get rid of the feeling that I need to leave this place and never come back." He huffed, catching Damian's reproachful stare. "Yeah, I know—a turn-away spell. I'm not gonna fall for it. You taught me well."

"Good, don't. I need you to keep it together..." Damian stared into the darkness behind the house and reached out to his brother through their blood bond. *"Cole, are you in position?"*

"Aye, aye, Captain. We're in position," Cole replied immediately, his voice sounding loud and clear in Damian's mind.

Damian stifled a sigh, thinking about his brother's inability to stay serious no matter how severe the situation was. *"You're a lot closer to the house. Can you detect any supernatural presence?"*

For a few seconds, Cole remained silent, then his voice sounded in Damian's mind again, humorous vibes replaced by tones of concern. *"A few vampires. Not mine. Either rogues or visi-*

tors from other states... Well, that's a big problem, and I need to handle it later." Cole stopped talking, and the short pause he took felt like an hour-long silence to Damian's stretched nerves. "Do me a favor, big bro. If you come across vampires, keep at least one of them alive if possible. I would like to ask them a few questions..."

"You got it," replied Damian. "Any other supernatural presence?"

"Yes," replied Cole. "Demons, at least two or three, judging by the amount of demonic essence they're emitting. Oh, and Atticus thinks there are a bunch of shifters among them. Most likely swords for hire."

"Jeez," muttered Damian, wondering why this completely unremarkable suburban house was guarded like a medieval fortress. "Okay. I believe there are wards around the place, so Jamie and I go first. If River is right, there could be humans inside. So, be careful. Don't go happy-go-lucky on me."

"Oh, no, and here I was going to rush in, guns blazing." Cole snickered, and Damian could almost see his brother rolling his eyes.

"You and Atticus stay back and wait for my signal," he replied, ignoring Cole's sarcasm.

"What signal?"

"You'll know it when you see it." Damian severed their link and seized Jamie's elbow, directing him toward the house.

They crossed the road, and Damian halted by the decorative fence surrounding the property. The house was large—eight to nine thousand square feet, if not more by the looks of it. The only two-story building on the block, it stood out like a sore thumb, and he had to wonder why someone would pick this place if they wanted to stay under the radar of local human and supernatural authorities. The windows of the house were dark, shaded by thick curtains, and nothing seemed to be moving either inside the building or in its front yard.

Damian squatted, placed his palm flat against the ground, and sent a touch of his elemental energy through it. The small area of the fence in front of him lit up with a barely perceptible purple glow, and a chain of tiny, shimmering runes shone along the perimeter of the property for a heartbeat before vanishing.

Damian got up and turned to Jamie. "Did you see it?"

"Wards?" replied Jamie, shoving his hands into the pockets of his track pants.

Damian noticed his move but managed to stop himself from smiling. A few months ago, Jamie had touched the wards and activated them, giving away their presence to their enemies. He had obviously learned his lesson, and now he kept his hands firmly locked in his pockets to make sure he wouldn't touch anything he wasn't supposed to.

He got up, straightening his jeans, and nodded at Jamie. "Well, they are wards, but they are not built to keep anything supernatural out. They're built to alert whoever is inside as soon as someone with magic crosses the property line." He brushed his palms together, getting rid of the sand. "It's a supernatural alarm system."

"Can you disable it without activating the alarm?" asked Jamie, his troubled gaze traveling across the property, settling on the dark house.

"No. I need to use my magic to disable the wards, but these wards are designed to react to anything magical." Damian frowned, considering different options, but none of them looked good. "Unfortunately, this protective magic also blocks my other sight, so I have no idea how many monsters are waiting for us on the inside or where they are."

Jamie shrugged, and his eyes lit up with the soft reddish glow of his magic, determination reflected on his face. "Then we do what we always do," he said quietly. "We make an entrance they will never forget."

"You are learning." Damian tapped Jamie's shoulder and reached out to his brother. *"Cole, there are alarm-type wards around the property. There is no way to get in quietly. Tell Atticus to be ready. We're going to go in first."*

"Ready." Cole's voice sounded in his mind like the low, dangerous growl of a predator.

"Jamie, now." Damian channeled his magic to his hands and shouted, pointing at the fence, "*Exitius!*"

The fence blew up with a thunderous bang, showering them with shards of wood, dust and debris. The wards crashed, and the ear-splitting sound of the supernatural alarms rang through the sleepy neighborhood. A few dogs replied with gut-wrenching howls that made the small hairs rise on the back of Damian's neck. A flock of birds went up in the air, their screeches adding to the cacophony of the alarm.

Damian held out his arms, and his daggers materialized in his hands, blazing in the surrounding darkness. He stepped through the opening he had created, registering from the corner of his eye that Jamie was following him. Opening his second sight, he ran soundlessly across the front yard toward the entrance into the house.

Halting on the circular driveway, he channeled more of his magic toward his hands, ready to break the door, when it opened with a soft squeak and remained ajar, exposing a lightless room behind it. Jamie came to a screeching halt, grabbing Damian's elbow.

"It's a trap," he exhaled, staring into the black rectangle of the doorway as if it were the maw of a monster.

"Of course, it is," murmured Damian, unable to hide his amusement. "Let's see who'll get trapped, though. I bet you a hundred dollars, it's not us."

"Make it two," replied Jamie, his hands clenching into fists.

"Perfect. Now, give me some light, boy!" Damian laughed, adrenalin surging through him. He planted his feet firmly on the ground and spread his arms, connecting with his element. As the energy of Earth flowed freely through his body, he redirected it toward the house.

The entire building shook, tremors running through its

walls. Damian took a step forward and twisted his arm, drawing a shining circle in the air with his blazing dagger. The tremors became stronger, the front wall wobbling as if it were made of jelly. Damian whispered a spell and drew another circle in the air.

A part of the front wall surrounding the doorway separated from the house, ripped by his magic. Deep fractures ran in every direction, but the building didn't collapse. For a brief moment, Damian held the chunk of wall suspended in mid-air, every muscle of his body tense with strain. Then he screamed and pushed his arms forward. The piece of wall flew through the opening into the house, exploding into a cloud of wood slivers and pieces of concrete. Loud screams of horror and cries of pain followed his move.

Jamie raised his arm, muttering a spell, and a swarm of tiny light orbs materialized over his hand. He flicked his wrist toward the building, and the orbs obeyed his command, zooming into the house.

"Ask and you shall receive." A winning grin split Jamie's face. "Light for you, my lord."

The light orbs illuminated a large hall covered in pieces of wood, slivers of glass, dust and other debris. There was no furniture in the room and the space was wide open with no place to hide. Two hallways ran in opposite directions, leading into the darkness. A group of dark figures cowered by the back wall, their eyes igniting with an angry glimmer as they started to recover from the initial shock. Jamie's magical orbs hovered above them, throwing flares of light against their blades and firearms.

Damian didn't need to use his other sight to know they were shifters for hire, their powerful energy signatures unmistakable from such close proximity.

"Shifters," hissed Jamie, unsheathing his sword.

"You're better off with your gun. Use the silver bullets,"

Damian whispered and crossed the threshold. At the same time, the clatter of broken glass and a furious slew of profanities sounded at the other end of the house. Damian's mouth twisted into a dark smile as the sound of an ongoing fight confirmed that his brother was in, too.

The noise ripped the shifters out of their stupor, and the air around them shimmered as they started to transform. Soon, a pack of desert wolves stood before him, their light, sandy fur raised on their backs. With blood-curdling howls, they charged Damian and Jamie.

Damian spun in place, ducking the first monster as it leaped in the air. His arm went up, and the shining dagger cut through the wolf's side and stomach, ripping it open. The monster fell to the floor next to his feet, his body convulsing as it transformed back into human form. The man's hands clutched at his front and side, blood and entrails spilling out of the terrifying wound.

The sound of a gunshot rolled across the house, and another wolf fell, turning into a man on its way down. Damian didn't wait to see what would happen next. Deadly and precise, his daggers worked their way through the pack of shifters, leaving disfigured bodies in their wake. The screams of pain and howls of anger filled the house, and the nauseating stench of spilled blood permeated the air.

Damian wasn't sure how many shifters he killed. It was hard to count, especially since they kept shifting, taking on a different form every chance they had, but it seemed like they kept coming. Throwing a quick glance around, he noticed that the shifters outmaneuvered him, separating him from Jamie. A gunshot boomed on his right, letting him know that the young wizard was still standing. He sharpened his senses, and over the howls of the wolves, he heard the cacophony of a battle unfolding in the other part of the house, suggesting that Cole and Atticus were still fighting.

"*On your left, Commander!*" A tiny, high-pitched voice

sounded in Damian's head, causing him to flinch. He knew it wasn't Cole, and he had no idea whose voice invaded his mind, but he had no time to think about it. Jumping aside, he spun to the left just in time to see the giant body of an honest-to-God lion rising in the air, its massive paws with hooked claws aimed at him.

He yelped and ducked out of the way, but one of the paws caught his shoulder, sending him tumbling to the floor slick with blood. He skidded on his back, hitting the wall with his injured shoulder and arm. His fingers unlocked, and the daggers fell on the tiled floor, their metallic clatter swallowed by the deafening roar of the monstrous animal. A cry of pain escaped his lips as he struggled to get back to his feet. Another roar rolled through the room, and then his brother's furious voice rose over the mayhem.

"Hey, lion! King of assholes!" Cole shouted somewhere at the other end of the room. "Why don't you pick on someone your own size."

The lion snapped around, its thick mane flowing with its move, and now Damian could see Cole standing with the glowing sword in his hand, a giant black wolf by his side. The wolf growled, exposing its terrifying fangs dripping with fresh blood, and Cole laughed in response, his ominous, dark laughter promising nothing good to the remaining shifters for hire.

Using the opportunity to regroup, Damian pushed off the floor, rising to his feet with a strenuous groan. The lion snapped back to him, baring its fangs in a low growl, his foul breath engulfing Damian's senses.

"*Procedia Amnia!*" Damian shouted, pressing his back against the wall as he summoned his daggers.

Cold perspiration covered his forehead when he realized that if the lion charged him now, he wouldn't be able to deflect the attack, praying for his basic protection spell to hold back the powerful supernatural animal. At the same time, the black wolf jumped forward. Cole screamed, terror in his voice, and sped toward him.

As the lion leaped in the air again, the boom of a gunshot echoed through the house. Like in a slow-motion video, Damian watched a silver bullet fly through the lion's head, exiting through its eye with a splatter of blood. The animal yelped and fell dead to the floor in front of him, slowly turning into a man. The remaining three shifters assumed their human forms and froze in place, their faces contorted with fear.

Damian searched the room and saw Jamie lying on the floor, his Glock in his hands, his sword on the floor by his side. With a groan of pain, the young wizard threw the body of another dead shifter off his legs and got up, his blood-smeared left arm dangling powerlessly by his side, four deep claw marks running across his bicep.

"A goddamn lion?" he yelled, blood mixed with sweat dripping down his face. "A lion? What the fuck?"

Cole winked at Jamie and snapped his fingers at the wolf. Before Damian had a chance to say anything, the remaining shifters fell dead to the floor, beheaded and torn apart by the mighty jaws of the purebred werewolf.

With a loud roar, the black wolf shifted, taking his human form, and a heartbeat later, Atticus stood next to them, his wide chest rising and falling with heavy breaths. His clothes were torn and soaked with blood and sweat. His body was covered in bite marks and lacerations. Red and brown splatters coated his face and arms, and Damian had no doubt some of this blood was his.

"Damian, we should go upstairs," said Cole, approaching him. He frowned, and a muscle twitched in his tightly pressed jaw. "Atticus and I dealt with a few vampires and demons in the family room. He pointed toward the dark hallway on his right. "There is a staircase to the second floor, and they were willing to do anything to stop us from going there." He raked his fingers through his blood-soaked hair, throwing it off his face. "Whatever they're hiding there must be important."

"Let's go." Damian headed toward the hallway, gesturing for Jamie and Atticus to follow them. "Cole, were the vampires yours? Did you manage to capture them?"

"No," replied Cole. "Not mine. I wish I could've asked them a few questions, but unfortunately, I couldn't capture any of them alive."

Stopping in front of a wide staircase leading to the second floor, Damian glanced over his shoulder and pointed up, gesturing for his friends to follow, remaining behind him. Cole frowned but didn't object.

Damian channeled his magic and opened his second sight, but just like before, he could see nothing. It seemed as though the walls of this strange house were soaked through with some magic that blocked his magical sight. Shaking his head, he slowly moved up, all his senses stretched to the maximum. As he reached the last step, he found himself in front of a doorway leading into a narrow hallway. He was about to move forward when the same tiny, high-pitched voice he'd heard before sounded in his mind again, making him flinch.

"Commander, be careful! Above you!"

Damian raised his eyes but could see nothing. Holding his breath, he approached the threshold, but instead of crossing it straight, he stepped slightly to the right, summoning one of his daggers. A dark figure dropped from above, aiming to crush him with their weight, but Damian was ready. In one fluid motion, he jumped to the side and spun around, catching the man, his fingers wrapping around the attacker's throat in a deadly grip.

A low growl rumbled in Damian's chest as he slammed the man against the wall and pinned him with his dagger. The assailant hissed, his eyes glowing with a menacing scarlet light, and his dangerous fangs expanded, betraying his vampiric nature. He grabbed the blade, trying to pull it out of his chest, but cried out and let go, the palm of his shaking hands covered in blisters of burns.

"Hey, Cole," Damian reached out to his brother. *"You wanted to capture a vamp? Here, I got you one, little bro. Don't ever say I don't get you any presents."*

Cole walked inside and stopped by his side, his glowing eyes narrowing into angry, scarlet slits. The vampire's jaw dropped as he stared at Cole, his face contorted with fear.

Damian gestured for Jamie to come in and whispered in his ear, "Do you have the silver cuffs with the runes that I made for you? I can't leave my dagger stuck in this moron."

The wizard nodded and pulled out a pair of handcuffs from his pocket, offering them to him. Damian took the cuffs and restrained the vampire, ignoring his groans of pain. The few runes engraved into the cuffs lit up with a brilliant white light as soon as the lock clicked, and the vampire cried out, his head dropping powerlessly to his chest. Then he grabbed Jamie's sword and thrust it into the vampire's chest before pulling his dagger out. Cole leaned forward slightly and seized the vamp's hair, yanking his head back.

"Don't go anywhere, asshole," he hissed, his voice shaking with barely contained fury. "The King wants to have a word with you."

Damian touched his brother's shoulder to attract his attention. *"Cole, my other sight is still blocked. Can you detect any human or supernatural presence?"*

Cole straightened and turned around, staring into the long, dark hallway lined up with closed doors on either side.

"Four heartbeats," he projected. *"Yes... three heartbeats behind the first door on the left and one heartbeat behind the door at the very end of this hallway."*

Damian approached the first door on the left and halted,

listening intently. He had no idea what the little voice in his head was, but at this moment he wasn't sure he cared. Whoever it was, it had saved him twice in one day. Since the voice remained silent, he assumed it was safe to open the door.

"*It is safe,*" peeped the tiny voice in his mind. "*I would tell you if it wasn't.*"

What the hell? Damian gasped, his hand reaching up to his head.

"*Hello, Commander—*"

Who the hell is talking in my head?

"*Don't you know?*"

No, goddammit!

"*Ew... Language, please—*"

What the fuck???

"Damian, are you okay?" whispered Jamie, touching his hand. "You look like you saw a ghost, and your tattoo is glowing a little, by the way."

Damian flinched and glanced at his arm. Under the layer of dirt and dried out blood, the runes and the words in Dragon tongue entwined with the intricate lines of the tattoo were glowing with a soft bluish light. Yakov had given him this tattoo six months ago, but he had never explained what it was and how it was supposed to work. Now it was glowing, and a strange voice was tormenting his mind, yet he had no idea how to deal with it.

I'll kill Yakov when he shows up again... Damian swallowed hard. The time now wasn't right for all that.

"I'm fine," he replied to Jamie and added for the pesky, little voice in his head, "*Shut the hell up. I still have work to do here. So, unless you have something important to tell me, keep your goddamn mouth shut. I'll figure out what you are and how you're able to invade my mind later when I get home.*"

"*Yes, my lord, Commander. I'm as silent as a mouse.*"

Grrrr...

Damian pushed on the handle, but the door was locked. Without thinking twice, he pulled his leg back and kicked it, placing all his aggravation into a single push kick. The door flew off its hinges and crashed to the floor with a loud bang.

The air conditioner wasn't working, but because he was either too preoccupied with the fight or got used to the smoldering heat outside, he didn't notice it until now. The thick odor of unwashed human bodies and excrements assailed his senses as a hot wave of stuffy air unfit for breathing hit him in the face like a sledgehammer. He staggered back, burying his nose and mouth into the crook of his elbow.

A large bedroom with a boarded window was dimly lit by the light of a single lightbulb hanging from the ceiling in the place where a ceiling fan used to be. Three mattresses were thrown on the tiled floor, and three young women lay motionless on top of them. Their eyes were closed, and they appeared to be sleeping, their chests moving up and down with shallow breaths. While they weren't restrained, it didn't appear as if they had tried to escape at any time.

Damian sucked in a deep breath and walked inside, taking a knee next to the woman closest to him. Her face was pale, and deep, dark shadows lay under her eyes. Her long dark hair covered part of her face and chest, but as Damian moved it to the side, his heart gave a painful jolt. Multiple puncture wounds on her neck told him all he needed to know.

He got up, pressing his hand over his mouth, and his gut twisted with the realization of what had transpired in this dirty room with unbreathable air.

"Are they drugged?" asked Jamie, his hoarse voice breaking.

"No," Damian managed to say, his eyes darting to the other two women. He couldn't see their necks, but their arms were covered in the distinctive puncture wounds of vampire bites.

"Vampires," whispered Cole. "They're not drugged, Jamie, but they are addicted." He bit his lip, shaking his head. "To the pleasure of a vampire bite. It's worse than any drugs." Then he punched the air with his fist, a haunted expression hiding in his eyes. "Goddammit! How could I miss it? Arizona is my territory! I'm responsible for all this." He pointed at the women.

"We'll figure it out, brother." Damian moved past Cole and walked out of the room, pulling Jamie and Atticus with him. "Let's check who is in the last room, and then we need to call River. These three women are human. They lost a lot of blood and need medical attention and memory adjustments... not necessarily in that order. Cole can take care of the latter. The vampire's glamor will be safer for them than my memory modification spell."

He walked through the dark hallway, everything inside him shaking with suppressed fury. As he reached the last door, he didn't slow down but kicked it open right away. The door flew off its hinges, revealing a large, dark room behind it. Unlike the previous room, there were no mattresses on the floor, and the window wasn't boarded. In the silvery light of the moon, he saw a woman chained to a metal chair with iron chains so thick, they could hold a cruise ship moored during a hurricane.

She was dressed in a black shirt and jeans. Her clothes were partially ripped, exposing ugly welts and bruises on her arms, chest and stomach. Her head was bowed low to her chest, and her short, golden hair was covered in brown stains of dried blood. Slowly, she lifted her head. Her emerald eyes swept from one face to the next, and her full lips twitched slightly.

"A vampire, a werewolf, a wizard and... a Destiny Enforcer," she rasped, her voice too deep for a woman. A short burst of laughter escaped her lips, but her eyes remained cold and angry. "It does sound like the beginning of a bad joke."

CHAPTER 2

~ DAMIAN BLAKE ~

"Who the hell are you?" growled Damian, fighting his exasperation.

She took a deep breath and snapped her fingers before Damian could say anything else. The iron chains fell off, crashing to the floor with a loud clatter. She rolled her head from left to right and stretched her arms.

"Well, boys, I must say—your timing couldn't be any worse." The woman crossed her legs at the knee and folded her arms, cocking her head. "I've been tailing these assholes for the last few days, trying to figure out what they were up to. I was almost done interrogating them when you and your Merry Men showed up and spoiled the whole cha-cha for me."

"What are you talking about?" asked Damian.

The woman got up with ease, as if she hadn't been tied up to a chair for God knows how long, and that raised a warning flag in Damian's mind. He opened his other sight, quickly scanning her with it. Even though she had a glow similar to that of a human soul surrounding her, he was positive she was at least a witch and a powerful one at that. However, she was concealing her energy signature so skillfully that he couldn't detect it.

While her face wasn't beautiful by the publicly accepted standards, there was something fascinating about her sharp, angled features that were a bit too hard for a woman. But it was her eyes—bright green and large, framed with long, black eyelashes—that made up for everything else, giving her an exotic and striking appearance.

She approached him, her eyes gliding up and down his body as if sizing him up, and one corner of her mouth lifted ever so slightly. Being an average height for a woman, she barely reached to his shoulder, but the way she moved and spoke projected a vibe of self-assurance bordering on arrogance.

"I'm talking about a bunch of assholes who are trafficking witches all over the country," she replied, rolling her eyes. "For a Destiny Enforcer, you sure are uninformed." She moved around Damian and walked out the door, heading toward the first room where she halted in the doorway and threw her hands up. "It's not only that you interrupted my interrogation, but you were also too late to help these poor souls."

"What are you talking about?" Damian repeated through gritted teeth. "These women are not witches. They have no magic."

"And you are not a Destiny Enforcer just because I can't detect your energy signature?" she retorted, not without a fair load of sarcasm in her words. Dismissing him with a light flick of her wrist, she walked into the room and squatted next to one of the victims, shaking her head. "But you're right. They have no magic. Not anymore." She got up and turned to Damian. "But just a week ago, they used to be powerful witches. Good witches, too. Now the entire Superstition Mountains covenant is gone. Ten witches—all drained and dead."

Damian stilled, staring at the woman in shock, his heart pounding against his rib cage. About a couple of months ago, a new case had landed on River's desk—a Missing Persons Report. A young woman went to work in Phoenix and never returned. Soon after, her car was found abandoned on the side of a highway leading to Blue Creek. No damage, no signs of struggle. Everything inside the vehicle was in perfect order, but the owner was nowhere to be found.

A few days later, another woman disappeared under similar circumstances. The police department doubled their efforts, but no matter what they did, they couldn't discover anything that would help them find the missing women.

When two more Missing Persons Reports had been filed at the Blue Creek police precinct just a week later, the Police Captain started to consider the necessity of contacting the FBI, suspecting a serial killer on the loose.

River spent all her time at work, coming back home for a few short hours to get some sleep and change. While she agreed with the Captain that all these disappearances were linked to the same person or a group of people, she wasn't convinced they were dealing with a serial killer or a human trafficking organization. On the contrary, she was positive the perpetrator wasn't human. She had no idea what made her think that the World of Magic was somehow involved, but she was sure all these abductions had a supernatural origin.

So, when she received a report about a violent incident involving a young woman on the west side of Blue Creek, before sending her team there, she had called Damian, asking him to check the neighborhood and the address in question for any supernatural presence.

"Perun almighty," whispered Damian, wiping cold sweat off his forehead. "River was right…"

"Who is River?" asked the woman, staring at him with curiosity. "And what was she right about?"

"How about you tell us who you are first?" Damian snapped, seizing her elbow and pulling her out of the room.

She yanked her arm out of Damian's grip, placing her hands on her hips. "My name is Zabava," she announced with a look of superiority on her face, as if her name was common knowledge, and they were supposed to know it without asking. "I'm a supernatural PI, hired to investigate this situation."

"No, seriously?" Cole turned to her, a bemused grin on his face. "Are you saying your name literally means *'fun'* in old Russian?"

She measured him with her cold, green eyes and tapped her index finger against her lips. "Let me see," she mused. "A tall, blond vamp who speaks Russian and fights on the side of the Light. Your hair is not long enough, so you're not Yaroslav Potemkin. Then you must be Cole Adams, also known as Nikolai Chernov, ancient Slavic warrior, turned sometime in the tenth century, and now the reigning King of the Arizona Vampire Court."

Cole's jaw dropped, and he gaped at her, unable to say a word. She flicked her eyebrows at him and turned to Damian.

"If I was right about the vampire, then it would make you"—she pushed Damian in his chest with her finger—"Dmitri Chernov, his overprotective, helicopter older brother. Unfortunately, I don't have any information on you, giant. The only thing I'm certain of is that you're a Destiny Enforcer."

Without waiting for Damian's response, she walked up to Jamie and Atticus and gave them a quick once-over. Lifting her hand, she brushed her fingers over Atticus' cheek, tracing the shape of his chiseled jawline, her eyes getting foggy for a moment. A low growl rumbled in Atticus' throat as he threw her hand off. She laughed, amused, and glanced back at Damian, her eyes turning icy.

"What were you thinking, Enforcer? A baby wolf and an inexperienced wizard?" she asked, shaking her head. "You and your brother—two ancient giants—brought these two kids into this mess? Where were your brains? You could have gotten them killed!"

"We can hold our own," muttered Jamie indignantly. "I don't need anyone's permission—"

"I've had enough," growled Damian, interrupting him. "I don't have time for your bullshit, Zabava. How do you know who we are, anyway?"

"I'm a supernatural PI, jackass," she replied, her deep voice filled with sarcasm. "Knowing things is a part of my job."

Damian took a deep breath to get his aggravation under control. "Fine, Zabava, you had your fun—no pun intended," he said, mirroring her sarcasm. "Now, let's take care of this situation, and then we'll go somewhere we can speak uninterrupted."

She held his steady gaze for a few seconds and then just nodded, her smugness gone.

Damian turned to his brother. "Cole, since these women are witches, we don't need to modify their memories." He bit his lip, frowning. "But they still need medical help, and since River has responded to the alert about the disturbance in the neighborhood, she needs to be here to take care of the legal side of this situation. After all, it is her case. We were supposed to just check the house." He thought for a moment and then added, "Before I can call her, I have to summon the cleaners, though. It's a bloody mess downstairs."

"Oh, really?" Zabava's eyes lit up with excitement, and she headed toward the stairs, throwing an indifferent glance at the vampire pinned to the wall next to the exit. "I could hear the sound of a fight downstairs, but I didn't want to blow my cover. I needed these assholes to think they had me." She shrugged with a dismissive wave of her hand. "Well, let's see then."

Damian sighed, throwing his hands up, and followed her downstairs, motioning for Cole, Atticus and Jamie to get moving. Zabava marched briskly through the hallway and halted in the doorway into the entrance hall. She observed the room that resembled a medieval style battlefield and whistled.

"Whoa," she exhaled, turning to Damian, her eyes darting

from him to Cole and then gliding over Atticus and Jamie. "I must give it to you, boys—impressive. I didn't realize there were so many shifters here."

Damian didn't reply but seized her shoulders and moved her back into the corridor, away from the doorway. He made his way to the middle of the floor, pushing the dead bodies aside with the tip of his boot. Then he drew a glowing rune in the air and infused it with his power, connecting it with his Shadow Enforcer rune. A small communication window opened up in midair, and an older man in long, navy-blue robes answered his call.

"Commander Damian Blake, what can I do for you?" he asked, but as he stared over Damian's shoulder, his mouth dropped open, shock imprinted on his round face. "Never mind, Commander. I know what I need to do. Please make sure you and your team are out of the room before I start the cleaning process." He fell silent for a moment, furrowing his brow, and then added, "And Commander, if you have vamps in your team, make sure they are at least a few feet away from my light."

Damian inclined his head, pressing his fist to his chest. "My gratitude, Ivor."

It had been a while since he had to work with Ivor and his department, and not without surprise, he realized he was glad to see this battle-hardened man who was always nothing but helpful and supportive to him. Ivor and Cossack were the only two people from the Destiny Council Realm who had always been there for him, no questions asked.

He raised his hand to close the communication window, but Ivor gestured for him to wait. "How many people are in your team nowadays, Commander?" he asked, observing the hall.

"Four," replied Damian, "including myself."

"Four?" mumbled Ivor, his eyebrows rising, but then he rubbed the back of his neck, humorous sparkles appearing in the depth of his steel eyes. "Nice to have you back with us,

Commander. Knowing you, this is not going to be your last call to my department." He laughed and gestured for him to get out before closing the communication window.

Knowing how the cleaners worked, Damian wished there was a door blocking the entrance into the hall, but since there wasn't, he waved his hand and muttered a spell, erecting a protective shield over the doorway.

"Take a few steps back and turn away." He seized Cole's elbow and pulled him a few feet back, away from the hall, motioning for everyone to follow. As a blinding white light flooded the hall, spilling into the corridor, he wrapped his arms around his brother, shielding him with his body.

A few seconds later, the light dwindled, submerging the house into darkness. Blinking red and white spots from his vision, Damian made his way back into the hall. As expected, he found it empty and virginally clean, nothing suggesting that less than an hour ago, a brutal battle unfolded here, leaving blood and gore in its wake.

Making a split-second decision, Damian moved his hand in a circular motion, and a portal rotating with shimmering blue lights opened next to him.

"Atticus, I'm about to call River, and I think before she arrives with her team, we should clear the area and let her do her job," he said, switching his attention to the werewolf. "This portal will take you to the gates into your father's property. Thank you for your help, my friend."

Atticus smiled, dimples appearing on his cheeks, making him look like a mischievous teenager. "Any time, Commander." He threw a quick glance at Jamie, giving him a pointed stare. "Are you coming with me?"

Jamie sent a guilty look to Damian, inching his way to the portal, but Damian pointed at his wristwatch, suppressing the desire to roll his eyes. "Go already," he said with a dismissive flick of his wrist. "I can't keep this portal open forever. See you tomorrow for training." But then he changed his mind and grabbed Jamie's elbow, stopping him. "Wait, Jamie, you're in pain. Let me heal you first."

Ignoring the young wizard's objections, he channeled his element and placed his hand over the ugly welts on his friend's arm. Slowly circulating the healing energy of Earth through the wound, he waited until it closed completely and removed his hand, releasing the connection with his element.

"Better?" he asked softly, feeling slightly lightheaded.

"Thank you," replied Jamie. "You didn't have to do it. You're wounded yourself, and healing magic takes a lot of your energy."

"I'll be fine. Now, go." Damian waved at the portal. "I'll see you tomorrow."

As soon as the portal closed behind Jamie and Atticus, Zabava turned to Damian. "Now that the kids are in bed, adults should have a serious conversation," she said, tapping her foot, laced in a heavy combat boot, and since neither Damian nor Cole moved, she threw her hand up and added, "Now is as good a time as any."

Damian glanced down at her, working hard not to allow his annoyance to break free, but her behavior and the tone of superiority in her voice were playing on his nerves.

"Oh, we'll have a word," he promised icily, and if he could sound any colder, it would probably start snowing in the room. "We will speak when I say I'm ready. In the meantime, you're going to keep your mouth shut and let me do my job." Without waiting to see what her next witty remark would be, he turned to his brother. "Cole, do you need my help with that vamp upstairs?"

"No, I'll be fine," Cole replied, a dark shadow crossing his face. "But if you could open a portal to Luciano's mansion, I would appreciate it."

After Luciano's death, Cole had discovered that since the

ancient vampire had no one in his life except for Cole and Ruslan, he had left all his assets to him, including his enormous estate in Paradise Valley, naming him the sole beneficiary. Even though Cole didn't need another piece of real estate, he refused to sell it, and when Damian asked why, he made an elaborate tap-dance around the question without actually answering it. Since it was clear that his brother wasn't in the mood to discuss it, Damian decided to leave it alone.

Since Luciano's estate was located on the outskirts of Paradise Valley and far enough from prying eyes, Cole had been using it for everything to do with the Arizona Vampire Court affairs, including the weekly assembly of his council. Even though the mansion was surrounded by a tall fence and had a gated entry with a twenty-four-seven security guard on duty, Damian had placed a light turn-away spell on the entire property to protect both sides—unsuspecting humans from running into the thirsty vampires, and vampires from exposing the World of Magic to overly curious humans.

Cole zoomed upstairs and came back a moment later with the captured vamp hanging limply over his shoulder. Catching Damian's puzzled gaze, he just shrugged.

"He passed out when I pulled the blade out." He gazed heavenwards, returning Jamie's sword to Damian, and muttered with disgust, "What a wuss."

Damian opened a portal for his brother, and as Cole walked through it, disappearing on the other side, he turned to Zabava.

"Are you ready?" he asked, placing his hand on her shoulder.

She nodded, and he snapped his fingers, teleporting them out of the house. They manifested behind an empty one-story building with a real estate sign in front of it. Damian glanced around and pressed his finger to his lips, asking Zabava to be silent, and then gestured for her to follow him. Keeping to the shadows, he circled the house, heading toward the front yard from where he could easily see the large two-story building across the road.

Crouching behind the fence, he reached in his pocket and produced his phone. He found River's name in his short contact list and pressed the dial button. Expecting his call, River answered her phone right away.

"River, you were right. The case is supernatural," said Damian quietly, throwing a warning glance at Zabava as she shifted closer to him. He quickly told River everything that had happened in the house, asking her to call an ambulance and cover the legal side of the incident.

"I'll be there in five minutes with my team," she replied after he finished. "If you and Cole are still in the house, you should leave now."

"We're out," he said, unease spreading numbness through his chest. "River, please be careful. I have no idea who these people are and what kind of operation they're running, but they're powerful and ruthless. They had an army of mercenaries protecting the house, and what they did to these poor women…" He bit his lip and swallowed. "From what I've been told, they're abducting witches and stripping them off their powers. Perhaps this is nothing more than a modern-day witch hunt, but it could be something entirely different—scarier and a lot more dangerous. So, get in, help the victims and get the hell out of there. You understand?"

"I understand. If there is anything I can do to help you with your investigation, let me know," she replied, anger ringing in her voice, and the sound of an engine coming through the phone line told Damian that River was on her way.

"Yes, you can." He lifted his head, staring at the empty road, expecting River to show up any minute. "Keep the police from digging deeper into this case until I find out what we're really dealing with."

"That's not going to be easy." River sighed, the soft ticking of the turn-signal sounding too loud through the phone line. "The Captain thinks we're dealing with a serial killer, so he's ready to call the FBI."

"Try to stall him for as long as you can." Damian exhaled with a groan. "I don't need humans to get caught in the crossfire."

"I'll do what I can," she replied and then added at length, her voice trembling with concern, "Dima, are you okay? Did anyone get hurt?"

"We are fine," he replied. "I have to go now, River. I'll see you at home in a few hours."

He hung up the phone and watched for a couple of minutes as a few police cruisers stopped in front of the house. Rising to his feet, he moved away from the fence into the shadow of the house and waited until River walked out of her vehicle, following her with his eyes.

"Oh, my friggin' God." Zabava's amused voice made him snap around. "You're totally hot for Detective Redhead, aren't you?" She gave him a quick once-over and tittered. "All this time, I thought the Destiny Enforcers were… um… eunuchs… you know… junk-less sorta."

Damian's jaw dropped as he stared at her, not sure if he should be angry or amused, but before he could make up his mind, her hand landed on his crotch.

"I guess I was wrong. You seem to be fully functional," she said, giving him a not-so-gentle squeeze, eliciting a furious groan out of him.

He seized her wrist, forcing her to unlock her fingers. "You try something like this with me again," he growled, leaning down slightly to invade her personal space, "and you'll find your fingers broken. Am I clear?"

"You're hurting me, asshole," she hissed, struggling to free her wrist from his iron grip. "Let go, or I will make you."

"I'm hurting you? Good." He laughed icily but let go.

"Oversized jackass…" She yanked her hand back, rubbing her wrist.

He ignored her words and continued lightly as though nothing happened, "Now, Zabava, we seem to work on the same side, so there is something I want you to think about—if you know how to do it, of course—and make a decision right now."

"What's that?"

"You're going to drop your juvenile shenanigans, because maybe you can fool my young friends, but you can't fool neither my brother nor me. All your despicable behavior from the moment I opened that door was nothing but a stupid act. Starting right now, you're going to treat me and my team courteously and with respect," he said calmly. "Or you *will* find yourself outside my state with no way to come back." He folded his arms over his chest, staring down at her with narrowed eyes. "Since knowing things is a part of your job, I'm sure you're aware that as a Commander of the Destiny Enforcers, I have the power to do that. So, the choice is yours. What is it going to be, Zabava?"

She stared at him for a few long seconds, a chain of emotions crossing her face. Then she pursed her lips and looked away.

"Fine. I don't start wars I can't win and fighting with the Destiny Council is like pissing against the wind," she grumbled.

"Good choice," he muttered, barely able to contain the wild laughter bubbling up in his chest. "Now we can have a word."

CHAPTER 3

~ DAMIAN BLAKE ~

They materialized a block away from *The Midnight Shift* in a dark, narrow alley. Damian quickly scanned the area, and since he didn't detect anything alarming, he headed toward the well-lit main street. Despite the late hour, the bar was still open, and a few last-minute visitors—all of them werewolves, judging by their energy signature—sat on tall barstools, chatting with Kaleb, the bartender.

"A sanctuary?" Zabava arched her brow at Damian as he opened the door for her. "I guess you still don't trust me, Commander."

"I don't know you," Damian replied calmly, directing her to a table at the far corner of the bar. He raised his hand, greeting Kaleb, and then sat down across from Zabava. "You're hiding your supernatural identity, and taking into account the latest developments, I prefer to err on the side of caution." Then he glanced down at his torn, dirty shirt and his injured arm covered in brown stains of blood and added with a shrug, "Besides, do you know any mundane restaurant that would allow me in looking like this?"

"Fair enough." She leaned back in the soft seat of the booth, staring out the window at the empty street.

"Damian, my friend. Long time, no see." Kaleb approached the table, wiping his hands on a white hand towel. His gaze slipped to Damian's wounded arm, and his eyes widened, but he didn't ask anything and continued, sounding as friendly and even as before. "I know what your preferences are," he said and turned toward Zabava. "What would you like, my lady?"

For a moment, she stared at the brawny werewolf, a desire to say something sarcastic clearly written all over her face, but then her eyes darted to Damian, and she mirrored Kaleb's smile instead. "Whatever his poison is, I'll take double."

If Kaleb was surprised by her statement, he didn't show it. He left and came back a few seconds later sporting a tray with a bottle of vodka and a few clean shot glasses. He placed napkins in front of them and put an empty shot glass atop each napkin. With quick, habitual moves, he filled the glasses with the clear liquid and put the bottle on the table between them.

"Take it, Damian," he said, holding out his hand with a small blue pill resting in his palm. "It will numb the pain for at least an hour."

Damian glanced at the pill but didn't take it, shaking his head. "Thank you, my friend, but I know how to block physical pain, and right now, I need my mind clear."

A part of the Destiny Enforcers' training was dedicated to learning how to deal with the pain of physical wounds. During a combat situation, healing wasn't an option, and every Destiny Enforcer had to know how to function despite their injuries without slowing down until the opportunity to take care of the wounds presented itself.

Kaleb shrugged and put the pill back in his pocket. "As you wish." He pointed at the bottle, and a wide grin split his face. "This is also a pretty good painkiller. I trust you know how to refill your glasses?" He winked at Damian and walked away, returning to his conversation with the group of werewolves at the bar.

The harsh odor of alcohol wafted through the air, and Damian inhaled it, closing his eyes for a brief moment. Adrenalin, spiked up by the previous events, started to dwindle, leaving him sore and tired, and he had no desire to play a twenty-questions game with Zabava. All he wanted was to find out who she was and what she was doing in his state.

Zabava took a shot glass, holding it between her thumb and index finger and lifted it, waiting for Damian.

"This wolf-boy called you his friend. You're the first Enforcer I've ever met who has friends. Usually, everyone hates your kind or are scared of you shitless," she said, staring at him over the rim of her glass. Then she leaned back slightly, narrowing her sparkling eyes. "Here is to making new friends."

She didn't wait for him and flipped the glass upside down, swallowing its contents in one gulp without so much as a cringe. Then she put it on the table and exhaled, closing her eyes for a moment. Without taking his eyes off of her, Damian downed his vodka and also leaned back, enjoying the feeling of the liquid burning down his throat.

"It seems you know everything about me and my kind," Damian started calmly, folding his arms. "I think it would only be fair if you told me who you are and what you're doing in my territory."

All mirth vanished from her eyes abruptly, and she leaned forward, resting her arms on the table. "I told you," she replied icily. "I'm a supernatural PI, and I was hired to investigate the disappearance of witches. If you think it is happening only in Arizona, think again, Enforcer. But Arizona seems to be at the epicenter."

"Who hired you?" Damian took the bottle and refilled their shot glasses.

She moved her glass closer but didn't lift it, her fingers

tracing the edge absentmindedly. He didn't rush her, allowing her to take her time with the answer. After a few seconds, she lifted her face. Her facade of cockiness and arrogance was gone, replaced by discomfort and a semblance of bitterness.

"Damian," she said, her deep voice wavering slightly. "I need you to swear that everything I'm going to tell you will stay between us."

"That depends on—"

"No conditions." She slammed her hand on the table, spilling some vodka. "Unless you give me your word, I can't disclose anything to you."

She's trouble. Just say no and don't do anything you'll regret later. A thought zoomed through his mind, and he frowned, exploring her tense features. *Keep your friends close, keep the little dark horses...*

"Fine, I promise that anything of any importance you say to me here will stay between us," he said at length. "Do you need me to swear on my blade?"

She glanced around, catching Kaleb's friendly nod, and shook her head. "No, Damian. Something tells me you're a man of honor. So, no more games. I need your help, and I believe you need mine, even though you don't know it yet. Let's talk."

"So, who hired you?" asked Damian.

"You're not going to like the answer to that question," she murmured as she refilled Damian's glass and moved it closer to him. "The Sisterhood of the Sun."

Damian froze in place, unable to move a muscle. The Sisterhood of the Sun was an ancient organization of powerful witches who dedicated their lives to exterminating vampires and anything without a heartbeat. Skilled not only in witchcraft but also in martial arts, combat magic and a few other, more obscure branches of the Light and Dark Arts, these women were forceful and ruthless in anything to do with the undead.

It wasn't enough to be magically gifted to be even considered for the Sisterhood. The candidates had to possess certain trades as humans and witches to be accepted into this highly secretive, ancient Order, and once accepted, their training was harsh and vigorous, turning them into merciless killing machines. When it came to vampires, they preferred to shoot first and ask questions later.

She probably read the expression of horror in his eyes, because she reached forward and touched his arm, causing him to pull back.

"Relax, Damian," she said softly. "They are not after your brother. Cole Adams is not on their list. I would know if he was."

Damian grabbed the glass and downed its contents in one gulp, exhaling a rugged breath. "Why did they hire you?"

"I already told you," she whispered, glancing toward the bar. "The disappearance of witches and the events surrounding them. It started a while ago, but what attracted the Sisterhood's attention was that whoever runs this show was using vampires to keep their victims subdued."

Damian nodded, his fingers crumpling the napkin as an image of the room they had discovered in the house flashed before his eyes. The three women, dazed or unconscious, were addicted to the vampire bite so severely, they probably couldn't distinguish dream from reality.

"Cole captured one of the vampires," he said at length. "Hopefully, he'll be able to get some information out of him."

"I doubt it." Zabava glanced out the window, a flare of light crossing her face as a lonely car rushed along the empty street, disappearing into the darkness. "I think the vamps are just doing someone else's bidding, and until we find out who's at the top of this evil pyramid, we won't be able to stop whatever it is they're doing."

"Cole has his… skills," muttered Damian, wincing inwardly

at how cold he sounded when he said it. "If this vamp has any information, my brother will know it by tomorrow."

"That's good." Zabava averted her eyes, staring at her clenched hands. "At first, I thought it was a witch-hunter, you know?" She chuckled mirthlessly. "It's hard to believe, but these evil bastards still walk the human realm as if we never left the Dark Ages." She massaged her wrists where the iron chains had chafed her skin. "Believe it or not, they're still using *Malleus Maleficarum*—the Hammer of Witches—as their go-to handbook."

Her teeth squeaked as she pressed her jaws, anger darkening her green eyes. For a few endless seconds, she remained silent, visibly fighting to keep her emotions under control.

"Anyway," she proceeded at length, "I don't think we're dealing with a witch-hunter. I think it's a lot worse."

"How so?"

"They don't torture the witches. There is no evidence that any of them were burned at the stake either," said Zabava. "And why would any witch-hunter need vampires to keep their victims compliant and submissive? They never work with anyone outside their clans." She pulled back and lifted her hand to stop him from interrupting. "And here is the most important fact that makes me believe it has nothing to do with the witch-hunters. All witches that I've discovered so far—dead or alive—were completely drained of their magical energy."

She glanced around and lowered her voice, speaking so softly that Damian could barely make out her words. "Someone is abducting witches to collect their magical energy, and we need to figure out who it is and why they need so much of it."

"Magical energy, as well as the energy of a human soul, is an expensive commodity. Not easy to come by," said Damian, trying to shuffle through the sudden disarray of thoughts in his mind. "Some supernatural entities would pay a pretty penny for that, and in some locked realms like the Dark Nav, for example, the magical energy can buy you a way out to freedom." He rubbed his cheek, frowning. "It could be anyone, anywhere."

"You're right," Zabava agreed with a short nod. "But maybe we could narrow it down a little. My investigation led me here, to your territory. Just like in every other state, there are a few powerful but shady supernatural organizations in Arizona. I have reason to believe that the head of one of these organizations is directly responsible for this... witch-hunt, for lack of a better word. Unfortunately, I couldn't find a way to breach their defense and security mechanisms. To make a long story short, I couldn't get past the lowest levels of their organization, and the man I'm searching for is at the very top."

She chuckled humorlessly and looked away, two bitter wrinkles materializing around her mouth.

"What organization are you talking about?" asked Damian. Deep inside, he already knew the answer, but somewhere even deeper, he hoped he was wrong, and it wasn't the case.

"Underground fighting circles," Zabava replied, a dark shadow of anger darkening her face. "I believe the man we're looking for is the mysterious Head of the Arizona House."

"Dammit," Damian muttered, his fingers rubbing the edge of his bracelet absentmindedly.

"A few years ago, someone was able to bring down two underground fighting Houses—California and Florida," she continued, drilling him with her unnaturally bright eyes. "It didn't stick, but at the time, this person was able to get to the very top. With his help, the Head of the Florida House was arrested, and the Head of the California House was killed."

"I heard about that." Damian huffed, shaking his head. "Do you know what it took for this man to achieve that?" he asked. "He went deep undercover and sold himself into slavery to become one of the captive fighters. Sorry, Zabava, but I'm not willing to do something as stupid and reckless as that. Underground supernatural fighting pits are a dangerous place, and as a captive fighter, you may never meet the Head of a House at all. Too big of a risk with a possibility of zero reward."

"Who's talking about you becoming a slave?" Zabava rolled her eyes. "I don't think anyone in the Arizona House is stupid enough to enslave a Destiny Enforcer. Even if you conceal your power and go deep under, I don't think you're the best candidate for this mission, anyway. But an ancient vampire—"

Before she could finish her sentence, Damian's arm snapped forward, seizing her wrist. He yanked her across the table and leaned closer to her. "You finish that statement, and I swear to all the gods I know, I'll smash your head against this wall," he hissed through gritted teeth, his glowing eyes just inches away from hers. "I will not risk my brother's freedom and safety. I don't care what's at stake. If you want to work with me, get it through your thick skull—Cole is off-limits."

He pushed her arm away, releasing her, and fell back in his seat. Rage locked his body, spiking the elemental power around him, and the walls of the building rattled slightly, causing Kaleb and the werewolves to turn around and stare at him in shock.

"Shish," she huffed, massaging her bruised wrist. "Relax, dude. You need to lighten up a little. If you don't want Cole involved in this, I'm not gonna say anything to him." She thought for a moment and added, "But don't you think you got him involved already?"

Damian took a deep breath, getting his anger and power under control. "Yes, he is involved, but you don't know my brother the way I do." He couldn't help but smile. "He is stupidly brave and reckless, and it's impossible to keep him away from a good fight. This is why I don't want you to say anything to him about going undercover. He'll jump at this opportunity without thinking twice."

Especially since Cole has a reason to believe his maker is held against his will somewhere in the pits. Damian sighed, thinking about what he had to do next.

"Fine." Zabava pursed her lips, raking her fingers through her short hair. "Do you have any other ideas?"

Damian was going to reply, but the persistent vibration in his pocket interrupted him. He raised his hand and held out his index finger, asking her to wait. Then he pulled out his phone and glanced at the screen, his eyes widening in disbelief.

"I'll be damned," he muttered, shaking his head. "Who said the gods are not watching and listening? Sneaky bastards…" He glanced at Zabava and added in a quick whisper, showing her the phone with Ricardo Torres' name on display, "This could be our key to unlocking the door to the upper levels of the Arizona House without anyone going into slavery."

Damian answered his phone, and as Ricardo proceeded to talk, he rose slowly, his fingers nearly crushing the device. A few seconds later, he hung up and put the cellphone on the table. Leaning forward, he propped his fists against the tabletop and stared at a photo of Cole and River on the lock screen.

He had taken this picture a few weeks ago on the driveway in front of Paradise Manor. Cole and River had a mock fight, and his brother had lifted her, holding her in his arms, while she tried to free herself, fighting the vampire's grip with all she had. Damian had captured this moment with his phone's camera, and right now, looking at their smiling faces and sparkling eyes, he thought that he managed to freeze a small piece of happiness forever.

Zabava got up and walked around the table, touching his shoulder. As he straightened and raised his head, running his fingers through his hair to cover his scar, she tapped his cellphone with her finger, pointing at Cole.

"I thought Destiny Enforcers weren't supposed to have personal attachments," she said softly. "Is that going to be a problem, Commander?"

He took the phone and shoved it in his back pocket, looking down at her icily.

"You're right," he said, his voice a dangerous growl. "Destiny Enforcers are not supposed to have personal attachments. But Cole isn't that at all. He is—" He cut himself off, pressing his lips into a firm line. "He's my only brother. My flesh and blood. He's the only *alive* part of me. Everything else has been dead for centuries. You kill him, and you're not going to like the man left standing. So, the next time you get a bright idea of throwing my brother into modern-day slavery, you think twice."

"Got it. The King of the Arizona Vampire Court, who happens to be your brother, is off-limits." Zabava looked at him without trying to conceal her curiosity. "How about Detective Redhead?"

"What about her?"

"Who is she to you? And if push comes to shove, is she going to be a liability?" Zabava touched his hand, but he pulled it away. "I'm not trying to pry into your private life, Damian, but I need to know that in a dangerous situation, you won't take a knee because some evil dude dangles the life of your brother or your woman's safety over your head. I need to know I can count on you to do your job no matter what."

Damian sighed, recognizing the truth in her words. This was exactly the reason why Destiny Enforcers didn't have a personal life. They either worked alone or with a small team of other Enforcers.

"She's a friend," he replied, staring to the side, his chest too tight to speak louder. "My happy memory… A dream of what could have been if I wasn't—" He shook his head and exhaled, closing his eyes. "Don't worry, I know how to do my job."

He reached into his pocket and pulled out his wallet. Placing a few twenty-dollar bills on the table, he waved goodbye to Kaleb and headed toward the door, motioning for her to follow. Once they were outside the bar, he turned the corner, moving briskly toward the dark alley he used as his teleportation point.

"You never told me what you are, by the way," he said, barely glancing at her. "I know you're a PI, but what's your supernatural identity?"

"I didn't tell you because I didn't believe you needed to know," she replied calmly. "For now, all you need to know is that I'm a powerful witch who's here to help. When the time comes—if it comes at all—I promise I'll show you my entire pedigree."

Damian stopped in the middle of the alley, quickly scanning it with his other sight.

"Fine," he replied, his mind racing. "I'm going to need a few days to do some checking around. How can I find you once I'm ready?"

"I'm staying at the Night Owl Inn." She beamed and winked. "I believe you know where that is?" He nodded. She extended her hand to him, wagging her finger impatiently. "Give me your cellphone, big boy."

He reached into his pocket and produced his phone, unlocking it. She grabbed it and took a quick selfie, giving a flirtatious wink and a lopsided grin to the camera. Then she opened his contact list and added her phone number, applying the photo she had just taken to the new contact.

"When you're ready, call me." She gave him his cellphone back, but before he could say anything, she snapped her fingers and vanished.

For a moment, he stood with his jaw dropped, but then shook his head, rubbing the back of his neck. "Witch my ass. Whatever this woman is, she is lying through her teeth. Witches don't teleport."

With a light snap of his fingers, he vanished from the dark alley.

CHAPTER 4

~ COLE ADAMS ~

Cole walked through the dark hallways of Luciano's mansion, the hollow sound of his steps bouncing from wall to wall. Even though it had been a while since Luciano's death, he couldn't get used to his absence, and every time he entered this house, decorated in Tuscan style from the early fifteen century, he couldn't help but think about the man who had stood by his side for over a thousand years. A familiar sweet scent of jasmine touched his nostrils, and his still heart gave a painful jolt as it reminded him of a trusted friend whom he would never see again.

He made his way to a large room at the back of the house. Kicking the door open, he walked inside and dumped the vampire to the floor by the wall. The man stirred, a tortured moan escaping his lips. His eyeballs moved under his tightly shut eyelids, and finally, he cracked his eyes open, staring somewhere at the ceiling without blinking.

His cuffed arms jerked up to the bleeding wound on his chest, and he moaned again. Cole seized his shoulders and hauled him up into a sitting position, resting his back against the wall. As the vampire's eyes settled on Cole's face, an expression of shock crossed his features, quickly replaced by that of fear. He struggled to get to his knees but fell back, a groan of pain breaking through his tightly pressed lips.

"I know who you are," he said, trying to change his position, but Cole pushed him back against the wall with his foot. "You're the King of the Arizona Vampire Court." He looked around wildly, confusion written all over his face. "Where am I?"

"Arizona," Cole replied, squatting in front of him.

The vamp gasped, his eyes bulging. "How did I get here? What am I doing here?" His eyes fell on the bleeding wound on his chest, and just now Cole noticed a small rune partially destroyed by the injury burned into the vampire's skin. "Why am I not healing?"

Cole stared at him in shock, thousands of thoughts crowding his mind. It appeared as though this man couldn't remember anything that had happened to him at least in the last few hours, and he couldn't help but wonder if that strange rune had something to do with it. Even though it looked familiar, he couldn't remember where he'd seen it, and that just added to his sense of foreboding. Since he hoped to get some information about the people who abducted these witches, the man's amnesia wasn't helping him to achieve this goal either.

"Let's take one step at a time." Cole walked away and pulled a chair closer to his prisoner. He sat down and leaned forward, resting his arms on his knees. "You're not healing because of the restraints I placed on you. Look at the handcuffs. The runes engraved in them are partially suppressing your essence. They're not going to kill you, but you can't self-heal, and you're no longer as fast and strong as you used to be."

"Your Majesty, please." The vampire raised his hands, pressing them together in a pleading gesture. "I don't understand. What did I do to—"

"For now, let me be the one who asks questions," Cole interrupted him, raking the vampire with a heavy stare.

"As you wish, Your Majesty," the man whispered, dropping his hands.

"What is the last thing you remember?"

The vampire lowered his head, his shaking fingers clenching and unclenching uncontrollably. "I don't…" he mumbled, staring down. "The last thing I remember is coming to see my king in his office." He raised his face, his eyes wide with fear like that of an animal caught in a hunter's trap. "I don't recall anything after that, my lord. I swear. I don't remember traveling to Arizona, or how I was wounded."

"Who is your king?" asked Cole, realizing that one of his questions had just been answered. This vampire wasn't rogue, but he also wasn't a part of his Court.

"Santiago del Castillo," replied the vampire. "The King of the Nevada Vampire Court, my lord." As Cole frowned, leaning back in his chair, the vampire moved forward, raising his hands pleadingly. "Please, Your Majesty, I swear I'm telling you the truth. You can call him and verify my words."

"What's your name?" asked Cole, reaching for his phone.

"Rob Miller. I am His Majesty's executive—"

With a loud bang, every single window in the room exploded, slivers of glass flying in every direction. Instinctively, Cole dropped to his knees, knocking his chair down. He bent forward, covering his head with his arms. A few pieces of glass cut his arms, leaving long, bleeding lacerations in their wake. With a low growl, he jumped to his feet and spun around to see six figures in dark tactical uniforms barging into the room through the glassless windows.

Dressed in all black with black masks over their faces, it was impossible to say who or what they were in the darkness of the room. Without saying a word, they pulled out their swords and hastened forward, moving with the grace and force of experienced swordsmen. Cole stepped back, positioning himself between his prisoner and the attackers, and unsheathed his sword, his eyes never leaving his opponents.

They stilled for a heartbeat to exchange a quick look. The person upfront gave a curt nod, and without saying anything, they attacked all at once. Cole spun in place, moving as fast as he could in the limited space he had. But despite his sword skills and his speed, the assailants deflected all his strikes with ease, and he couldn't get rid of the feeling that they were toying with him like a bunch of alley cats with a tiny mouse.

A sharp pain spiked through his body as a blade ran through his side, and he cried out, staggering backward just to run into his prisoner, tripping over his leg. He fell to the floor, but jumped to his feet right away, ignoring the burning pain under his ribs. Glancing down, he noticed that the wound wasn't healing, dark red blood gushing from the deep laceration, soaking his shirt and pants. He had no time to worry about it. His attackers didn't give him a chance to regroup, and judging by their behavior, they weren't here to negotiate or take prisoners. It was a kill or be killed situation, and he'd never considered himself easy prey.

Cole screamed, swinging his sword in a desperate attempt to parry the next strike. Metal clashed against metal with a loud clang, sparks flying. He pushed down on his blade, looking directly at his opponent's face. A pair of dark eyes stared back at him through the slits of the mask, the taunting twinkles mocking him. The attacker retreated, skillfully avoiding the bind. Fast and forceful, Cole followed, and his sword finally found its target, the blade sliding through his assailant's chest, missing the heart by no more than an inch.

The attacker cried out in a high-pitched voice and fell to the floor, hands rising to cover the wound. Cole closed the distance between them in one long stride and ripped the mask off, exposing their face.

"But you're a woman," Cole whispered, staring down at her

in shock. A derisive sneer stretched her lips coated in bubbling, red liquid, her brown eyes shining with disdain as she glowered at him.

"Yes," she hissed and coughed, blood spilling from her mouth, running down her chin. "And you're nothing but a stupid, disgusting vamp who just got played."

Cole snapped around, realizing his mistake too late. A long blade pierced his stomach, and the person wielding it twisted it in his gut, moving it up slightly before pulling it out. As debilitating pain ripped through his insides, he screamed and fell back, hitting the tiled floor with his head.

The attackers stopped and lowered their weapons, taking their masks off. Tall and athletically built, all of them were women. The front one—most likely their leader, judging by the way she held herself—took a knee next to Cole and seized his hair, yanking his head up. Then she took a dagger and stabbed him in his stomach again. He groaned, his hands rising to his bleeding wounds involuntarily.

"Cole Adams," she said softly, her voice barely above a whisper, "today is your lucky day, vamp. We're not here for you. In fact, we have orders to keep you alive for a little while longer."

She glanced over her shoulder and gave the other four a quick nod. One of her teammates reached behind her back and produced a wooden stake. Cole tensed, raising his hand covered in red splatters of fresh blood.

"Please, don't kill him—," he started, but before he could finish, the woman thrust the stake through his prisoner's heart.

The vampire's mouth opened in a silent cry of pain, and his widened eyes locked with Cole's for a brief moment before his body disintegrated, turning into ash. The enchanted handcuffs fell to the floor with a loud clatter, and the woman picked them up, observing them with interest, her finger following the flow of runes.

"What a neat little toy," she murmured, sliding the handcuffs into a small hip purse attached by leather straps to her belt and her thigh. "I think I'll keep it." She winked at Cole and added with a shrug, "Spoils of war."

The leader patted Cole lightly on his cheek. "Our job here is done," she said, making a circular motion with her finger. "In case you were wondering, your wounds are not healing because of the poison circulating through your body. All our blades are covered with it. But don't worry. It's not going to kill you. It's designed to make you weaker for a few hours. After that, your wounds will heal, and you'll be back to your normal self." She got up, staring down at him with unconcealed disgust. "Whatever that means."

She pivoted on her heels and headed toward the window without as much as giving a second look to him or her fallen teammate. The other four women followed her, and they left the room the same way they came in.

Cole moaned and fell back. His eyes closed and darkness, hot and sticky, enveloped him, strangling his every desire. He wasn't sure how long he lay like this, motionless, subdued by crippling pain. After a while, he opened his eyes and reached for his cellphone. He brought the device up and cursed, dropping it. The phone was broken, a thin web of fractures covering the screen.

His arm fell to the floor with a dull thud, and his head lolled to the side powerlessly. Right in front of his face, he saw the arm of the dead woman. The sleeve of her uniform was torn above her wrist, and through the hole, he could see a small tattoo drawn in red ink—a stylized Ankh symbol that looked like a sword with a serpent coiling around it.

He closed his eyes, swallowing hard, and opened his mind to the blood bond with his brother.

"Dima, I need you," he projected. *"I'm in serious trouble, brother."*

There was no answer…

CHAPTER 5

~ DAMIAN BLAKE ~

At first, Damian teleported to Paradise Manor, but as his arm responded with a sharp twinge, he glanced down at the four long welts left by the shifter-lion that cut deep into his flesh. Despite his ability to control his pain, the gruesome look of the injury made him shudder, sending waves of weakness and aches through his battered body. He glanced at the house, but as inviting as it looked, he changed his mind. He didn't want River to see him like this. Even though she had witnessed a fair share of injuries in her line of duty, when it came to him and Cole, she couldn't tolerate seeing them hurt.

"It's okay," he mumbled to himself. "All I have to do is heal myself and go back home to get some sleep. A few hours of uninterrupted rest, and I'll be like new."

Despite the exhaustion he felt, he snapped his fingers again and teleported to his favorite place in the desert. Isolated by a few large rock formations, the natural amphitheater he had found when he moved to Blue Creek was secluded enough to provide some privacy. A while later, however, he had added a few more large rocks, making sure that the area he chose wasn't visible to anyone from outside. So even if some crazy human decided to take their dirt bike for a spin in the middle of the night, they couldn't see him there.

With a low groan, he lowered himself to the ground and ripped the leftovers of his shirt off. Then he lay down flat on his back and folded his hands over his stomach, enjoying the touch of the cold sand to his bare skin. Closing his eyes, he channeled the elemental energy of Earth and started the healing process. As the energy of his element rushed through him, surrounding him with its warm, welcoming embrace, he moaned softly, feeling weakness assailing him once again.

While healing magic could take care of any injury and relieve pain, it demanded a lot of magical and physical energy. After performing healing, Damian always felt so drained and tired that the only thing he could think of was sleep. Today, it was the second time he had to do it, and he knew it would take a toll on him. Besides, keeping his pain under control for such a long time had its price tag as well.

As the pain gave up its hold, and all welts, lacerations and bruises disappeared, his eyes closed of their own accord, and a peaceful oblivion took hold of him.

* * *

"Damian... Daaa-mi-aaa-n..."

He jolted into a sitting position, staring around in shock. He was still in the same place, surrounded by the rocks and the endless desert, yet everything looked different. The sky shone with a soft, purple glow, and a few white clouds had a shining purple lining. The sand and the mountains reflected the color of the sky, shimmering with purple and lilac sparkles.

"What the hell?" he mumbled, rising to his feet.

As he glanced down at himself, his jaw dropped. His body was clad in ancient Russian armor, the links of chainmail reflecting the purple shades of his surroundings. He ran his fingers over it, feeling the slick coldness of metal under his touch, and spun around.

"What the hell?? Mara! I know it's you. Show yourself! Goddammit!" he yelled, throwing his hands up.

A sound of soft, musical laughter rang behind him, making him twirl around, his chainmail producing a soft jingling sound with his every move.

"Aw, Damian, a girl just wants to have fun. What's wrong with that?" She giggled, her fingers tracing the shape of his chest plate. "Can't I see my handsome Russian warrior in his full regalia?"

Damian stared down at the Slavic goddess of Nightmares, flabbergasted. She rose on her tiptoes and brushed his cheek with her fingers. Damian seized her wrist and forced her arm down.

"Are you trying to flirt with me, Mara?" he asked with an exasperated sigh, watching her grin grow wider.

"And is it working?" she asked, batting her long, black eyelashes at him.

"Not in the slightest. What do you want?"

She snapped her fingers, playful twinkles shining in her eyes. He glanced down, realizing that even though she had restored his normal appearance, it only made the situation worse.

"Dammit..." he mumbled, assessing his state of undress.

She laughed, and for a moment, she didn't look like one of the most powerful dark deities in the Slavic pantheon, but like a young girl who truly did have fun flirting with him.

He sighed and sat down, pulling his knees to his chest. She lowered herself to the ground next to him, readjusting the folds of her long black dress.

"What can I do for you today, Mara?" he asked, sounding slightly softer. "To be honest, I'm exhausted, and it's the middle of the night. Unlike you, I have a human body, so I need food and sleep. And I know until you say your piece, you're not going to let me out of this illusion. So, let's get to business."

"I can sense how drained you are magically, Damian, and I'm truly sorry to be the bearer of bad news. I know you've been through hell in the last few hours, but the night is not over yet," she said in full seriousness. "Anyway, this is not why I'm here. You fell asleep in the middle of nowhere, and I seized the opportunity to speak with you."

"About?"

"You," she replied, gently following the flow of his bicep with her slender finger. "You seem to be a magnet for trouble, boy."

"What do you mean?"

"The last time we met, you had a Fallen toying with you," she continued. "This time—" She cut herself off and looked away, staring at the bright, purple desert. There was something so plaintive in her expression that it sent icy waves down his spine.

"What's going on, Mara?" he asked softly, turning toward her. "You went through the trouble of creating this illusion, so you may as well give me your warning."

She scrambled to her knees and readjusted her position to face him. Sitting back on her heels, she took his hand into hers, her thumb rubbing his knuckles absentmindedly. His first reaction was to yank his hand out of her grip, but he suppressed it.

"Damian," she said at length, "you know how it all works. I can't tell you what's going on. All I can do is give you a vague warning."

"I know that," he replied, giving a gentle squeeze to her tiny hand. "It's frustrating, but I've been around long enough to know the limitations. I also know that you wouldn't do anything without getting something in return."

She shook her head no, a deep vertical crease appearing between her thin, black eyebrows. "I already have what I want from you. You gave me your word that you'll speak with Chernobog on my behalf, given the opportunity."

"I stand by my word, Mara."

"Well, then you understand that I have a vested interest in keeping you alive and well, right?" She gave him a half-hearted shrug. "So, here is my warning. You're on the right path, my Russian warrior, but this path is too dangerous to walk alone—even for someone as powerful as you."

"Are you talking about my brother?" he asked.

"Yes, but no," she replied, shaking her head. "Your brother always stands by your side, anyway. You two are bound by destiny. I'm talking about a different person in your life. When the time comes, don't say no to an offer of help, no matter who this offer comes from. Do you understand me?"

Damian nodded, wondering if the goddess was talking about Zabava. But since he knew that asking her about that was pointless, he inclined his head in a slight bow. "Thank you, my lady. I'll try to remember that."

"I guess it's time for you to wake up." She raised her hand, but he seized it, holding it in his grip.

"Wait," he said, releasing her. "Can I ask you a question before you leave?"

"Oh?" She raised her eyebrows, curiosity gleaming in her large, black eyes. "Go ahead. What would you like to know?"

Damian nibbled on his lip, searching for better words. Then he averted his gaze, staring at his hands covered in bloodstains. "In the last few months, I can barely get any sleep," he said, his voice hoarse. "I see the same nightmare over and over with slight variations that make it only harder and more painful for me to watch. The same vision you showed me a while ago. Are you doing it to me?"

"No, Damian." She pressed her hands to her chest. "I swear it isn't me. Why would I do that to you if you promised to help me? You're my only hope to find my way home… the only hope to see my—" She cut herself off and added, "Besides, I'm not the only dream-walker as you probably know."

"You're right," he agreed calmly. "You're not the only dream-walker, but you are a dark deity, and it takes true evil to do something like this."

"Good. Evil." Mara huffed, gazing heavenwards. "After walking this puny realm for the last thousand years, you still didn't learn your lesson, did you, Damian?"

"And what might that lesson be?"

"There is no such thing as unadulterated evil or pure good." Mara shrugged with a light flick of her hand. "The world is not black and white, my boy. There are all sorts of shades in between. The mesmerizing canvas of life is painted with these shades, and every one of us is the artist who wields the brush." She fell silent for a moment, exploring his face. "Sometimes, good people do bad things for the right reasons. Sometimes, an evil being does something completely selfless because they believe it's what they need to do. I don't believe that throughout your long life, you've never witnessed something like that." She looked up at him, her face absolutely serious, but then her lips twitched ever so slightly. "Besides, without evil, you won't know what good is."

"You have a point, but I've never seen a dark deity playing on the side of the Light. Not without an ulterior motive, that is. And I'm sorry, but you're not an exception to this rule." Damian sighed. "The other reason I thought it was you was because you were the one who showed me this vision in the first place." He fell silent and raised his eyes at her, a flicker of hope igniting in his chest. "I think if you break the mystery of this vision and tell me who that man is, the nightmares will stop."

She looked away, a soft pink shade rising to her pale cheeks.

"Sorry, Damian, but I can't do that," she said and added hastily, "Not because I don't want to help you." She met his eyes, tugging at the collar of her dress uncomfortably. "This vision is real, but I have no idea who this man is. I lied to you to force you into a deal with me. Just like I lied to your brother when I told him his maker was dead. I did it to hurt him, and I think it worked." She threw the long black strands of her hair off her face and shrugged nonchalantly. "I'm not going to apologize for that. I did what I had to do at the time. As you pointed out many times, I'm a dark deity. It's in my nature."

She winked at him and got up. Leaning down slightly, she cupped his cheek. He held his breath and stiffened to stop himself from shying away from her touch.

"If you trust me, I'll find out who's messing with your dreams—," she offered, but cut herself off, and a dark shadow crossed her face. She straightened, listening to something intently.

"What is it?" he asked, looking around, but everything remained the same.

Her gaze focused on him, and she frowned. "It's time for you to wake up, Damian," she said in a hoarse whisper. "As I mentioned before, this night isn't over for you."

"Mara—," he started, but she wasn't listening.

"Goodbye for now."

She touched his forehead with two fingers, and the world around him spun in a whirlpool of colors. He screamed and woke up, lying on the cold sand of the midnight desert.

"Dima, I need you..." Cole's voice sounded shaky and weak in Damian's frazzled mind, and a wave of fear surged through their blood bond. *"I'm in serious trouble, brother."*

CHAPTER 6

~ DAMIAN BLAKE ~

Damian jolted to his feet, and the world around him swirled and tilted, making his stomach heave. He dropped to all fours, realizing belatedly that after all the events of this day and the double healing he had performed in a matter of a few hours, he was too weak and too drained to do anything except for returning to Paradise Manor and dropping on his bed, dead to the world.

"*Dima...*" Cole's voice sounded in Damian's mind again, and a wave of despair and fear rushed through their connection, taking his breath away. "*Brother... I hope you're okay...*"

"*Nikolai, I hear you,*" he replied, his chest shuddering with laborious breaths. "*Where are you? What's going on?*"

"*Luciano's estate. Council room.*" A surge of hope flooded their psychic link. "*Can you come here? I'm alone now, but I can't...*"

His brother's voice faded for a moment shorter than a heartbeat, but to Damian, this fleeting pause was longer than forever.

"*Cole—*"

"*Dima, I can't move on my own. I've been poisoned,*" continued Cole. "*I need your help.*"

"*On my way,*" replied Damian, cutting their line of communication to make sure Cole couldn't perceive how he felt at the moment.

Still on all fours, he dropped his head and took a few deep breaths, trying to pull himself together. With a strenuous groan, he forced himself to his feet and swayed a little as the desert spun around him again. He closed his eyes, cold sweat dripping down his back, and channeled his magic. Then he snapped his fingers and teleported, praying to all the gods he knew that he had enough strength and magical energy to help his brother.

* * *

DAMIAN MATERIALIZED IN front of the entrance door into Luciano's mansion and reached out to his brother but received no answer. A wave of pain, raw and all-consuming, assailed him through their connection, and the blood froze in his veins, his heart beating somewhere in his throat.

He didn't remember running through the dark, empty hallways, focusing only on the weak connection with his brother, and when he finally reached the main hall, sweat was running down his face, plastering long, uneven strands of his hair to his face. He kicked the door open and stopped dead, observing the room, every little detail telling him the story of the battle that had unfolded here just a few minutes ago.

All windows were broken, and slivers of glass covered the floor. A dead woman in a black uniform lay sprawled on the tiles, her eyes with dilated pupils staring at the ceiling. Cole sat by the wall in a pool of his own blood, his hands clasped over the bleeding wounds on his stomach. His head was bowed to his chest, and gray shadows lay under his eyes and cheekbones, making him look older and tired. Dark blood was seeping slowly from another wound on his side, trickling from under his arm.

Damian crossed the distance between them in a few strides and dropped to his knees next to him, realizing with horror that he barely had enough strength to keep an upright position, let alone teleport with a passenger.

"Nikolai," he whispered, brushing his brother's blood-soaked hair off his face. "Open your eyes…"

Cole cracked his eyelids open, his eyes resembling a black void filled with torment, and the corners of his mouth quirked up in a pained grimace. His lips parted as he tried to speak, but he couldn't say a word, blood spilling from the corner of his mouth.

"The Sisterhood of the Sun is after me..." he projected, his voice sounding weak and unsteady even through their blood bond. *"Their blades are poisoned... they lied, they said they weren't after me, but..."*

Damian turned around and glanced at the dead woman, his eyes halting on the tattoo on her wrist, his heart thundering in his chest.

"Cole, hang in there, brother. I'll get you help. We'll figure it out," he said, turning to him. "It's probably going to hurt. Sorry about that."

As gently as possible, he lifted his brother into his arms but remained in a kneeling position for a few seconds to give himself a chance to deal with the weakness. Cole cried out, and his arms dropped powerlessly, exposing two deep cuts on his stomach. With a low growl, Damian rose to his feet and leaned his back against the wall, taking short breaths as his vision went out of focus.

"Dima... you're drained... you can't teleport," Cole projected. *"That's okay. Let's come up with a different plan."*

"No," Damian exhaled and pushed away from the wall. "I can do it."

He opened himself to the flow of magic and elemental power, hoping to gather enough for one more jump. He didn't have enough strength to channel magical energy from the outside, and his internal resources were almost depleted. He knew it, but he refused to think about it.

Perun almighty, give me the strength... just one more time... It's my little brother. Take my life if you must, but let me save him...

Tapping into whatever was left of his internal energy, he snapped his fingers. The dark room twirled around him, making wild somersaults. Nausea rose to his throat, and his stomach clenched. As his vision blurred, he pressed Cole to his chest, focusing on keeping his arms locked.

He materialized in front of the entrance to Paradise Manor, but the ground slipped from under his feet, and he fell, hitting his head on the marble steps.

DAMIAN REGAINED CONSCIOUSNESS and attempted to lift his head, but as a splitting headache responded to his move, he moaned and dropped back. Turning to the side, he saw his brother, and his heart gave a painful jolt. Cole appeared to be unconscious. His lips were slightly parted, and he looked like a boy who fell asleep, ready to wake up at any moment. The bleeding had stopped, but Damian wasn't sure if it was good news or bad.

With sheer effort of will, Damian turned to his stomach and pushed himself to all fours. After a few breaths, he scrambled to his feet and made his way to the door. He rang the doorbell and leaned against the wall by the entrance, counting his heartbeats as he waited for River to open it. When the lock finally clicked, he pushed away from the wall, meeting River's flabbergasted stare.

"Dima, what happened?" she whispered, an expression of horror imprinted on her face.

"I'll explain later. Help me bring Cole inside." Damian headed toward his brother, every move taking serious effort.

With River's help, he lifted Cole again and opened his mind to their blood bond, but no matter how hard he tried, Cole wasn't responding, a giant empty hole remaining in the place where he used to feel his brother's presence. Damian crossed into the house and headed toward the right wing, barely able to move his feet. He reached only as far as the end of the foyer and stopped, his legs trembling with strain.

Lowering Cole to the floor by the wall, he dropped to his knees next to him and raised his eyes at River, guilt shredding his insides.

"This is as far as I can manage," he said, his every muscle buzzing with exhaustion. "Cole has been poisoned, and I'm too drained to do anything." He reached for his magic but found none, his body refusing to function properly. "Dammit…" He slammed his hand against the hard tiles, shaking his head. "I need to summon Luc de la Crosse, but I can't perform even the tiniest spell."

"Luc de la Crosse?" River muttered, reaching into her pocket. "I can summon him."

Damian glanced up at her and smiled faintly. "You can't. To perform a summoning spell, you need to use magical energy. You're human, River. You have no magic."

"Oh, yeah?" She cocked her eyebrow. "Watch me. I'm going to use a very complicated and obscure branch of magic. It's called dialing a goddamn phone number." She showed him her cellphone, pursing her lips reproachfully. "Doofus. If you would learn how to use your cellphone, maybe I'd sleep better at night."

"But how—"

"Cole gave me a few phone numbers in case of emergency," she murmured, searching through her contact list. "Luckily, he is not as archaic as you are and doesn't count on magic to do basic things in life, like getting in touch with people he needs."

She dialed a phone number and pressed the device to her ear. Even though she didn't put the phone on speaker, Damian could hear the beeps and then a raspy male voice as Luc answered the call.

"Mr. Luc de la Crosse?" asked River, her voice strong and calm. "This is detective River Evans. I'm sorry for the late-night call, but I need your help, sir. I'm going to put Damian Blake on the phone, so he can brief you in."

She passed her cellphone to Damian, and he took it, barely able to wrap his fingers around the device. "Luc," he said, cringing inwardly at how empty his voice sounded. "Cole has been poisoned by the Sisterhood slayers. I'm too drained to do anything to help him." Trying to be as brief as possible, he told the Master Warden everything that had happened earlier today and everything that Cole had told him.

"Are you sure those were the Sisterhood slayers?" Luc asked, doubt clear in his voice. "The Sisterhood reports to the Destiny Council. Cole couldn't be on their list, *mon ami*. Something doesn't sound right."

"I don't know, Luc. I saw their mark on the wrist of the dead slayer." Damian threw a desperate look at his brother, his chest tight with the expectation of a brewing supernatural storm. "I'm going to find out the first chance I get. In the meantime, can you do anything to help Cole?"

"I assume you're at Paradise Manor," said the Warden.

"Yes."

"I'll be with you in ten minutes. I need to get the antidote for Cole."

As the Master Warden hung up, Damian gave River her phone back and leaned forward, resting his elbow atop his bent knees. Ten minutes wasn't a long time, but in the current situation, it was ten minutes too long. He took Cole's hand, slightly squeezing it, but Cole didn't respond.

"He'll be all right. A while ago, he told me that as long as he's not a pile of ash, he can recover from any injury," said River.

Damian snorted, shaking his head. "Sounds like Cole. Only he can say something like this while keeping a straight face."

"Well, it's true, isn't it?" She sat down next to Damian, resting her back against the wall, and tapped her lap. "Lay down, Dima. You look like you're going to drop dead if you have to remain in the upright position for another minute."

He averted his eyes, staring to the side at the old silver mirror. She chuckled and grabbed his arm, pulling him closer. Feeling too tired to resist, he lay down on the cold concrete floor, placing his head on River's lap, and closed his eyes.

"Why don't you get a few minutes of sleep while we're waiting for Luc?" she suggested, her fingers threading through his hair in slow, even strokes.

"I'll wait," he mumbled, folding his hands over his stomach. "I'm afraid if I fall asleep in my condition, you won't be able to wake me up." He glanced up at her, meeting her warm, blue eyes. "Tell me something… anything to keep me awake. What happened in that house after I called you?"

"We found three victims on the second floor, but unfortunately, we discovered nothing about the perp. No prints, no DNA, nothing. We have zero leads," she said, the movements of her hand slowing down. "The women were alive, but they suffered severe blood loss and appeared to be under the influence of some kind of substance. We're waiting for a report from the hospital, and hopefully, the doctors will be able to identify what drug they were on."

"It's not a drug," objected Damian faintly. "They were addicted to a vampire's bite."

"That would also explain the blood loss," murmured River, resuming her even strokes through his hair.

"River, you were right," he said, catching her hand and pressing it to his cheek. "It is a supernatural case." Damian sighed, his thoughts traveling back to his conversation with Zabava. "Even though I still don't know who is behind these abductions, I have no doubt this person is extremely powerful and dangerous. It's not easy to abduct a witch in the first place, but to drain her of her magical energy is next to impossible. Trust me, not everyone can perform this kind of dark magic." He glanced up, meeting River's troubled gaze. "Please, do whatever you have to do to give me enough time for my investigation. If local human authorities get involved deeper before I find this person…"

He let go of her hand, and his arm dropped to the floor with a dull thud.

"I'll do what I can, Dima," she replied, gently caressing his cheek, "but I can't promise anything. I can't stand in the way of an active investigation."

"I know." He closed his eyes, exhaling with a low groan. "Where is Gypsy, by the way? I'm surprised she's not here to make fun of me while I'm down."

River giggled, sounding like a little girl. "I still can't get used to the fact that you can talk to animals. Don't worry, she's sleeping in your bedroom. She'll get her chance to poke her feline jokes at you."

Detecting a slight fluctuation of magical energy field outside the house, Damian raised his head. "River, Luc is here. Open the door for him, please."

As River rose to her feet and headed toward the entrance, Damian forced himself into a sitting position, moving closer to Cole. Luc, dressed in his usual black pants and shirt of a priest, stepped into the foyer, and his jaw dropped. Getting in control of his initial reaction, the Master Warden made his way to Cole and lowered to his knees, placing a black backpack on the floor by his side.

"I thought it was bad, but I didn't realize how truly bad it was," he murmured, mostly to himself.

He opened the bag and pulled out a small plastic bag with a few paper strips inside. Muttering something under his breath, he quickly explored the opened wounds on Cole's stomach and side. Then he took one of the strips and dipped it into the vampire's blood. As the strip turned blue, the Warden exhaled, frowning, and put the used strip in a separate plastic bag.

Throwing a quick glance at Damian, he said, "You were right. The poison belongs to the Sisterhood. They developed it a while ago, and it's available only to the members of their organization. It's not supposed to kill vampires but put them out of commission for a few hours. As you can see, it's quite effective." He grabbed his backpack and produced a small, clear vial with a thick, shimmering liquid inside. "Luckily, it's not deadly, and I do have an antidote that can counter its effects right away."

He uncorked the vial and lifted Cole's head slightly, shifting to find a better position. Then he looked back at River, a vibe of doubt lingering over him.

"River, you may want to leave this room or at least turn away," he said. "It's not going to be pretty."

"I'm not going anywhere." River folded her arms, planting her feet firmly on the floor. "I'm not a delicate flower, and Cole is… like a brother to me. He's family."

"As you wish, my lady," Luc murmured, returning to the task at hand.

He rested Cole's head on his lap and forced his jaws apart. Pressing the vial to his lips, he let a few drops of the liquid slip into his mouth. The Adam's apple in Cole's neck moved as he swallowed the antidote. At first, nothing happened. Then suddenly, Cole's eyes flew wide open, shining with a bright scarlet glow. His every muscle tensed, and his body arched, his hands locking and unlocking spasmodically at his sides. His fingers elongated and turned into claws, leaving long scratches on the polished surface of the floor. As his terrifying fangs expanded, a blood-curdling howl of unbearable torment erupted from his lips.

River gasped and pressed both hands to her mouth, a horrified expression on her face. Damian reached for his brother, but Luc intercepted him.

"Stand back, Commander," he shouted, struggling to hold the vampire in place. "I swear he's going to be all right."

It was over as fast as it started. Cole stopped screaming, and his body relaxed, falling to the floor limply. His eyes moved to Damian, and as he looked at his brother, the scarlet glow vanished, replaced by his natural deep blue. But as his gaze shifted to River, his lips parted, and his eyes widened. He pressed his hand to his mouth to cover his fangs just to realize that his fingers were still elongated into claws. His face turned even paler, his skin looking almost translucent, and with a soft moan, he closed his eyes and turned away.

Luc de la Crosse gently moved Cole from his lap and quickly gathered all his plastic bags, placing everything in his backpack. Then he rose to his feet and pulled a few medical blood bags, offering them to Damian.

"Commander, your brother will need some blood, and you're not in any condition to donate," he said calmly. Damian took the bags, placing them on the floor next to Cole, and Luc continued, "I can see how drained you are, Damian. Please, get some rest tonight, but as soon as you wake up, call me. I believe we have a serious problem, and I must know everything there is to know."

"Yes, sir. I'll call you first thing tomorrow morning." Damian scrambled to his feet and held out his hand for a handshake. "Thank you, Luc."

Luc shook his hand and headed toward the exit. Stopping by the door, he turned to River, sending a reproachful gaze her way.

"Just for the record, Detective," he said softly. "I never thought you were a delicate flower. I didn't ask you to leave because I thought you couldn't handle it. I asked you to leave because I thought Cole wouldn't want you to see him like this."

He bowed slightly and walked out the door, closing it behind himself with a soft thud.

CHAPTER 7

~ DAMIAN BLAKE ~

By the time Damian woke up, the sun was blasting through the open window, and the scorching afternoon heat invaded his room. He cracked his eyes open, staring at the bright rectangle of light on the ceiling, and pulled his left arm across his chest, gently stretching it. The injury he had received the night before was gone, and he felt rested and refreshed after a full ten hours of uninterrupted sleep.

Damian sat up, lowering his feet to the floor. He didn't recall having any nightmares while sleeping, and it made him wonder if it had been Mara after all who was tormenting him in his dreams. His mind flashed back to the last conversation he had with the Slavic goddess of Nightmares, her every word imprinted in his memory. He frowned, rubbing the edge of his bracelet as he stared down at the slithering lines of the tattoo on his right arm. Mara was right. She had no reason to cripple him with nightmares if she was counting on his help to find her way back home. Besides, she had helped him twice already.

Maybe she kept her promise to find whoever had been playing with my dreams and blocked them from entering my mind? The thought popped in his head, and he facepalmed at how ridiculous it sounded even to himself. Maybe Mara was gracious enough to help him twice, but dark deities weren't known for their selfless deeds. They used others to get what they needed, giving back nothing or as little as possible. *No, it couldn't have been her. Then who and how?*

"*Finally! The first intelligent thought since you woke up,*" a high-pitched voice peeped in his head, making him flinch and jump to his feet, staring around wildly. "*It was me, of course. Who else?*"

"What the hell?" Damian stood in the middle of the empty room. Even Gypsy was gone. The memory of the voice in his head warning him of the upcoming danger crossed his mind, and he added, "I've had enough of your games since yesterday. It's time you showed yourself."

"*Aw, Commander, come on. My friend told me you were a smart man. This was one of the reasons I agreed to serve you. But so far you are doing everything to prove him wrong,*" the voice spoke up, tones of humor ringing in his words. "*Look at your right arm.*"

Damian glanced at his arm and swallowed hard. His tattoo glowed with a soft blue light, the ink slithering slightly under his skin as if the vines were alive. He channeled a little bit of his magic and ran his fingers over the design, detecting a gentle energy signature that wasn't his. It didn't appear to be dark or evil. On the contrary, it felt warm and friendly.

"*You're getting warmer, Commander...*" the voice sang in his head.

Yakov gave it to me. He said I needed it... It can't be anything evil.

"*Warmer...*" The voice giggled.

"Dammit." Damian threw his hands up. "Just show yourself, would yah?"

"*Ew. You have such poor manners, Commander. Didn't the Destiny Council teach you anything? I shall have a word with them the first chance I get.*" Damian couldn't see the owner of the voice, but he was positive the speaker was grinning from ear to ear, and that just added to his aggravation. *"You forgot to say the magic word."*

"The magic word, huh?" Damian folded his arms over his chest, staring at the glowing tattoo with nothing but the worst intentions. "How about three magic words? Laser. Tattoo. Removal." He held out three fingers.

"Ha-ha. Very funny. I'm bound to a comedian," the voice grumbled, and an image of a cartoonish-looking dog rolling its round eyes flashed in Damian's mind. *"You know as well as I do, I'm not a tattoo. This ink is just a visual representation of the spell that binds us together."*

Next time I see Yakov, I'm going to kill him, Damian thought, his aggravation rising to a dangerously high level. *Come to think of it, I should summon him right now and rip him a new one.*

"A blood-thirsty comedian with the manners of a medieval peasant," the voice summarized snidely. *"I think I'm going to summon Yakov myself and ask him what he was thinking, talking me into serving an ogre."*

Realizing that this verbal battle could stretch on forever with no favorable outcome, Damian sat down on the bed and rested his arms on his lap, shaking his head. He took a deep, cleansing breath and said as peacefully as he could muster, "Please, show yourself. If you're right, and indeed, we're bound by a spell, let's meet face-to-face and get to know each other better."

"Aw, Commander," the voice mumbled tearfully. *"I'm touched. Are you asking me on a date?"*

"I've had enough." Damian got up and headed toward the bathroom.

He stripped everything off, throwing the dirty, torn clothes into a garbage can, and opened the faucet, waiting for the water to warm up. Yesterday, when he returned to his room after making sure his brother had completely recovered, he had been too drained to do anything else but sleep. So he'd dropped on the bed without undressing or taking the cover off, dead to the world in a matter of seconds.

Damian grabbed a fresh towel out of the cabinet and hung it on the handle of the shower door, ready to get in.

"Commander, turn around!" the voice shouted, causing him to flinch again.

Damian spun around, and his jaw fell to the floor. Right in front of him, reflected in the polished, white tiles, sat a German Shepherd puppy. He was no older than three-four months, judging by the looks of him. One of his black, furry ears stood straight up, but the second one was tilted to the side, resting against the first one. His round, black eyes stared at Damian with humorous twinkles, and a wide doggish grin stretched his muzzle, showing a long pink tongue.

The puppy shifted from paw to paw, his long, black tail brushing the floor from side to side eagerly. *"Nice to meet you in person, Commander."*

Damian's eyes widened, and he pressed his hand to his mouth, staring at the pup incredulously. *Uhhh... Gypsy is going to kill me for bringing a dog into the house...* He squatted and reached forward, patting the dog's warm fur carefully.

"I knew as a Child of Earth you wouldn't be able to resist my beauty and natural charm," the puppy announced proudly, stepping closer.

Damian chuckled, warmth suffusing his chest. He took the dog with both hands to pick him up, but to his shock, he couldn't move him even an inch. The puppy's tiny body seemed to be as heavy as a ton of bricks.

"Oh, damn," Damian mumbled as realization dawned on him. "I know what Yakov gave me. I know what you are…"

"Oh, yeah? Let's hear it then." The puppy's grin grew wider.

"A gargoyle," Damian replied, stifling his laughter. "You're a gargoyle. I think Yakov gifted me a personal bodyguard."

"Ding-ding-ding!" The puppy spun in place, chasing his tail.

"*Hallelujah! Not all is lost. There is some intelligent life inside that ungroomed head of yours after all, Commander.*" He shook like a dog shaking water off his fur, and two large, webby wings expanded behind his back. Wagging his eyebrows, he added, "*You like me. You really, really like me! Am I not awesome?*"

Damian got up, laughing. "You are as awesome as gargoyles come." He opened the shower door, glancing at the little monster over his shoulder. "Now, Mr. Awesomeness, as fun as all this is, I need to take a shower, and something tells me I have a busy day ahead. Can you hide back in that tattoo until we have more time for small talk?"

"*Um... no can do.*" The puppy folded his wings and tilted his head to the left, his softer ear flapping with his move. "*Well, if you want to be in charge, you must complete the binding spell.*"

"What?" Damian turned toward the gargoyle. "What do I have to do?"

"*It's simple.*" The puppy waved his paw dismissively. "*All you have to do is name me and seal it with—*"

"If you're going to say what I think you're going to say, I'm done with you, and you're going back where you came from," muttered Damian.

"*Hmm... no, Commander,*" replied the puppy with a sizable amount of sarcasm in his voice. "*That wasn't what I was going to say, but I do like your train of thought.*" He hopped closer to Damian, staring up at him in that sweet doggish manner with his tail working like a fan. "*I was going to say seal it with fresh ink, okay? Now, be nice. Can you give me a strong, powerful name? Like Bulat, Yakov's gargoyle. Please, please, please...*" The puppy danced in place. "*Pretty please?*"

Damian laughed softly and squatted to scratch the little dog behind his ear. "You got it, buddy," he said, rising. "Give me a few minutes to take a shower and clear my mind. It'll give me a chance to think of a strong name for you. Then we'll go to the kitchen so I can introduce you to my family, and I'll name you at that time. Deal?"

"*I see,*" the gargoyle murmured thoughtfully. "*Now, I think I understand why humans take showers every day. When their brain gets dusty, they can't even think of something as simple as a name.*" He waved his paw, nodding approvingly. "*In this case, take a nice, long shower, Commander.*"

Damian stumbled, almost choking on the suppressed laughter. He nodded at the dog and finally stepped into the shower stall.

* * *

THIRTY MINUTES LATER, Damian walked out of the shower but didn't find the gargoyle where he had left him. Cursing quietly, he toweled his body dry, got dressed as quickly as he could and rushed out of the room. Halting by the doorway, he scanned the house with his other sight and detected the gargoyle's energy signature somewhere around the kitchen area.

Cursing Yakov for his gift and all the gargoyles in the world, he ran into the kitchen. But as soon as he got there, he came to a screeching halt and pressed his hand to his mouth, flabbergasted. Cole was crouching on top of the kitchen table, his fangs fully expanded. Hissing in that eerie vampire's way, he stared down at something. River stood by the refrigerator, tears of laugher glistening in her eyes. Jamie was next to her, a wide grin splitting his face.

Damian took a step forward and saw what the commotion was all about. The gargoyle, in his German Shepherd form but with the wings opened, was parading around the table with Gypsy riding proudly on his back, sitting between his wings. As soon as he saw Damian, the puppy rushed toward him.

"Gypsy, up." Damian tapped his shoulder, gesturing for the cat to jump, putting all effort into keeping his laughter down.

Gypsy gave him a reproachful gaze but hopped up, landing softly on his shoulder.

"Normally, I don't like dogs," she purred into his ear, rubbing against his cheek, "but I'll make an exception for this one. He's too cute to hate him."

"Uh-huh," murmured Damian. "He's very cute in that lethal gargoyle way." He switched his attention to his brother, laughter bubbling up in his chest again. "Cole, would you mind telling me what you are doing on top of the table, hissing like a wild cat?"

"Only after you tell me what moved you to bring a gargoyle into our home," Cole hissed, raking him with an angry stare. "Tell your pet to stop harassing me, and I'll gladly get off the table."

Damian snorted, making his way to his brother. "He's not my pet, Cole," he said, throwing a stern glance at the puppy. "He's my bodyguard, but unfortunately, until I name him, I can't fully control him."

"Commander, I'm innocent," the puppy assured him, his black, round eyes flooded with guilt. "He's a vampire, and he started it."

"I don't give a damn who started it. Cole is a vampire, but I'm sure your senses told you he's not evil," said Damian, folding his arms. "Besides, he's my brother, so you better treat him well."

A wide grin appeared on the gargoyle's face. "I know he's your brother, and of course I've detected that he's as good as a vampire can be," the puppy replied. "But I just couldn't help it. I had to show him who's the alpha male here. Besides, it's in my nature, you know? It's like when dogs bark at a mailman, or cats hunt birds."

"Watch your tongue, dog," purred Gypsy. "We queens don't hunt. We have our meals delivered to us by peasants, fresh and ready to consume. Observe me carefully and learn how it's done."

She jumped off Damian's shoulder and approached the refrigerator. Stretching her paws up against the door, she threw the sweetest glance at River and uttered the clearest meow Damian had ever heard from her. River petted Gypsy's head and opened the cabinet, reaching for a can of cat food. She opened the can, put its contents on a plate and placed it on the floor in front of Gypsy.

"*You see? And that's how* my *regal nature works,*" Gypsy said, getting busy with her food.

Damian clasped his hand over his mouth, realizing that besides the gargoyle, he was the only one in the room who knew exactly what had just happened. River sent a puzzled gaze his way, throwing her hands up.

"Dima, what's up? What did I do?" she asked. "What did Gypsy say?"

"Nothing of any importance," replied Damian, offering his hand to Cole, but the vampire glanced down at it irritably and jumped off the table. "I just need to name this gargoyle, so he doesn't have to show Cole who's the alpha male here." Cole threw a scorching gaze at him, and Damian finally burst out laughing.

"Do I have to remind y'all that I'm the *only* alpha male in this house," said River, placing her hands on her hips and tapping her foot. She pointed at Damian and Cole. "You two sit down and shut up."

Cole and Damian exchanged a quick look and said, "Yes, ma'am." Damian pulled a chair out and sat down, watching his brother do the same.

"Good boys," River murmured, wild sparkles of laughter dancing in her eyes. She turned toward Jamie and pointed at an unoccupied chair. "Jamie, take a seat. Takeout should be here in a few minutes. In the meantime, I believe Damian has some naming to do, and then we need to discuss everything that happened yesterday." She squatted in front of the puppy and petted its soft fur, her blue eyes sparkling with joy. Then she looked up at Damian with a guilty smile. "Dima, do you mind if I name him for you? I think I have the perfect name."

Damian glanced at the gargoyle and shrugged. "Sure, why not?"

"When I was little, I had an old dog," started River. "It used to belong to my mother…" She fell silent, a fleeting shadow of sadness crossing her face. "Anyway, playing with this dog was one of my earliest childhood memories. His name was Zhulik, so I thought… It's kind of appropriate for this little guy. What do you think, Dima?"

Damian glanced at Cole, and they both laughed.

"Do you know what this word means in Russian?" Cole asked when he stopped laughing. "Even though I do think it's appropriate for this little monster, I want to make sure you know the meaning."

"Of course I do," replied River, pressing her lips into a straight, reproachful line. "I don't speak Russian, but my father explained the meaning of the name to me. It means swindler or a conman."

"Commander, I like this name," the gargoyle pleaded in Damian's mind. *"I want it."*

"You can have it," replied Damian, surprised. "But you do realize this is not a name of power as you wanted earlier?"

The gargoyle approached River and sat down next to her feet, wagging his tail. *"I know that… But it's a name given with love, and I think love is more important than power."*

"So be it," Damian concluded. He channeled some of his magic and ran his fingers over his tattoo. "Let's make it official then. I name you Zhulik."

The tattoo lit up with a bright bluish light, and Damian hissed as pain shot through his arm. The design came to life, slithering and weaving under his skin, and a few more words in Dragon tongue materialized between the vines. He let go of his magic and took a deep breath, wiping sweat off his forehead.

"Why does everything to do with magic have to be so painful," he mumbled and switched his attention to the gargoyle. "Now, Zhulik, I need you to go home." He pointed at his tattoo. "The adults need to have a serious, uninterrupted conversation."

"I am *an adult*," grumbled the gargoyle. *"For your information, I'm older than you and your blood-sucking brother put together. But fine... Since I'm supposed to obey all your commands, no matter the level of stupidity, I'll do what you asked."* With a light pop, the winged German Shepherd vanished from the room, melting into the tattoo.

Damian sighed with relief and placed his arms on the table, leaning forward slightly. His eyes halted on Cole's face for a moment, then slipped to Jamie and finally stopped on River.

"River is right," he said, his fingers fidgeting with his bracelet. "We must have a serious conversation about what happened yesterday. Since it involves all of us in some way, I believe I must share the information I have."

He quickly went over all the events that took place in the last twenty-four hours, including some parts of his conversation with Zabava he believed he could disclose without breaking his promise to her.

"Who's this Zabava?" asked River dryly. "I want to meet her."

"You will," promised Damian, "but right now, I have something else to tell." He pulled his phone out, staring at the picture on the lock screen a moment too long. Then he sighed and added, turning to his brother, "Cole, last night, I received a call from Ricardo that we've been expecting for a while."

Cole got up slowly, moving his chair back with a loud screech. "Tell me he found Ruslan."

"He believes so," replied Damian, a heavy weight settling in the pit of his stomach as he observed his brother's reaction.

Cole loved his maker, and Damian was positive he was loyal to Ruslan through and through. That made the situation a lot more dangerous and unpredictable. With his brother's bravery that bordered on recklessness, he would do anything to save his maker.

"Dima—," Cole started, but Damian frowned, shaking his head, and Cole fell silent.

"Zabava believes that all the leads she has on the missing witches' case are pointing toward the underground supernatural fighting circles," he said. "So, if Ricardo can get me in, I can kill two birds with one stone. I'll do my investigation, and I'll find your maker. But I have to be extremely careful. As you're well aware, underground pits are not a safe place to be for anyone with magic."

"Jesus…" River whispered, her face turning ghostly white. "We have supernatural underground fighting pits in Arizona? Are you serious?"

"We have them all over the country," replied Damian. "Every state has its own Fighting House, each owned by a different supernatural asshole who makes their millions on the slave trade and suffering of others." As River's eyes darkened, and she took a step forward, Damian shook his head warningly. "River, you must stay out of it. Human authorities can't get involved in this. It's enough that the FBI is monitoring them, putting all of us in danger. I can't have Arizona police get involved. That would lead to hundreds of human casualties and the exposure of the World of Magic. No matter what you hear during this investigation or how angry it will make you, you must stand down and let me do my job."

"Fine," she said, pulling a chair out, her moves sharp and angry. "I understand. You are the supernatural cop, so anything that starts with the word *supernatural* is not my jurisdiction. It's yours."

"That's right," replied Damian, turning to Jamie, and the wizard shrunk under his heavy gaze, his shoulders hunched as if he knew what Damian was about to say. "Jamie, I'm sorry, my friend, but you're going to hate what I'm about to tell you."

"Go on." Jamie waved his hand weakly, averting his gaze. "I already know. I'm too inexperienced as a wizard, and I'm nothing but a liability in a combat situation." He raised his eyes at Damian. "You are right. When it comes to combat magic, I'm good for nothing. I don't even know where my sword is. I think I lost it yesterday."

Damian chuckled, tilting his head a little as he gazed at his pupil with warmth. "No, Jamie," he said. "That wasn't what I was going to say. As a matter of fact, it's the opposite. Yesterday, you handled the situation perfectly well. You saved me from the lion. Come on, Jamie, give yourself credit. And as far as your sword, I was the one who lost it after we left the house. I believe I dropped it somewhere in the front yard of the house across the road when Zabava and I were hiding there."

He caught River's scorching gaze and raised his hands in a placating manner. She frowned, pursing her lips. "I definitely want to meet this Zabava and have a word with her."

Damian threw a pleading gaze at his brother, but since Cole just grinned at him without coming to the rescue, he raked his fingers through his hair on the front to cover the left side of his face and switched his attention back to Jamie.

"Anyway, Jamie," he continued, "I was going to tell you that until I get to the bottom of this and find whoever is abducting the witches, you're not safe. I need you to call your boss at the library and take a two-week vacation. Since I don't think you're safe in your own house, I'll give you a choice. You can stay here, in Paradise Manor. You can go to Hawk's ranch if the pack master doesn't mind you hanging around there. Or you can stay with Yakov and the Wardens and help them with the research they're doing to find Koschei the Deathless."

"Damian," started Jamie, "but why? I'm not a witch."

"Semantics," Damian muttered. "You're a wizard, and I don't think these assholes care about your gender. They are after your magical energy. I wish it were different because I would like to have you by my side, but I do believe you're in danger, my friend. So, tell me what you want to do, and I'll open a portal for you."

Jamie bowed his head, a vibe of helplessness hovering over him. "The Wardens," he said at length. "At least, I'll still be useful while working with Yakov."

Damian got up and channeled his magic. With a light wave of his hand, he opened a portal, gesturing for the young wizard to go. Jamie got up and headed toward the rotating vortex, his shoulders slumped. Damian watched him step through it, disappearing on the other side, and dread surged through him, squeezing his heart in its iron grip, whispering that losing Jamie as a fighter was just the beginning.

He sat down heavily and hid his face in his hands. Feeling a light touch to his shoulder, he raised his head to find his brother standing next to him.

"You did the right thing, Dima," he said. "Jamie is the most vulnerable among us."

Damian chuckled bitterly. "I know. But it doesn't make me feel any better." He patted the empty chair next to him. "Sit down, brother. We need to have a word."

Cole lowered himself on the chair, his blue eyes widening. "Don't tell me... You want me under the Warden's protection, too?"

"No. I don't believe you're in more danger than you were yesterday," replied Damian. "But if Ricardo set up a meeting with the Head of the Arizona House, I don't want you to go with me."

"Why?" asked Cole, iron tones ringing in his voice. "Because I'm an ancient vamp with sword skills? I understand it makes me a priceless commodity as a captive fighter, but I'm not planning to sell myself into slavery any time soon."

"No, that is not the reason," Damian objected quietly. "But it does add to my resolve to keep you away from the fighting circles." He averted his gaze, staring at his clenched hands. "You are emotionally involved, Cole. Supposedly, the Head of the Arizona House holds your maker imprisoned. When it comes to Ruslan, your judgment is compromised, and I can't take a chance of you doing something..." His voice trailed off, and he exhaled, searching for a better word.

"Stupid? Reckless?" Cole supplied snidely, but his voice trembled with defiance.

Damian looked at his brother, reading in his eyes just how pointless his attempt to keep him safe was. "Cole..." he started, but then cut himself off and added in a firmer voice, "Both of the above. You are not coming with me. Period."

"No." Cole got up and bent down slightly, bracing his fists against the table. "You're right. I love my maker, and I'm willing to give my life for him just the way he would do for me. But you're forgetting I'm not human, Dmitri. I know how to keep my emotions under control. So, this conversation is over. I'm coming with you whether you like it or not. Besides, I would never let you go into the lion's den alone. You hear me?" He slammed his fist against the table, and deep fractures ran across its polished surface in all directions. "This fucking conversation was over before it started, and you know it!"

Cole turned to River and inclined his head in a traditional bow, his moves unusually jerky. "My apologies, my lady," he said, his voice shaking with anger. "I'll buy a new table for you tomorrow."

Damian got up sharply, sending the chair flying back. His blazing eyes met Cole's, and he slammed his hand against the table, too, adding a few more fractures to the already wide web. The floor shook, and the dishes in the cabinets responded with a soft jingle.

"Sit down," he growled through clenched teeth, his chest

rising and falling with heavy breaths. "I'm not done talking to you." Cole turned to him, and his lips parted. "I said sit your ass down! Now!"

River jumped to her feet and stepped between them, holding her arms up. "Both of you sit down and shut the hell up," she yelled. "And if you need to go and take a cold shower then do it, because right now, your anger is cooking your antique brains." She threw her hands in the air, a cloud of desperation rising over her. "Don't you see? You're both trying to protect each other, but instead of figuring out the best way to approach the situation, you're at each other's throats."

Damian took a deep breath and bent down, picking up his chair, his anger simmering down. He sat down and watched Cole lower himself on the chair next to him, the scarlet glow vanishing from his eyes.

"River, thank you," he said as evenly as he could muster. "We need to figure out the best way to approach this dangerous situation." He tapped his brother's shoulder, and Cole turned to him. "Here is what I suggest we do. Get dressed, and we'll pay a visit to Zabava and Ricardo. He's waiting for us. We'll take it from there."

"I'll be ready in ten minutes." Cole got up and walked out the door.

CHAPTER 8

~ DAMIAN BLAKE ~

Damian opened the door of Cole's SUV and climbed onto the passenger's seat, locking the seatbelt. Without looking at his brother, Cole started the car, driving it slowly toward the gates out of Paradise Manor, his fingers squeezing the steering wheel.

"Where to?" he asked, his voice raspy and quiet.

"Night Owl Inn," replied Damian, staring straight ahead.

"Dima, I'm sorry…" Cole pressed the button on the built-in remote control, watching the gate open. "You are right. I *am* emotionally compromised, so I understand why you don't want me with you. But please, try to understand my side, too. Ruslan is like a father to me. I actually do call him Father. I've been searching for him for the last few years, and I can't sit and wait now that we possibly know where he is. Please—"

"Cole." Damian shifted in his seat slightly, readjusting his seatbelt. "I understand, but I can't take a chance that your feelings toward your maker will cost you your life."

Cole turned to him, a deep wrinkle appearing between his eyebrows. "Dima, no. I'm not going to do anything that can—"

"What you fail to understand," Damian interrupted him, "is

that I watched you die once, and I still see it in my worst nightmares. I can't do it again, Nikolai." He took a pause, a dull ache tightening his chest. "You are *my* personal attachment. Do you think I don't know that? I'm just as emotionally compromised as you are, and I have no idea what I will do if…" His voice faded into silence, and he looked away.

Cole nodded, his wrinkle becoming deeper. As they approached the hotel, he took the car off the road and parked it on a small parking lot in front of the main entrance. Unlocking the seatbelt, he turned to face his brother.

"You won't have to watch me die because it's not going to happen," he objected softly. "But what *you* fail to understand is that even though I love my maker, you're my brother. Nothing and no one can compare to that. Yes, I want to save Ruslan, but even more so I need to be with you because someone has to watch your giant back. And no one can do it better than me. Just put it through your thick skull—I'm with you. No matter what. You will never be alone again. Do you understand me, you stubborn jackass?"

Damian glanced at his brother's tense face, and the corner of his lips lifted just a touch. "Fine… Dracula Junior. But we do it my way," he said, swallowing the dread that had never left him since this morning. Since Cole didn't change his position, still staring at him intently, he shrugged and added, trying to sound as lightheartedly as he could, "What? Do you need me to give you a hug?"

"Doofus." Cole chuckled and pushed the door open, stepping out of the vehicle.

* * *

Damian dialed Zabava's phone number, but before he heard the first beep of the dial tone, she answered the call.

"What took you so long? Room two-ten," she said and hung up.

"It has to be the second floor," muttered Damian, heading toward the building. He made his way upstairs and stopped in front of the door, ready to knock.

"Unlocked," Zabava's deep voice sounded from inside of the room.

Damian pushed the door open, allowing Cole to walk in first. The small hotel room was dark with the only window covered by thick panels. The closet door was opened, displaying an absolutely empty space behind it. Zabava lay on the bed with her arms folded under her head, observing them with her calculating, slightly sarcastic eyes.

"Look who's here." She pushed herself up and sat down, lowering her feet clad in heavy combat boots to the floor. "What can I do for you, boys?"

Damian pulled a chair and sat down, facing her. "You can start by telling us why the Sisterhood of the Sun is after my brother?"

"Impossible." She frowned, her eyes darting to Cole. "Your brother is not on their list, Damian. I would've known if he was. It's not my first job with the Sisterhood, and whenever they send me to a new territory, Grand Master Elony herself provides me with a list of all the rogue vampires in the area. Why do you think the Sisterhood slayers attacked him?"

"Because I recognized the tattoo on one of them." Cole leaned against the wall, folding his arms. "I hope you believe I can identify the Sisterhood signature symbol and their fighting style." Cole told her about the attack on Luciano's mansion and the poison the slayers used to disable him.

"Impossible… I can't believe—"

She fell silent and looked up, her eyes turning milky white, her lips moving as if she was reading something out loud, but no words came from her mouth. A moment later, she took a deep breath, and her eyes returned to their normal green. She got up and approached Cole, placing her hand on his arm.

"Cole, I don't want you to be alarmed, but Grand Master Elony wants to speak with you," she said, her gaze darting to Damian.

"If the Sisterhood still works with the Destiny Council, fighting on the side of Light, I have no reason to worry," Cole replied calmly, giving her a dismissive wave of his hand. "Go ahead."

Zabava channeled her magic, its soft, bluish glow enveloping her body. She drew a rune in the air, whispering a summoning spell. A glass-like oval of a communication window replaced the rune, and a woman stepped forward from the darkness. She was tall and muscular, her military fatigues just adding to her less than feminine appearance. Her pale gray eyes shone brightly against her ebony skin, and it seemed as if they lived a life of their own on her hard, emotionless face.

She crossed her arms behind her back and quickly observed every person in the room, a vibe of superiority surrounding her. Her eyes lingered on Damian a moment too long before moving to Cole.

"Mr. Cole Adams," she said icily, disgust curving her lips into a snarl, "you dare claim that my people attacked you for no reason?"

"I claim nothing, Grand Master." Cole stepped closer to the communication window, his face just as cold and void of emotions. "I'm stating a fact. A red tattoo on the wrist—a stylized Ankh symbol that looks like a sword with a serpent coiling around it. Are you going to say this is not the brand all your slayers wear?"

"A red tattoo on the wrist?" Her full lips parted, and her blazing eyes widened, an expression of confusion replacing that of arrogance. She ran her fingers through her short-cropped, curly hair and frowned. "It's impossible. Only members of my special team have red tattoos."

"Then you may want to assemble your special team and see if one of them is missing," Cole retorted so frostily that Hell could freeze over from the mere sound of his voice. "They attacked me in my own Court for no reason, and I killed one of them. It was self-defense, of course."

Grand Master Elony hooked her thumbs in the hoops of her belt, giving Cole another once-over. "I don't believe it," she objected, shaking her head. "It just can't be." She pointed at Cole, the heavy ring of the Sisterhood's Grand Master decorating her index finger. "Mr. Adams, your reputation precedes you, and all my fighters are well aware of who you are. Besides, your name has never been in our books. Your claims have no—"

"Are you calling me a liar?" Cole shoved his hands in the pockets of his pants, his voice becoming softer. Damian stepped closer to his brother, recognizing the signs of an upcoming storm.

Grand Master Elony took in Damian's massive frame and tilted her head, narrowing her eyes. "On the other hand, Mr. Adams, I believe you." She took a long pause, looking like she was about to choke, and uttered, "I apologize for this unfortunate mistake."

"You apologize?" Damian stepped closer to the communication window. "Isn't that swell, Grand Master? My brother could have been killed by your people, and all you can do is apologize?"

For a brief moment, fury distorted her features, but she took a deep breath and inclined her head. "You're right, Mister..." she said, raising her voice at the end as she expected Damian to introduce himself.

"Commander Damian Blake," offered Damian, stressing his title, and pressed his fist to his chest, inclining his head in a formal Destiny Enforcers' bow while suppressing the desire to rip her apart with his bare hands.

"Commander?" she repeated, staring at him in disbelief. "I don't think I've ever heard of you. I know only of Commander Moore..."

"I guess you're not as well informed as you think." Damian brushed his hand over the rune on his shoulder, and as it lit up with a soft white glow, she gasped and squared her shoulders, crossing her arms behind her back.

"The Shadow Enforcer..." she whispered in awe, but quickly composed herself and continued, "You're absolutely right, Commander Blake, apologies are not enough. As Mr. Adams recommended, I will gather my special team and run an investigation myself."

"Thank you, Grand Master," said Damian. "I hope to hear from you soon. Cole Adams is not only my charge, but also my brother. I must know if he is in danger."

"Yes, Commander. I'll keep you updated on the progress of my investigation." Grand Master Elony inclined her head in a formal bow and waved her hand, closing the communication window.

"Goddammit!" Cole threw his hands up. "She treats me like vermin! She's not going to do anything to figure out what's going on. In the meantime, I have slayers breathing down my neck. As if we don't have enough problems without it."

"She treats all vampires like disgusting parasites, kiddo. Don't flatter yourself. But she will do as promised, trust me," objected Zabava, lowering herself on the bed. She leaned back, propping herself on her elbows, and a sneaky feline grin crossed her face. "I think your big bro put the fear of God in her." She laughed, throwing her head back. "I've never seen good old Elony squirm like that."

Damian shrugged indifferently, his mind on the upcoming mission. He didn't like the idea of them diving into the supernatural swamp of the underground fighting pits while Cole had to constantly look over his shoulder for a possible attack of the slayers.

"Shadow Enforcer, huh?" Zabava's voice brought him back to reality. She gazed at him with unconcealed curiosity. "I knew you were a Commander, but you didn't bother to mention your status."

"I didn't tell you because I didn't believe you needed to know," Damian replied, sarcasm lacing his words as he gave Zabava the exact same speech she had given him just yesterday. "For now, all you need to know is that I'm a Destiny Enforcer who's here to do his job. When the time comes—if it comes at all—I promise I'll show you my entire pedigree."

"Fair enough," she murmured. "For such an old geezer, you have a good memory."

"What can I tell you," replied Damian. "Maybe I'm old, but my memory is still intact as well as everything else."

She pushed herself up into a sitting position. "So, what's your next move, Commander?"

"We're going to meet with the Head of the Arizona House," replied Damian. He tried to sound confident, but all sorts of doubts crowded his mind. He rubbed the bridge of his nose, exhaling. "Dammit, not the thing I wanted to do."

"Do you want me to come with?" asked Zabava lightly. "Going into a place like that, you'll want to have a strong team with you. Keep in mind, it's not only your mission, but also mine."

"I would love to have a team, but it has to be a team I can trust entirely," replied Damian, motioning for Cole to get up. "Thank you for the offer, Zabava, but I prefer to have my brother by my side. He's the only team I need." He thought for a moment and added, "Besides, I need to have a person who knows where I'm going on the outside. If Cole and I don't come back in time, you know what to do."

She nodded, all mirth gone from her face. "That's fine, Damian. I understand. Trust is not given. It's earned, and so far, I haven't really given you a reason to trust me." She looked at the heavy panels covering the window and stifled a sigh. "Do me a favor and call me right before you go in, so I know when to expect you back."

"You got it." Damian turned around and walked out the door, followed by Cole.

CHAPTER 9

~ DAMIAN BLAKE ~

For the entire way to Ricardo's house, Cole didn't say a word. Even though Damian wasn't sure what bothered his brother more at the moment—the idea of returning to the house where he had been treated like a slave, or the fact that the Sisterhood slayers were after him—he didn't try to push him into a conversation, giving him some space.

He didn't worry about meeting with Ricardo in his house since they were bound by a mutual interest. As far as the Sisterhood of the Sun, he believed the safest place for Cole was by his side. The slayers wouldn't dare assault a Destiny Enforcer protecting his charge. Besides, Zabava had a point—Grand Master Elony hadn't looked happy with the situation, so whether she liked it or not, she would take care of it and run the investigation as she had promised.

Cole stopped the car in front of a tall gate next to a guardhouse and rolled down the window, staring at a guard who stood with a phone squeezed between his ear and shoulder. The man lifted his hand, gesturing for them to wait a moment. Cole grunted, and a muscle twitched in his tightly pressed jaw, aggravation breaking through in his every move. But as soon as the guard stepped out of the booth, a wide, friendly smile split Cole's face, and he looked as relaxed as ever.

The guard approached their car and bent down slightly, giving Damian and Cole a quick once-over. "What can I do for you?" he asked once satisfied with his observations.

"We have a meeting with Mr. Torres," Cole answered calmly. "Cole Adams and Damian Blake."

The guard brought up his cellphone and stared at the screen, swiping across it. Then he lifted his head and gestured toward the gate with a nod of approval.

"Please proceed, Mr. Adams. Mr. Torres is expecting you and Mr. Blake in his office." He returned to the guardhouse, and a moment later, the gate slid to the side, opening slowly.

Cole drove across the property and parked the car in front of the main entrance. He shut down the engine but didn't move, staring at the door without blinking.

"Hey, Cole." Damian touched his brother's shoulder, causing him to flinch and snap toward him as if he had just woken him up from a nightmare. "If you don't want to go with me, you don't have to. I can take care of everything on my own."

"No." Cole unlocked his seatbelt and opened the door. "The meeting with Ricardo doesn't bother me. I'm worried about what he may say to us. What if the man he found is not Ruslan?"

"No what-ifs. If that's the case, we'll keep looking for him," promised Damian. "In the meantime, we also have the situation with the witches, and Ricardo has connections that will open a door to the top layers of the Arizona underground fighting pits."

"And then there is that," Cole murmured, stepping out of the car. He shut the door and turned toward Damian, looking at him across the top of the vehicle. "There is something else we need to look into, brother, and I don't think you're going to like it."

"Oh, yeah?" Damian shrugged. "Is there anything in the

current situation I may like?" He chuckled humorlessly. "Spit it out. What's going on?"

"Remember that vampire you captured yesterday?" Damian nodded, and Cole continued, "Well, before the Sisterhood slayers showed up and killed him, he said something... interesting in a disturbing kind of way."

"What did he say?" asked Damian.

"He had a strange amnesia, and something tells me a rune inscribed on his chest was the cause of it. It didn't look like the necromancy rune I'd seen on Luciano, but for the life of me I couldn't place it. Anyway, he had no idea what he was doing in Arizona, but most importantly, he had no recollection of leaving Nevada in the first place." Cole walked around the car and halted next to Damian. "From what I understood, he was Santiago del Castillo's executive assistant, and that tells me he would never betray his king. Santiago is an ancient vampire, probably close to my maker or Luciano in age. He doesn't surround himself with people he doesn't trust entirely."

For a heartbeat, Damian stared at his brother, all sorts of troubling thoughts and worst-case scenarios flashing in his mind.

"Perun almighty," he whispered, frowning. "Why now? Why are all these events happening at the same time? They must be connected somehow, even if we don't see the connection yet." He took Cole's elbow, directing him toward the steps to the house. "Have you called Santiago yet?"

"No." Cole raised his face, a haunted expression hiding in his blue eyes. "When? I barely had time to—"

"That's okay," Damian interrupted him. "We'll call him together after we speak with Ricardo." He tapped his brother's shoulder. "Let's get it over with."

He walked up the steps, reaching for the button of the doorbell when the door opened and a short, stout man in a black business suit with a bow tie appeared in the doorway. He bowed, gesturing for them to come in. Despite his refined appearance and manners, his lips twitched slightly as if he had just smelled something foul as his icy gaze halted on Cole. A carnivorous light ignited in his shifty eyes, but he quickly switched his attention to Damian.

Catching his reaction, Damian cursed inwardly, hoping his brother didn't notice that, but since Cole remained emotionless and calm, at least on the outside, he let it go. The butler took in Damian's appearance and blanched, but quickly composed himself and pointed toward the hallway on the left.

"Mr. Blake, Mr. Adams." He bowed again, a smile as sweet as honey appearing on his face. "Allow me to show you to Mr. Torres' office."

As they walked through the wide, well-lit hallway in silence, Zhulik's tiny voice emerged in Damian's mind, adding to his overall unease. *"Commander, I don't like this place,"* the gargoyle peeped. *"You know you can't use magic here? And this short man... I can't tell you what it is, but something is off about him."*

"I know," replied Damian, fighting the desire to turn around and leave the house. "But—"

He stopped talking with Zhulik as the butler halted in front of a door, knocked, and then pushed it open with a slight bow. Stepping out of the way, he gestured for them to come in.

"Be careful..." Zhulik whispered.

Damian glanced at the opened door, and his eyes darted to the butler, a dark sense of foreboding spreading through him. He cursed inwardly at the magic detectors and other anti-magic tech installed in Ricardo's house that prevented him from teleporting or channeling magical or elemental energy without triggering unwanted consequences.

Giving a short nod to the butler, Damian walked into the office, feeling as though he were crossing enemy lines. As the door closed behind him with a soft thud, he winced inwardly, his intuition screaming bloody murder in his mind.

Ricardo sat on the leather sofa, his normally manicured hair in disarray, his white shirt unbuttoned halfway down his chest. His jacket and tie lay on the floor, and the entire office looked like it had been vandalized. Papers were scattered all over the carpet, and his computer monitors lay by the desk, cracked.

He lifted his face, and his dark eyes filled with raw anguish halted on Damian. "Thank God, you're here," he whispered, his voice hoarse.

"What happened?" asked Damian, taking a step forward, his dread intensifying tenfold. "I spoke with you yesterday, and you were fine. What happened between now and then?"

Ricardo rose to his feet, his every move heavy and torturously slow. "I think I made a mistake, Damian," he whispered even softer, averting his eyes. He took a couple of steps forward and halted. "Now, you and your brother are my only hope." He dropped to his knees and hid his face in his hands. "Please, I'm begging you—"

Exchanging a shocked look with Cole, Damian seized Ricardo's arm and yanked him to his feet, directing him to the sofa. He pushed him onto it and stopped, folding his arms.

"Stop the drama. It doesn't work on either of us. Especially since we know what kind of operation you've been running for years. So cut the crap and tell me what's going on," said Damian through gritted teeth. He grabbed a chair and moved it closer to the sofa, lowering himself on it. Cole sat at the other end of the couch, half-turning toward Ricardo.

"Right. I'm sorry." Ricardo cleared his throat, looking away. "I did everything the way we discussed," he started at length, still keeping his voice low, "and everything was going just the way we planned. My efforts paid off, and I was able to meet with my sister in person. First time in years…" He looked up at Damian, shaking his head bitterly. "And I thought, this is it. Here it is—the light at the end of the tunnel."

"You called Damian and told him that you found Ruslan. Why?" asked Cole icily.

"Because I did find him. I'm many things, Mr. Adams, but I'm not a liar," Ricardo snapped back, but then raised his hands in a peaceful gesture. "Your brother and I had an agreement. Damian helps me break my Mephistophelian deal and set my sister free, and I help him find your maker. I fulfilled my part of the deal. I found Ruslan. The reason I called was that I also found a way to get both of you into the House HQ without triggering any suspicions. We were going to go tonight—"

"Something tells me your best laid plans of mice and men backfired?" murmured Damian.

Ricardo nodded and swallowed hard. "Damian, I swear I was careful, and I didn't rush. I did everything the way you told me to do. I have no idea how he found out. The only thing I can think of is that I made a mistake somewhere, but for the life of me, I don't know what I've done wrong..."

Damian got up and walked toward the window. Pulling the heavy curtain aside, he glanced outside at the view of the desert, thousands of thoughts rushing through his mind.

"What now?" he asked without taking his eyes off the view. "Since you're begging on your knees, I believe you're in serious trouble." He turned around and rested his back against the wall. "Tell us the truth and don't turn it into a two-part story. What's going on?"

Ricardo got up and looked around, his face darkened by fear. "He called me in this morning," he whispered.

"Who?" asked Cole.

"The Head of the Arizona House, of course," replied Ricardo. "When I arrived, he told me straight that he knew I betrayed him and now our deal was off." He pinched the bridge of his nose, averting his eyes. "Now he wants a new deal, but not with me. He wants it with you and your brother, and if you don't comply—"

"Let me guess," Damian interrupted him. "He'll kill your sister?"

Ricardo nodded. "Yes, and Ruslan."

"Goddammit, Ricardo!" hissed Damian, slamming his fist against the wall. "Why didn't you warn me?"

"I have no idea how he found out." Ricardo threw his hands up. "I told no one about it. Not even my sister. Like I said, I followed every instruction you gave me." He bit his lip, shoving his hands into the pockets of his pants. "I couldn't warn you, Damian. I swear I would if I could. While I was meeting with the Head of the House, he sent his people here, and now, all the magic-detecting and repelling tech is activated. Everywhere. You can't teleport. You can't use magic. They installed anti-magic tech even in my office. They are watching my every step, and if I tried to warn you…" He threw his hands up again, desperation radiating around him. "I'm sorry, Damian, but you walked into a trap, and this time, I am not the one who set it up."

Damian took a deep breath and bowed his head, processing everything Ricardo had said.

"Do you know what this new deal is?" he asked after a while. "What does he want from me and my brother?"

"He didn't give me any details," replied Ricardo. "He told me to bring you to his office, and if you comply with his demands, he'll release me from our agreement and free my sister and Ruslan. He said he wants you, Damian, to run an errand for him."

"Me?" Damian chuckled coldly. "He picked the wrong person to blackmail. Not going to happen. I'm not an errand boy for every evil bastard out there."

Cole froze in place, his blue eyes staring at Damian without blinking, his fingers ripping through the leather upholstery, but he said nothing.

"Damian, please… you can't." Ricardo stepped forward, his

shoulders slumped powerlessly. "He'll kill my sister. Please! I destroyed my life… I sold my soul to give her a future. Please—"

"No," Damian snapped, his jaw clenched. "I'm not going to be blackmailed into doing something that could potentially endanger both the realm of humans and the World of Magic. You have no idea who I am and what kind of power I wield. I cannot allow some evil bastard—a slaver, to boot—to force me into submission. Because of what I am, my actions have serious consequences." He shook his head slowly and repeated, "No."

Ricardo grunted and spun toward Cole. "Cole, please!" he pleaded. "Please, talk to your brother. If he doesn't agree, come tomorrow morning, your maker will be dead. Please! I'm begging you…"

Cole lifted his eyes, meeting Damian's steady gaze, and a muscle twitched in his tightly pressed jaw. "As much as I want to, I can't ask him to do it, Ricardo," he said, barely moving his lips, his face becoming almost translucent. "Damian is right. He can't allow an evil being to command him. It's too dangerous."

"I don't understand!" Ricardo yelled, raising his voice for the first time since they arrived here. He turned to Damian, breathing hard. "Who the hell are you that you think your power can destroy the world? You are just a Child of Earth and your brother is a common vamp! Get off your high moral horse and save the lives of two people. I understand you don't care about my sister, but how about your brother's maker? I believe he's like a father to him."

Suddenly feeling exhaustion settling in his very bones, Damian sighed and made his way to the sofa. He sat down by Cole's side and bent forward, hiding his face in his hands, thousands of thoughts crowding his mind. Crumbling inside, he glanced at his brother sideways, and besides endless sorrow, he found the warmth of support in his eyes. Damian lowered his hands and looked up at Ricardo.

"Ricardo, I'm truly sorry," he said quietly. "But I can't allow myself to get into a subservient situation to an evil being of magic because I'm not only a Child of Earth. I'm a Destiny Enforcer."

"A Destiny Enforcer?" Ricardo repeated, sweat beading his forehead. For a moment, he stilled, staring at Damian in shock, but then he punched the air and yelled, "I don't give a fuck what you are! You can be Lord Jesus himself for all I care. To me, you are the only person who can save my sister but too full of himself to do it!"

"Ricardo—," Damian started but cut himself off as a familiar headache started to build up behind his eyes. He threw a glance at Cole, feeling chills running down his back, and then switched his attention back to Ricardo. "Ricardo, someone is summoning me. I need to use my magic to answer the call. I can't ignore it. Can you shut down the magic tech in your office?"

"A summoning call?" A wild burst of laughter escaped Ricardo's lips as he slapped his thighs. "Perfect timing. Guess what, asshole? Even if I wanted, I couldn't deactivate the magic tech. I'm no longer in control. And if you try to answer the summoning call, you'll get this room filled with the dust of gray stones and silver, killing your brother. So, yeah..." He laughed again, and there was so much hatred and pain in his laughter that Damian flinched. "Enjoy the pain. And while you are emasculated by the summoning call, I'll summon the people who will deliver you to the Head of the House. They are just one call away."

As the pain of the unanswered call intensified, Damian stared at his brother with wide-open eyes, unable to say a word. A loud buzzing filled his ears, and he squeezed his head with his hands, a tortured howl erupting from his lips. The room swam around him in nauseating waves, and the last thing he remembered was his brother's arms catching him as he started to fall to the side.

CHAPTER 10

~ DAMIAN BLAKE ~

He couldn't see or hear anything except for the raw, pulsating anguish that had become his entire world. It ripped him from within, leaving nothing but a bleeding heap of flesh twitching on the floor, unable to do anything to stop it, to help himself. It merged with the darkness and wrapped around him, squeezing tighter and tighter, and all he could do was scream, tearing his vocal cords, his fingers clawing spasmodically into his own scalp.

"Dmitri!"

Somewhere far—too surreal to be true—he heard a familiar voice, a sound other than horrifying screams of pain he couldn't recognize as his own. Holding on to the last spark of hope, he reached for it. A soft touch to his forehead followed, and suddenly, the pain was gone, leaving him hollow and drained. The darkness, soft and mushy, came right after, enveloping him into a gentle embrace.

"Dmitri, open your eyes." Someone's hand slapped his cheek gently. "Open your eyes, Commander."

Damian moved his arm, and his every cell responded with an overwhelming soreness. He swallowed, his throat raw and scratchy as if filled with hot sand. With effort, he cracked his eyelids open and blinked a few times at the eye-watering white light somewhere right above him. The light also blinked, and as realization dawned on him, he forced his hands up and rubbed his eyes.

"You used a forbidden summons on me…" He could not help but feeling betrayed. "Why? How could you?"

The blinding light blinked faster, slowly dimming down, and then vanished. A hand touched his forehead again, and a wave of warmth spread through him, taking away the soreness and weakness.

"Sit up, Commander," the same voice said. "We need to talk."

"We used a forbidden summons because you refused to answer our original summoning call," another voice sounded somewhere above him.

Damian opened his eyes fully and pushed himself up into a sitting position. His vision cleared, slowly adjusting to the semi-darkness of a large round hall illuminated by the shimmering, blue light of numerous magical orbs. He recognized this place, and an expectation of trouble twisted his gut. He was back in the Destiny Council realm, in their main hall that was used mostly to hold trials. Magnus stood next to him, his silvery eyes gazing down at him with concern. A man and woman stood by a tall desk, their eyes blazing with a brilliant, white light.

"Forbidden summons, as unpleasant as they are, allowed us to zero in on your location and bring you here, Commander," the woman said, sounding flat and indifferent.

"I didn't answer your call because I couldn't," Damian growled, meeting the woman's shining eyes. "I was locked in a room stuffed to the brim with anti-magic tech, and if I attempted to channel even an ounce of my magic, the consequences would have been more than I was willing to pay." Thinking back, fear clawed at his heart, and he switched his attention to Magnus. "Did you bring me here alone and leave my brother unprotected in a hostile environment?"

"Yes, but your brother is going to be fine. While you're with us, the time in the human realm stands still," replied Magnus. "We have to talk, Commander."

"About?"

"You will take the deal," the woman cut straight to the chase, her loud voice echoing through the hall.

"When we send you back," the man standing next to the woman started, "you will tell Ricardo Torres that you changed your mind and are willing to meet with the Head of the Arizona House."

"And why would I do that?" Damian asked through clenched teeth, anger slowly rising within him. "Whoever this person is, he's evil to the core. What do you think he's going to ask me to do? Do his produce shopping? Whatever he wants me to do is most likely the one thing I shouldn't be doing."

"You're a Destiny Enforcer," the man growled, his eyes igniting brighter. "You will do as you're told, no questions asked, Commander, or suffer the consequences. Am I clear?"

"Yeah, no… Not this Destiny Enforcer," replied Damian. He got up and folded his arms, meeting the man's furious gaze without flinching. "If you want blind obedience, go to Moore. I'm not going to make a move until I understand why you're giving this order to me. It's reckless, and depending on what this so-called errand is, it may endanger the realm of humans as well as the World of Magic, which I swore to serve and protect when I accepted the mantle of a Destiny Enforcer."

The woman huffed, throwing her hands in the air. "Magnus, he's your Shadow Enforcer," she yelled. "Deal with him, or I swear, I'll throw him in the deepest, darkest dungeon I can find in our holding facilities, and he'll never see the light of day again."

Magnus took a deep breath as if getting ready for a deep dive, the expression on his face speaking louder than any words.

"Dmitri," he started. "I need you to trust me."

"I trust you, Magnus," replied Damian, his anger simmering down as he got in control of his emotions. "But I still want at least some kind of explanation."

The woman gasped, and her entire body ignited with an eye-watering light. She headed toward them, fury contorting her features. As she approached them, she rose on her tiptoes and slapped Damian across his face with the back of her hand. As a bright light exploded behind his eyes, his head jerked to the side, and his hand went up involuntarily, but he stopped himself and dropped his arm, silently staring down at her, his jaw set.

"Heaven and Earth, Magnus!" the woman squealed, stamping her foot. "He doesn't even address you properly. He has no respect for you or his own position. Please explain why you're keeping him around. And this is the mongrel we're stuck with for such an important mission? We may as well give up now."

Magnus took a step closer to her, his face ashen. "You touch him one more time," he hissed, his voice shaking with poorly suppressed rage, "and this will be the last thing you do. Am I clear, Miranda?"

She paled and raised her hands, shaking her head, resigned. Muttering something under her breath, she turned on her heel and marched back toward the desk.

Magnus turned to Damian, placing his hand on his shoulder. "Dmitri, you've been around long enough," he started peacefully. "You know that there are things I can tell you, and there are things I can't tell you."

Damian nodded, glancing at the other two members of the Destiny Council over Magnus' head. They conversed in hushed tones as Miranda kept throwing murderous stares in his direction.

"Here is what I can tell you," Magnus continued quietly. "The

Head of the Arizona House is not your regular slaver. He's not like the rest of his kind. Highly secretive and evasive, he doesn't let anyone he doesn't trust fully come close to him. No one has ever seen his face or been able to identify his supernatural identity. We know he is not mundane, but we have no idea what kind of being of magic he is. This is the first time we have the opportunity to come in close contact with him and find out what he's doing."

"He's a slaver who makes money on the suffering of others. What else do you need to know? I should destroy him the first chance I get," Damian said quietly. He dropped his head, remorse clawing its way through his heart. "Magnus, he holds Ruslan, my brother's maker. He tried to blackmail me into submission, holding Ruslan's life over my head, and I refused to submit... Cole was crushed, but he accepted my decision. And now you're telling me to do that?"

"You did what you were supposed to do as a Commander of the Destiny Enforcers, and I'm sorry for what I'm about to tell you..." Magnus sighed, squeezing Damian's arm. "Dmitri, my child, you *will* accept his deal, and you *will* do whatever he wants you to do," he said quietly. "And you're going to have to sell it, too, so this insidious person will have no reason not to believe you. Do you understand me, Commander?"

"Yes, sir." Damian nodded, unable to speak louder than a whisper.

"We must know who and what this man is," Magnus continued, "and you will do whatever it takes to get us this information. Also, we want to know what he wants you to procure for him, so keep close contact with me. I must know your every step."

"Yes, sir," Damian whispered, barely able to breathe.

"Go, save the man who's important to your brother," he whispered so softly only Damian could hear him. "Trust me, you won't regret doing that." Then he tapped his arm and added louder. "Commander, you have your orders. I'm going to send you back to the human realm now. Are you ready?"

"Yes, sir…"

"Dmitri." Magnus frowned, giving him a pointed stare.

Stifling a sigh, Damian lowered to one knee and pressed his fist over his heart, bowing his head. "I'm yours to command, my lord."

"Aw, Magnus, you do know how to tame your wild beast after all," Miranda sang, her voice overflowing with sarcasm. "Commendable."

Magnus didn't even flinch. Bending down slightly, he whispered for Damian's ears only. "Ignore her, my boy." He chuckled softly. "And remember that phone call to Santiago del Castillo?" Damian nodded. "Make it before you leave Ricardo's house."

He touched Damian's forehead with two fingers, and the Destiny Council's main hall melted into the darkness.

* * *

"Dima!"

Cole's desperate voice rang in Damian's ears, and he opened his eyes, jolting to his feet, disoriented. Breathing hard, he spun around to see both Cole and Ricardo standing next to him.

"Dima, are you okay?" asked Cole, his face beyond pale. "I've never seen a living person in so much pain."

"I'm fine. Some assholes tried to use a forbidden summons on me. You know how the forbidden summons work…" He threw a guilty glance at his brother. "They melt your brain until you answer. Anyway, I was able to block them." Damian turned to Ricardo, thinking how to tell this extremely perceptive man that he changed his mind and make it believable enough so he wouldn't question it.

"Ricardo—," he started, but Ricardo pressed his hand to his mouth, his eyes watering slightly, and Damian fell silent.

"Damian, I'm sorry." Ricardo lowered his arm, his fingers trembling slightly. "I didn't lie. I had no way to shut down the magic detectors." He looked away, wrinkles etched deeper around his tightly pressed mouth. He shook his head slowly, his hand tugging at the collar of his shirt as if it were suffocating him. "I'm truly sorry... The things I said to you. I should never have said anything like that. You know I would never betray you?" He exhaled a ragged breath, rubbing his forehead. "I gave you my word that you were safe in my house, and I stand by it."

"I know, Ricardo," replied Damian. "But you were right. I have the opportunity to save two good people—your sister and Cole's maker. Destiny Council be damned with their rules and their methods of enforcing them." He glanced at his brother and then at Ricardo. "Let's do it. I'm going to take the deal."

"*Ay, Dios mio...*" Ricardo exhaled, his lips parting slightly in disbelief. "Are you sure?"

"I'm sure," replied Damian.

"*Dima, you just lied to him, and I want to know why,*" said Cole, using their psychic link.

"*Not now, Cole,*" replied Damian. "*I am planning to save your maker and Ricardo's sister if I can, but there is more to this story, and I can't go into any explanations now. Just do what I say and pray to whatever God you pray to nowadays that we all survive what's coming.*"

"Ricardo, before we leave, there is something Cole and I must do. It'll take just a few minutes." Damian lowered himself on the sofa and patted it next to him, gesturing for Cole to sit down. "Cole, dial Santiago del Castillo. We'll speak with him now because after we leave, it will be too late."

"Santiago del Castillo?" Ricardo mumbled. "As in the King of the Nevada Vampire Court?"

Damian pulled out his phone, unlocking it, and offered it to Cole.

"The one and only," Cole muttered, taking the phone from

his brother. Then he raised his face, giving Ricardo a sarcastic stare. "What can I tell you? We royalties love to chat once in a while."

He punched in the phone number and pressed the dial button, putting the phone on speaker. After two beeps, Santiago answered the call, his rich baritone sounding clear in the silence of the room.

"Cole, what an unexpected surprise," he said calmly. "It's not like I'm not happy to hear your voice, my friend, but to what do I owe this pleasure?"

"To Rob Miller," replied Cole. "Do you know who he is?"

"Of course, I do. He's my executive assistant. A loyal servant." Santiago's voice shook, becoming deeper with concern. "He was following a lead for me but disappeared a few days ago, and I haven't heard from him since. Is there something I should know?"

"I'm sorry, Santiago, but Rob is dead." Cole glanced at Damian, moving the phone closer to him. "He was killed by the Sisterhood slayers in front of my eyes."

"In Arizona?" Santiago hissed, sounding shocked even across the line. "What the hell was he doing in your state?" He grunted and something fell with a dull thud. "And why would the slayers kill him? I'm in peace with the Sisterhood of the Sun."

"So am I. Yet I was attacked in my own house, and Rob was killed. My brother and I contacted the Grand Master of the Sisterhood, and she had no idea what that was all about." Cole fell silent, tracing the shape of the phone with his finger absent-mindedly. "Anyway, we'll figure it out. But if I may ask, what lead was Rob following in my state?"

For a few long seconds, Santiago remained silent, and when he spoke again, he sounded strained, tones of pain hiding in his deep voice.

"Who's in the room with you, Cole?" he asked. "I can hear two heartbeats."

"My brother Damian and our friend Ricardo," replied Cole. "They're helping me with the investigation. I swear anything you say is safe with us."

Something screeched, and heavy steps sounded on the other side of the line. "Cole, Sylvana is missing," said Santiago. "My only child... As her maker, I know she's alive, but something is partially blocking our connection, and I can't locate her. I can't find her anywhere..." His voice broke, and a pregnant pause hung in the room. "Rob was searching for her on my orders, but he never told me that the trail led to your state, otherwise I would have contacted you right away."

"How long since she disappeared?"

"Over two months," replied Santiago.

"Why didn't you say something?" Cole asked, slamming his hand on the sofa. "Dammit, Santiago! Sylvana is not easy prey. As a vampire, she is old, fast and strong. Besides, she's an ex-slayer with all the infamous training of the Sisterhood under her belt. Whoever was able to take her..." He cut himself off, shaking his head.

"Ruslan has been gone for three years," replied Santiago, "and you still have no idea where he is. I hate to sound skeptical, but your maker is a lot more powerful and a more skilled warrior than Sylvana. There is a chance..." His voice trailed off as if he didn't want to say his thoughts out loud.

"There is always a chance." Cole glanced at Damian, raising his eyebrows, and Damian gave him a curt nod, understanding his brother without extra words. "Santiago, I found Ruslan," Cole continued. "At least, I believe I know where he is. If it is indeed the same individual who captured Sylvana, I'll do everything I can to free her and reunite her with you."

Santiago chuckled, and there was something so despondent in the sound of his laughter that shivers ran down Damian's back.

"Cole, you are old enough to know that baseless optimism

brings nothing but pain," he said softly. "I appreciate your words, my friend, but I prefer not to bring my hopes up." He fell silent for a moment. "Farewell, my friend. Stay in touch and good luck. Something tells me you're going to need it."

For a few seconds, Cole stared at the phone, nibbling on his lip. Damian glanced at him, a weight settling in his chest, spreading numbness through his arms.

"Maybe Santiago is right, but you're not him, Cole. I don't care how old you are, optimism is the natural state of your mind." Damian offered his hand to his brother. "It's not a good time to lose it. Keep it up for both of us, little bro. You know how I am—my glass is always half-empty."

He winked, and as Cole took his hand and got up, Damian gave him a quick tap on his arm and turned to Ricardo. "Give me one more minute, Ricardo."

Damian took the phone from Cole and dialed River's number, counting the beeps. As the call went to voicemail, he grunted, stifling a sigh. He hated leaving messages, still feeling uncomfortable speaking to a machine.

"River," he said quietly, "I wish I could speak with you and not your recording machine..." He fell silent, searching for better words. "Anyway, if Cole and I don't come back home tonight, don't worry. We're going to be all right. I'll try to call you as soon as I get an opportunity."

Damian hung up the phone and put it in his pocket, turning to Ricardo. "We can go now."

CHAPTER 11

~ DAMIAN BLAKE ~

Damian walked through the hallway toward the entrance, barely paying attention to his surroundings. Silently cursing the Destiny Council for putting him in this dangerous and precarious situation, he tried to set his mind on the upcoming meeting with the mysterious Head of the Arizona House, but all he could see were problems, holes, and potential downfalls.

It wasn't the first time he had to carry out an order he didn't understand fully or agree with, but never had he felt so helpless and vulnerable starting on a new mission. Since becoming a Destiny Enforcer, he had always felt the power of the Destiny Council behind him, facing any foe—no matter how scary and dangerous—from a position of strength. Now, he was about to come face to face with an unknown evil, and his position was that of weakness.

Walking a few steps behind Cole, Damian glanced at his brother's back, and his fingers formed tight fists of their own accord, his hands unusually clammy. He hadn't lied when he said he was just as much emotionally compromised as Cole. His brother has been his biggest weakness since they were kids, and now, so many years later, nothing had changed. If anything, their bond had become stronger. For Cole, not only would he take the shirt off his body to keep him warm, but he would give his life in exchange for his brother's safety. He knew this, but there was nothing he could do about it.

Pushing the troubling thoughts away, Damian sped up to catch up with Ricardo and Cole in the lobby. But as soon as they reached the door, the same butler, who had escorted them to Ricardo's office earlier, emerged from the shadows, blocking their way out. He inclined his head and crossed his hands behind his back.

"Mr. Torres," the butler said calmly, but the iron tones in his voice left no doubt—he wasn't here to serve. "Did you and your friends make your decision?" A grimace of superiority settled on his face as he glanced at Cole, but as he turned to Ricardo, his expression changed to icy contempt. "As you're well aware, Mr. Amaris doesn't like to wait. I suggest not to test his patience."

Ricardo stiffened for a heartbeat, but before he could say anything, Damian put his hand on his shoulder, stopping him.

"We will meet with Mr. Amaris and hear him out," he said dryly, staring down at the man. "As far as everything else, it's between us and your master."

A tight-lipped sneer crossed the butler's face, and he opened the door with a barely noticeable bow.

"Your ride is ready. Please, follow me." He headed outside toward a black limo with tinted windows parked on the driveway. Opening the passenger door for them, he gestured at it, a smile too sweet to be sincere appearing on his face. "Make yourself at home."

Following Cole and Ricardo, Damian got into the limo and lowered himself onto a soft, leather seat. The vehicle had enough space to easily fit in at least three more people, but as soon as the butler shut the door, darkness engulfed the cabin, and his usual claustrophobia reared its ugly head, pressing on his mind. He groaned and closed his eyes, trying to deal with it, but no matter how hard he tried, the overwhelming feeling of being trapped sent his heart into a wild frenzy. As the vehicle took off, his fingers dug into the seat, cold sweat covering his forehead.

"Dima, I'm here. You're fine. You know it's just your claustrophobia. Open your eyes and look at me," Cole's voice sounded in his mind, demolishing the walls of rising panic in him.

Listening to his brother's soft voice, Damian forced himself to breathe and cracked his eyelids open. Cole sat next to him, his eyes glowing in the darkness of the cabin. A wave of tranquility spread through him, and he exhaled a ragged breath.

"Did you use your glamor on me?" asked Damian.

Cole flicked his eyebrow and shrugged. *"It worked, didn't it?"*

"I hate having you in my head..."

"You're lost without me, doofus." Cole tapped his brother's shoulder but quickly sobered up. "Your claustrophobia is a real deal," he muttered with a slight shake of his head. "Until now, I had no idea how it made you feel."

"I hope the ride is not too long." Damian bent forward a little to see Ricardo. "How far are we going?"

"Not far. Downtown Phoenix," replied Ricardo through clenched teeth, his voice so tense that Damian had to do a double-take. Ricardo sat with his shoulders lifted, his face so pale, it was a sickening yellow.

"Is there anything you forgot to mention?" asked Damian quietly.

Ricardo flinched as if Damian had just slapped him. "No, Damian. I swear I told you everything," he replied. "I'm just..." His voice melted into the soft hum of the engine, and he bowed his head. "What if you can't do what he demands of you?"

He raised his eyes, his dark gaze pleading. Then he glanced

forward at the raised partition between the driver's area and the passenger cabin and took a ragged breath.

"Damian, I'm done," he whispered barely audibly. "You have no idea what I had to do for that man last week... His every next request is worse than the previous one. I can't do it anymore." He swallowed, dropping his head. "I'm disgusted with myself to such a degree that I'd rather die than continue—" He cut himself off, his hands resting powerlessly on his lap.

Before Damian could answer, the limo came to a soft stop, and a heartbeat later, the butler opened the door, announcing that they had arrived. As soon as Damian stepped out of the car, his breath caught, and he cringed inwardly, feeling like a tiny mouse in front of a mousetrap. He stood in the middle of Downtown Phoenix, surrounded by high-rises—all glass and concrete.

"I'll be damned," he muttered, following the butler as he walked up the steps and headed across a small plaza paved with concrete tiles toward a tall building with mirrored windows reflecting a blue, cloudless sky.

Damian walked through a tall glass door and halted in a giant lobby in front of an elevator, his nerves stretched to the limit. As the door opened with a soft ding, he practically had to force himself to step inside. Feeling Cole's cold fingers grasping his arm above the elbow, he snapped his head toward him.

"Hang in there, big bro," Cole projected, giving him a barely visible nod. *"I know you're not going to enjoy what's coming next."* Then he switched his attention to the butler, glowering down at him with unconcealed aversion. "Which floor?"

The butler glanced at him, and his eyes ignited with a menacing glow. "Twenty-four." He stepped closer to the panel and pressed the button with the number twenty-four on it.

"Cole, I'll be powerless there... Less than human. It's too high above the ground." Damian rested his back against the wall, clutching

the railing with both hands. *"I'll do my best to hide my weakness, but we both know if push comes to shove..."*

"If push comes to shove, I'll fight for both of us," Cole replied. "I'll never let anything happen to you."

And that's exactly what scares me the most... Damian suppressed a sigh, giving a short nod to his brother.

The doors closed with a soft swoosh, and as the elevator took off, Damian closed his eyes and held his breath. Being confined in a tiny box, the panic of claustrophobia roared to life, but it wasn't as bad as the overpowering weakness that settled in his body, increasing with each floor they passed. He felt as if he was standing at the top of Everest, worn out beyond his limit and deprived of oxygen. His knees trembled, and his heart thudded somewhere in his throat.

As the elevator came to a stop with a soft jerk, Damian groaned and pushed away from the wall, forcing the nausea down. He took one unsteady step forward, and the booth spun around him, his vision blurry. He caught Ricardo's troubled gaze and chuckled with a dismissive wave of his hand.

"I hate elevators. This is one of the modern inventions I can never get used to," he muttered and walked out the door, the floor slipping and wobbling under his feet, his body buzzing with weakness.

The butler rolled his eyes but said nothing and marched briskly along a wide hallway. He stopped in front of a black door at the very end and placed his hand on the door handle. Turning toward Damian, he gave him an arrogant once-over, and a look of smug superiority appeared on his face.

He knows my supernatural identity. But how? A thought rushed through Damian's mind, sending a jolt of unease through him.

"This is where I leave you," the butler said, pushing the door open. "Mr. Amaris will see you in a minute."

* * *

Damian crossed the threshold and came to a sharp halt, looking around in shock. He stood in the middle of a tiny room with a low ceiling. Between the three of them, there was barely enough space to turn around, and with his height of six-foot-four, he touched the ceiling with his head.

Everything inside was black. The walls were painted with matte black paint and the ceiling resembled a starless night sky. There were no windows, and the only source of light was a small, round lamp attached to the ceiling on his left, its faint fluorescent glow barely enough to reach the opposite wall.

Cole crossed the room and brushed the tip of his middle finger over the wall. "It's a one-way mirror. Somebody is watching..." He smiled and waved at his dark reflection on the black surface of the glass.

"Ricardo, have you ever been in this office?" asked Damian.

"No," replied Ricardo. "Usually, I meet with him in the underground facility where he keeps his captive fighters. I don't really know its location, though. The only way I could get in and out was through a portal entrance located Downtown, but in a different building."

Damian nodded. Now, he had no doubt that the Head of the Arizona House knew his supernatural identity and wanted him sufficiently weakened before the meeting. Between constantly spiking fits of claustrophobia and being at a significant distance from his element, he could barely keep an upright position, but he straightened his shoulders and put all his effort into projecting a calm and relaxed image for whoever was standing behind the black mirror. There were no chairs in the room, so Damian headed to the wall across from the mirror and rested his back against it, folding his arms.

No one talked, and since the room had neither windows nor a clock, time seemed to stand still. Damian wasn't sure how long they had waited when the glass wall lit up with a deep ultramarine glow, and a pleasant female voice said, "Please, come in. Mr. Amaris will see you now."

A small door Damian hadn't noticed before opened next to the one-way mirror with a metallic click, but there wasn't any light coming from the other side either. Damian approached the doorway first and raised his hand to stop Cole and Ricardo. Channeling his magic came with a significant effort, weakening him even more, but as soon as he opened his other sight, he was glad he did.

The space behind the small door felt like a dark void filled with nothing. The absolute emptiness glared at him from beyond the doorway, stretching its sinister tentacles to him, feeding on his energy like a hungry vamp. With a strangled groan, he staggered back, clutching at his throat.

"I have no idea what lies behind this door," he said to Cole and Ricardo without looking at them. "If I didn't know any better, I would say it's a gateway into the Void."

"I'm glad you know better. I didn't sign up to be a schoolteacher for a C-minus Destiny Enforcer student," a small voice grumbled in Damian's head sarcastically. *"The place behind this door is not a void, but it's not of this world either."*

"*The* Void?" echoed Ricardo. "I remember my father talking about it when I was just a boy. It didn't sound good."

Damian nodded, gesturing for Ricardo to be quiet.

"Zhulik, do you know what this place is?" asked Damian. He thought for a moment and added, *"Please, my friend, I need your help."*

"Aww... You do know how to be nice after all, Commander." The gargoyle snickered in his mind. *"Well, in this case, I'll try to help. The place behind this door is"*—Zhulik hummed as if searching for a better word—*"a tiny, pocket dimension, and my guess is that it's been created especially for you, Commander, since there is no elemental or magical energy there. It's like a miniature version of the Dark Nav. You're already weakened, so as soon as you cross the*

threshold, you'll feel as if someone just punched you in the gut. But the worst part of it is that once inside, you won't be able to summon me in case you need help."

Dammit... Damian rubbed the back of his neck and turned toward Cole and Ricardo. "To make a long story short, behind this door, there is a mini-dimension that was created by the Head of the House or someone who works for him. I don't know what we're going to find there, but it can't be any good. Ricardo, Cole—"

He met his brother's eyes, but Cole shook his head no, and his face hardened. "Don't even think about it. I'm coming with you."

"I have no choice on the matter." Ricardo shrugged. There was no fear in his eyes, just endless exhaustion.

"Here goes," muttered Damian and stepped across the threshold.

* * *

AS SOON AS Damian passed through the doorway, he felt as though all oxygen was sucked out from his lungs. He froze in place, gasping for air with his mouth open. His eyes widened, and he doubled up, pressing his hands to his stomach. Zhulik was right when he compared this place to the Dark Nav.

Throughout his long life, Damian had visited the Slavic realm of spirits and demons only once, but he could never forget how it had made him feel—powerless, despondent and lost. Deprived of all elemental energy, the Dark Nav was unfriendly to all beings of the Elements, feeding on their energy and life force until there was nothing left. Everything inside that dark realm was created to eradicate the desire to live, to fight, to survive.

"You'll feel better as soon as you adapt to an environment deprived of the elemental energy," a cold male voice sounded somewhere in front of him. "I'm sorry, but my safety is my highest priority. You'll survive."

"You're sorry? I'm touched." Damian straightened despite the lightheadedness and shortness of breath. Once the initial shock started to wear off, he forced himself to breathe in and look around. The only problem was, he wasn't sure where he was.

He stood in a barely lit room, surrounded by hundreds of mirrors. He couldn't say how many mirrors were there, but everything around him was reflecting. Even the floor was made out of a few large pieces of black mirror. Different shapes and sizes, they were positioned at various angles, creating endless corridors that ran in all directions, disappearing into the dark nothingness. A kaleidoscope of broken images, fragments of reflections, and flares of purple lights moving from one mirror to the next were mind-bending and eerie.

Damian spun around, searching for Cole and Ricardo. He could see their distorted and shattered reflections repeated in the mirrors over and over, but he had no idea how far his brother and Ricardo truly were.

Out of habit, he reached for his magic to open his second sight but found none. A loud guffaw followed his attempt, and the sound of this sinister laughter rushed over him like icy water, making him wince inwardly. Taking a deep breath, he forced himself to calm down.

"I assume you are Amaris, Head of the Arizona House," he said, sounding as even as he could muster in the situation.

"Yes, I am. But it's *Mister* Amaris to you," replied the bodiless voice snidely. "And you are Damian Blake, a Child of Earth who's commonly known in the supernatural circles as the Shadow Slayer." He giggled as if he found the sound of Damian's name amusing.

"Yes, I am, and now that we got that out of the way, stop playing your friggin' games and tell me what the hell you want from us," growled Damian.

"Mr. Blake, good manners can take you a long way," the voice hissed, and every mirror in the room vibrated as though reverberating the sound. "First, you're here because I wish you to be here. And believe me—if I didn't want to speak with you, you'd never find me."

"I believe that," replied Damian with a nonchalant shrug. "So, if you brought us here, you obviously want something from us. What is it?"

For a few seconds, the voice kept silent, and Damian started to wonder if the man had left. But just as he was going to call him, the voice spoke up again, sounding flat, almost as if he was bored.

"Second. From all of you, I want nothing. What I want is related to you only, Mr. Blake," he said frostily. "I want you to run a little errand for me."

"So I've heard," replied Damian, folding his arms over his chest. "And what might this errand be that the all-powerful and mysterious Head of the Arizona House can't do it himself?"

The voice snickered. "I can do it myself, alright. I just can't be bothered," he replied, not without a hefty dose of sarcasm in his voice. "So, what is it going to be, Mr. Blake? Yay or nay?"

Damian huffed, shaking his head. "First, you have to tell me what you want me to do, and then I'll give you my answer."

"No can do," replied the voice. "My house—no pun intended—my rules. If you say yes, I'll tell you what I need you to do. If you say no…" He cackled, his laughter too high-pitched compared to the deepness of his voice. "Well, the consequences will hurt in all the places that matter."

Something clicked, the sound bouncing off of every mirror in the room. Then one of the mirrors lit up with a soft bluish light. For a heartbeat, the seamless chain of corridors and reflections was broken, and Damian could see his brother and Ricardo standing just a few feet away from him. He grabbed Cole's arm, pulling him closer. The light was replaced with a photo of a dark-haired, dark-eyed man. Although Damian didn't think he'd ever met him in person before, his face looked familiar. Cole gasped and took a step closer to the image.

"Mr. Adams, I believe you recognize this man?" asked the voice.

"Yes," Cole whispered, staring at the image of the man in the mirror without blinking. "This is my maker, Ruslan."

"Wonderful." The voice tittered happily, and even though Damian couldn't see him, he was positive the man was rubbing his hands in delight.

Another mirror lit up with the blue light, which was quickly replaced by an image of a young woman. No older than twenty-five, she was beautiful in an exotic way. Her long black hair framed the tender oval of her face, falling to her back and chest in rich waves. Her large, brown eyes seemed to be sad even though a soft smile played on her coral lips untouched by lipstick.

"Mr. Torres, would you mind telling our friends who this gorgeous woman is?" asked the man, his voice morphing into a soft hiss.

"Damian." Ricardo turned to him. His ashen face reflected the bluish light of the screen, making him look like he was a step away from crossing the veil. "This is my sister, Camila."

Damian looked at Ricardo and then at Cole, but said nothing, remaining absolutely emotionless, at least on the outside, in the hope that the man behind the mirror would make the first move. A heavy silence enveloped the room, pressing on his nerves.

"Damian, whatever you decide, I understand and support you," Cole's voice sounded in his mind. His brother tried to sound firm, but his voice trembled slightly, betraying the pain and despair he felt.

A soft click reverberated through the room, and the images of Ruslan and Camila vanished.

"I will give you until sunrise tomorrow to make your decision, Mr. Blake," Mr. Amaris' voice sounded somewhere above Damian, causing him to look up.

"Before making any kind of decision, I want proof of life," replied Damian. "You showed us photos that could have been taken a long time ago."

The voice chuckled, its sound shifting somewhere to the right. "I expected that," he replied snidely. "This is why until tomorrow morning, the three of you will remain in my care." He took a short pause and continued, "Mr. Blake, you and your brother…" Damian stiffened involuntarily, and the man snickered. "I always do my homework. I know everything there is to know about you, Mr. Blake."

"I doubt that," growled Damian but waved his hand, motioning for Amaris to continue.

"You and your brother will spend this time in Ruslan's company," Amaris proceeded, his voice turning frostier with each next word. "Mr. Torres will get a chance to speak with his sister. After that, you will give me your answer, Mr. Blake." He fell silent again, but since Damian said nothing, he asked, "Do you agree?"

Dmitri, my child, you will accept his deal, and you will do whatever he wants you to do… Magnus' voice sounded in Damian's head, and he took a deep breath.

"I agree," he replied flatly.

With a metallic click, the weak light vanished, replaced by an impenetrable darkness. A heartbeat later, a portal rotating with dim purple lights opened in front of Damian.

"Proceed through the portal," the voice sounded somewhere so close that Damian could swear Amaris was standing right next to him. "I'll see you on the other side."

I hate the Destiny Council… The thought flashed in Damian's mind as he stepped through the portal.

CHAPTER 12

~ DAMIAN BLAKE ~

Damian had never been inside a high-security prison, but he sincerely doubted that even the most secured prisons of the human realm had so much security tech installed or so many guards on the premises. Even the Destiny Council holding facilities weren't guarded as heavily as the underground bunker where Amaris kept his captive fighters.

Amaris' portal opened up into a large hall the size of any good warehouse. Four well-lit corridors led away from the central area, doors constructed of heavy steel bars blocking the entrance into each corridor. A few massive metal desks were positioned in the center of the room, surrounded by digital display walls, every screen displaying a different cell with a single person inside or the area outside the building. He couldn't say how large the entire bunker was, but the idea of so many supernatural beings suffering in slavery sent a jolt of anger through him.

A man dressed in a black uniform similar to military fatigues —most likely a guard—got up, saying something to the other guards. Then he grabbed a digital tablet from the desk and approached them, giving them a quick once-over.

"Please, follow me," he said coldly, motioning toward the desks. "Mr. Amaris wishes to speak with you."

Damian exchanged a quick look with Cole and Ricardo and followed the man. The guard halted in front of one of the monitors and pressed something on the tablet. The monitor lit up with a dark-purple glow, and the silhouette of a man appeared on the screen. The guard bowed to him and stepped a few feet back, crossing his hands behind his back.

"Mr. Blake," Amaris said, his voice coming through loud and clear. "You and your brother will follow my guard"—he waved at the man standing behind Damian—"to the cell where I hold Ruslan. As promised, you have a few hours to discuss the situation and make your decision. However, I must warn you, if you think you have enough power to break free and take Ruslan with you, think again. This facility is equipped with anti-magic tech the likes of which you have never seen. What you experienced in Mr. Torres' house is nothing compared to what we have here. Am I clear, Mr. Blake?"

"As day," muttered Damian through clenched teeth.

"The room where I hold Ruslan allows only for the presence of vampiric essence," Amaris continued. "If you try to use your magic, channel your elemental energy, or even as little as open your second sight, the consequences will be dire. So, unless you don't mind losing your brother and his maker, I suggest you think of yourself"—he twirled his hand and snickered—"as a mere human and nothing more. Do you understand me?"

"Yes," replied Damian.

"Good." The silhouette shifted in his chair, readjusting his position. "One more thing, Mr. Blake. Ruslan's life is strictly regimented, and I am not going to change anything just because you and your brother are in the cell with him. But I must warn you—do not interfere and don't try to stop my guards, or I will have to remove you both from the cell and demand your decision immediately. Is that clear?"

"Yes," Damian grumbled, wishing to tear this man limb from limb with his bare hands.

"Yes…?" Amaris raised his voice as if expecting Damian to add something.

A breath caught in Damian's throat as an explosive wave of fury washed over him. "Not in your lifetime, evil bastard," he growled through gritted teeth. "I'm not going to bow to you or kneel before you. Neither will I address you as *'my lord'*. Am I clear?"

"We'll see about that. The night is young, Mr. Blake." Amaris cackled with a dismissive flick of his wrist. "Mr. Adams, was that clear to you, too?" he asked, turning slightly toward Cole, carnivorous delight in his voice.

"Yes, you're exceptionally articulate," replied Cole, sounding as calm as ever.

Amaris got up and waved for his guard to approach. "Jeff, escort Mr. Blake and Mr. Adams to Ruslan's holding cell." He thought for a moment and added, "When you come back, direct Mr. Torres to his sister's chamber. He's not to leave her room until further notice."

Jeff snapped his fingers at another guard, and he got up immediately, nearly running to him. "Make sure Ricardo Torres goes nowhere until I return."

"Yes, sir." The guard inclined his head and headed toward Ricardo.

Ricardo threw a troubled gaze at Damian, but he couldn't say anything to him in the presence of the guards.

"See you soon, Ricardo. Be careful." Damian gave him a curt nod and followed Jeff toward the corridor on his right.

* * *

Ruslan's holding cell was at the very end of the corridor, and as Damian followed the guard, he kept his head down, trying not to think of what kind of supernatural beings were locked up behind the heavy, reinforced doors and the torture their lives were, day in and day out.

The guard stopped in front of the last door and swiped his magnetic card over the security dial pad. The lock clicked, and Jeff pulled the heavy door open, gesturing for them to walk in. As soon as Damian and Cole crossed the threshold, he slammed the door shut without saying a word. The lock clicked again, its metallic sound sending shivers down Damian's back. He took a deep breath and observed the cell, focusing on every little detail.

Everything inside the room was absolutely white, and unlike in Ricardo's house, the boxes of anti-magic tech were visible everywhere. There was no bed or any kind of furniture. Instead, two iron polls were erected in the center of the room. A man dressed only in black sweatpants was sprung up between the polls, his arms attached to them by thick iron chains. Under the manacles, his wrists were raw and bleeding, his skin covered in blisters and patches of burns. He was on his knees, and his head was bowed low to his chest, his thick, black hair falling over his face in disarray.

"Father," Cole whispered and took a tentative step toward the man.

Ruslan lifted his head, his movement torturously slow. His gaze halted on Cole, but there wasn't even a shadow of recognition in his glowing, scarlet eyes. Then he looked at Damian, and a feral growl escaped from his mouth, his upper lip rising in a snarl, exposing his long, blade-like fangs. He pulled on the chains, fighting against his restraints to no avail.

"Damian, stay back," Cole hissed, pushing Damian toward the wall. "I don't know how many days they haven't fed him, but he's mad with thirst. He can hear your heartbeat, and it's driving him crazy."

Slowly and carefully, Cole approached Ruslan and lowered

to his knees in front of him. Pushing his long hair off his face, he tucked a few strands behind his ear.

"Father," he called, "it's me, Nikolai... Can you hear me? Can you understand?"

The vampire hissed and pulled back, shying away from Cole's touch. Swearing under his breath, Cole rose to his feet and turned toward Damian. He lifted his arm, his fingers trembling slightly, but then dropped it and lowered his eyes, staring somewhere at level with Damian's chest.

"If we want to speak with him, we have to get him some blood," he said, his voice hoarse and shaky. "I would never ask you for something like that, but it has to be yours, Dima. Ruslan bled for me more than once, and I would give him every last drop of mine, but I know it's not going to help him."

Damian stiffened, everything inside him screaming against doing what his brother was asking for. He glanced from Cole to Ruslan and then quickly observed the cell again, registering every white box of magic detectors installed along the perimeter.

"That's fine." He nodded, his throat too tight to speak. He swallowed and continued, forcing himself to sound all business-like. "I trust you to control Ruslan. By the looks of him, he won't be able to control himself, and I'm too weak to stop him on my own without using my magic," he said softly, pointing up at the boxes. "You can't let me die a human death, Cole. If I die, the elemental energy of Earth will take over to resurrect me and heal my body, and that will trigger the anti-magic tech, killing you and your maker. Do you understand?"

Cole nodded, his arms hanging limply at his sides. "Dima, I'm sorry."

Damian didn't reply but headed toward Ruslan, halting a couple of feet away from him. The vampire growled and jerked forward, pulling on the chains. Turning toward Cole, Damian gestured for him to come closer.

"I need you to bite my wrist," he said flatly. "I can't summon my daggers here."

Cole approached him and took his wrist, his fingers cold against Damian's skin. He lowered his face, and his fangs expanded before he sunk them into Damian's arm. Blood spilled from two puncture wounds, permeating the air with its metallic odor, and Ruslan hissed, thrashing violently in his restraints. Damian approached the ancient vampire and seized his hair, yanking his head back. Then he lifted his bleeding arm, pressing it to Ruslan's mouth.

A groan escaped his lips as Ruslan's fangs cut into his arm. The pain was sharp but short-lived, replaced by the sensation of warmth and content almost immediately, and Damian moaned, closing his eyes. Dizziness assailed him, and he would have fallen if his brother hadn't caught him.

"Cole, please…" he moaned but was unable to say anything else. His head dropped back powerlessly, and darkness, soft and sticky, wrapped around him, taking him over.

* * *

"Dmitri, open your eyes."

A voice sounded somewhere above him, and someone slapped his cheek gently. It wasn't the voice of his brother, and even though he had never heard Ruslan's voice, he expected him to sound deeper.

"Dmitri, look at me…"

Damian cracked his eyelids open and gasped, struggling to scramble into a sitting position. As far as he could see, there was absolutely nothing around him. He could feel a hard, slick surface under his back, but he couldn't see it. A wispy, white mist flowed low over the invisible floor, its long, curly tendrils slithering over his legs. There were no walls or ceiling—nothing but eerie darkness all around him. The air lacked the freshness and scents of nature, and even though he couldn't see anything that would help him identify where he was, he was positive there was nothing natural about this space. It was man- or magic-made.

A man kneeled next to him, his silvery-white eyes glowing dimly, concern reflected on his face.

"Magnus," Damian whispered, reaching for the man in the long white robe. "What are you doing here? Where am I?"

Magnus exhaled with relief and sat back on his heels, dabbing sweat off his forehead with a white handkerchief. He stuffed it back in his pocket, grumbling something under his breath. Then he took Damian's bleeding wrist and touched it with two fingers, whispering a short spell. The bleeding stopped, and the wounds closed.

"You're nowhere," replied Magnus in a quick whisper, "and I don't have time to explain. While you are here with me, time in the human realm stands still, so I don't want to keep you here longer than I have to."

Damian tried to push himself up again but felt too light-headed and let go.

"You lost too much blood," Magnus pointed out, pursing his lips. "When you come back, make sure Cole stops his maker from taking more of your blood." He seized Damian's shoulders and helped him to sit up.

"What do you want from me, Magnus?" Damian shifted to adjust his position and leaned forward, wrapping his arms around his bent legs. "You literally threw me into the lion's den, giving me no wiggle room and leaving me no choice but to do whatever this evil asshole wants, no matter how dangerous or reckless that might be. What more can you possibly want from me?"

Magnus sighed and averted his eyes, his fingers fiddling nervously with the official ring of a high member of the Destiny Council, turning it around his finger.

"Goddammit, Magnus." Damian slammed his hand against the invisible floor. "If you're going to tell me that I have to become one of Amaris' captive fighters, I'll demand the *'no one'* status again, and this time, I'm not coming back. I'll never wear a collar again."

"No, I would never let you do that," Magnus objected quickly, too quickly for Damian's liking. "But what I'm about to ask you is not much better. In your case, I believe it's actually worse."

"Spit it out," Damian growled, his teeth clenched so hard, his jaw hurt.

"It's about Cole—"

"No!" Reaching forward, Damian seized Magnus' robes, yanking him closer. "I said, no. Leave my brother out of this."

"Sorry, Commander." Magnus raised his arms in a placating manner. "But your brother is neck-deep in all of this already. And let me remind you—it's his maker's life Amaris holds over your head."

Damian exhaled and let go of Magnus' robe. "No, Magnus," he said quietly, slightly shaking his head. "I already told you. Cole loves his maker like a father, but he was ready to give up on him if I chose not to deal with Amaris." He rubbed his face, looking away. "It's not Cole's desire to save his maker that forced me into this dangerous situation. It's you and the rest of the High Council. So, tell me what else I need to do and get the hell out of the nightmare my life has become."

"I understand why you are not happy with the situation, but unfortunately, I'm not authorized to give you any more information than I have already given," said Magnus, his voice void of emotions. "I wish I didn't have to—"

"Not authorized? Oh, cut the crap, Magnus," hissed Damian. "You are the Head of the Destiny Council. You could've stopped the other two. We could've come up with some other way to find out what Amaris' deal is."

"No, I couldn't, and you know it, but you're too upset or too lightheaded to think clearly," objected Magnus. His voice shook, and he looked away for a brief moment. "The Destiny Council is not a monarchy, and I'm not a king. The three members of the High Council are equal in rights, and it has to be a majority vote on all important decisions. Please trust me, my boy, I've done everything I could to avoid putting you in this situation, but this is the only way. I swear."

"Fine." Damian shook his head bitterly. "Just tell me what I need to do, and how it is going to affect Cole."

"In the morning, when you tell Amaris that you have decided to comply with his demands, he may ask for your brother to remain in his care as a hostage until you return," started Magnus, speaking quickly, his eyes following Damian's every move. "You're going to agree to this condition."

For a heartbeat, Damian's vision became blurry, and he felt as if the invisible floor disappeared from under him.

"So, let me get this straight... You want me to leave Cole—an ancient vampire with unmatched fighting skills—in the hands of a monster who makes a living by enslaving supernatural beings and forcing them to fight in gladiatorial events?" he whispered, fighting to keep his fear and anger under control. "Are you out of your fucking mind? It's like giving a dog a treat and asking it not to eat it. As soon as I step out of the building, Amaris is going to put a collar on Cole's neck and throw him into the octagon."

"Yes, there is always the risk of that, of course, but most likely, it's not going to happen," Magnus said, iron tones ringing in his voice. "You will do whatever this man demands of you, Commander. You must find out what he's after and retrieve it."

Damian stiffened, pressing his hand to his mouth. "Magnus, you're asking me to willingly kill my brother. You know that, right?" he said, everything inside him frozen with dread. "And you're putting me in a no-win situation."

"How so?"

Damian dropped his arm on his lap, raising his eyes at the Head of the Destiny Council. "Give me some credit, Magnus," he whispered, unable to speak louder. "I'm not an idiot. We don't even know what Amaris is after. If it is some kind of powerful magical artifact, I'm sure you don't want me to deliver it to him, do you?"

"Absolutely not. No matter what it is, you will deliver it to the Destiny Council realm as soon as you put your hands on it," said Magnus, frowning. "Also, you can't release anything evil into this world on his orders. If he demands something like that, you must report to the Destiny Council immediately and wait for our decision."

"Then how am I going to get my brother back? I'm sure if I don't deliver on my promise, Amaris is not going to let Cole go out of the evilness of his heart." Damian shook his head, his hands lying powerlessly on his lap. "Like I said—it's a no-win situation for me, but I understand, the life of my brother doesn't matter to the Destiny Council. Purpose justifies the means, so to speak?"

"Dmitri." Magnus leaned forward and touched his shoulder, but Damian shied away from his touch, raising his hand. "I promise, we'll figure out how to get Cole out, but no matter what, you must comply with my orders." He glanced around. Even though they were in some timeless, spaceless void, Magnus looked fearful. "Right now, I'm not speaking with you as your master. I'm asking you as... a friend. Please, trust me, my boy. The future of this world depends on it."

"The needs of many versus the needs of one... Yeah, I know." Damian bit his lip, numbness spreading through his chest. "Just send me back, Magnus."

"Dmitri—"

"I'm a Destiny Enforcer. I do as I'm told," Damian interrupted him and pressed his fist to his chest. "After all, I'm yours to command, am I not?" A pained smile touched his lips as he added, "My lord."

"Dmitri, please—"

"Magnus... have mercy on my soul and send me back," Damian said, barely able to speak. "I need to be alone now. I have to figure things out."

"As you wish. But before I send you back, I wanted to tell you that I have Cossack on standby in case you need his help," Magnus said quietly, his shoulders slumped.

"May Perun strike me with his lightning bolt if I drag another innocent soul into this mess," growled Damian, clenching his fists.

With a deep sigh, Magnus reached forward and touched Damian's forehead with two fingers. The darkness became absolute, and when Damian could see again, he was back in Amaris' holding cell, Ruslan's fangs tearing at his arm.

CHAPTER 13

~ DAMIAN BLAKE ~

"Ruslan, stop!"
Cole's voice sounded somewhere above him. Loud and strong, it broke through the wall of fog obscuring his mind, delivering him back to the unpleasant reality.

"Cole," Damian moaned, feeling indifferent and weak as the toxic vampire essence circulated through his bloodstream.

Suddenly, the hold on his arm loosened up, and the fog in his mind started to clear, bringing forth the pain. Wincing, Damian opened his eyes and found himself lying on the floor, his head resting on Cole's lap. His brother punctured his own finger with his fang and smeared some of his blood over the wound on Damian's wrist, instantly healing it.

"Dmitri Chernov. We meet at last," a deep male voice said his true name, pronouncing it slowly and clearly as if savoring every syllable. "I've heard... too much about you over the centuries."

Damian turned his head, a swirl of dizziness accompanying his move, and his gaze fell on Ruslan. Even though his lips were covered in blood, the ancient vampire no longer looked like a trapped, feral animal. His brown eyes shone with intelligence, tiny twinkles of humor dancing in their depths. Like all vampires, he had a pale complexion, but his skin was still darker than Cole's and Damian's with shadows etched under his high cheekbones. His bloodied lips curved as he stared down at Damian without blinking.

"All these years…" Ruslan mused, his gaze traveling up and down Damian's body. "I thought you were an immortal Child of the Elements the first time I laid my eyes on you, back in Kievan Rus. And your brother"—his eyes darted to Cole, and warmth suffused the hard features of the ancient warrior—"just as special as you are. Now that I've tasted your blood, I'm positive you're a Child of Earth, but there is more to you than just that. What are you, Dmitri?"

Damian turned away and closed his eyes for a second, taking a breath to deal with the lightheadedness. "I was right… He does have a deep voice," he murmured to himself, but both vampires heard him. They exchanged a quick look, and Ruslan chuckled.

"He's still slightly groggy after the effects of the vampire bite," he said to Cole. "You know how it is. He'll get over it soon."

"My brother *is* special." Damian pushed himself into a sitting position and pressed his hand to his mouth as the room swam around him. "What can you tell me—"

"Hush, Dmitri," Ruslan whispered so softly that Damian could barely make out his words. Ruslan's eyes darted toward the entrance door, and his straight, black eyebrows snapped together. "These walls have ears and eyes, even though you can't see them."

Damian nodded. Getting up with a strenuous groan, he stilled, swaying slightly on his feet. Then he made his way to the wall and sat down, resting his back against it. Cole threw a somewhat guilty look at his maker and lowered himself to the floor next to Damian.

"We need to talk," Damian whispered without looking at his

brother, numbness spreading through his limbs as he thought back to his conversation with Magnus.

Slowly raising his head, Ruslan looked at him from under the dark strands of his hair and gave him a barely visible shake no, his eyes igniting with a furious scarlet glow. For a few seconds, he listened to something intently. Then his entire body shuddered, and his fingers gathered into tight fists, muscles bulging on his shoulders and chest.

"If it's anything important, I suggest using your blood bond. Cole is my son, and I can sense that you two are connected," he whispered even softer than before, his jaw clenched. "But you'll probably want to wait a few minutes, anyway." His eyes flashed to Cole, widening for a heartbeat, and then darted toward the door, hatred shadowing his tense features. "Son, turn away. I don't want you to watch—"

The lock clicked, interrupting him, and two guards walked into the room. Damian recognized Jeff as one of the guards and swallowed hard as the warning Amaris had given them about Ruslan's life being *strictly regimented* surfaced in his mind. Jeff approached Cole and Damian and halted, staring down at them with narrowed eyes.

"You two stay here and don't move," he said icily, his hands moving down toward the guns holstered on his hips. "Just a friendly warning—my guns are loaded with silver."

Without waiting for their reply, Jeff turned around and gestured for the other guard to proceed. He approached Ruslan and wrang his long hair around his wrist, yanking his head backward.

"Hello, Ruslan," he said, a derisive sneer on his round, freckled face. "Did you miss me, buddy?"

Ruslan didn't reply, but as he met the guard's mocking stare, every muscle in his body tensed, his eyes overflowing with loathing. The guard snickered and let go of his hair.

"I have no idea why, but Mr. Amaris insists on me asking

you this question every time. Since I know your answer already, it's just a formality." The guard unclipped a bullwhip attached to his belt, letting its long thong fall to the floor, pieces of silver embedded into it reflecting the lights. "Are you ready to submit to your master's will and bend your knee, old-timer?"

Ruslan lifted his face, and his lips stretched, showing off his terrifying fangs. "Never," he hissed. "Do what you must and get the hell out of here. I prefer the sound of your whip to the sound of your voice."

"As you wish." The guard shrugged and stepped behind Ruslan, the thong of his whip slithering on the floor.

Cole met his maker's dark gaze and stiffened, locking and unlocking his fingers at his sides, an almost palpable fury radiating from his body. Damian seized his brother's elbow, squeezing it.

"Do not move," he projected. *"You try to stop them, and you'll make it worse for all of us. If you can't watch it, close your eyes. Trust me, brother. The time for payback will come, but it's not today."*

The whip whistled through the air, biting into Ruslan's back. The ancient vampire pulled at his restraints, but no sound came out from his tightly pressed lips. Damian dropped his head to his chest, keeping his hand on Cole's arm. With each strike of the whip, Cole jerked slightly as if the silver-infested thong was landing on his back.

The guard counted ten lashes and stopped, staring at Jeff with a question in his eyes. Jeff turned to Cole and Damian, a menacing grimace on his face.

"I'll see you in a few hours, boys." He snickered and headed toward the exit, motioning for the other guard to follow him. On his way out, he halted and turned toward Ruslan, pointing at him. "We'll see you, Ruslan, in another twelve hours." He pushed the door open, and both left.

As the lock clicked, Ruslan moaned and hung limply, supported only by his chains. Damian got up and walked around him, barely able to move his feet. He stopped behind the vampire and clasped his hand to his mouth, holding his breath. It wasn't the first time he'd seen a man flogged. Looking back, he couldn't count how many times a whip had struck his own back. But whenever he was forced to watch this barbaric form of physical punishment, he couldn't help but feel sick thinking about the pain and humiliation a person had to endure at the hand of another being, human or supernatural.

Angry, red welts crisscrossed Ruslan's back, his skin pulled and torn by the silver whip. The damage was significant, but the healing process had started already, slowly closing the gruesome wounds as the bleeding gradually dwindled to nothing. The process was a lot slower than it would have normally been, undoubtedly affected by the silver in the whip and the iron in Ruslan's restraints.

"Like what you see?" Ruslan groaned without lifting his head

Damian walked back and stopped in front of him, the horror of Ruslan's situation making his blood run cold in his veins. "They do it to you—"

"Twice daily, on the clock. Every single goddamn day," Ruslan replied, a deep line etched between his brows. "That's how I know I've been imprisoned for exactly eleven hundred and thirty days."

"Perun almighty," whispered Damian, sweat covering his forehead. "Over three years of this torture, and you're still fighting... Have you ever considered giving in?"

"I've had plenty of time to consider that..." Ruslan gave him a barely visible shrug and winced. "Roxana sold me to the slavers, and I wasn't going to give her the satisfaction of watching me wear a collar and fight in the pits."

"Roxana is dead," said Damian flatly. "Cole is the King now."

"Oh?" Ruslan raised his gaze at Cole, a true fatherly pride gleaming in his eyes. "The best news I've heard in the last three years."

"Damian killed her," Cole said in a hoarse whisper. "I hope It'll make you feel better to know she was beheaded by my brother's whip."

"Live by the sword…" Ruslan muttered, shaking his head. "I guess I missed a few things while being imprisoned." He glanced at Damian, and his tense features softened. "Thank you for taking care of my son."

"Your son is my only brother. What did you expect?" Damian headed back toward the wall and sat down, stretching his legs. "I hope you don't mind if I get a quick nap. Blood loss is kicking my ass, and I can't self-heal in this shithole."

He tapped the cold floor next to him, gesturing for Cole to sit down.

"There is something I must tell you," he projected, using their blood bond, *"and you're not going to like it."*

Cole lowered himself to the floor next to him, bending his knees, and wrapped his arms around his legs. *"What's going on, brother. You're not yourself."*

"Damn right, I'm not myself," muttered Damian, throwing a sideways glance at his brother. Then he frowned and looked away, his fingers tracing a net of fractures on the white tiles. *"I don't think I can do it, Cole."*

"Do what?" asked Cole, furrowing his brow. Before Damian could reply, Cole's lips parted, and his eyes widened. *"Magnus pulled you to his realm, didn't he?"* Damian nodded. *"Let me guess, Amaris wants me to stay behind as his hostage, and Magnus wants you to agree to that."*

Damian nodded again, barely able to meet his brother's eyes.

"I'm okay with it, Dima."

"You're okay with it because you don't know everything." Crumbling on the inside, Damian told Cole about his conversation with Magnus. *"I can't leave you here knowing ahead of time that I'm not going to deliver on my word to Amaris."* He threw a glance at Ruslan and bit his lip, anger searing through him. *"This fucking*

animal... What he's doing to Ruslan is beyond..." He swallowed hard, finally meeting his brother's calm gaze. "I can't take a chance of him doing something like this to you."

"Dima, I need you to relax and think clearly—the way you always do." Cole changed his position, turning half-way to his brother. "You're looking at it the wrong way."

"How so?"

"Amaris has been torturing Ruslan for over three years, but he still didn't kill him," replied Cole. Damian moved, shaking his head, but Cole put his hand on his arm to stop him from interrupting. "It means Amaris knows the true value of an ancient vampire with a sword in his hands. I hate to sound like this, but someone like me can make a fortune for him. He's not going to kill me either."

"Do you think the idea of Amaris flogging the skin off your back twice daily makes me feel any better?" Damian stared in the direction of the exit, quietly cursing the Destiny Council for his current predicament.

"Dima, you're not thinking straight. Amaris wanted you to see what he's doing to Ruslan to make sure you stay true to your word. It's a scare tactic." Cole fell silent, nibbling on his lip. "It's not going to happen if we play it right, anyway," he continued at length. "Also, don't forget, saving Ruslan wasn't our only goal. We still need to discover who abducts witches and why they steal their magical energy, as well as to find out if Santiago's daughter is here. If I stay behind, it'll give me the opportunity to do all that and possibly more."

"Come on, Cole," Damian all but shouted through their blood bond. "Your unrealistic optimism blinds you. Please tell me, how are you planning to do all that if you're locked up in a cell without windows with twenty-four-seven security?"

"Lighten up, brother." Cole laughed softly, gazing at him reproachfully. "Jamie is right. You're always doom and gloom." He tapped Damian's knee. "You need to learn to look on the bright side, and I need you to trust me. I survived Roxana and her Court. I can *handle Mr. Amaris, especially since I have a feeling he's more inclined to deal with me than with you."*

Damian took a deep breath, slowly shaking his head as thousands of possible worst-case scenarios flashed through his mind.

"Dmitri, I don't know what Nikolai just told you, but you should trust your brother," Ruslan whispered, the chains clanking as he pulled slightly against his restraints. "I know you spent many years apart, but I've been by his side since the moment I turned him. Believe me when I tell you, Nikolai is quite capable of dealing with any sticky situation."

Damian glanced at Ruslan with curiosity, a twinge of envy spiking through him as for the first time, he realized that this ancient vampire probably knew his brother a lot better than him, having spent all these years by his side. He gave Ruslan a nod and switched his attention to Cole.

"Cole, our blood bond allows us to communicate from any place and any realm, correct?" he asked, his voice sounding strained even to his own ears.

"Yes," replied Cole. "And I promise that if I'm in trouble, I'll let you know right away."

"Swear to me..."

"I swear on my undead life." A sadness clouded Cole's face. "Who else am I going to call for help if I need it, anyway? I have you on speed dial."

"Your phone is broken," Damian murmured and closed his eyes, folding his hands over his stomach. *"I need to get some rest before facing Amaris again. He's a slippery bastard, so I need to have a clear mind. Besides, I'm sure you want to spend the few hours we have left with Ruslan without me hovering over your shoulder."*

"You're welcome to hover over my shoulder any time you wish, big bro." Cole got up, a wave of warmth washing over Damian through their psychic link.

Damian closed his eyes, allowing his drained body to take over his racing mind.

* * *

THE SOFT, metallic click of the lock ripped Damian out of his sleep, and he jolted to his feet, his mind on high alert. Jeff promenaded toward Damian and halted, giving him a demonstrative once-over. Damian took in his facial expression and the arrogant posture, and his stomach twisted with the expectation of more bad news.

"Damian Blake, Mr. Amaris is expecting you." He motioned toward the exit, but as Cole got up, he pushed him on his chest with a menacing scowl on his face. "Only Blake. Both vampires will remain here until further notice."

"*Dima, I'll be all right,*" Cole projected, staring at the guard with murderous intent in his eyes. "*Remember what we talked about and watch your back.*"

"*I swear I'll get you out of here,*" Damian replied to his brother and gave a reassuring nod to Ruslan as he turned toward the guard.

"Let's go," he said to him, but as Jeff made a move toward the door, he seized his arm, yanking him back. "And Jeff, if I find out that you put your hand on my brother again, I'll break it." Damian squeezed his fingers tighter, eliciting a cry of pain out of the guard. Then he smiled—a dark and dangerous sneer that left his eyes icy cold—and gestured at the door with a mocking bow. "After you."

Jeff escorted him along the corridor into the central room but didn't stop by the desk and headed toward the opposite wall. He swiped his magnetic card over the digital lock, and a small trapdoor opened up with a high-pitched squeak.

"Go on, buddy." Jeff snickered. "Mr. Amaris is expecting you. Let's see whose arms are going to get broken first."

Ignoring the guard, Damian bent down and walked through the low doorway. As soon as he crossed the threshold, the door behind him closed, and he found himself in complete darkness.

"Amaris." Damian folded his arms over his chest, planting his feet wide. "Stop playing your twisted games and let's have a chat."

A dim purple light ignited at the other end of the room, outlining the dark silhouette of a man sitting in a wide armchair.

"Good morning, Mr. Blake. How do you do? I hope you had a pleasant stay in my establishment," the man said in the best manners of a fifties sitcom. Damian couldn't see his face, but the amount of sarcasm he was emanating was hard to miss. Since Damian remained silent, the man laughed, and continued, "Did you make your decision?"

"Yes," replied Damian icily.

"Pray tell." Amaris leaned forward slightly.

"I'll take your deal. As soon as you set Ruslan and Camila free, Cole and I will do what you want." A chain of shivers ran down Damian's spine, locking his jaw, as he expected Amaris' answer.

Amaris laughed frostily. "Nice try, Mr. Blake, but that wasn't the deal."

"Excuse me?" Damian took a step forward and ran into an invisible barrier. Cursing under his breath, he stepped back, followed by Amaris' giggles that sounded completely inappropriate for a man.

He cut his giggles abruptly and leaned forward again. "First of all, the deal was that you do something for me, and only after that I'll set Ruslan and Camila free," he said in a no-nonsense tone. "Second, I hate to be rude, but I don't trust you, Mr. Blake. So, while you run this little errand for me, your brother will remain here, in my underground facility." He straightened, giving a dismissive flick of his wrist. "Don't worry, I'll take good care of him. If it makes you feel any better, I swear to return your brother to you as soon as you deliver on your promise."

Even though Damian expected that, it still came as a bit of shock, sending his thoughts into a wild frenzy for a few seconds. He dropped his head, forcing himself to calm down.

"That's fine," he said at length. "But in this case, I have a few conditions of my own."

"Really?" Amaris' voice was laughing, arrogance polluting his every word. "I don't think you're in any position to negotiate, but I feel charitable today. So, name your conditions, Mr. Blake, and I'll see what I can do."

"Let's agree to disagree. If I don't get what I want, you don't get what you want. I think I'm in a perfect position to negotiate," replied Damian, trying to sound as self-assured as he could but feeling none of it. Deep inside, he knew he didn't have a leg to stand on in this negotiation since now Amaris held hostage not only Ruslan and Camila, but also Cole and Ricardo, and his facility was overflowing with guards and anti-magic tech. "So, my first condition is that I want my brother to remain with his maker at all times."

"Done."

"Also, I want you to—," he started to say, but Amaris interrupted him.

"I think I can guess what you want," the Head of the Arizona House said. "You want me to remove the restraints from Ruslan and stop"—he waved his hand—"his daily punishment. Is that what you want?"

"Yes," replied Damian.

"How predictable." Amaris snickered, leaning back in his chair. "Consider it done. Anything else?"

"Under no circumstances can you use Cole as one of your fighters, either captive or unattached."

"Do I look like an idiot to you? I wasn't planning to." Amaris shrugged. "He's too well-known in both the supernatural and mundane communities. Having him fight in the pits, even in high-class events, is bad for my business."

"Perfect, then just one more thing—"

"You're pushing it, Mr. Blake," Amaris hissed, slamming his hand on the armrest of his chair. "And I'm losing my patience."

"And I don't give a damn. You meet my every condition or no deal," Damian continued calmly. "After I deliver whatever it is you desire so deeply, you give Ricardo Torres his contract back. He and his sister are free to live their lives as they wish."

"No." Amaris got up sharply, moving his chair back with a loud screech. "Ricardo Torres is one of my best suppliers. I can't replace him easily."

"I don't care." Damian folded his arms. "It's a deal-breaker for me. So, what is it going to be? Yes or no?"

Amaris muttered something and dropped back in his chair with a dismissive wave of his hand. "Fine. I'll do it. You're driving a hard bargain, Mr. Blake, but it better be your last demand."

"It is," replied Damian. "Now, tell me what I need to do."

"Finally," Amaris muttered, annoyance breaking through his even voice. "What I need from you is… um… How can I explain it so someone as unsophisticated as you would understand?" He fell silent, thinking. "You see, Mr. Blake, what I want you to do is simple in its complexity, but complex in its—"

"Simplicity?" Damian supplied snidely.

"No one likes clowns—"

"Suffering from coulrophobia, Mr. Amaris?" Damian lifted an eyebrow, watching Amaris hop to his feet, his aggravation setting his eyes ablaze with a purple glow, clearly visible against the darkness of his silhouette.

"What I was going to say," Amaris growled through gritted teeth, "is that what I need you to do is simple in its complexity, but complex in its execution."

"I don't care about your verbal acrobatics, Amaris. Stop speaking riddles and tell me what I need to do."

"Insolent peasant." Amaris sat down and crossed his legs. "I need you to go there—I don't know where, and bring me that—I don't know what."

Damian stilled with his jaw dropped. "You can't be serious," he mumbled. "I have to go somewhere, but you can't tell me where this place is. Also, you don't know what it is I need to find for you?"

"Something like that, but no. Not really." Amaris snickered. "If it were an easy quest, I wouldn't need to go through the trouble of blackmailing you and pushing you into the tightest corner I could find, now would I?" He leaned forward, reaching into the dark. Something clicked softly, and Amaris waved his hand in a circular motion. "I shut down the magic detectors in this room, so you can use your magic to teleport. Now, off you go."

"Wait." Damian stepped closer to the barrier separating him from the Head of the Arizona House. "How can I find you after I'm done? I have no idea where we are right now, so I can't teleport back."

"When you are done, you will go to Ricardo Torres' estate," said Amaris. "You'll find the man who escorted you here. He runs Ricardo's business in his absence. Now, be a good boy and fetch!"

Amaris laughed, the sinister purple glow in his eyes igniting brighter. Without saying another word, Damian snapped his fingers and vanished from the room, followed by the ominous outbursts of Amaris' laughter.

CHAPTER 14

~ DAMIAN BLAKE ~

Damian materialized on the steps of Paradise Manor. He halted, unable to make a move, staring wistfully into the desert where the pink rays of the rising run caressed the mountains with their warm embrace. Then he ran his fingers over his overgrown stubble and lowered himself on the steps. Resting his arms on his knees, he dropped his head and closed his eyes.

He wasn't thinking. He couldn't gather his scattered thoughts, so he just sat, staring at his boots, trying to take one breath at a time. A soft touch to his shoulder brought him back to reality, and he raised his head. Jamie stood next to him, his blue eyes filled with his usual curiosity.

Damian patted the cold surface of the steps next to him, gesturing for him to sit down. "Go ahead," he said with a sigh. "What would you like to ask?"

"Why do you think I want to ask you anything?" Jamie sat down, a wide grin splitting his face, turning his eyes into two narrow arches.

"It's written all over your face," murmured Damian.

"I always wondered why you never teleport inside the house?" the young man asked, looking sideways at him. "Sometimes you're so hurt and drained, you can barely stand. Why wouldn't you teleport directly into your own room? I'm sure River won't mind. Luc also never teleports inside a house, and Yakov doesn't open his portals. Why is that?"

Damian chuckled, shaking his head. "What can I tell you?" he said, tapping Jamie on his knee. "We're the knights of the old code. The World of Magic has certain rules that have been established centuries ago. Some of them are in place for your safety, but some of them are just etiquette. You know? Good magical manners? Like all the bowing and kneeling…" He rolled his eyes, stifling a shudder at the thought of some archaic manners that still existed in his world. "Anyway, one of the rules of the World of Magic states that you don't teleport inside a person's house without a warning, and you don't teleport out of a person's house without their permission. The same applies to opening a portal."

"I had no idea." Jamie turned slightly to face him.

"Don't worry, the Wardens are going to instill good manners in you with iron and fire, whether you like it or not." Damian glanced at the young man and frowned. "Speaking of which… What are you doing here, Jamie? I thought I told you to remain with Luc and Yakov?"

"I don't know how to explain." Jamie spread his arms slightly with a guilty shrug. "I had a feeling you needed my help. So, I told Luc about it, and he opened a portal for me." He gazed at him, a shy smile playing on his lips. "I know you well enough, and right now, you look like you're in some serious trouble. I want to help you, Damian."

"Jamie, thank you, but no." He rubbed the back of his neck, moving his head from left to right as his muscles responded with soreness. "Everything is so complicated. I'm afraid to bring another person into this mess. Especially not you. What kind of mentor would I be? I'm supposed to teach and protect you. Not throw you into the thick of things unprepared…"

"What kind of friend would *I* be if I left you in a tough situation alone?" Jamie asked quietly.

Damian glanced at the young man, expecting to find defiance in his eyes, but found none of it—just understanding and sympathy.

"When the time comes, don't say no to an offer of help, no matter from whom this offer comes..." The words Mara said to him a while ago surfaced in Damian's mind, and he glanced at his young friend with renewed interest.

"Alone is what I do best, Jamie," he continued quietly. "I don't even know what to do next. I was ordered to retrieve"—he fell silent and exhaled, nibbling on his lip—"something. But I was given neither directions on where to find it nor the description of what the actual entity is." He pinched the bridge of his nose, feeling a light headache building up behind his tightly shut eyes. "My brother's life depends on the success of this mission, and God knows what else. Are you sure you want to go with me?"

"Why is it even a question?" Jamie asked, gazing at him with reproach. "Especially if Cole's life is on the line. Where you go, I go."

Damian looked at his young apprentice as if he saw him for the first time. "Then we do it together. Thank you, my friend."

"Speaking of help." Jamie got up, offering Damian his hand. "You have a guest, waiting for you in the kitchen. She knocked on the door an hour ago and announced that she needs to speak with you and it's important. Since then, she's been nothing but pure entertainment."

"Let me guess." Damian got up, taking Jamie's hand. "Zabava?"

"The one and only." Jamie headed toward the front door and opened it for Damian, allowing him into the foyer first.

Damian walked inside and halted, staring at his own reflection in the antique silver mirror. A shadow moved inside, and an image of a young woman replaced his reflection, staring back at him, tears brimming her large blue eyes.

"Zerkalitsa, please don't," he mumbled to the spirit of the mirror. "I already know how fucked up my situation is."

She wiped her eyes and pointed toward the hallway on the right. Her entire body lit up with a soft, white glow, and a bright disk resembling a halo appeared over her head. Damian frowned, trying to figure out the message the spirit was attempting to convey. Probably noticing the confusion on his face, she rolled her eyes and stomped her foot, visibly aggravated by his inability to understand her. With an exasperated sigh, she pointed at the hallway again and motioned for him to go, giving him a reassuring node.

"What are you trying to tell me?" he asked in a soft whisper.

The image of the woman flickered on and off and vanished. Damian glanced at Jamie, but the wizard looked just as confused as he felt. Shaking his head, he made his way to the kitchen and halted in the doorway, observing an unusual view. River sat next to the table, her face flushed with laughter. Gypsy stretched on the chair next to her, her round eyes following Zabava's every move.

Zabava, dressed in her usual black jeans and a shirt, had a kitchen apron with a photo of Gypsy printed on it over her clothes. She was frying pancakes, handling a spatula like the chef of a five-star restaurant. A large stack of them already towered on the plate next to the stove, but she kept adding more, flipping each of them in the air as she did it.

Damian inhaled the bitter aroma of freshly made coffee entwined with the scent of pancakes and leaned his shoulder against the doorframe, closing his eyes. The kitchen smelled warm and homely, and everything looked so normal that his heart skipped a beat. After everything he had been through in the last twenty-four hours, he had a hard time believing that normality like this was possible in his life.

"Damian." River got up, her warm gaze brushing over him.

Zabava stopped what she was doing and turned to face him. Her eyes moved from him to River and then settled back on him, a tiny lopsided smile appearing on her lips. Wiping her hands on a piece of paper towel, she pointed at an empty chair.

"Sit down, Damian. You look like you can do with a nice, hot breakfast." She winked at him playfully, but her green eyes turned cold and alert.

Damian walked inside and pulled a chair out, lowering himself onto it. River filled two cups with hot coffee and placed one in front of him and the second one in front of Jamie before moving the plate with all the pancakes from the counter to the middle of the table. Zabava shut down the stove and took the apron off, hanging it over the back of a chair. Then she pulled the chair back and sat down across from Damian.

"Dig in," she said, moving a few pancakes to her plate, but he didn't move.

"What are you doing here, Zabava?" he asked coldly. "I don't remember giving you my address or inviting you to visit me here for that matter."

"Damian, behave." River gave him a pointed stare.

"Yeah, Sasquatch, behave." Gypsy lifted her head, staring at him with her round eyes without blinking. *"You know River doesn't cook. So, be quiet and enjoy the ride while you can. If things go well, she may end up staying with us. Mmm-mmm-mmm."* She winked and stretched, a blissful feline grin on her face.

"I told you already." Zabava took a bottle of maple syrup, pouring it over her pancakes. "I'm a supernatural PI. Knowing things is what I do." She took a sip of her coffee and closed her eyes, inhaling its aroma. "Anyway, the only reason I'm here is that the Grand Master of the Sisterhood called me. She wanted me to deliver you a message." She put her cup down and took a fork, twirling it in her fingers. "Fair warning—you're not going to like it."

"I've been told this statement one time too many in the last twenty-four hours." Damian pushed away the plate with pancakes and folded his arms on top of the table. "And every time it ended up being worse than I expected, so cut the bullshit, Zabava, and tell me what's going on."

"Fine." Zabava got up and propped her fists against the table, leaning forward slightly. "Here is what's going on. Elony gathered all her teams, not only her special team. She even went as far as recalling her undercover slayers. Guess what?"

Damian swallowed, staring out the window. "They're all accounted for," he whispered at length.

"That's correct," replied Zabava, straightening. "Every single one of them. No one is missing. I don't enjoy giving 'I told you so' speeches, but in your case, give me a moment to savor it, because I will enjoy every second of it." She closed her eyes with a smug look on her face and exhaled. "Ahh... it will feel good." She walked around the table, halting behind Damian, and placed her hands on his shoulders, bending down to his ear. "I told you, Cole Adams wasn't on their list. The Sisterhood slayers didn't attack him." Her warm breath brushed his skin as she touched his earlobe with her lips. But then she stepped away and crossed her arms. "So, if your brother said he killed one of his attackers, who were they?"

"Ahh... God damn it all..." Damian groaned, hiding his face in his hands. His brother's already dangerous situation just became tenfold more complicated.

"Oh, almost forgot," Zabava continued. "Since the impostors used the poison, which formula is a high secret of the Sisterhood, Grand Master Elony wanted you to know that she will continue her investigation, working on your territory whether you like it or not. Don't worry, she already ran it by the Destiny Council, and they gave her their blessing. She also asked me to tell you that if you find the impostors first, you're obligated to deliver them to the Sisterhood, and that she will personally hold you responsible if you don't comply with her orders."

For a moment, Damian stared at her with his mouth open, unable to say a word. Then he pressed his hand over his eyes and exhaled, his breath coming out as a moan. "Ahh... why now... goddammit..."

River moved her chair a little and took his hand, forcing it down. "Damian, what's going on?" she asked softly, her troubled gaze darting to Jamie and back. "God knows I witnessed you fighting through tough situations before, but never have I seen you so... despondent. What happened?"

"I would like to know that, too. As a Destiny Enforcer, you have no luxury of falling apart. So, would you care to tell us what's going on, Commander?" Zabava sat down. Her sarcastic expression vanished, replaced by a cold, business-like determination. "And where is your fanged mini-me? Where is your brother? The last time we spoke, you two were going to visit the Head of the Arizona House. You were supposed to call me before going in, but you never did."

"I didn't call you because I couldn't." Damian got up and motioned for Jamie to follow, half-turning toward the exit, but before he had a chance to move, River blocked his way, placing her hands on her hips.

"Sit down," she ordered in the best tone of a police detective. "And don't give me your usual 'conversation is over' bullshit, because it's not over until *I* say it's over."

Jamie snorted, but pressed his hand to his mouth and shut up under River's icy stare. Damian froze in place, stifling a sigh.

"What do you want me to tell you, River?" he asked, speaking slowly and evenly. "That I'm stuck between a rock and a hard place? Then yes, I am. An evil monster holds my brother hostage, and there is nothing I can do about that because my superiors force me into complying with his demands. Is that what you wanted me to say?"

"Damian, I'm sorry…" River reached for him, but he stepped back without realizing what he was doing. "I don't understand. If this man is evil, then why are your superiors forcing you to comply with his demands? All this time, I thought the Destiny Council was supposed to be good."

Zabava chuckled, her laughter void of any humor.

"You're too new to all this, River. So let me explain to you the best I can, because your inarticulate buddy here"—she pinned Damian with a heavy stare—"doesn't understand the importance of a clear line of communication." She rolled her unnaturally bright eyes and turned to River. "The Destiny Council is neither good nor evil. They do fight on the side of Light, but they work in mysterious ways, darling. When it comes to Damian and the likes of him, they don't explain themselves. The Destiny Council just tells them to jump, and they are supposed to ask how high. Destiny Enforcers are a special breed—they have no mercy, no remorse, no regrets, and no choice. Free will doesn't apply to them. They do as they've been told. Period. Once an order is given, the choice is removed from their hands."

Damian sucked in a sharp breath as if someone had just punched him in the gut. Slowly, he turned around and headed toward the exit, feeling River's and Zabava's eyes on his back.

"Damian, what does the Head of the Arizona House want you to do?" Zabava called after him, making him stop half-way through the threshold. "Does it have anything to do with my investigation?"

He glanced back, debating if he should just leave while he still could, but then turned around unwillingly to face her.

"No, it has nothing to do with the abduction of witches or the Sisterhood impersonators, at least as far as I can see." He read the mistrust written all over her face, and the desire to be as far away as he possibly could from this forceful woman roared through him, increasing tenfold. "You'll be happy to know that since my brother had no choice but to stay behind, it may give him the opportunity to look around. If the Head of the House is somehow involved in the disappearance of witches, Cole will figure it out."

He stopped talking, going over his conversation with Amaris in his mind.

"I'm not happy about Cole's situation, or that you're forced into doing something against your better judgment. I'm sorry if I gave you that impression, Damian, but I have to do my job. I hope you can understand that," said Zabava. "So, what does the Head of the Arizona House want from you? It has to be something important. Otherwise, he wouldn't go through so much trouble just to force you into submission. He has more than enough supernatural slaves on-premises who can do his bidding."

"That's the problem." Damian rested his shoulder against the doorframe and shoved his hands into the pockets of his pants. "I have no idea what he wants me to do. He gave me a riddle and refused to tell me any details. I'm supposed to figure it out on my own."

"Maybe between the four of us, we can figure it out?" suggested River, pointing at a chair. "What was his riddle?"

"I doubt that," Damian murmured, but since he had nothing to lose at this point, he changed his mind. "He wants me to go somewhere and find something, but he didn't tell me what that is and where it's located. That's the riddle."

"That makes zero sense," said Jamie. Then he looked at River and shrugged. "River, do you have a computer? I can try to look it up. You never know what you can find on the internet."

"Wait." Zabava buried her fingers into her short, golden hair, her eyes moving up and to the side. "Wait..." She moved her hand to her cheek as if she had a toothache, her face turning ashen. "That can't be right. Can you repeat his *exact* words? Don't add anything, say everything the way he said it."

"He said, I need you to go there—I don't know where, and bring me that—I don't know what," Damian repeated with a sigh. "Does it ring a bell?"

For a moment, Zabava stared at him, her jaw slacked, her eyes resembling two green plates. "Yeah," she managed to say after a short pause. "It rings a bell, alright. A bell the size of the two-hundred-sixteen-ton Tsar Bell."

"Do you know what that is and where I can find it?" Damian asked, a spark of hope igniting in his heart for the first time since he met Amaris.

"No and no," she replied, rising from her chair. "But I know someone who knows someone." She gave Damian a quick once-over and shrugged. "Your mission, since you have no choice but to accept it, takes you outside of the realm of humans and to the magical nexus, the Land of Dreams. I'll escort you to the person who can point you in the right direction. But as always, I don't take any responsibility for what may happen to you or your little buddy"—she sent a veiled gaze filled with mockery to Jamie—"during our journey. Since your brother is not here to go with you, I assume this baby wizard will take his place by your side."

Damian nodded, giving a warning stare to Jamie to prevent him from getting into an argument with Zabava. She followed their silent communication with a humorless look on her face.

Gazing heavenwards, Jamie muttered to Zabava, "Please say that you'll self-destruct after this message. Make my friggin' day."

"So, do you agree with my terms, Commander Blake?" Zabava asked, ignoring Jamie's remark.

Dammit, what am I getting myself into? I swear if I ever see Magnus again...

"You will do what?" Zhulik's voice sounded in Damian's mind, causing him to stiffen and hold his breath. *"Oh, wait. Don't tell me. I know that one. You'll kneel and kiss his ring? Right? Am I right?"*

"Ha-ha. You are supposed to be my guardian. So shut up and guard," Damian snapped.

"I'm not your guardian. I'm the only voice your malnourished, suppressed conscious has," the gargoyle muttered. "Take the deal, Commander. This is the only way."

"I agree to your terms," Damian said, offering Zabava his hand.

CHAPTER 15

~ DAMIAN BLAKE ~

"Let's get going then." Zabava shook Damian's hand, but didn't let go and raised her free hand, ready to snap her fingers.

Damian pulled his hand out of her grip, giving her a tiny shake no. "Not so fast. We're going outside the human realm. Would you mind if I take a few minutes to get ready?"

Zabava looked at him with curiosity. "I thought Destiny Enforcers have no worldly possessions, travel light and can leave on the spur of the moment." She cocked her head, looking up at him.

"I guess there is something you don't know about Destiny Enforcers after all. Give me ten minutes," muttered Damian, turning toward Jamie. "Jamie, call Luc and let him know what's going on." He headed toward the exit, but as he caught River's widened eyes, he halted and returned to her, taking her hand in his. "As much as I hate to admit it, Zabava is right. In my line of work, I sometimes have to get up and leave on the spot."

"I understand," she replied, quickly composing herself. Giving a gentle squeeze to his hand, she added, "It's going to be all right, Dima. You know that, right?" There was so much calm confidence in her voice, his chest tightened.

"I'll be right back," he promised, giving her a reassuring nod.

Pivoting on his heel, he headed out of the kitchen and didn't stop until he reached his room. He stripped his clothes off, quickly changed and sat down on the bed, lacing his combat boots. Once he finished, he sat upright and took a few deep breaths, disconnecting from everything that troubled him at the moment. He opened his mind to his connection with his brother and stilled, listening intently. Cole responded immediately.

"*Cole, are you okay? Where are you?*" Damian asked, lowering his face into his hands. "*Listen, little bro... The errand Amaris wants me to run for him takes me to the Land of Dreams. I have no idea what to expect and how long it'll take me to come back—*" He fell silent, his fingers digging into his scalp. "*Before I leave, I wanted to know you were okay and our blood bond could keep us connected no matter where I have to go.*"

"*Dima, our blood bond is fine, but not for long,*" replied Cole, speaking faster than normal.

"*What do you mean?*"

"*As soon as you left, Amaris moved Ruslan and me to a different wing of his underground bunker,*" Cole continued, but even though his normal calm confidence flooded their connection, Damian could tell something was off. "*Good news—Ruslan is no longer being abused. Bad news—I believe Amaris knows I have a bond with you, so he sent some wizards over to work their mojo. I know nothing about runic magic, but as far as I can see, a few more runes on these walls, and this room is going to look like an art gallery.*"

Damian cursed, slamming his hand on the bed. "*This asshole will block our connection.*"

"*Yes, he will, and not only in my room. From what I understand, the same runes have been placed all over the bunker.*" Cole's voice wavered, breaking and cracking as if they were speaking on cellphones with a bad connection. *"Dima, I'll be all right. Trust me, I can hold my own. Watch your back, brother. You know how the magical nexuses are—you must expect the unexpected."*

"Always..." Damian fell silent, thinking how to bring the news to his brother. Making a split-second decision, he chose to tell him straight. *He's a big boy, he can handle it...*

"You're thinking out loud, brother mine." Cole chuckled in Damian's mind. *"What can I handle?"*

"The Sisterhood's Grand Master spoke with Zabava," said Damian. *"The women who attacked you are imposters. They don't belong to the Sisterhood of the Sun."*

"Then how did they come into possession of their poison? From what I remember, it's quite unique."

"Beats me." Damian frowned, rubbing his chin. *"At this point, there are more questions than answers. So, I suggest we take one step at a time and see where the investigation leads us. I'm going to travel to the Land of Dreams and try to find—um—I have no idea what. And you just go with the plan and see if you can learn more about Amaris, his true business and what he's doing with the witches. He's a dangerous and conniving man, Cole, so don't take him lightly. There is a reason he surrounds himself with all this mystery. I have a feeling these Sisterhood copycats may have something to do with him, too. Just proceed with caution."*

"Always... Dima—" Cole's voice broke and disappeared.

"Cole?" His brother didn't respond, emptiness flooding the place where their connection had once been. *"Nikolai..."* There was no answer.

For a few long seconds, Damian just sat on the bed without moving, feeling hollow on the inside. Then he took a deep breath and got up, observing every detail of his room one more time. After years of constantly moving from place to place and living on the run, this was the first place he called home. Despite everything he had to deal with in his line of duty, Paradise Manor was his safe haven, a place where he could relax, at least to a degree, living a semblance of a normal life. But no matter what, he could never get rid of the feeling that it was as temporary as everything else in his existence, always waiting for the other shoe to drop.

"I guess this is it," he murmured to himself and walked out of the room, softly closing the door behind himself.

He wasn't sure why he did it, but instead of going to the kitchen, he turned in the opposite direction and headed toward Cole's room. The door was cracked open, and he pushed it, walking inside. As always, everything in his brother's room was in perfect order, not a thing out of place. A weight settled on his heart as he observed it. Unlike him, meticulous and punctual by nature, his brother couldn't stand any mess, whether it was his bedroom in Paradise Manor, his corporate office, or his giant mansion.

Damian's eyes halted on the half-opened door of the closet, and he frowned. Quickly crossing the room, he walked into the closet and halted. Cole's trench coat hung on a plastic hanger. With his heart beating in his throat, Damian pulled the side of the coat open and saw the leather scabbard with Cole's sword inside.

In the whirlwind of events, he hadn't noticed that his brother went to the meeting with the Head of the Arizona House unarmed. Damian's heart wrenched even though he knew it was the right thing to do.

Smart boy, he thought, heading out of Cole's room. *He didn't want to take the chance of Amaris learning about his unusual abilities.*

As soon as he walked into the kitchen, Zabava got up, giving him a quick once-over. "Are you ready to go now, Commander?" she asked, but even though a slightly sarcastic expression appeared on her face, her voice was serious bordering on tense.

"Almost," muttered Damian.

He approached River and stopped in front of her, ignoring Zabava's curious gaze. River got up, her movements slow and measured, which wasn't like her. He took her hand and brought it to his lips, kissing her knuckles gently.

"As always, you were right," he said, caressing her hand with his thumb. "Everything is going to be all right. I just spoke with Cole. He's fine. I'll be okay, too. It's just a quick trip. Jamie and I will be back before you know it."

"For someone so old, you sure have no idea how to lie convincingly, Commander Blake." Reaching up, she cupped his face, forcing him to bend down. Her lips found his, and for a moment shorter than a heartbeat, the world around him disappeared. Even though his body ached with the need to feel her touch, he pulled away, taking a step back.

"Come back to me?" she whispered.

"Always," he replied and bowed to her in the best traditions of the World of Magic.

"I thought you don't bow, and you kneel before no one." She laughed softly, shaking her head.

"I don't," he replied in full seriousness. Seizing Jamie's arm, he turned to Zabava, offering her his hand. "I'm ready now."

She took his hand and snapped her fingers, teleporting them out of Paradise Manor.

* * *

THE SHEER AMOUNT of magical and elemental energy was so overwhelming that for a moment, Damian couldn't breathe. Feeling lightheaded and intoxicated, he bent forward and propped his hands against his knees, struggling to keep upright. He stood like this for a few seconds until the effects of the magical nexus started to dwindle, clearing his mind.

"Ahh," he exhaled, rolling his shoulders like after a long sleep. "I already forgot how great it feels to be here."

He looked around for Jamie and found him lying on his back, staring at the perfectly blue sky. His eyes were foggy, and a drunk smile played on his lips. Damian glanced at Zabava, and they both laughed.

"He really is new to the World of Magic, isn't he?" she asked, shaking her head.

"You have no idea," murmured Damian, lowering to his knee next to Jamie. "Are you okay, my friend?"

"Whoa…" Jamie lifted his arm, trying to touch Damian's face but missed it by a few inches. "What's this place? All the colors and smells and sounds… And your eyes are glowing orange… so pretty…" He tittered. "I feel—"

"Drunk?" Damian seized his shoulders and yanked him to his feet. He placed his hand over Jamie's forehead, gently blocking some of his magical energy. As his glowing eyes cleared, Damian let go and waved his hand around. "Welcome to the Land of Dreams, one of three magical nexuses in the realm of humans."

Damian observed his surroundings, slowly turning in place. They stood in the middle of an enormous clearing that was surrounded by a thick, dark forest from every direction. A light breeze played with tall, lush grass, sending wave after wave across the clearing, and a chorus of birds chirped loudly somewhere in the depth of the woods. The bright rays of sunshine caressed the ground, kindling sparkling flares in the drops of the morning dew. The scent of wildflowers mixed in with a slight odor of damp earth and foliage lingered in the air, adding to its crisp freshness.

At the far end of the clearing, a tiny house nestled against the trees. Built in the classic old-Russian style, it had a tall A-frame roof, and even from this distance, Damian could see a wind vane crafted in the shape of a rooster.

"I need to check in with the Lady Gatekeeper first." Zabava jerked her chin toward the house and snickered, taking in Jamie's state of awe. "Can you walk without tumbling down, baby wizard?"

"I'm fine," grumbled Jamie, taking a few unsteady steps forward.

Damian chuckled, grabbing his arm for support. "You'll get used to it," he said, heading toward the house. "Compared to the magical nexuses, the human realm is low on magic. The flow of magical and elemental energy here is so concentrated that every time you arrive in a nexus, your senses will get overwhelmed for a little bit. It's an adjustment, you know. You'll learn to deal with it." He shrugged, throwing a humorous glance at his young apprentice.

"I don't think I'd ever want to leave this place. It truly is magical," Jamie murmured, looking around in wonderment.

Damian stifled a sigh, reminded why he was here in the first place. "It's magical, alright, but it's not a safe place, Jamie. All the monsters of your childhood nightmares, all the fairy tales and legends you've ever heard—everything is real here. So, you must be vigilant at all times, no matter where you are in the nexus, and remember that human logic doesn't always apply here."

"Human logic?" Jamie scratched the back of his head. "I'm not sure I had one in the first place. So, nothing to worry. I'll be perfectly fine."

Zabava slowed down a little, falling in step with them. "And Jamie, whatever you do, don't look into the Lady Gatekeeper's eyes. She's blind, but she's an ancient seer, and she can see better than any person with twenty-twenty vision. Take my word for it—soul reading is an unpleasant procedure."

They approached the small house, and Zabava ran up the steps, raising her hand to knock, but the door opened up before she could do it. An old woman dressed in a long black skirt and white blouse with lacy sleeves walked out onto the porch and halted. Her eyes were closed, but somehow Damian felt as if she was looking into his very soul. Jamie gasped and squirmed next to him, taking a step back.

"Zabava, my child, I'm so glad to have you here." The woman

beamed, a web of small wrinkles manifesting around her tightly shut eyes. "Please, come in." She stepped aside, ushering all of them into her home.

Inside, the house was just as beautifully crafted as on the outside. Built of solid wooden logs, it was light and spacious with a tall, vaulted ceiling. Lacy curtains adorned the windows, and the morning sun came into the room unobstructed, bouncing against a large mirror on the opposite wall.

The Lady Gatekeeper made her way to a table and sat down on a wooden bench with a soft groan, gesturing for them to join her.

"So, Zabava, what brought you here?" She turned toward her, inclining her head slightly. "You wouldn't visit your old friend just to say hello, would you?" She turned her head slowly as if she could see Damian and shook her head. "Fascinating. If I am not mistaken, you brought a Destiny Enforcer into my domain. Why is that?"

She got up heavily and made her way around the table. Halting behind Damian, she placed her hands on his temples and stilled. Damian tilted his head up and gasped as her extremely powerful magical energy overwhelmed his senses, turning his muscles into powerless mush. Her milky blind eyes opened wide, gazing deep into the depth of his soul.

"My lady, please," he whispered, unable to break their eye contact, "if you want to know something, just ask me. I swear I'll be honest with you."

"Hush, boy," the old seer murmured. "I know the process of soul reading is not fun, but I'll be honest with you, too. I'm not a fan of your kind, so I want to know who I'm dealing with."

"I am Commander Damian Blake, Lord Magnus' personal Shadow Enforcer," he hissed through clenched teeth. "I'm here because—"

"You need to go there—you don't know where and find that —you don't know what?" she finished his sentence and let go.

Damian exhaled in relief, his chest still shuddering with laborious breaths. "Yes, my lady," he managed to say.

She tapped on Jamie's shoulder. "Please let me sit down here, young wizard," she said, motioning for him to move over.

As Jamie got up and took a seat next to Zabava, the Lady Gatekeeper lowered herself on the bench next to Damian, turning toward him. She raised her hand covered in thin slithering veins, and her fingers, deformed by arthritis, brushed over his face, pushing his hair away. Her hand lingered over the scar, and she shook her head again.

"You're a Destiny Enforcer, but your heart"—she pressed her slightly trembling fingers over his chest—"is not hollow. How is that possible?"

"My lady." Damian took her hand, gently removing it. "Can you help me find—er—this mysterious magical entity? The life of my brother depends on it."

"A lot more than just the life of an ancient vampire depends on the success of your mission," she said, patting his cheek in such a motherly manner that his breath caught in his chest. "I know, your brother is your world, but in the grand scheme of things, his life means nothing."

"I know this magical entity is the real deal, but I have no idea where to find it," said Zabava. "Can you point us in the right direction?"

"I wish I could," the Lady Gatekeeper replied, rising, "but I can't. I know it's located on an isle, but this isle doesn't stay in the same place long. It moves all around the nexus, changing its location every so often."

"Perun almighty…" Damian bowed his head. Despite the old seer's words, his thoughts returned to Cole and his dangerous situation.

"As powerful as Perun is, he can't help you, Enforcer," replied the Lady Gatekeeper, "but another deity of the Slavic pantheon can be quite helpful if the right person asks the right question."

"Who is this person, and where I can find him?" Damian asked quietly.

"Her, not him." The old lady cocked her head, staring at Zabava, the corners of her mouth lifting just a touch. "Luckily, you won't have to go far since she's sitting across the table from you. But the real question, is she willing to put her enormous pride aside for the greater good?"

Damian got up slowly. "Zabava, why?" he asked, his voice husky. "If all this time you knew where I needed to go, why did you waste my time? You know the gravity of the situation—"

The Lady Gatekeeper laughed, the sound of her cracked, elderly laughter bouncing in his ears. "No, Enforcer," she said, readjusting her flowery kerchief to tuck a strand of gray hair under it. "She doesn't know where the isle is located, but she knows someone who can identify the location. All she has to do is ask. The problem is, I don't think she's willing to do it."

Damian's jaw tightened as he stared at Zabava without blinking. "Zabava," he exhaled, and the ground shook beneath his feet as he failed to control his power.

"I wasn't wasting your time, Damian. I was hoping that as a seer, she could have given us directions," Zabava yelled, throwing her hands up. "Fine! Stop staring at me like this. I'll do it." She snapped toward the old lady, her eyes igniting brighter with the glow of her magic. "Just so you know, it has nothing to do with my pride." She stomped her foot and opened her mouth to add something but then changed her mind and marched around the table toward Damian and Jamie. "Jamie, get up. We're leaving now."

The Lady Gatekeeper chuckled. "It took the manipulation of some evil bastard to get you to do the right thing, but it's about time."

"Ugh." Zabava stamped her foot again, reaching for Damian's arm.

The old seer raised her hand, stopping her. "Hold on,

darling," she said, turning toward Damian. "There is something I want to tell you, Commander Blake." She chuckled as if she found the sound of his title and name amusing. "Choosing someone like you as his Shadow Enforcer? Magnus is as eccentric as always, but I can *see* why he did it."

"What do you mean?" asked Damian, sending a puzzled look Zabava's way, but she just shrugged, lifting her arms.

"Magnus knows what I mean. You don't have to." She stepped back, staring directly ahead at Damian's chest. "Commander, maybe you're not a common Destiny Enforcer who obeys every command blindly, but that's one of the things that makes you special. Nevertheless, what I was going to tell you has nothing to do with your job." She lifted her arm, placing her hand over his chest. "When the time comes, don't be afraid to show what you have here."

"Do you mean his sizable pecks and washboard six-pack?" asked Zabava snidely. "I don't think there is anything else there to look at."

"Aw, Zabava, how sweet. Don't tell me you're infatuated with this boy? It's been a while since I've seen you showing any kind of affection to anyone." The corners of her mouth lifted, but a thin layer of sarcasm was clear in her voice.

"In his wet dreams," Zabava grumbled. "And just for your information, the last time he could have been called a boy was about a thousand years ago or more."

"Compared to you and me, he is a boy," the old lady objected and gave her a dismissive wave of her hand. "Now, off you go."

"Thank you for your help, my lady," said Jamie with a bow.

"At least one of you has some manners." As the Lady Gatekeeper glanced at Jamie, a warmth changed her features, wiping out the sarcasm. "I'm glad you're here, young Warden. Your mentor needs you."

"I'm not a Warden." Jamie glanced at Damian for support, confusion written all over his face.

"You're marked by Guardians, but here and here"—the old lady touched his forehead and his chest—"you're a Warden. Luc de la Crosse is your Master, I believe." Jamie nodded. "He'll tell you soon..." Her eyes moved from Jamie to Damian and then halted on Zabava. "Godspeed, all of you."

Rolling her eyes, Zabava stepped between Damian and Jamie and pushed her arms through the crooks of their elbows. Then she snapped her fingers, and everything around them swirled into a continuous blur as she teleported them out of the Gatekeeper's house.

* * *

They materialized in the middle of a forest, the trunks of tall leafy trees covered in a thick cloak of moss rising all around them. At the far end, a dim light broke through the thickets, and Damian headed toward it. Halting at the edge of a clearing, he turned to Zabava, rubbing the back of his neck.

"Whoa…" Jamie exhaled, carefully pulling shrubbery apart to get a better view. "I don't know if modern movies or fantasy books are a reliable source, but that can't be any good."

A small hut with a straw-covered roof stood in the center of the clearing. Lacy wooden frames surrounded the windows in an intricate design, and a wind vane, similar to the one on the Lady Gatekeeper's house, topped the tip of the roof. But the most unusual part of the house architecture was that it was supported by two massive chicken legs.

"Are you kidding me?" Damian hissed, jerking his thumb at the hut. "As if I didn't have enough problems without that!" He waved his hand in a wide arch, muttering a spell under his breath, and a power field lit up with a dim bluish light, running all around the clearing. "Only a god can conjure this kind of protective magic! And not just any god. If I'm not mistaken, these wards were placed by Veles, the god of the Three Realms and one of the most powerful deities in the Slavic pantheon."

"I'm more than sure Veles isn't here, so stop shaking in your pants. You wanted directions?" Zabava huffed, taking a step closer to him. "This is the only place where you can find them. Deal with it, Enforcer. And if you think I want to be here, think again."

"And what directions might that be?"

Damian heard a female voice and turned around to find a tall woman dressed in a black leather outfit and motorcycle boots standing in front of him. She threw her long, dark-brown hair off her face and cocked her head slightly, her honey-colored eyes exploring every inch of Damian's body. Then her gaze darted to Zabava, and her coral lips twisted into an icy grimace.

"Well, hello, daughter. Long time no see."

CHAPTER 16

~ DAMIAN BLAKE ~

"There is no need for such a dramatic entrance, Mother," Zabava muttered, but shrunk under the woman's heavy stare and fell silent.

"Whoa…" Jamie exhaled, staring at Zabava. "Now I know where your sweet personality came from. Are you saying Baba Yaga is your mother?"

The woman glanced at him, a shadow of displeasure crossing her face. "I prefer Yaginya if you don't mind," she said coldly. "Thanks to Russian fairytales, the image of Baba Yaga has been turned into some kind of bogeyman that is used to scare misbehaving children."

She grabbed Jamie's arm, pulling him closer to the invisible barrier of protection magic. Jamie threw a pleading glance at Damian, but she probably noticed it because she laughed, shaking her head.

"Don't be afraid, little wizard. I don't eat children for breakfast." She touched the barrier, whispering something, and it lit up with a dim blue light. Giving Jamie an arched stare, she pushed him through the shield and added with a snide smile on her lips. "Children are on my dinner menu." She glanced back and jerked her chin toward the hut. "What are you two waiting for? A special invitation?"

Damian threw a scorching stare at Zabava. "You couldn't tell me earlier that you're a demigod and your mother is Yaginya?" he hissed.

"What makes you think I'm a demigod, Enforcer?" she snapped back, invading his personal space.

Damian froze in place as the image of Zerkalitsa with a halo over her head flashed before his eyes. He opened his mouth, but before he could say anything, Zabava seized the shirt on his chest and yanked him through the barrier.

As soon as he crossed inside the protected area, the view changed. The hut on chicken legs was replaced by a contemporary home built of glass and concrete. A clearing covered in tall grass had turned into a perfectly manicured front lawn with blooming flowerbeds by the side of the building. Yaginya and Jamie had already reached the house and stood on the marble steps in front of the entrance.

The ancient goddess pushed the door open, inviting them inside. "Please come in," she said dryly, her frosty eyes lingering on Zabava. "I wish I could say my daughter's friends are my friends, but I can't. She has really bad taste in men."

"Now you see why I didn't want to come here?" Zabava muttered, poking Damian in his ribs.

"Sorry, not sorry," murmured Damian. "She's your mother. Kiss, make up, and be happy you still have her." He fell silent, thinking about his mother whom he barely remembered, wondering how his life would have turned out if she had lived longer.

He crossed the clearing and halted in the doorway indecisively, observing a sizable open room with a tall ceiling and giant windows taking most of the wall space. A large dining table covered with a white tablecloth stood at the other end of the room, reflected in perfectly polished marble tiles.

A few pictures in modern frames depicting mountains, rivers and forests hung on the wall. In each picture, he saw Yaginya either sitting on or standing next to a beautiful Harley-Davidson motorcycle. Just like now, she was dressed in biker's gear, including a leather jacket, pants, and motorcycle boots. With her rich, long hair blowing in the wind, she looked like one of those high-end models, posing for a photo in a fashion magazine.

"Nice bike," murmured Damian before he could stop himself.

Yaginya walked Jamie toward the table, gesturing for him to sit down, and turned to Damian, lifting a brow.

"What can I tell you," she said. "A girl has a need for speed." She chuckled, shaking her head. "Or did you think I ride around in a mortar with a pestle in my hands? Or maybe on a broom?"

"Nothing like that, ma'am," Damian replied cautiously, approaching the table. "Just admiring your taste in transportation."

"Uh-huh," she hummed, looking up at him.

Even though she was tall, at least six feet, he still towered over her, and judging by the expression on her face, she wasn't fond of it—or of him in general. She didn't invite him to sit down, and her slightly downturned eyes flashed to her daughter, igniting with annoyance.

"Zabava, I haven't seen you for centuries, and then you show up here, unannounced, accompanied by this brute?" She pointed at Damian, and his jaw dropped.

He had expected anything from the old goddess-slash-sorceress, but this kind of frosty welcome wasn't something he had foreseen.

"I didn't know I needed a special invitation to come home, Mother," Zabava growled, folding her arms. "Trust me, if I had a choice, I wouldn't, but the future of the human realm is more important than my grievances about the way my mother treated me when I was a child."

"The way I treated you?" Yaginya threw her hands up, and the walls of the house trembled slightly as the magical energy field spiked around her. "How about what you did? Running off with a man—a filthy human to boot—to live in a world deprived of magic? And if that wasn't enough, you warded yourself, so no one, including me and your father, could detect your presence. Every night, I had nightmares about you being burned at the stake by witch hunters! Do you know what it feels like for a mother not to know what happened to her child?" She nodded mostly to herself, mirroring Zabava's position. "Wait, one day you'll have children of your own, then you'll understand how you made me feel."

"Mo-o-the-er—," Zabava started but didn't finish the statement.

"Don't mother me!" Yaginya yelled, pointing at Damian over her shoulder. "And now, centuries later, you show up accompanied by this? An Enforcer?" She seized Damian's arm, pulling him closer. "Don't tell me he's your new object of affection. Destiny Enforcers have empty hearts, Zabava. They're not allowed to fall in love, have families, live normal lives. I thought you were smarter than that, daughter."

"I'm not—"

"And this one..." Yaginya continued, completely ignoring her daughter, and frosty laughter escaped her lips. "Oh, this one is truly the cream of the crop. Why would you bring an Enforcer into my home in the first place? You know I can't stand their kind."

"He's not my lover, Mother!" Zabava was finally able to put her words through. "He's a good man who's trying to do his job, even though he's a Destiny Enforcer, and I want to help him because it's the right thing to do! Because witches all over the human realm are being chased, captured and drained of their magical energy. Because he's the only one who can help me stop the monster who's doing that!"

"But did you know that he's marked?"

"Marked? By what?" Damian and Zabava asked at the same time.

Before Damian could react, Yaginya seized the hair on the back of his head and slammed his head against the table, adding her godly power to her physical strength. Damian yelped and blacked out for just a moment. When he regained consciousness, he was lying on his stomach on top of the table, invisible ties of magical energy binding him to it. With one sharp move, Yaginya ripped his shirt, exposing his scarred back.

"That's what I mean," she exhaled. "He's marked by the beast."

Her finger moved lightly over his back, tracing the shape of his scars, and Damian jerked, struggling in the restraints of her magic to no avail.

"Let. Me. Go!" he growled.

Anger spiked through him, and the entire building shook as he no longer cared to control his power. But the ancient goddess touched the back of his head, severing his connection with his element, and weakness spread through him.

"Let him go!" Jamie yelled.

In his position, Damian couldn't see his apprentice, but the sound of a fallen chair and his shaking voice told him how truly angry the young man was.

"What is wrong with you?" continued Jamie, his voice rising higher. "You tell us Destiny Enforcers have empty hearts? Look in a mirror, lady! What you're doing to Damian makes me believe you have no heart at all!"

Complete silence enveloped the room. Even the birds stopped chirping in the forest. Damian glanced at Yaginya, feeling the hair rise on the back of his neck. The goddess stood rigid, her pale face contorted by unadulterated fury, her blazing eyes staring at Jamie without blinking.

"No, my lady, please," Damian whispered, but in the surrounding silence, his soft voice sounded louder than thunder. He swallowed, realizing that he was begging and pleading, but at this moment, he didn't care what he needed to do as long as it would help him save Jamie. "He's a modern man—too young and inexperienced in everything to do with the World of Magic. He doesn't even know he's talking to a goddess of the Slavic pantheon. The only thing he knows about you is what he learned from reading Russian fairytales and watching modern TV. Please forgive him, my lady. If you feel the need to punish someone, then punish me."

Yaginya winced as if he'd just slapped her. She looked down at Damian, anger slowly dwindling in her eyes. Then she snapped her fingers, and the restraints of her magic vanished. Unable to look into Jamie's eyes, Damian pushed himself into a sitting position and stepped on the floor, throwing his torn shirt on the table. Without saying a word, he turned around and walked out the door.

As he moved down the steps, he heard Jamie shouting, arguing with Yaginya, but he didn't listen and kept walking. He stopped at the edge of the clearing by the barrier and lay down on his back, folding his arms over his stomach. The elemental energy of Earth engulfed him, partially restoring his strength, and he closed his eyes. But a moment later, something cold and wet poked him in his side, and he turned his head, cracking his eyelids open. A German Shepherd puppy sat next to him, his sad, brown eyes gazing at him with affection.

"Zhulik?" he murmured, reaching for the puppy to pet his soft, thick fur. "I don't remember summoning you."

"It's hard to remember something you haven't done." The puppy tilted his head, a doggish grin on his muzzle. *"I thought you could*

do with something warm and fuzzy right now. To make you feel better, you know?"

"Thank you, my friend." Damian chuckled. "But right now, I would rather have something hard and sharp, preferably with god-killing powers. Do you have anything like that in your arsenal?"

"I always knew you had a proclivity for becoming a serial killer," murmured Zhulik, his tail working faster. *"I'm sorry. I couldn't help you, Commander. She locked me inside your tattoo."*

"It's okay." Damian sat up, bending his knees, and the puppy shifted closer to his side, allowing him to pet his back gently. "Not the first time..."

"Not the first time?" Jamie's voice sounded behind him, and Damian turned his head, watching the wizard approach him with a new shirt in his hand. Jamie lowered himself to the ground, throwing the shirt on his lap. "Put it on."

"Thanks." Damian took the plain black T-shirt and put it on, noticing with interest that it fitted him perfectly. "You know that Yaginya is an ancient goddess and a powerful sorceress. As much as I appreciate you standing up for me, it was reckless, my friend. She could have killed you with one touch of her pinky."

"I knew it, and I didn't care," Jamie replied softly, staring down at his clenched hands. "I couldn't just stand and watch her torture you..." His voice trailed off, and he raked his fingers through his hair, a vibe of awkwardness lingering over him. Then he peered at Damian, and a tentative look crossed his face. "Can I ask you something? Just don't get upset."

"By saying that you already made me upset," murmured Damian.

"Jamie, don't push the red button." Zhulik snickered in his head.

"What do you wish to know, pupil of mine?" asked Damian, throwing a warning stare at the gargoyle.

"These scars—on your back and your face... why do you have them?" asked Jamie. "I've seen your healing power in action. You can self-heal or heal any injury with no scars left behind."

"I don't know." Damian shrugged, pulling a blade of grass from under his foot. "At first I thought they didn't disappear because I accepted the *no one* status and lost my healing power, but later on I realized it wasn't the case. I have no answer to this question."

"Yaginya said you were marked by the beast. Was she referring to the beast that injured you?"

"I don't know." Damian shrugged again. "To be honest, I don't recall most of what happened that night. I was a powerless chew-toy for a giant monster, and all I remember is the anguish. Not the physical pain of the injuries, but—" He cut himself off and dropped his head, hiding his face in his hands. A moment later, he lifted his head and glanced at his friend. "I really don't want to talk about this, Jamie."

"I'm sorry." Jamie glanced back at the house. "But maybe you're here for a reason other than just finding whatever it is we're looking for," he said quietly. "You told me yourself—there are no coincidences in the World of Magic. Maybe it's your chance to shed some light on your past. If Yaginya could sense"—he shifted uncomfortably—"that you're marked by the beast, maybe she can tell you something about your scars that you don't know?"

"Aww... The student surpasses the master..." Zhulik sniffled, wiping his eyes with his paw. *"Our little boy is all grown up and ready to kill monsters."*

"Zhulik, shut up." Damian frowned at the gargoyle, eliciting a burst of laughter out of Jamie.

"What did he say?" asked Jamie, reaching to pet the puppy.

"He said you're right, and we should go and talk to Yaginya." Damian got up, offering Jamie his hand, and as Jamie took it, rising, he squeezed it in a firm handshake. "Thank you. I won't forget."

Damian crossed the clearing and halted in front of the door, doubt tearing at his soul. Besides the fact that for some reason Yaginya hated Destiny Enforcers in general, he was positive there was something about him personally that she disliked. He cringed, thinking how easily she could disable him, and how powerless he was against her magic.

"I'm with you, Commander," a deep, rumbling voice sounded in Damian's head, and he spun in place, searching for his gargoyle. A fully grown German Shepherd sat next to him, baring his large fangs. *"She took both of us by surprise, but this time we're ready."*

Giving a short nod to his gargoyle, Damian pushed the door open and walked inside. Yaginya and Zabava sat at the table, discussing something calmly. As soon as he stepped into the living area, both stopped talking and turned toward him. Seemingly, there was no more animosity between them, and that gave him hope that he could speak with Yaginya in peace.

"Aw, look what the dog dragged in," sang Yaginya, cocking her head. "Do you seriously think that your gargoyle has what it takes to stop me if I decide to kill you, Enforcer?"

"No," replied Damian calmly. "But between the three of us, we can at least slow you down."

Yaginya chuckled and pointed at the chairs. "Sit down, both of you," she said, gesturing at him and Jamie. "My daughter told me why you're here, Enforcer, and as rarely as it happens, I must admit she's right."

"And what is she right about?" asked Damian calmly, his hand resting on Zhulik's head.

"She's right in saying that you do have a commendable physique," replied Yaginya nonchalantly.

"Mother," Zabava hissed, kicking her leg under the table. "I said no such thing!"

Damian's jaw dropped, his eyes darting from one woman to the other. They didn't behave like powerful old gods but like two sorority girls, gossiping about boys. Zabava had lost her cockiness and gruff superiority, and for once, she looked relaxed and happy.

"Fine, fine." Yaginya snickered, pulling a safe distance away from her daughter. "She didn't say that. I did. But she did tell me about your situation, and why you're here, Enforcer, and I agreed with her. So, as much as I dislike your kind, it *is* my duty to help Zabava save our sister-witches." She waved her hand at Zhulik. "You can send your pet-gargoyle home. As tempting as it sounds, I'm not going to whoop your ass. We need to have a word."

"Not a pet." Zhulik growled, baring his fangs.

"*It's okay, Zhulik.*" Damian tapped the ink on his arm. "*I believe I'm safe now. Thank you, my friend.*"

With a low growl, Zhulik took a step closer to Yaginya and snapped his fangs at her for good measure. Yaginya frowned, backing away slightly. The gargoyle turned around and headed toward Damian, a giant grin playing on his muzzle. With a look of innocence and deep satisfaction, he winked and vanished, morphing soundlessly into his tattoo.

Damian pulled a chair out and sat down across from Yaginya and Zabava, motioning for Jamie to sit next to him.

"Before we get to business," he said, folding his arms on the table, "can I ask you a question?"

"You want to know about your scars," said Yaginya. She sighed, staring out the window at the green wall of the forest. "The beast that left these scars behind marked you for life. You two are connected for as long as the both of you are alive. Have you ever asked yourself why you have these scars? You're a Child of Earth. You have the power to heal any injury without leaving any marks."

"I did. Not once," replied Damian. "You know as well as I do that scars left by magic always leave a mark. So, I assumed that was the case."

"No." Yaginya chuckled, shaking her head. "Even you're not dumb enough to believe that. Haven't you seen normal scars left by magic before? They look like thin white lines. Your back looks like something out of a modern horror movie."

Damian dropped his head, rubbing his bracelet absentmindedly. "I made many mistakes over the course of my life," he said without looking at her. "When I took the mantle of a Destiny Enforcer for the second time, Magnus healed me, but he told me that he wanted to leave the scars on my back and my face as a constant reminder of my mistakes and failures."

"Oh…" Yaginya exhaled, exchanging a look with her daughter. "Are you the Shadow Enforcer to Lord Magnus?" Damian nodded, and she continued, "He must be really fond of you. The old wizard never lies, but he lied to you to protect you."

"Protect me from what?" asked Damian.

"From…" She fell silent, a deep frown settling on her face. "It's not my place to tell you, Damian. You have to ask him." Damian's jaw slacked as he realized that the goddess used his name for the first time. "If he doesn't want you to know, I'm not going to be the one to tell you. But there is one thing I want to mention, anyway." She leaned forward, placing her hand over his. "Even though you carry the mark of the beast, it's the Beast Master that you need to worry about."

She pulled away, leaning back in her chair, and folded her arms, her entire demeanor telling him that this conversation was over.

"Thank you, my lady," he replied, inclining his head respectfully, which elicited a wild snort out of Zabava.

"Don't believe his fake politeness, mom," she said, shaking her head. "The man is a wild beast himself. Trust me."

Yaginya laughed softly and got up. She approached Damian, and raked him with her gaze, appearing amused. "Taming wild beasts is what I do best, daughter," she murmured and walked out of the room.

She returned a few minutes later, changed into a long silk dress, her hair styled into an elaborate updo on the back of her head. Halting behind Zabava, she placed her hands on her daughter's shoulders, and a dreamy smile lit up her face.

"And now we're going to summon the only person who can help you find what you're looking for, Damian," she said and closed her eyes, the magical energy around her rising to an unbelievable level.

Yaginya drew a complicated rune in midair and pressed her palm against it, infusing it with the shining blue glow of her magic.

Throwing one more glance at Zabava, she whispered, "Husband, I summon thee…"

CHAPTER 17

~ COLE ADAMS ~

The room was a tiny box with a low ceiling and dreary, gray walls. The entrance door was reinforced by so much iron and silver that even the briefest connection with it would have left any vampire scorched to the bone. A one-way mirror took the entire space next to it, reflecting the gray color of the walls. Besides that, the boxes of magic detectors and anti-magic tech were installed all around the perimeter of the space. There was no visible source of light, and the dim illumination didn't change no matter what time of the day it was.

Ruslan lay on a narrow bed with his hands folded under his head. His long, black hair fanned around his face, accentuating his strong features, and his brown eyes stared at the ceiling without blinking.

Cole glanced down at the gray medical scrubs he was wearing and threw his hands up, frustrated. Then he dropped onto his bed, pressing the heels of his hands to his eyes. For a few long minutes, he lay without moving, a disarray of thoughts and images crowding his mind.

"Amaris blocked your blood bond with your brother," said

Ruslan without changing his position. It wasn't a question. He just stated the fact.

"Yes," Cole replied, his voice just a whisper.

"Don't tell me you didn't expect him to do that?" Ruslan sat up, lowering his bare feet on the gray concrete floor.

"Of course, I did." Cole sat up on his bed and turned to face his maker. "As a matter of fact, I was positive he'd do that."

"But you didn't tell your brother, did you?"

"No."

"Why not? I assume you trust him?"

"With my life." Cole dropped his head into his hands.

"Then why didn't you warn him?" Ruslan got off his bed and lowered himself next to Cole. Gently lifting his chin, he forced Cole to look at him. "Oh, son, you lied to your brother, and it's killing you now. Why did you do it?"

"Because if I told him the truth, he would never have left me behind," Cole whispered, his throat clenched. "He would rather break his deal with Amaris than leave me behind without any means of communication. I knew he would pay dearly for that, so I told him what he needed to hear."

"I don't understand. Why couldn't he break his deal with Amaris? He's a free man."

"He's anything but free... Father, you don't understand because you don't know what my brother is." Cole glanced around the room, looking for listening devices. "Just take my word for it, I did what I had to do to keep him safe."

"Say no more."

Cole nodded. "A lot happened since you've been gone," he whispered. "Luciano is dead... I'm sorry, Father."

Ruslan winced, a pained expression darkening his features. His shoulders dropped, and his lips pressed into a straight line, but he said nothing. Raising his finger to his lips, he glanced at the door, turning his entire body toward it. As Cole sharpened his hearing, soft steps reached his ears, and he got up, positioning himself between the entrance and his maker. A moment later, the lock clicked, and the door opened soundlessly. A guard walked into the room and halted by the door, his hand lingering over his gun at his hip.

"Cole Adams?" he said, his cold eyes halting on Cole. "Mr. Amaris summons you."

Cole gave a barely visible nod to his maker and headed toward the exit. The guard waited until he walked out and closed the door, locking it. He gave Cole an arrogant once-over and gestured for him to follow. The guard led him all the way to the central area, but he didn't stop there and proceeded into another hallway.

All corridors and hallways in this facility looked alike—the same gray walls and shimmering gray light. However, this one, instead of coming to a dead-end, merged into another hallway, running ninety degrees to it. The guard turned to the right and stopped in front of a tall double door. With a crooked sneer on his face, he pushed the door open and stuck his head through the doorway.

"He's all yours," he yelled. Then he seized Cole by the scruff of the neck and pushed him inside.

Cole stumbled a few steps forward before he could stop and looked around. He was in a large, empty room. Just like everywhere in the facility, there were no windows, but this room didn't have a one-side mirror, at least as far as he could see. The space was poorly illuminated, and shadows gathered in every corner, obscuring the far end of the room.

Sharpening his hearing, Cole stilled. Even though all his heightened vampiric senses told him he was alone, he was positive he wasn't. He couldn't see, hear, or smell anything, yet he detected a slight fluctuation in the magical energy field. He had no idea how he could sense it or how he was doing it for that matter, but he knew what it was instantly. The wave of magic was weak, and it felt as if a light current of electricity grazed his skin. Everything inside him tensed as he prepared for an invisible attack.

The air shimmered with purple sparkles a few feet away from him, and three women stepped out of the shadows. All three were armed with swords, but their blades remained sheathed in the scabbards attached to their belts. They halted, observing him with silent hatred.

The Head of the supernatural fighting House wants to test my fighting skills. How original. A thought rushed through Cole's mind, and his eyes swept around the perimeter of the room, searching for anti-magic tech. He wasn't surprised when he didn't find any, but he saw a few cameras installed under the ceiling and that just confirmed his suspicion. *Enjoy the free show, bastard.*

"I'm unarmed," he said, raising his hands, "and I have no desire to fight you."

The women exchanged a quick look and burst out laughing.

"There will be no fighting, vamp," the taller one of them said. Stepping forward, she raised her arm and pulled her sleeve up, exposing a red tattoo on her wrist. "We'll just kill you right away."

Cole glanced at the tattoo, but he knew what it was without looking—the Sisterhood of the Sun symbol.

Damian was right—the imposters are working for Amaris... His eyes darted from one face to the next, quickly registering every detail. *But how did they come in possession of the Sisterhood's secret poison recipe? And their fighting style, too... Who taught them?*

"I'm sure you will give it your best," he said calmly. "Since I'm unarmed and alone against three armed and well-trained opponents, you may think you actually have a tiny, itsy-bitsy chance..." He tilted his head, regarding them with frosty contempt. "But even though the fight won't be fair, I sincerely doubt you can win it."

"I guess we'll see." The woman cackled, extending her hand toward him. "*Moderius*," she shouted.

Even before she said the spell, he felt the spike of magical energy around her. Reacting immediately, he ducked to the side. Picking up as much speed as he could in the limited space, he switched into a brutal attack. Before they realized he wasn't affected by the spell, he punched the woman on his left. To him, it was a light jab, but her nose cracked, blood gushing down her chin. She yelped and blacked out, falling backward. Before her body hit the floor, he seized her sword, pulling it out of the scabbard. In one fluid motion, he thrust the blade through her heart and turned to the other two.

"Now, ladies," he said in a hissing whisper, raising the blood-smeared weapon to his shoulder, "shall we dance?"

For a heartbeat, they stared at him, stunned, their widened eyes darting from the sword in his hands to the dead woman sprawled on the floor. Then one of them screamed, an ear-piercing shriek of anger, and all hell broke loose. Even though they were moving with the speed and fluidity of Sisterhood slayers, Cole clearly saw they didn't have the self-control and mental focus the slayers had, and that told him that they couldn't have been training long. Driven by anger, they spread apart just to attack him from opposite directions, each of them moving in a straight line without much care about his position.

He spun out of their direct line of assault, knowing full well that even with their minds clouded by their raging emotions, they still presented a dangerous force. Underestimating his opponents wasn't his style. Between their poisoned swords and their magic, it was only a matter of time before one of them would reach him if he wasn't faster and smarter than them.

Suddenly, something changed. He didn't hear them saying a spell, but the magical energy spiked around them, and both women vanished. Their cloaking magic was so potent that he couldn't hear their heartbeats either. He didn't wait to see what would happen next and darted back into the shadows. Since his eyes were useless, he closed them and tensed, sharpening his other senses. It didn't come as a surprise that he didn't hear them approach but detected them with the strange, magical sixth sense he had developed in the last few months.

He dropped to one knee and swung his sword to the side. A cry of pain announced that his blade had found its target. The heavy thud of a body falling to the floor followed, and a moment later, a woman materialized next to him. Her hands were pressed to a wound on her side, dark-red liquid streaming from under her trembling fingers. The metallic odor of her blood permeated the air, and Cole growled, fighting the relentless thirst. His lips curved into a snarl, displaying his long fangs, but he didn't follow his instinct. Keeping all his senses trained on the invisible opponent moving in the shadows behind him, he stilled and waited.

As he sensed her approach him from behind, he didn't turn but thrust his sword backward. She yelped and grabbed his blade, but he didn't let go. In one swift motion, he rose to his feet and pulled the sword out, eliciting another cry of pain out of her. Following the direction of the sound, he spun around, moving his blade parallel to the ground. The blade bit into human flesh, and something fell to the floor with a dull thud, rolling. The air shimmered, and the last woman—or rather, what was left of her—materialized in front of him. For a brief moment, her headless corpse just stood there. Then she swayed and fell to the side, a puddle of blood spreading under the body.

Without any rush, Cole wiped the blade on his blood-splattered gray scrubs and approached the only one of his attackers who was still alive. Taking a knee next to her, he seized her hair, jerking her head up. She stared at him, her anger and cockiness gone, her lips moving in a silent plea.

"Who taught you the Sisterhood fighting skills and magic?" he asked, pronouncing every word loud and clear.

"I used to be one of them," she whispered, turning her hand to expose her wrist with the tattoo.

"It's a nice tattoo, but it's not the real one," he objected without giving it as much as a second look. "Tell me the truth, and I may consider leaving you alive. Who taught you? Who gave you the recipe of their poison?"

She didn't reply. Her eyes rolled back, and her head lolled to the side. Her heart gave a couple more weak thuds and silenced forever.

"Dammit," Cole hissed, staring at the dead woman.

A soft shuffling noise was barely detectible, yet he heard it and rolled to the side on his shoulder, coming out of the roll to his feet. A blade hissed through the air in the place where he had stood just a moment ago. The new foe was visible just for a heartbeat and swiftly disappeared into the dark, moving as fast and soundless as he did.

A vampire? He sharpened his senses but couldn't detect any magical energy. *I can deal with a vampire—*

Something impacted his Achilles tendon with a tremendous force, sending him tumbling to the floor. His fingers unlocked, and his sword fell, sliding across the concrete tiles and out of his reach. He did a kip-up, rising to his feet, but before he could make his next move, a strong arm wrapped around his neck, pressing a sharp edge of a knife to his throat. While the person who held him was tall and strong—vampire strong—he had no doubt it was a woman.

He reacted immediately. Seizing the assailant's wrist with both hands, he raised his shoulder while pulling her arm down sharply to create a space between his throat and the blade. Tucking his chin, he slid under her arm, escaping her hold. Still holding her hand with the knife, he stabbed her a few times in her side with her own weapon, pushing her forward. A choked scream erupted from her lips as she collapsed to the floor, clasping her wound with both hands.

Cole dropped to one knee next to her, grabbed her head and slammed it against the concrete floor. She yelped, and the scarlet glow vanished from her eyes as she lost consciousness. He yanked the ski mask off her head, and his jaw dropped, his blood running cold.

"Sylvana..." he whispered, slapping her cheek gently.

She moaned and opened her eyes. "Cole," she whispered, a chain of emotions flashing across her face, starting with happiness and ending with horror. "What are you doing here?"

He didn't reply. Turning her to the side, he explored the injuries he inflicted and growled, slamming his fist against the floor. As he expected, the cuts weren't healing, bleeding profusely, and he didn't need to guess—the knife was smeared with the Sisterhood's poison.

"Sylvana, I'm sorry. I had no idea it was you," he whispered. "Why did you attack me?"

He glanced down at her. The thin band of a metallic collar wrapped around her neck. He moved his hand over the collar and jerked it back, a hiss escaping his lips. Even though the collar wasn't silver, it emitted a strange wave of magical energy. While he couldn't identify what it was, it sent a wave of weakness through him.

"Gray stone jewelry?" he guessed, flabbergasted. "But gray stone magic doesn't affect vampires. I don't understand."

She chuckled humorlessly and winced, clutching her side. "After so many years of being one of the slayers, this is the first time I'm on the receiving end of their poison... and their runic magic..."

She raised her hand, covered in dark red liquid, and pulled the collar of her shirt down, exposing a glowing rune imprinted on her chest. Cole frowned, exploring the design of the rune. While it was slightly different than the one he had seen on Santiago's assistant's chest, it was close enough to have the same purpose.

"You're right," Sylvana continued in a weak whisper. "The gray stone jewelry is just a reminder of my status. What keeps me under Amaris' control is this." She pointed at the rune. "Necromancy." Large, red drops gathered in the corners of her eyes and slipped down her pale cheeks. "You have no idea what he makes me do… and there is absolutely nothing I can do to fight his control. He ordered me to fight you, Cole… I recognized you as soon as you walked in, but I—"

She cut herself off and fell silent, biting her lip, her tender face contorted by unimaginable pain.

"Sylvana, I'll find a way to help—"

"Kill me, Cole. This is the only way you can help me. I'm begging you," she interrupted him, her hand finding his. "I can't live like this… I broke the sacred oath, and I'm ashamed of…" Her voice faded, her entire body shuddering with silent sobs.

"Oh, Syl, no," he whispered.

The sound of steps reached his ears, and he fell silent, listening. Reaching over Sylvana, he grabbed her knife and straightened, raising it. She stared at him with widened eyes, red tears still running down her face, but there was no fear there. If anything, she looked relieved.

"Syl, I'm not going to kill you, but I must play my part," he whispered so quietly, only she could hear. "Hang in there, my friend. It'll be all right."

He screamed, ready to plummet his blade down when the door opened with a loud bang.

"Cole Adams, stop at once!" Jeff rushed toward him, his silver-loaded gun in his hand.

With a ferocious growl rumbling in his chest, Cole jumped to his feet and bared his fangs at the guard, hoping that he was playing the blind fury convincingly enough.

"Mr. Adams, please stop." Jeff halted a few steps away from him, his chest rising and falling with heavy breaths, his gun trained at Cole's head. "There has been a mistake. The guard was supposed to take you to a different location. We apologize for the inconvenience. Mr. Amaris is waiting for you."

Cole stared at him for a few seconds. Then he dropped his knife, and it fell to the floor with a loud clang. Leisurely, he wiped his blood-splattered hands on his dirty scrubs, and a slow, lazy smile crossed his face.

"Inconvenience?" he asked, lifting his shoulders in a half shrug. "Not at all. I needed some exercise." He glanced back, the scarlet glow vanishing from his eyes. "Too bad your little mistake cost the lives of three of your fighters." He raked Sylvana with his gaze and added, "Nearly four." He approached Jeff and gave him a patronizing tap on his shoulder. "Lead away."

CHAPTER 18

~ COLE ADAMS ~

Following Jeff, Cole barely paid attention to where he was going, his mind set on everything that had just happened. It wasn't hard to put two and two together, and he had a pretty good idea how the fake slayers came in possession of the real Sisterhood's poison.

Centuries ago, Sylvana had been a decorated slayer, holding one of the highest positions in the Order. She knew how they operated, how they trained, as well as all the weapons and spells used by the fighters. Even after Santiago turned her, many years ago, she had never betrayed the slayers' sacred oath, keeping all the secrets to herself. Cole wasn't sure what kind of deal she or Santiago had struck with the Sisterhood, but the slayers had never tried to assassinate her, letting her live in peace. So, he was positive that nothing would turn Sylvana into an oath-breaker and a traitor. Nothing but necromancy.

"Right here, Mr. Adams."

Jeff's voice, too sweet to be genuine, sounded next to him, and Cole halted, turning toward the guard. They stood in front of a tall door without any nameplates or numbers on it, nor did it have a digital keypad.

"Please, go in," Jeff said, pushing the door open before him. "Make yourself comfortable. Mr. Amaris will be with you momentarily."

He waited until Cole walked inside and closed the door behind him without locking it. Cole observed the surroundings with interest. He was positive he was still in the underground bunker, but this particular room was nothing like what he'd seen before. Even though it was still windowless, the spacious chamber was furnished with comfort and luxury in mind, but a little too opulent for Cole's taste.

A large crystal chandelier hung from the ceiling, illuminating the area with a soft electric light. A black bar with four barstools was located on his right, multiple shelves with expensive liqueurs and wines embedded into the wall above it. At the opposite end of the room, he noticed a few leather sofas and recliners. But what struck him as something unexpected was a beautiful grand piano in the center of the room.

Since there was no one in the room, Cole approached the piano and brushed his fingers over the polished surface of the musical instrument, following the curves of the design. Gently, he touched a key and closed his eyes, enjoying the clarity of the sound.

Before he realized what he was doing, he pulled the piano bench back a little and sat down. He placed his hands over the keyboard and closed his eyes. Music and reading had always been his escape from reality, and for a moment, he forgot where he was and what he was doing here. His fingers flew over the keys, his soul singing in tune with the beautiful sound this one-of-a-kind instrument produced at his touch.

"Bravo, Mr. Adams," a male voice said somewhere behind him. "You're quite a virtuoso."

Tensed to the limit on the inside, Cole got up and turned around, a light smile playing on his lips. A man dressed in a black business suit and a black shirt stood a few feet away from him, his hand in the pocket of his pants. He wasn't tall, no more than five-foot-seven, and it was impossible to guess his age since most of his face was covered by a leather mask.

"An interesting choice," he said, approaching the piano. "Lacrimosa. The Requiem Mass in D minor by Wolfgang Amadeus Mozart. A little morbid, perhaps?"

"No, I don't think so. Lacrimosa means 'tearful' in Latin, and I agree, it is filled with sadness and internal torment. But at the same time, it is moving and powerful—the kind of power that lifts your soul… forever…" Cole glanced back at the piano with regret. "One of my favorite pieces by Mozart."

"Fascinating." The man chuckled. "You know that Mozart never delivered this piece," he said softly. "He passed away before he had a chance to finish it. There is an interesting legend associated with the Requiem, you know." He motioned for Cole to follow him and proceeded toward the bar. He circled the counter and took a bottle of whiskey off the shelf. "Please sit down. What can I get you, Mr. Adams?"

Cole lowered himself on one of the barstools and leaned to the side slightly, resting his elbow on the countertop.

"A negative, please," he replied, observing the Head of the Arizona House with open interest. Except for the black mask, there was seemingly nothing special about this man, yet there was something unsettling in the way he moved and spoke.

Amaris took a crystal whiskey glass and moved it below the counter. He pressed something, and the metallic odor of blood permeated the air. He placed the glass filled with a thick, red liquid in front of Cole and filled another glass with whiskey.

"Legend has it that Death himself visited Mozart to place an order for the Requiem," he said, sitting down on a stool behind the bar, his long, elegant fingers tracing the design on the glass. "It was a dark, stormy night when a stranger knocked on Mozart's door and commissioned him to compose a Requiem. He was dressed in all black, and the hood of his long, black cloak concealed his face completely. After the visitor left, Mozart was convinced that the stranger was, indeed, Death, and he was writing the Requiem for himself…" Amaris' lips twitched ever so slightly, and even though Cole could see only the bottom part of his face, there was a vibe of a strange satisfaction that the man exuded. "As we both know, Mozart was right. He died before he finished the Requiem." He lifted his glass, clinking it with Cole's. "Cheers."

Cole lifted his glass and took a small sip of the blood, putting effort to suppress his vampiric nature as much as he could. He placed the glass back down on a coaster and grabbed a napkin, dabbing his lips.

"You have amazing self-control, Mr. Adams," Amaris said, putting his glass down. "Your fangs didn't expand."

"Well, thank you, Mr. Amaris." Cole inclined his head in an elegant half-bow, his expression hardened for a brief moment. "I'm an old vampire. I know what I am and how to keep some parts of my nature under control."

"You're nothing like your older brother, though." Amaris propped his elbow on the bar, making a steeple of his fingers. A flair of light bounced against a polished black stone embedded into the silver ring on the middle finger of his right hand. "He's a bit rough around the edges, wouldn't you agree? A little abrupt."

"I can't imagine why he would be a little *abrupt*." Cole's eyes narrowed slightly as he tilted his head. "You… Well, how can I put it delicately, without making you feel uncomfortable…" He glanced heavenwards, rubbing his chin. "Oh yes, you blackmailed him, forcing him to do something he most likely didn't want to do. So, I'm sure he wasn't in the mood for social pleasantries." Then he smiled as charmingly as ever and added, "My apologies if I sounded a little vulgar, my lord."

Amaris laughed, shaking his head slightly. "I do like you, Cole." He took a pause. "May I call you Cole?"

"But of course, Mr. Amaris," Cole replied with a dismissive wave of his hand. "After all, I am your prisoner. You can call me number five hundred twenty-six, for all I care."

Amaris took another sip of his whisky. "When I spoke with your brother the last time, he made certain demands of me regarding your safety, Cole," he started, his eyes shining with a dim, purple light through the slits of his mask. "But truth be told, I never contemplated anything harmful toward you."

"What did he ask for?" Cole took another swig of blood, carefully watching Amaris' every move.

"For some reason, he thought I was going to enslave you and use you as a captive fighter," Amaris said, his voice calm and even. "It wasn't even in my thoughts. Preposterous, if you ask me."

"My brother loves me and is a bit overprotective." Cole chuckled. "I'm a public figure—a rich entrepreneur, Arizona's most eligible bachelor, and the King of the local Vampire Court." He flicked his eyebrow at Amaris. "Putting a collar on my neck and throwing me into the octagon during one of your events would be a bit problematic for you, wouldn't it?"

"Yes, you are quite a celebrity... and I can see why," Amaris murmured. "You're as clever as you're suave, well-read and diplomatic. And I do agree with your brother—you're an unmatched swordsman. This brings us to the subject I wanted to discuss."

"Oh?" Cole raised his glass, drinking the rest of the blood. *I was right. This evil bastard was watching me fight.* "What can I do for you, Mr. Amaris?"

"What I asked your brother to do for me is not easy. It'll take him a while." Amaris got up, his mouth pressed into a tight line. He took a deep breath, tapping his fingers on the bar. Then he glanced at Cole, and the corners of his well-shaped lips turned up. "I thought, since you're going to be my guest for at least a few weeks, why don't we make this time mutually pleasant and beneficial for both of us."

Cole met his strange, purple eyes without blinking. "I'm listening."

"You were unarmed and alone, but it took you only a few minutes to kill three of my best slayers," said Amaris, his fingers clutching the edge of the counter with hungry anticipation.

"They weren't the *real* Sisterhood slayers." Cole laughed softly. "We both know that. So, I'm wondering why you needed this"—he twirled his hand as if searching for a better word —"charade."

Amaris nodded, a thoughtful expression crossing his face. "You're right, Cole," he said at length. "These women weren't the real Sisterhood slayers, but they were powerful witches who were trained by an ex-slayer. You still disabled them in no time." He thought a moment and added, "As far as why I needed this pretense, it's complicated, but I'll try to explain."

He got up and refilled his glass with whisky, taking a large gulp. Then he pointed at Cole's glass, offering him more blood, but Cole raised his hand, shaking his head.

"I run quite a few business operations that have nothing to do with the supernatural fighting pits," Amaris continued, speaking lightly as if he were talking to his best friend during a social dinner event. "Some of them require assistance and the cooperation of vampires—local as well as from the other states. So, I need to have trained fighters who can hold their ground against the undead, just in case things go wrong for whatever reason. Until I met you, I thought I made all the right arrangements."

Amaris chuckled, taking another sip of whisky. "How wrong was I... Wow!" He shook his head slowly. "To be completely honest, you took my breath away, Cole. I've never seen anyone move and fight like you, and I just couldn't take my eyes off of you. Trust me, I've seen my fair share of fighters since I took over the Arizona House."

Cole clenched his jaw, fighting the rising anger. "You took a huge gamble, Mr. Amaris. Your slayers could have killed me, and that would cause my abrupt brother to become even more unpleasant than before."

"No, Cole, I would never take such a chance, and not because I'm afraid of your brother. All my slayers had strict orders not to kill you," he said. "You have quite a reputation in the supernatural circles. I apologize, but my curiosity got the best of me. I wanted to see if all those crazy rumors were true."

He leaned forward and touched Cole's hand, his soft, warm fingers brushing over his knuckles. Cole stilled, staring at him with widened eyes, but Amaris pulled back as if nothing happened, relaxing on his stool.

"Please tell me what I can do for you, Mr. Amaris." Cole shoved his hair away from his face, slipping him a curious glance. "The suspense is killing me."

"Oh, Cole, something tells me you already know what I'm about to ask," said Amaris, his lips quirking up in a playful grin. "Don't disappoint me."

"You want me to train your fake slayers," said Cole, his face turning a shade paler.

"For now… Yes, that and a few of my captive fighters," added Amaris. "While your brother is away, it'll keep you occupied. Also, if you agree, I will provide you and your maker with different accommodations." He gestured at Cole. "A lot more suitable for your status."

Cole nodded, suppressing the deep shudder running through his body. "If I agree, will you allow me and Ruslan to move around your facility freely, or are we still going to be locked in our cell. I'm not fond of prison-like environments."

"Not a cell, Cole," Amaris objected, sounding almost reproachful. "More like a luxury suite. Are you suggesting that

Ruslan will join you in training? I'm sure being as old as he is, he must be quite a mighty warrior."

"Ruslan is the best warrior I've ever met," replied Cole coldly. "He taught me everything I know. I believe I can persuade him to join me in training. After all, he spent three years strung up between two poles. He'll welcome some physical exercise."

Even if Amaris noticed some sarcasm in Cole's voice, he didn't flinch, his smile remaining as sweet as ever. "If both of you agree to train my people, I will gladly allow you some freedoms within the walls of this facility," replied Amaris, excitement igniting brighter in his purple eyes. "Besides, I wouldn't mind spending a few evenings in your company. You're quite an entertaining conversationalist."

Cole got up, pulling down his blood-splattered shirt. "Then you got yourself a deal, Mr. Amaris."

CHAPTER 19

~ DAMIAN BLAKE ~

For a short while, everything remained unchanged. The rune shone in midair, and Yaginya stood in front of it with her hand pressed to her chest. Then the air shimmered with soft, blue sparkles. They started to rotate, moving faster and faster with each passing second until the rune vanished, replaced by the large, whirling vortex of a portal.

A tall man walked out of the portal and halted, his bright blue eyes moving from one face to the next. His gaze lingered on Damian a moment too long, and his eyebrows drew together, his hand inching its way down to the pommel of his large sword. But no matter what his thoughts were, he didn't act upon them.

Throwing his long, golden hair to his back, he turned to Yaginya. Without saying a word, he approached her and pulled her into a tight embrace. She rose on her tiptoes, encircling his neck with her arms, and placed her head on his chest. A quiet sigh that sounded almost like a moan escaped his lips as he lowered his cheek atop her head and closed his eyes, barely breathing.

For a few seconds, they just stood like this, ignoring everything around them. Then Yaginya pulled away, her fingers brushing his face as she lowered her arms, regret reflected in her honey-colored eyes. She turned toward Damian and Jamie, her cheeks still slightly flushed.

"Allow me to introduce my husband." She glanced at the brawny man with affection. "Veles, the god of the Three Realms, the Guardian of the Veil, the Dark deity who fights the Darkness, my one and only love."

"Oh, my God," Jamie exhaled, his eyes becoming round like two blue plates. He blanched and dropped to one knee, inclining his head.

Veles gave him a short nod, motioning for him to rise, and turned to Damian who inclined his head in a respectful bow but didn't kneel. The Slavic deity folded his arms, the corners of his lips lifting beneath his thick, golden mustache.

"How about you, Enforcer?" he asked, his deep, rumbling voice filling every corner of the large room. "Aren't you mine to command?" He raised his eyebrows, expecting Damian's answer.

"Of course, my lord. I *am* yours to command," Damian replied without blinking an eye. "But after years of being a Destiny Enforcer, I realized that carrying out your commands from a kneeling position is quite uncomfortable."

Veles' eyebrows rose dangerously close to his hairline. He threw a baffled glance at Yaginya and burst out laughing, slapping his massive hands on his thighs.

"Yaginya, my love," he managed to say through bursts of laughter, "where did you find"—he waved at Damian—"this… him."

"Take a wild guess." Yaginya gestured with her thumb over Veles' shoulder.

He glanced back and just now noticed Zabava. Warmth suffused his face as he turned to his daughter and hugged her tenderly, pulling her to his chest.

"Zabava, my little girl," he whispered, kissing the top of her head. "You're just as beautiful as your mother. I miss you so…" His voice shook and trailed off. With a deep sigh, he stepped back and jerked his chin toward Damian. "I remember when you were a little girl you used to bring home baby wyverns with broken wings. Now, you're all grown up and bringing home a broken Destiny Enforcer?" He chuckled, patting her cheek gently.

"He's not broken, Dad. He is just a little offbeat compared to the others of his kind." Zabava paused, staring at the enormous sword sheathed at Veles' hip. "But to be honest, if he wasn't the way he is, I would never have brought him here, and Mother would never have summoned you to help him."

"Really? Yaginya wants to help a Destiny Enforcer? That's a first." Veles looked back at Damian with a curiosity that hadn't been there before. "And why would any Enforcer need the help of a Slavic god, anyway? Don't you people work only with your own kind?"

"He's a Shadow Enforcer to Lord Magnus, my love," replied Yaginya before Damian could say a word. "He works alone… Well, not entirely true. He arrived with this young wizard, who doesn't know his arse from his elbow, but is apparently ready to forfeit his life for him." She threw a sarcastic gaze at Jamie that made him shrink and shift closer to Damian. "I've summoned you because I believe his mission is of extreme importance to all of us. Please hear him out."

Veles pulled a chair and sat down, stretching his legs in front of him with a light flick of a wrist. "Speak."

As concisely as possible, Damian told him everything without holding anything back. After he finished, the god of the Three Realms propped his elbow on the table, leaning against it, and didn't say a word for a few long seconds. Then he stroked his long, thick beard, regarding Damian thoughtfully.

"Let me ask you, Enforcer," he said, narrowing his eyes

slightly. "If you were in a situation where your brother's life was in grave peril, but at the same time, your entire city was about to perish. Who would you save? Your brother or the thousands of people of Blue Creek?"

Damian smiled, holding the deity's heavy gaze without blinking. "I'll let you know as soon as I am in that situation... my lord."

Veles' lips quirked up a little as he inclined his head. "It is a wise answer indeed, Enforcer. It's hard to predict how one will act until one is in the described situation. But please, humor me. Give me the best answer you can."

Damian dropped his head, his thoughts traveling back to his battle with Mara and Morok where he nearly lost his brother to save River Evans and the world by preventing two dark deities from ascending to their full power.

"I understand you're testing my morality, and it *is* a tough philosophical question, my lord," he said, lifting his eyes. "But I have already been in this situation, and I chose plan C, so to speak. Both the city and my brother are still alive and well."

"How so?" Veles leaned forward, the coldness in his eyes replaced with disbelief.

In general details, Damian outlined the gist of his confrontation with the dark gods and what he had to do to resolve the situation.

"Interesting," murmured Veles. "So, you were *no one,* and you managed to capture the god of Lies. I'd heard the rumors, but I had a hard time believing them. Commendable... I know Morok is somewhere in the Destiny Council's dungeons, but where is Mara?"

"I've spoken with Mara on a few occasions, and as shocking as it sounds, she helped me," replied Damian, telling the god of his previous encounters with the Slavic goddess of Nightmares. "She's partially stripped of her powers and tired of roaming the Yav alone. Now, all she wants is to come back home. She realizes that the path to the Prav is closed to her forever, but I wonder if you will accept her in the Dark Nav, my lord?"

"I feel like the world flipped upside down today," murmured Veles, giving his wife a puzzled gaze. "Did a Destiny Enforcer just ask me to help a dark deity?"

Zabava chuckled, all but rolling her eyes. "I told you, Father. He's not like the others. Meet Commander Damian Blake."

"A Commander, eh?" Veles arched his brow, switching his attention back to Damian. "If you truly wish to help Mara, you have to speak with Chernobog, the King of the Dark Nav. These kinds of decisions are in his hands, not mine. But I must warn you..." He paused, darkness gathering in his eyes. "Chernobog can't stand the Destiny Council, and for him, the only good Enforcer is a dead one."

"Since I'm immortal, Chernobog is going to like me even less, but I guess I'll take my chances with him." Damian shrugged half-heartedly and paused for a moment, but since being disrespectful toward one of the most powerful Slavic deities wasn't in his plans, he inclined his head and added, "Thank you for hearing me out, my lord."

"Not like I had a choice in the matter," muttered Veles, sending a veiled gaze to his wife. "Now..." He crossed his legs at the knee, leaning back in his chair. "Your current mission, however, is a different story. It's not going to be easy to locate the Sacred Isle, but I believe I can help you with that. If my wife is willing to work with me, that is."

He looked at Yaginya, and her face lit up with happiness, making her appear younger and breathtakingly beautiful. Instead of answering, she stepped closer to her husband and offered him her hands. He took them, her small, elegant fingers disappearing in his massive palms, and got up to his feet. For a few seconds, they stood, silently gazing at each other, and even though they looked like any couple in love, Damian was sure they were communicating telepathically.

"Let's do it then?" Veles asked at length, caressing her hands with his thumbs. She nodded. Veles turned toward Jamie and Damian and added, "I suggest you both close your eyes. Especially you, young wizard. Two gods are about to wield their full power."

They channeled their power at the same time, and the magical energy field spiked around them with an incredible strength the likes of which Damian had never felt before. In one fluid motion, he seized Jamie and turned him around, shielding him with his body.

"*Procedia Amnia,*" Damian whispered, erecting a shield of basic protective magic around himself and Jamie. To make it stronger, he channeled his elemental power, infusing his shield with it. Then he wrapped his arm around the wizard and covered his eyes with his hand.

"Don't open your eyes, Jamie," he groaned, struggling to sustain his protective magic.

As the amount of magical energy spiked around him again, he felt as if his skin was set on fire, sweat dripping down his back. The light kept growing brighter and brighter, and soon, even though his eyelids were tightly shut, white and red spots started dancing in his vision. Veles' and Yaginya's voices became one as they chanted louder, but Damian couldn't make out their words, blood pumping forcefully in his ears.

All of a sudden, everything ceased. The pressure on his shield vanished, and the brightness of the light dwindled to nothing. Removing his shield, Damian opened his eyes and blinked a few times to restore his vision. Carefully, he unlocked his arms, releasing Jamie, and turned around to find all three gods staring at them without hiding their amusement.

"Oh, ma-a-n... You should've seen your face," Zabava sang, tears of laughter sparkling in her eyes. "So, how was it? I mean dealing with *real* gods for a change, puny Enforcer?"

Damian took a deep breath, finally able to fill his lungs with oxygen, but he still couldn't say a word, his throat dry and constricted. He glanced at Jamie and stifled a sigh. The young man's face was gray, sweat beading his forehead, and he was gasping for air like a fish out of water, taking short breaths. With his eyes half-closed, he looked like he was ready to faint, so Damian decided not to give the family of gods a new source of entertainment and pulled a chair closer, helping Jamie to sit down.

"Are you going to be okay, Enforcer?" asked Veles, a slight layer of sarcasm in his deep voice. Damian nodded. The god of the Three Realms approached Jamie, touched his head with two fingers and leaned down, exploring his face. "Feeling better?"

"Thank you, my lord," Jamie croaked, wiping the perspiration off his forehead. "I'm sorry, I've never… experienced anything like that."

Veles chuckled, tapping his shoulder. "It's okay. There is a first time for everything. The path you and your companion are about to take is not going to be any easier, though, and probably a lot more dangerous. Are you sure you're ready for a quest like this, young wizard?"

Jamie glanced back at Damian, and his usual friendly grin turned his eyes into two narrow arches. "I'm sure, my lord," he said, switching his attention back to Veles.

Yaginya stepped from behind her husband, and just now Damian noticed that she was holding a small ball of red yarn in her hands. She offered it to him, and he took it gingerly, expecting pretty much anything. As soon as he touched the yarn, a powerful wave of magical energy assailed him, and he sucked in a sharp breath, his eyes igniting with a bright, orange light.

"It's powerful, isn't it?" said Yaginya with pride in her voice, her fingers lingering over Damian's hands. "At first, I thought a guiding spirit would do the job, but then I realized that all these modern gimmicks are not strong enough to survive a quest like yours." She glanced at Veles as if searching for his affirmation, and he gave her a slight nod. "So, we decided to go the old way. The oldest way there is." She brushed her fingers over the yarn with affection. "This enchantment is as old as Creation, and nowadays, I'm the only one who can wield it. My husband infused the ball of yarn with his magic, so it knows exactly where you need to go."

"Thank you, my lady." Damian bowed, pressing his hand to his chest. "How do I activate the magic?"

"Just throw the damn ball in front of you and follow its every move," replied Zabava, tittering. "It works like the GPS in your car, but unlike GPS, it's not going to take you on a wild goose chase. As my mother said—it knows exactly where you need to go." She tilted her head, sarcastic twinkles dancing in her eyes. "Didn't your mom tell you any Slavic bedtime stories when you were a child? Tell me you were a child at some point… in some century."

"Of course, I was a child, but my childhood didn't include bedtime stories and cuddles…" Damian replied, trying to sound calm, but his voice shook slightly, and he frowned, swallowing a lump in his throat. Zabava's mouth opened, and she blushed a bright red, discomfort lingering over her.

"Sorry, Damian," she said. "I shouldn't have said that." Scratching the back of her head, she shifted slightly. "I'll go with you and Jamie, anyway, and help you find what you're looking for."

"No!" Yaginya and Veles shouted at the same time.

"Well, that didn't sound good," mumbled Jamie, throwing a bewildered look at Damian.

"No," Veles repeated, clearing his throat. "My daughter is a goddess. Where you're going, Damian, gods are not welcome. She won't be able to cross the river *Smorodina*."

"Wait… What?" Damian staggered back a step, goosebumps rising on his arms as if the temperature in the room had dropped a few degrees. "Please tell me this Isle is not located in *Peklo*?" He rubbed his forehead, trying to organize his chaotic thoughts. "I'm a Child of Earth, my lord. *Peklo* will bring me down to my knees even before I finish crossing the river, and I won't be able to complete my mission."

He shuddered, and despite his effort to remain calm, his chest tightened with fear. The Dark Nav—the Slavic realm of the dead—was deprived of all elemental energy. His one and only trip to the Dark Nav had left him drained and weak, and he could never forget how helpless and vulnerable he was there. But compared to *Peklo*, the Dark Nav was child's play. Just like in Hell, the worst scum of human and supernatural worlds found their way to *Peklo* after their death, cursed to suffer unimaginable torment for all eternity.

Even though Damian was immortal, he knew *Peklo* would feed not only on his elemental energy, but also on the energy of his human soul, suppressing and destroying everything he was, leaving behind nothing but a walking corpse. The flaming river *Smorodina* encircled Slavic Hell, cutting all ways in and out of this grim and twisted realm. Filled with smoldering flames, which weren't elemental by nature, it incinerated the spirit of anyone who dared cross it. Leaving them weak and defenseless, it wiped out whatever leftovers of humanity those twisted souls still possessed.

Needless to say, the idea of crossing the river of eternal torment didn't give Damian warm and fuzzy feelings. He pressed his hand to his mouth, his mind racing. As his eyes darted from Veles to Jamie, he held his breath, a terrible realization dawning on him.

"Jamie," he said, his voice hoarse. "I'm sorry, my friend, but this is as far as you can go." He glanced at Zabava, silently pleading her for help. "Zabava will take you home—"

"But why?" asked Jamie, interrupting him, his voice rising.

"You're too human. A lot more than I am," Damian explained

quietly. "I may survive it... in some shape or form, but you won't. Crossing the river *Smorodina* will destroy your human soul, and I can't allow it."

"I don't care." With a stubborn shake of his head, Jamie got up, his fists clenched at his sides. "This trip doesn't sound like a walk in the park, and I'm not letting you go alone."

"Jamie, I appreciate it, but my answer is still no. You're too inexperienced to understand how truly dangerous it is and the consequences of you going with me. This discussion is over," said Damian, bringing forth the commanding iron tones in his voice, and then turned to Yaginya and Veles for support. "Can someone, please, reason with him? He's a good man, and he's too young to suffer through something like this..." His voice trailed off as both ancient gods remained motionless. "I have my orders, so I have no choice but to go. He has a choice!"

Yaginya inclined her head just a little, two deep wrinkles appearing around her tightly pressed mouth. "You're right. Unlike you, Jamie is not a Destiny Enforcer, so he has a choice," the goddess said, placing her hand on Damian's arm. "But it seems to me your friend made his choice, and you should respect it."

"I second that," added Veles. "Besides, even though you'll have to cross the river *Smorodina*, you're not going to *Peklo*. Don't get me wrong—your quest is not going to be a walk in the park as your young friend pointed out, but given the right circumstances, I believe both of you have a good chance of surviving it."

"I'm sorry, my lord, but I don't understand," said Damian. "I thought the river *Smorodina* flows only through the Dark Nav, making a full circle around *Peklo*."

"Yes and no," replied Veles, stroking his thick beard. "River *Smorodina* takes its beginning in the Dark Nav, but under rare circumstances, it makes its way into the Yav. Protecting the Sacred Isle when it appears on the border between two realms

—the Dark Nav and the Yav—is one of those occasions." He paused, observing Damian's reaction. "I guess it's your tough luck, Enforcer, that at the time when you need to find the Isle, it's protected by the flaming waters."

"Figures..." Damian exhaled, silently cursing the over five-hundred-year-long streak of bad luck he had. "So, what am I looking for on the Isle?"

"You're looking for a man," replied Veles. "The problem is, you can't see him unless he wants to be seen. So, when you get to the Isle, you better make a good case, or you'll never find him." He fell silent for a brief moment, a thoughtful expression crossing his face, and then added, "So just to be on the safe side—keep your supernatural identity hidden, though. No one likes Destiny Enforcers."

Dammit...

Damian pressed the heels of his palms to his eyes, feeling the ground slipping from under his feet. Over the years, he got used to the hate and open hostility toward Destiny Enforcers. Now, however, the stakes were higher than ever, and not for the first time since he had accepted the mantel again, he wished he had remained *no one*.

"Nothing new. I'll deal with it when the time comes," he said, lowering his arms. "What's his name?"

"I don't know," replied Veles. "He goes by different names. He's not a single person, you know? The Lord of the Isle is bound to the Isle. He guards everything that is hidden there, and for as long as he holds this position, he is immortal. However, once a suitable replacement arrives in his domain, he trains him and transfers the power. Usually, it's a thousand-year cycle, give or take a few centuries. So, I have no idea who's in charge today. It's been over two thousand years since I visited the Sacred Isle myself, and the last time I was there, Svat Naum was in charge." Then he shook his head, pursing his lips. "I'm sure he's no longer the Lord. It's been too long."

"It just keeps getting better and better," muttered Damian. *I hate Slavic fairy tales... The further you go, the scarier and more twisted they become...*

Veles chuckled in response, stroking his mustache. "What did you expect, Enforcer? That everything would be delivered to you on a silver platter?" The god of the Three Realms folded his massive arms. "That's why they call the Isle *'don't know where'*, and its Lord—*'don't know what'*."

Ignoring the hefty load of sarcasm in the god's voice, Damian inclined his head. "I guess it's time for us to go. I appreciate your help, my lord," he said to Veles calmly. Glancing at Yaginya, he added slightly softer, "My lady."

"Wait," said Veles, raising his hand. "Just one more thing."

Approaching Jamie, he took his necklace off and placed it around the young man's neck. Seemingly, there was nothing special about this necklace—a simple leather cord with a round, copper disk attached to it. But once Jamie touched the pendant, he sucked in a sharp breath and closed his eyes.

"Whoa," he exhaled after a moment. "What is it?" He glanced at the pendant, tracing the symbol engraved into it with his finger. "It looks like the Celtic triquetra... But you are a Slavic god, my lord, why would you—"

"It's not a Celtic triquetra, my young friend," Veles interrupted him. "It's a powerful Slavic protection symbol. Long before now, people recognized it as mine, calling it *Triglav*, and it represents my power over the Three Realms—the Prav, the Nav, and the Yav— and their connection. *Triglav* is a powerful amulet and has many magical properties. So, rest assured, it will protect you when it's time for you to cross the flaming river of torment."

"Thank you, my lord," said Jamie, deep gratitude reflected on his face.

It's true what they say— ignorance is bliss, thought Damian. Unlike Jamie, he knew all the possible consequences of crossing the river *Smorodina*, and this knowledge in combination with Jamie's resolve to stay by his side no matter what pressed heavily on his soul.

Over time, he had gotten used to Jamie's company and learned to appreciate his sharp mind and undying optimism that reminded him of his brother. Both Cole and River adored the young man, considering him a part of the family. With his easy-going personality, Jamie made it easy to like him, and even Damian with his habits of a loner accepted him as a friend. But until this very moment, Damian had never realized how deeply he cared about his young apprentice.

As he watched his friend bow to the Slavic deity, for the first time since he started this dangerous journey, he felt some relief. Before he knew what he was doing, he lowered to one knee and pressed his fist to his chest.

"Thank you, my lord," he said, meeting the god's curious gaze. "I'm yours to command."

"I see," murmured Veles, glancing back at his wife in awe. "As always, you were right, my wise wife." Noticing Damian's puzzled look, he placed his hand on his shoulder. "When it comes to reading human souls, my wife is never wrong. She told me that the only way to get your loyalty is through taking care of people you love."

"I'm not sure it's entirely true," replied Damian, "but I *am* deeply grateful for what you did for Jamie, and my loyalty and sword are the only things I can offer to you to express my gratitude."

Veles leaned down slightly and moved Damian's hair out of the way, carefully examining the scar on his face. Then he threw a troubled glance at his wife, and she gave him a barely visible shrug, slightly opening her arms.

"Please rise, Commander Blake," he said, taking a step back. "Something tells me our paths will cross again, and when it happens, your loyalty is something I want to have."

Damian got up, debating if he should ask the ancient deity for an explanation, but then decided against it. If he had learned anything since becoming a Destiny Enforcer, it was that the paths of the Board of Destiny were unpredictable, and in most cases, knowing what was coming without the ability to change it was nothing but a terrible burden to carry.

After saying his farewells, Damian turned around and headed toward the exit, motioning for Jamie to follow him. He walked out the door and took a deep breath, inhaling the fresh air infused with the scent of the forest.

He held the ball of red yarn, carefully moving his fingers over it. "I guess, it's time," he murmured to himself more than to Jamie and was about to throw the ball on the ground when the sound of the door opening touched his hearing. He turned around and found Zabava standing behind him, clutching her black backpack in her hands.

"Take it," she said, sounding slightly awkward. "My mother made it for me, but I think you need it more than I do."

Damian glanced at the small backpack, which appeared to be empty, and gave her an arched stare. "Sorry, but—"

She rolled her eyes. "Are all Destiny Enforcers so thick?" she grumbled, her former superiority and arrogance returning for a brief second. "Let me repeat for the specially gifted ones. My mother—*Baba Yaga*—made it. Anything ring a bell?" Since Damian remained silent, she threw her hands up. "Aw, come on, Damian. Think Russian fairy tales."

"It has magical properties?" asked Jamie tentatively.

"Of course, it does." Zabava switched her attention to Damian, shoving the bag into his free hand. "Why would I want to give you my backpack with a hot pink liner otherwise? Because hot pink goes so well with your charming personality?"

Damian pulled the zipper, opening the bag, and couldn't help but snort. The backpack was empty and everything inside was covered with bright pink silk.

"Pink doesn't seem to be your color either," he said, closing the bag.

"Don't tell that to my mother." Zabava threw an annoyed glance at the house and turned back to Damian. "Anyway, jokes aside. Do you know what *skatert-samobranka* is? The magical tablecloth that cooks better than a five-star restaurant chef?"

"Of course, I know what it is," replied Damian.

"You know, Baba Yaga is the only sorceress who knows how to make those," Zabava continued, "but she has no business sense whatsoever. I told her to start mass-producing them a long time ago. Humans would pay a small fortune to have one of those at home." She raked her fingers through her short, spiky hair, and sighed, unease almost tangible around her. "You know what she said?"

"No idea."

"She said if she did that, she would get slammed with antitrust lawsuits in no time, and that would be the end of her so-called business venture." Zabava pursed her lips. "She just doesn't like the realm of humans."

"She has a point," Damian objected carefully. "You said it yourself—she's the only one who can produce it."

"Never mind," Zabava grumbled, switching the subject. "Damian, your trip may take quite a few days, and you—being a Child of Earth and all—are probably not into hunting and killing cute furry things in the forest. So, I don't want you to lose weight. Besides, River will kill me if something happens to you and Jamie." She looked away, her cockiness gone. "This backpack works like any *skatert-samobranka*. Just think what you're in the mood for, and it'll cook for you. Got it?"

"Got it," replied Damian, trying hard to keep a straight face. He took her hand and squeezed it gently. "Thank you, Zabava. What are you planning to do now? Are you going to stay with your parents?"

"You're kidding me, right?" She laughed, throwing her head

back. "I love my father, but I don't think I can spend more than a few hours in the same room with my mother before being at each other's throat." She shook her head. "So, thank you, but no, thank you. As soon as my father is gone, I'm leaving the Land of Dreams." She winked at Damian. "Besides, even though the realm of humans is low on magic, it's high on fun, and I'm all about fun. Hence, the name."

"Yeah, I noticed," he replied, not buying her playful tone. "Keep an eye on River for me, will you?"

"I will," she promised, her bright green eyes darkening with a sadness she was working hard to conceal. "I don't think I'll hear anything from your brother, but I'll snoop around to see if I can find out anything." She fell silent, staring down at her clenched hands. "I'll hang around the area. You never know… Besides, I have to continue my investigation, and Grand Master Elony is arriving in a few days…"

Her mouth twitched, but her eyes remained hollow. Approaching Jamie, she pulled him into a quick hug.

"Jamie, you take care of him." She jerked her chin at Damian. "He's lost without you." She ran up the steps and halted there, turning toward them. "Ta ta for now, boys." Flashing them a quick grin, she disappeared behind the door.

"Here goes nothing," Damian whispered and threw the ball of yarn on the ground.

CHAPTER 20

~ COLE ADAMS ~

"Goddammit! Just stop it!" Cole pushed off the wall and walked briskly toward the center of the large training room where two vampires stood, staring at him with a mix of loathing and murderous hunger reflected on their faces.

Cole approached them and halted a few feet away, shaking his head in resignation. "If you fight like this against a real Sisterhood slayer, you'll be dead before you say 'blood.'"

He crossed the distance between them, seized the arm of one of the vampires and pulled him to the side, taking his position on the hardwood floor. Raking his hand through his hair angrily, he assumed a guarding stance and waved at his opponent to attract his attention.

"Attack!" he shouted.

The vamp moved forward with a skipping roundhouse, but Cole switched his stance and met him with a powerful kick to his side, easily avoiding his attack. The vampire fell, clasping his ribs, but quickly recovered and hopped to his feet, getting back into a fighting stance.

"Again!" Cole yelled, pointing at his bare torso. "I'm wide

open. You're a vampire. You have the strength and the speed. I'm not using mine. Move!"

The vampire roared, fury igniting his eyes with a carnivorous scarlet glow. Without giving a momentary thought to what he was doing, he stepped forward, chambering for another roundhouse.

Dumbass... Cole thought, easily avoiding and blocking the vampire's vigorous kicks and punches. *Does he even remember that he has two legs? Where did Amaris find these useless baby vamps?*

Moving at half of his speed, Cole turned around and met the unfortunate vampire's attack with a powerful back kick. His foot landed on his opponent's stomach, sending him flying a few feet across the floor. Without slowing down, he reached the young vamp in a few strides and seized the collar on his neck, yanking him to his feet.

"Have you ever fought in one of the captive events?" he asked, letting go of the collar. "Have you ever witnessed one?"

"No," the vampire hissed through gritted teeth.

"They are brutal, merciless, deadly. It's a kill or be killed world. So, guess what, asshole? If you continue sabotaging my training, I suggest you get ready to meet your true death," Cole growled, turning around. His eyes swept across the line of ten fighters, and he folded his arms across his chest. "This applies to all of you. Tomorrow, you'll be sparring with the top three fighters your master owns." He cringed inside at his own words but forced himself to continue. "Get ready for pain. I think pain is the only thing that can make you appreciate what I'm trying to do for you here."

He pivoted on his heels and marched toward Ruslan, who sat on a small stool by the wall with an expression of endless boredom on his face. Lifting a square piece of plastic attached to the wall above Ruslan's head, Cole exposed a communication panel and pressed an intercom button.

"Jeff, I am done for today," he said once the guard answered his call. Then he lowered himself to the floor next to his maker and stretched his legs, dropping his hands on his lap.

A few minutes later, the lock clicked, and Jeff, accompanied by four guards, walked inside. While they gathered the captive fighters and escorted them out of the training facility, Jeff made his way to Cole and Ruslan. Giving Ruslan a sarcastic once-over, he switched his attention to Cole, his shifty eyes raking him with deep distaste.

"Mr. Adams," he said, placing his hands on his hips, "Mr. Amaris would like to have the pleasure of your company tonight. Again." The guard glanced at his wristwatch, and a mocking sneer distorted his lips. "I hope thirty minutes is enough for you to make yourself presentable?"

"More than enough," Cole replied calmly, rising to his feet.

"I'll come by to escort you to his chambers in thirty minutes then," Jeff added, gesturing at the exit.

"That won't be necessary," Cole replied dryly, heading toward the door. "I know where his chambers are."

"You sure do," Jeff murmured with so much derision in his voice that Cole shuddered inwardly.

Before he could stop himself, he spun around to face the guard. "What did you say to me?" he growled, his hands clenching into tight fists.

"Nothing." A shadow of fear crossed the guard's face, and he took a defensive step back, raising his hands in a peaceful gesture. "I agreed with you, Mr. Adams. You've been a guest of Mr. Amaris long enough to know your way around. That was all I said."

"Son," Ruslan whispered so quietly that only Cole could hear, placing his hand on his shoulder.

Cole flinched at his touch, and for a brief second, his every muscle tensed. But he forced himself to relax and plastered a smile on his face.

"I'll see you tomorrow morning, Jeff," he said calmly, "for the next training session with the Sisterhood slayers."

"Yes, you will." Jeff opened the door, allowing Cole and Ruslan to leave the training facility.

* * *

Cole walked into his room and shut the door, sliding to the floor covered by a soft carpet. Amaris had kept his promise, and his new accommodations didn't look like a prison cell but rather like a Presidential Suite of a high-class hotel. It had two separate bedrooms, two bathrooms and a large living area with an enormous TV attached to the wall above an electric fireplace. The suite was stuffed to the brim with modern tech and expensive but completely unnecessary items of luxury and décor, but it lacked windows and clocks.

As far as Cole could see, there wasn't any anti-magic tech or runes on the wall, but since his connection with Damian was still blocked, he knew they were all around. He was also positive that security cameras had been installed everywhere, including the large walk-in closets and both bathrooms. Despite the comfort of his new room, he clearly realized he had neither privacy nor security here, and he couldn't relax even in his sleep.

"Cole, what's going on?" asked Ruslan, lowering himself heavily on the couch. "Don't you think you need to take a shower and get dressed for your meeting with Amaris?"

Cole glanced at his maker and averted his gaze, his scalp prickling. "How long has it been?" he asked, rubbing spatters of dried out blood off his knuckles.

Ruslan frowned, resting his arms on his lap. "Since they stopped torturing me, I have a hard time counting days," he said, his dark eyes never leaving Cole. "To be honest, I have no idea. A week? Probably more."

"It seems like years," Cole whispered, resting his head against the door.

"I think we should talk." Ruslan leaned forward and grabbed the TV remote control. Turning the TV on, he brought the loudness as high as the device allowed for.

"Some other time." Cole shook his head, rising. "You're right. I should get ready." He closed his eyes, biting his lip. "Oh, God… I'd rather die…"

He whispered the last words so softly that he wasn't sure his maker could hear him, but he did. Before Cole took a step, Ruslan was in front of him. He pushed him back and leaned closer, pinning him against the wall with the weight of his body.

"Keep… your mind… on the mission…" he hissed into Cole's ear, making short pauses between the words. "Do you understand me, son?" He let go, taking a small step back, and braced his arms against the wall on either side of Cole. "You owe it to your brother and to yourself. We already know the fake slayers work for Amaris. So, do what you must do, but you have to find out if Amaris collects the magical energy of witches, and why he does it. I have no doubt killing witches is just another day at the office for this asshole. So, get him to talk about his business affairs."

"Yes, Father…"

"It's not the first time you have to do something you don't want to do," Ruslan continued quietly. "If you think I don't know what Roxana was doing to you, think again." Cole nodded, barely able to face his maker. "Time moves differently in the Land of Dreams, but from everything you told me about your brother, I'm positive Dmitri will be back soon, so you don't have much time. I know it's not easy, but Amaris seems to drop his guard when he is with you, and you should use it. Get on with it, son. We must bring this evil empire to its knees, and you're the only one who can do it." Ruslan pulled back, gesturing at the bathroom. "A quick shower and be on your way."

Cole nodded and headed toward the bathroom. Trying to keep his mind blank, he took a shower as fast as he could, dried himself and walked into the closet. Amaris didn't go cheap, and his closet was filled with anything he could find useful while staying in the underground facility, starting with expensive business suits and ending with workout outfits. Without giving much thought, he took one of the business suits and quickly got dressed.

Still holding a tie in his hand, he walked out into the living area, slowly making his way toward the exit, but Ruslan stopped him. Giving him a quick once-over, he frowned.

"You're not going to like it, but your ensemble needs a few small adjustments," Ruslan murmured, narrowing his eyes. He took the tie out of his hands and threw it on the couch. Then he unbuttoned the collar of his shirt and opened a few more buttons down to the middle of his chest. Raking his fingers through Cole's hair, he made it fall around his face in a disarray of blond curls. "Now, go…" He dropped his head, rubbing his forehead.

"You know…" Cole whispered, barely moving his lips.

"Of course, I know." Ruslan's voice shook with suppressed anger. "I'm not blind, and I have a sharp sense of smell." He looked away, a muscle twitching in his tightly pressed jaw. "Do what you must do, Cole. His time will come."

"Yes, Father."

There was so much darkness in his maker's voice that Cole did a double take. With a stiff nod, he walked toward the door and placed his hand on the door handle, but before he could push it open, Ruslan stopped him again.

Seizing Cole's shoulder, the ancient vampire turned him around. Cole glanced at his maker, and everything inside him crushed, the room around him becoming blurry for a heartbeat.

Ruslan's face, normally cold and emotionless, was twisted with anger and anguish, his fingers digging painfully into Cole's shoulder.

"What am I doing? Cole... stop..." he whispered, his voice hoarse and unsteady. His hand rose to Cole's cheek and stilled there without actually touching him. "Forget everything I said. I can't have you—" He cut himself off, shaking his head, and dropped his hand powerlessly. "You're my only son... my boy. I can't stand by and watch this evil bastard abuse you in any way. There are always more ways than one to get things done."

"Yes, there are." A sad smile touched Cole's lips as he carefully pried his maker's fingers off his shoulder. "But most of them will take a lot longer. We have no time to find a better or easier way," he replied softly. "So, I'll do what I have to do. I know what Amaris wants from me, and I will use it to my advantage without actually giving it to him. You know I can do it, right? Two can play this twisted cat-and-mouse game." Ruslan nodded, but doubt was clearly reflected in his dark eyes. Cole averted his gaze, rubbing his chin. "So far, nothing happened, and I'm inclined to keep it this way. Trust me, Father, I'd rather be flogged twice daily than give this evil asshole what he wants."

Without waiting for Ruslan's response, he turned around and walked out the door into a well-lit hallway.

CHAPTER 21

~ COLE ADAMS ~

Moving like on autopilot, Cole barely remembered his walk to the room where he had been meeting with Amaris every night for a social conversation, the way the Head of the Arizona House loved to put it. Raising his hand with effort, he knocked on the door and pushed it open, hoping that Amaris wasn't there yet.

He hoped in vain. Dressed in his usual black suit, with a black leather mask on his face, Amaris sat on the piano bench, his strange purple eyes shining through the slits of his mask.

"Cole, come in, my friend," he said, rising, a hint of melancholy in his voice. He pointed at the piano bench, inviting him to sit down. "Would you play for me tonight?"

Suppressing his desire to run and hide, Cole offered him a bright smile and approached the piano, his fingers brushing over its polished surface. "What would you like me to play, my lord?" he asked softly.

"We spent quite a few evenings together, and I must say I enjoy your company immensely. There is no need for formalities," replied Amaris as Cole took a seat. "My full name is Frederick Luan Amaris, but you can call me Erick."

"Okay, Erick," replied Cole, cringing inwardly. "What would you like me to play for you this lovely evening?"

"The choice is yours, my dear friend." Amaris waved his hand dismissively and headed toward the bar.

Taking his jacket off, Cole threw it on the couch and sat down on the piano bench. He positioned his hands over the keyboard and stilled with his eyes closed, but he wasn't trying to choose what to play. He was trying to focus on the mission, shutting down all emotions to leave his mind cold and calculating. Without opening his eyes, he lowered his hands, his fingers —fast and light—touching the keys with perfect precision, as if he could see them.

After he finished playing, he lowered his hands to his lap and dropped his head, deep in his thoughts. A movement of air infused with the light fragrance of Amaris' cologne alerted Cole to his presence, and he opened his eyes but didn't turn around.

"Bravissimo, maestro," Amaris whispered behind him, his voice sounding strangely raspy and thick. "What a wonderful choice—*Sonata ao Luar*... It's perfect."

Portuguese... A thought flashed through Cole's mind. *Amaris speaks Portuguese.*

He didn't say anything. Instead, he forced a nonchalant smile and turned around, swinging his long legs over the bench. Amaris stood in front of him with two crystal glasses in his hands. He offered Cole the glass with red liquid inside but didn't sit down, gazing at him with unconcealed intensity in his purple eyes. Cole brought the glass to his lips, detecting the harsh odor of alcohol, and allowed his eyes to ignite a bright scarlet.

"Erick, you're playing with fire," he said softly, taking a sip of his drink. "A drunk vampire can be hazardous to your health."

"I'll take my chances," Amaris murmured, downing his drink in one gulp. Then he took a step forward and halted, standing between Cole's legs, barely a few inches from him. As he watched him drink, his lips slightly parted, and his eyes fogged, their purple glow dimming down. When Cole finished his drink, Amaris took the empty glass from his hands and placed it on the side of the bench. His hand brushed over Cole's shoulder, moving toward the collar of his shirt. Cole raised his eyes and froze, his hands clutching the edge of the bench. Amaris' fingers traced the shape of his jaw and moved down, halting on the small hollow of his neck.

After a moment, he exhaled a ragged breath and lifted his hand, taking a step back. "Every day, I watch you in training on my security monitors," he said softly and tugged at the collar of Cole's shirt. "You don't wear a shirt when you practice martial arts."

"An old habit of mine, thanks to Ruslan," Cole replied, sounding as evenly as he could muster.

Amaris giggled, his laughter sounding too high-pitched compared to the sound of his voice as always. "I should reward Ruslan for that," he said. "You have the body of a Greek god… a sight to behold…" He pointed at Cole's shirt and twirled his wrist. "Take it off. I want to see you closer."

Cole swallowed, rising slowly. His fingers found a button on his shirt, fumbling with it, but he couldn't bring himself to open it. Amaris noticed his hesitation and took a few more steps back, away from him.

"Oh, please, Cole," he said, shoving his hand into the pocket of his pants. "I'm not going to force you to do anything you don't want to do. I just want to see you. I admire beauty in all shapes and forms—whether it's a theater play, music, a painting or the perfectly sculpted body of an ancient vampire."

The corners of Cole's mouth lifted, forming a light and easy grin, and he quickly unbuttoned his shirt. Pulling it out of his pants, he shrugged it off, letting it fall to the floor and spread his shoulders, slightly flexing his muscles for added effect. With a playful flick of his eyebrow, he turned around and walked toward the bar. Supporting himself with his arms, he vaulted over the counter, landing soundlessly on the other side. He turned his back toward Amaris, exploring the shelves with alcohol.

"That's quite a collection you have here," he said, glancing at Amaris over his shoulder.

"Take anything you want," replied Amaris, his eyes never leaving Cole's unobstructed torso.

Taking a bottle of vodka, Cole filled a small shot glass with it, raising it. "Cheers," he said, downing its content in one gulp. Then he pointed at a small office phone with buttons of multiple lines and asked, "Do you mind if I make a quick call?"

"A call?" Amaris approached the bar, his lips set in a hard, unyielding line. "Where would you like to call? I believe there is no cell service where your brother is. Besides, he needs to focus on his mission, not on you. This is the reason I blocked your blood bond in the first place."

Cole chuckled and walked around the bar, halting next to Amaris. "I wasn't going to call my brother," he said reproachfully, brushing Amaris' arm with his elbow as if by accident. "I love Damian, but my life doesn't revolve around him. I have a successful business to run, and to be honest, I'm worried about the situation in the company with me being absent for so many days. So, I wanted to call my head developer to make sure things are moving along while I'm gone. But if I can't use your phone, I understand. I have no illusions about my position in your House."

He reached over the counter and refilled his shot glass with vodka. Bringing the glass to his lips, he smiled and downed the drink. As he did, a few drops of alcohol slipped down his chin, falling on his chest. Amaris sucked in a sharp breath and lifted his arm, but then lowered it before his fingers came in contact with Cole's skin.

"Your position in my house is that of a valued guest. To me, you're neither slave nor a hostage, as your brother thinks," he whispered, his eyes glued to Cole's body. "Go ahead, make your call. Just put it on speaker so I can hear."

Cole reached over the counter again and brought the phone up. He dialed the phone number and the extension of his head developer, putting the call on speaker.

"Dennis, this is Cole Adams," he said as soon as his developer answered the call. "How is everything going?"

"As planned," the young man reported without skipping a beat. "The product is in beta testing, and so far, so good." He paused and then added, "We have a Scrum stakeholders' meeting scheduled in two days. I hope you'll be back by then."

"I doubt it, Dennis." Cole stifled a sigh, sadness gripping at his chest. "Most likely, I'll be away for at least a couple more weeks, and I need you to take care of all the development activities while I'm gone. McKenzie will take care of everything else."

"No problem, sir," replied Dennis. "I'll record all the meetings for you, so you can review them later."

"Thank you, Dennis," said Cole, his fingers tracing the edge of his shot glass. "You won't be able to reach me on my cell, but I'll try to get in touch with you again as soon as I can."

Cole hung up and placed the phone back behind the counter. He lowered himself on the barstool, nibbling on his lip. Amaris sat next to him and put his hand on his wrist. Battling the urge to recoil, Cole raised his eyes, giving him an arched stare.

"I knew you owned a successful tech company, but I could never imagine you actually run it yourself," Amaris said, his thumb caressing Cole's skin. "How do you do it?"

"Do what?" asked Cole, slightly sharper than he intended. "I have a Master's in Computer Science, MBA, and years of experience running different businesses successfully. Also, I have a silent partner who does monetary infusions when or if I need them to support my R&D efforts. I'm more than capable of running any type of business."

"But of course, you are. From the first time I laid my eyes on you I knew, you're just as smart as you're breathtakingly handsome." Amaris gave Cole's wrist a gentle squeeze and removed his hand. "That's not what I was asking. Being a vampire, how can you spend the entire day among humans without ripping their throats out? What do you do to control your thirst?"

"My thirst?" Cole slipped off the stool and stepped closer to Amaris. His lips stretched into a slow, seductive smile, exposing his fully expanded fangs. "What thirst?" He lowered his face over Amaris' neck, grazing his skin with his fangs. "I can hear your heartbeat..." he whispered airily, his fingers moving up Amaris' arm. "It's fast... too fast... I can smell your blood and hear its sound as it rushes through your veins..." He seized the hair on the back of Amaris' head, keeping him steady, and Amaris held his breath. "Are you afraid of me, Mr. Amaris... my lord..."

"No," Amaris croaked. "I have no reason... Ahhh..." His voice faded into a strangled moan as Cole punctured his skin just enough to draw a single drop of blood.

Cole let go and sat back on his stool, smiling at him as if nothing happened. The tip of his tongue moved over his upper lip, his fangs gone now. "I can control my urges around humans, Erick. Ruslan taught me well."

Amaris touched his neck with his finger and brought his hand to his eyes, staring at the small, red drop on his fingertip, bewildered.

"Yes, you can," he exhaled, his breath quickening, his eyes shining brighter through the slits of his mask. Pressing his fingers to his face, he readjusted his mask. "I wonder..." His voice trailed off as he regarded Cole with a different kind of interest in his narrowed eyes.

"About what?"

"I mentioned I have a few businesses of my own," he said at length.

"I hope you forgive my forwardness, Erick, but I don't consider slave trade and gladiatorial fights a legit business," Cole cut off dryly.

"I assure you, it's quite a profitable venture, *Senhor* Adams, and there is nothing wrong with it." Amaris rose, a sudden flare of anger making his lips quiver with indignation. He cleared his throat and moved his head from side to side, a bright shade of magenta rising up his neck to his face.

Hmm... Portuguese again...

"My apology." Cole bowed his head, allowing his long curls to fall over his face while watching Amaris' every move with interest. "I forgot my manners, my lord."

Amaris took a deep breath and seized Cole's chin, lifting his face.

"I can't be angry with you even if I wanted," he whispered and let go. Brushing Cole's cheek with his fingers gently, he tucked his hair behind his ear. "When we meet tomorrow, I would like to discuss a business proposition with you, Cole." He leaned forward and whispered into Cole's ear, his lips touching his cheek on the way down. "You'll be pleased to know it has nothing to do with the underground fighting circles. I need a partner who's touched or exposed to the World of Magic, someone I can trust. You with your money and experience are a perfect candidate. Besides, a vampire-partner is not the worst I can do."

"Oh? You trust me?" Cole gave him an arched stare, barely able to contain his sarcasm.

"I don't trust anyone, Mr. Adams." Amaris laughed darkly. "But I have different levels of distrust for different people, and I believe I can handle you."

Yes... Let's see what else you're cooking here, asshole. Everything inside him flipped with excitement, but he calmly inclined his head and asked, "Is your business legit?"

"Define legit." Amaris narrowed his eyes, shaking his head.

"Although I run all my operations in this very bunker—I never leave it—not all of them involve gladiatorial fights," replied Amaris. "This particular venture is a legit trade for the World of Magic, but not for the realm of humans, unfortunately." He giggled in his weird manner. "Telling human authorities about this business will expose the World of Magic. So, as far as humans are concerned, my business doesn't exist. I hope it's not a problem for you."

"Not a problem at all. I'll be honored to hear you out," said Cole, suppressing his excitement. "We can discuss it right now if you wish."

Amaris glanced at him, a semblance of regret reflecting in his eyes. "No, let's meet tomorrow in my office." He got up, gesturing at the door. "I'm a little tired and drunk, and with you looking like this, my mind is anywhere but on business. Besides, I have a small gift for you. You'll find it when you return to your chamber."

"As you wish, my lord." Cole got up and headed toward the piano, wondering what that was all about.

He picked up his jacket and shirt, but before he could put it on, Amaris placed his hand on his bicep, stopping him. He didn't say anything, just caressed his arm, following the flow of his muscles, and shied away, lust darkening his strange eyes. Stifling the rising nausea, Cole lowered his head and brushed Amaris' cheek with his lips under the edge of his mask, barely touching his skin.

"I wish you didn't wear this mask," Cole whispered into his ear. "I just want to see you." Then he pivoted on his heels and walked out the door.

* * *

COLE STOPPED in front of the entrance into his room and looked around. The hallway was empty, a barely noticeable presence of magical energy lingering in the air. It was always here, on this side of the underground bunker. He had no knowledge of magic or experience wielding it, so he couldn't identify what it was, but the longer he stayed in this room, the more aware of its presence he had become.

He pushed the door open and walked inside. The TV was playing on the local news station, and Ruslan lay on the couch in front of it, but Cole was positive his maker wasn't listening to the news. His velvety eyes were distant and unfocused, and his hands, folded over his stomach, were clenched so tightly, his knuckles were white.

"Father," Cole called, dropping his unused shirt and jacket by the door.

Ruslan sat up sharply, taking in Cole's appearance, and dropped his head, a deep crease forming between his black eyebrows.

"Your brother is going to put a wooden stake through my heart, and he'll be right to do so. I shouldn't have allowed you to —," Ruslan started.

"First, nothing happened," Cole interrupted him. "Like I said, two people can play this cat-and-mouse game, and I played my part. Second, you didn't allow me anything. I'm not a little boy. I did what I believed needed to be done. Third, Damian will kill someone, but it's not going to be you, Father. Should I continue?"

Cole lowered himself on the couch next to Ruslan and leaned forward, propping his elbows on his knees. Speaking too fast and too soft for any modern tech to register his words, he told Ruslan everything he learned about Amaris.

Just when he finished, the door swung open, and Jeff walked inside, followed by Sylvana. She was dressed in a long, silk robe held together by a wide sash. With every step she took, the robe spread apart a little, exposing her beautiful, long legs. Cole got up, staring at the guard in shock, but before he had a chance to say anything, Jeff seized Sylvana's arm and pushed her forward. She staggered a few steps and would have fallen if Cole hadn't caught her. The guard snickered, waving his hand in her direction.

"Mr. Amaris thinks you need some entertainment," he said, derision dripping from his every word. "She is going to take you to a place you'll never forget, vamp. So, enjoy while you can." He brought his hand to his temple in a mock salute and left the room, snickering.

Cole let go of Sylvana, but she didn't move, standing with her hands on Cole's chest. "Syl, what's going on?" he asked, gently lifting her chin, realizing that the collar was no longer on her neck.

"You need to come with me, Cole," she whispered, barely meeting his eyes. "I must do what he said, or I'll be in a world of pain." She pulled the robe aside on her chest, exposing the rune glowing with an angry purple light. "Please, Cole, just follow me."

At the sight of her rune, Ruslan gasped and rose to his feet, his face an iron mask.

"That evil bastard," he hissed, anger making his voice deeper. Approaching Sylvana, he moved his fingers over the rune, shaking his head. "You poor child. I don't know if it's possible to remove it." He pressed his hand over his mouth and stilled for a brief moment. Then he covered the rune, readjusting the lapel of her robe. "Cole, if you manage to get in touch with your brother, tell him that if he needs help to take care of this monster, Santiago and I are more than willing to step in."

"I know someone who can possibly remove this rune," Cole whispered, his hands clenching into fists. "One step at a time, Father. We deal with Amaris first, and then we'll take care of everything else." He wrapped his arm around Sylvana's shoulder, sadness constricting his throat. "Let's go, Syl. After all, I'm supposed to be entertained tonight, and it seems like I'm getting more entertainment than I can handle."

Giving Ruslan a curt nod, he followed Sylvana toward the door where he picked up his shirt and put it on before leaving the room. They moved quickly along the hallway in silence. Sylvana was a ball of raw nerves, and knowing that she had no choice but to obey the orders Amaris had given her, he didn't want to ask anything. With all his senses heightened to the limit, he couldn't help but notice that the presence of the strange magical energy he had sensed around his room intensified, and the farther they moved, the stronger it became.

The hallway ended into another long corridor, and Sylvana turned to the right, pulling on his arm to follow, but Cole halted, closing his eyes.

"Do you feel it?" he whispered.

"No… what?" Sylvana looked around, her eyes wide. "We have to go, Cole. Please. There're cameras everywhere—"

"Hold on, just a second."

He turned to the left and came to a sharp halt. A few feet away from him, he noticed a tall white door, reinforced with iron and silver like everywhere else in this facility. Since he couldn't see any other doors, he assumed the entire left side of the hallway was one large room. The presence of magical energy here was so concentrated that he felt as if his skin was on fire. Sharpening his hearing, he stilled, listening intently. A soft moan and the sound of a woman crying reached his ears, and he pulled back.

"I'll be damned, Syl," he muttered. His eyes darted up, toward the security camera in front of the door. Grabbing Sylvana's arm, he pulled her closer and pressed her back against the wall. Leaning down, he kissed her and then whispered into her ear, "This is it… This place is what Damian and I have been looking for."

She laughed, escaping his hold, and tugged at his arm. "Let's go, darling. You made a wrong turn. We're almost there." She waved in the opposite direction, pulling him with her.

They walked all the way to the end of the hallway where Sylvana stopped in front of another locked door. She pressed six numbers on the digital keypad, and the lock clicked. Sylvana glanced at him, scarlet tears gathering in her beautiful eyes.

"After you," she said and pushed the door open.

As soon as they walked inside, the door closed behind them automatically, its soft click making Sylvana wince, and Cole halted with his jaw dropped. The room—or rather a luxuriously decorated bedroom—looked like something from the tales of one thousand and one nights, and mellow, sensual music flowing in soft waves through the air just intensified the resemblance. But it wasn't the opulent décor that stopped Cole in his tracks.

"Holy shit," he whispered, his eyes sliding across shelves with sex toys and the kinds of sexual devices he had never known existed. "What the fuck..."

The late Queen Roxana had prided herself on the knowledge of how to please her sexual partners of both genders, as well as an understanding of intimacy and erotism, but even she didn't have as many devices of pleasure and torture in her arsenal.

"I'm supposed to please you in any way you wish," Sylvana whispered, averting her pained gaze.

"Excuse me?" Cole mumbled, staring at her in shock. "Tell me his orders exactly the way he said it."

She raised her eyes, a red tear sliding down her pale cheek. "He said, I must do anything you ask for, anything that would please you." Her lips trembled, and she looked away. "Cole, I must obey... please, be kind..."

Cole shuddered, undiluted anger rattling through him. Then he took Sylvana's hand and planted a soft kiss on her knuckles.

"Sylvana, darling," he murmured, walking her toward the bed. "Please lie down and close your beautiful eyes. There is nothing in this world that will please me more, driving me straight into an earth-shattering orgasm, than watching you sleep. Sorry, I'm this kind of perverted creep."

"Thank you, Cole," she whispered barely audibly, slipping under the blanket. "I'll never forget your kindness."

Cole observed the room, and even though he didn't notice any cameras, he was positive Amaris was watching his every step. Moving slowly and seductively, he started to dance, his body flowing in soft waves, following the music. He put his hand under the collar of his shirt, gradually taking it off his shoulders. As the shirt fell to the floor, he kept dancing, his muscles rippling under his pale skin.

As he made his way to a large armchair, he opened the button on the waistband of his pants and pulled the zipper down. His hand slipped inside, and he half-closed his eyes, throwing his head back. His body was still moving and flowing with the music, just the way Roxana had taught him years ago. His other hand raked through his hair, throwing it off his face, and then progressed down his chest, halting over his stomach.

I hope you enjoy the show, evil bastard.

A touch of darkness shadowed Cole's face as he zipped up his pants and dropped onto the armchair, throwing his legs over its side.

"Dima, where are you?" he reached to his brother, even though he was positive their blood bond was still blocked. Something twitched in his mind, and his brother's voice broke through the emptiness their bond had become since it was blocked.

"Cole...? Nikolai!"

CHAPTER 22

~ DAMIAN BLAKE ~

As soon as Damian threw the ball of yarn on the ground, it took off, rolling at considerable speed. He exchanged a quick look with Jamie, and both sprinted to catch up with it. Being bright red, the magical yarn was easy to spot even when it rolled through the tall grass or shrubbery, and after sunset, it glowed with a dim red light, so finding it in the dark wasn't an issue either. Following it at that high of a pace, however, wasn't easy, and from time to time, Damian had to command it to stop, so they could take a fifteen-minute breather before continuing on their way.

It had been a few days since Damian and Jamie left Baba Yaga's hut on chicken legs, following the magical ball of yarn. They traveled as fast as they could, stopping for a few hours only when they needed to get some rest and grab a bite to eat. Thanks to Zabava's parting gift, food wasn't a problem.

Sleeping in the forest under the open sky wasn't new to Damian. He actually enjoyed this part of the journey since while he was surrounded by wilderness, he was in his element. Besides, he was trained to trust his heightened senses of a Destiny Enforcer to notify him of the smallest fluctuations in the magical energy field, waking him up instantly. Jamie, on the other hand, had a hard time relaxing, worrying about all the wild beasts—magical and mundane—circling their small camp.

Even though Damian reassured him that no forest animal could break through the shield of protective magic he had been erecting around their camp each time they stopped, Jamie kept staring into the dark with wide-open eyes, jumping to his feet at every sound. Hence in the end, Damian decided to take shifts, so at least one of them could get some rest while the other watched the area.

* * *

THE LAST COLORS of the late dusk were long gone when they reached a small clearing encircled by thickets of shrubbery. Damian caught up with the ball of yarn before it had a chance to disappear behind the bushes and ordered it to stop. He picked it up, brushed the dust and dried grass off of it, and put it in the outside pocket of the backpack Zabava had given him.

While Jamie gathered some branches and set up a fire, using his magic, he surveyed their surroundings, carefully checking the area for any magical or mundane presence. Except for a few wolves, he didn't notice anything hostile or dangerous. Nevertheless, he drew a circle around the clearing, infusing it with his magic, and conjured a powerful protective shield.

The night brought coolness, and the forest was filled with rustling noises and screeches of birds. Damian sat down on the ground and shifted closer to the flames, rubbing his arms with his hands. The warmth of the fire and the scent of burned wood had a calming effect on him, making his eyelids heavy and fogging his already frazzled mind. Besides, he was so tired after following the relentless ball of yarn for hours that he didn't feel the hunger, having only one desire—to assume a horizontal position and stretch his worn-out body. Since it was Jamie's turn to stay guard, he gave him the backpack, telling him to get something to eat for himself, and then lay down, turning to his side.

After that, he reminded Jamie to wake him up in two hours and closed his eyes. The elemental energy of Earth embraced him like a loving mother, pacifying his aching, buzzing muscles, and before he knew it, he was fast asleep.

* * *

DAMIAN WOKE UP before his two hours ran out but didn't get up. Instead, he sharpened his senses, carefully scanning the forest with his other sight. A slight fluctuation in the magical energy field that had awakened him seemed to be increasing rapidly now. While the energy wasn't pure dark, there was something unusual about it, and its presence was growing too fast for his comfort. He rose soundlessly to his feet and approached Jamie, who sat by the fire, poking the flames absentmindedly with a small twig.

Bending down, Damian touched Jamie's shoulder, causing him to gasp and snap around. Before Jamie could say anything, Damian gestured for him to be silent and straightened, pulling the wizard to his feet.

"Jamie, do you sense it?" he whispered into his ear.

"Sense what?" Jamie looked around, his eyebrows snapping together. "What should I be looking for?"

"Shh… just close your eyes and open yourself to the flow of magic." Damian moved his hand over the flames and whispered, *"Aquamius."* A stream of water erupted from his palm, extinguishing the fire, and complete darkness surrounded them. "I think we're close to our final destination. I'm just surprised I hadn't noticed it earlier."

"Hmm," Jamie murmured, slowly turning around in place. Damian sensed Jamie's magic spiking and wrapping around him, but a confused expression on his friend's face told him he had no idea what to look for.

Damian moved his hand in a wide arch, and a flare of glowing white light followed his move, slowly melting back into the dark. Then he touched the ground, whispering a quick spell, and the grass lit up with a dim purple glow.

"The Darkness and the Light," he explained. "They are both here. So, it's safe to assume we're standing right on the border between the Dark Nav and the Yav. If you recall, Veles said that currently, the Sacred Isle is located between two realms. It has to be somewhere close by, but—"

He cut himself off and fell silent. Opening his other sight again, he scanned the forest around them and frowned, scratching the overgrown stubble on his chin.

"What?" asked Jamie grumpily. "I don't like the expression on your face, and usually when you scratch your five o'clock shadow like this, it means nothing but trouble."

"It means I need to shave," murmured Damian, amused. "But you're right. Something is off here."

"I knew it!" Jamie's hand reached down to his belt where his new dagger was sheathed in a leather scabbard.

"Remember my explanation about the balance between the Darkness and the Light?" asked Damian, and Jamie nodded, his face turning almost blue, shaded by the colors of the night forest. "It's not the first time I'm standing on the border between two realms, and usually, both the dark energy and the light one are present in equal measures. But here, the darkness seems to be prevalent, and it's growing exponentially." He closed his eyes and moved his head from left to right, tuning his senses to the continuously increasing flow of the dark magical energy. "We need to go."

Keeping his other sight open, Damian took off running, relying only on his senses. Without slowing down, he connected with his element, commanding the thick shrubbery to give way, and it obeyed him immediately, parting before him. Long roots submerged under the ground, allowing him to move forward without the fear of tripping over, and the trees lifted their low-hanging branches. Under the cover of night, he ran, fast and soundless like a shadow, stepping softly on the carpet of leaves, and nature bowed to him, complying with his every command.

Damian didn't look back, but the heavy steps and an occasional slew of profanities told him that Jamie was following him. Soon, the presence of the dark energy became so heavy that it overwhelmed his senses, suffocating him. Struggling to fill his lungs with oxygen, he slowed down but didn't stop until he reached the edge of the forest.

"I can never get used to the way you run, man," Jamie panted, pressing his hand to his chest. "I swear, one day you'll give me a heart attack."

"Well," murmured Damian, spreading the shrubbery to peek outside, "if I don't give you a coronary, then this most certainly will." He motioned for Jamie to approach and take a look.

The forest opened into a long, narrow clearing ending on a steep chasm. He couldn't see far enough from where he stood, but he was positive that the flaming river *Smorodina* flowed at the bottom of it. Swirls of dirty, gray smoke rose into the dark sky, partially obscuring the view, but the pungent odor of sulfur and the reek of demonic essence left no doubt—they stood just a few feet away from the river of eternal torment bordering with the Slavic realm of demons and spirits.

Right by the chasm, a giant oak tree spread its massive branches, reaching high into the starless sky. Its hefty crown was partially hidden beneath low, gray clouds, and its trunk was so thick that it would have taken at least ten people to circumvent it. The harsh gusts of cold wind, which they hadn't felt under the cover of the forest, battered the oak, rustling its heavy foliage, and it looked as if the ancient tree was shaking in fear.

"Oh, God," Jamie exhaled. "What the hell is that?"

An enormous nest, roosting high on the thick branches of the oak, was as large as any one-bedroom apartment. At least Damian thought it was the nest of a bird, and the mere size of this contraption chilled his soul.

"Is that a… bird's nest? What kind of flying monstrosity would build a nest this size? A pterodactyl?" Jamie exhaled, mirroring his thought.

"I'm afraid the owner of this nest is a lot bigger than a pterodactyl."

Damian strained his hearing, but through the howls of the rapidly increasing wind, he couldn't hear anything else. Thick, low clouds gathered over the chasm, and lightning forked through the sky, followed by a heavy rumble of thunder almost immediately.

"I don't think mommy is home though, so this is not our biggest concern at the moment," murmured Damian, pointing at the tree. "But this is…"

Barely distinguishable from the whitish-gray bark of the oak, an enormous snake coiled its way up the tree. Its body was thicker than the torso of an adult man, and while Damian could see its tail wrapped around the trunk of the tree just above the ground, its head was already reaching the lower branches of the oak. Dark energy surrounded the monster like a dirty veil, and as it slowly progressed up, the flow of its magical energy kept increasing.

"Holy snake," Jamie gasped, his hand landing on the grip of his dagger. "What the hell is that?"

"Not sure," murmured Damian. "I think it's some type of an Aspid or maybe a Basilisk. From what I recall, these two types of serpents could reach this size or even bigger, and some of them have wings. The biggest problem is that both the Aspid and Basilisk can kill you by just looking into your eyes, so, if you don't want to decorate Paradise Manor as a nice marble statue, do me a favor and avoid eye contact."

"Thank you, but no, thank you," murmured Jamie, shaking his head. "I hate snakes. Trust me, I'm not coming anywhere close to this monster."

"Something tells me staying away may not be an option. At least for me," Damian muttered and channeled his magic, pressing his hand to the tattoo on his arm. "Zhulik, are you with me?"

"Where do you expect me to be?" the gargoyle grumbled in his mind.

"Can you do me a favor?" asked Damian and quickly added, "Please?"

"Hmmm, he said please," purred Zhulik, amusement in his high-pitched voice. *"This can't be anything good. What do you need, Commander?"*

"You see this giant nest on the tree?" asked Damian, pointing up. "Can you check and let me know if there is anyone alive there?"

Zhulik gasped, sending a low-voltage jolt of electricity through Damian's arm, causing him to hiss and clasp his tattoo. *"Are you out of your friggin' mind, Commander? You hate me so much already? There is a low-level Aspid over there. It can turn me into stone!"*

"Oh, come on, Zhulik," Damian whispered, throwing his hands up. "An Aspid can't turn you into stone because you're a stone already! You're a gargoyle, for crying out loud!"

"Aw, yeah, right." Zhulik snickered. *"I just wanted to check if you remembered."* With a light pop, he appeared next to Damian in the form of a German Shepherd puppy. Spreading his leathery wings, he wagged his doggish eyebrows at him. *"Let's kick the tires and light the fires. Wish me luck, Commander."*

With one flap of his wings, he rose high in the air and sped toward the oak. He made a few circles around it before vanishing behind the thick screen of foliage. He was gone no more than a few minutes, but even though the serpent was moving slowly, it was still progressing upward, and to Damian, this short time seemed endless.

Shivering from the touch of the cold wind, Damian stared intently in the direction the gargoyle had disappeared, when suddenly he popped out next to him, manifesting out of nowhere. Breathing heavily, he landed on the ground and raised his paw, asking for a moment to catch his breath.

"The nest is not empty," he managed to say finally. "There are three young birds inside, nestlings at best. They can't fly. I'm sure the Aspid thinks they're his easy breakfast. But between us, the birds are also emitting the energy of the dark, similar to that of the Dark Nav."

Damian nodded and bit his lip, staring at the nest and the well-camouflaged serpent as it slowly moved toward it. Then he looked toward the chasm and frowned, a crazy thought rushing through his mind.

"If you're thinking what I'm thinking you're thinking, then think harder," barked Zhulik, snapping at Damian's leg for good measure, and just now, Damian noticed that the gargoyle spoke out loud instead of using telepathic communications. "Each baby bird in that nest is the size of a small pony. How big do you think their mama is?"

"You can speak aloud?" asked Damian, staring at Zhulik, flabbergasted.

"Only when I have to, and your stupidity leaves me no choice," Zhulik growled, scowling angrily at him, but his high-pitched voice sounded anything but intimidating. "Hey, wizard!" He turned toward Jamie. "Would you please talk some sense into him? He can't go there. Period. Even if the Aspid doesn't turn him into a giant chunk of rock, the mama-birdie will make him wish he was never born."

"Damian, I think Zhulik is right—," Jamie started, but Damian shook his head, stopping him in mid-sentence.

"Of course, he's right, and that's the beauty of it, Jamie. Try to remember what we discussed a while ago and do the math," he said quietly. "There are no coincidences in the World of Magic, and the Land of Dreams is the embodiment of magic. So, there is a reason you and I are here at this very moment, and as far as I can see, this reason is staring us in the face." He motioned at the tree. "Think back to Slavic lore. Nothing is ever pure good or undiluted evil, and things are never what they appear to be. So, to me it's clear. If I want to cross the chasm, I have to save the birds. Besides, this serpent is shifting the balance toward the Darkness, and since I'm a Destiny Enforcer, keeping the balance intact is my direct obligation…"

"You're going to risk everything to save some birds? You're kidding me, right?" Jamie glanced at Zhulik, shock imprinted on his face, but since Damian didn't move, he threw his hands up. "You're *not* kidding me. You *are* going to go and fight this giant reptile."

"Jamie, trust me, my friend," muttered Damian, carefully surveying the area around the oak. "I wish I didn't have to, but I know this is the right thing to do."

"Don't tell me… the paths of the Board of Destiny, and blah-blah-blah," grumbled Jamie, and Damian nodded, suppressing a chuckle. "If I ever find this friggin' Board, remind me to bring the biggest sledgehammer I have." Jamie exhaled a ragged breath, and a chain of emotions crossed his face, starting with fear and finishing with cold determination. "I can't believe I'm about to say this, but…" He shook his head in disbelief. "What do you want me to do?"

"Fighting the Aspid is not an option—too hard to kill and too dangerous. Not only can it turn you into stone by just looking into your eyes, but it also breathes fire and has deadly fangs," said Damian, speaking in a fast whisper, his mind shuffling quickly through all possible options and outcomes. "It's not enough to decapitate it, you then have to burn its body, otherwise it'll regrow the head back. Regular fire magic is not going to cut it. You need the purifying energy of the fire... A Phoenix or a Fire Salamander could—"

He fell silent, nibbling on his lip, his fingers tracing the shape of his bracelet. Jamie shifted from foot to foot, his eyes igniting with nervous excitement.

"Here is what we are going to do," said Damian at length. "I'm going to take a flight to the nest and see if I can save the birds. You and Zhulik are going to stay under the cover of shrubbery and keep an eye on the Aspid. I need to know that if things go south, I can count on your help."

"Damian, you can't fly," said Jamie, his eyes sliding from the nest to the bottom of the tree, measuring the distance. "The farther you're from the ground, the weaker you'll become."

"I know," replied Damian. "I'll be all right, though. Since we're in a magical nexus, my connection with the element of Earth is a lot stronger than in the human realm. Besides, we're in the middle of the wilderness, so I'm surrounded by my element, unlike when I'm in Downtown Phoenix."

"Aw... how sweet. A *'divine wind'* reincarnated," murmured Zhulik, tilting his head from side to side, his long ears flapping. Catching Jamie's puzzled gaze, he rolled his eyes in an undog-like manner. "Kamikaze? I hope you've heard of those, little wizard? What he's planning to do is a suicide mission. Are you out of your friggin' mind, Commander?"

"If you have a better idea, I'm all ears," said Damian dryly, but since the gargoyle didn't say anything and lay down, placing his head on his paws, he turned around and stepped through the bushes into the clearing.

*　*　*

"OPRIMENTA AMNIA," whispered Damian, casting a cloaking spell as he ran stealthily toward the tree. He had no doubt that the serpent would see through his spell as soon as he opened his wings, but he was hoping that it would happen later rather than sooner.

The closer he came to the oak, the stronger the wind became. It blew through the branches, bending and shaking the tree, seemingly coming from everywhere at once. Through the howls of the wind, he isolated a soft, rustling noise accompanied by a loud hissing as the giant snake kept circling the oak, its scales rubbing against the bark.

A blinding flare of light made him halt and look up just in time to see multiple lightning bolts spreading through the dark sky in all directions like some nightmarish fireworks. Thunder boomed, filling the chasm with a long-lasting echo, and Damian shivered, swallowing hard.

Carefully, he approached the tree, stopping a few feet away from it, and craned his neck, staring at the bottom of the massive nest visible through the canopy of leaves.

Dammit, he thought, shaking his head. *There is no way I can fly straight into the nest. It's surrounded by too many thick branches and foliage.*

The flat head of the snake was just a couple of yards away from the nest, and he had no time to strategize.

Perun almighty, help me survive this suicide mission and save my brother... He channeled his magic, and his entire body lit up with a blinding white light, his black wings opening behind his back to their full extent. The hissing and rustling ceased immediately, and the Aspid's thick tail hit the ground, raising a cloud of dust.

Forcing himself not to look at the monster, Damian rose in the air, quickly picking up speed. With his peripheral vision, he noticed the snake's giant head separating from the tree and turning in his direction, its sinister eyes igniting with a deep red glow. The snake inhaled with a loud hiss and opened its enormous maw, two long, sharp fangs protruding from it. As it exhaled, a powerful jet of fire erupted from its mouth.

Since flying wasn't his favorite exercise, Damian wasn't

fast and flexible enough on his wings. He yelped and swung to the side, the flames grazing his skin. The snake hissed and screeched, getting ready for the next attack. Moving faster than Damian expected, it struck with its flat head. Damian screamed, ducking to the side. The Aspid kept striking and spraying him with fire, blocking his way to the nest.

"*Too s-s-s-low, too heavy... You can't win-s-s-s...*" A soft hissing voice invaded Damian's head, and he pulled back, halting in midair. "*Look at the nes-s-s-s-t... it's-s-s too far... You can never pass-s-s-s me... Just look into my eyes, little human-s-s-s.*"

Everything inside Damian ignited with the burning need to look up, to meet the Aspid's eyes. He groaned, forcing himself to look away. The Aspid cackled in his head, and the small hairs on the back of Damian's neck stood on end from the malignancy of the sound.

"*You can hear me, human-s-s,*" hissed the Aspid, its body slowly slithering around the tree. "*You're a Child of Earth-s-s-s. How unfortunate for you.*" It snickered, and its body stopped moving, only its ugly head swinging evenly from side to side in an almost hypnotic manner, like an ugly, oversized pendulum. "*You don't need to look-s-s-s at me... just lis-s-s-s-ten to my voice-s-s-s. Listen... listen... lis-s-s-s-ten...*"

"No!" Damian shouted, the sound of his own voice breaking the momentary trance. Fighting the monster's powerful influence on his mind, he channeled some of his magic and reached to his gargoyle. "*Zhulik, now!*"

The Aspid emitted a deafening sound resembling a roar, which morphed into a long hiss, and then showered Damian with another jet of fire.

"*Aquamius!*" Damian extended his arms, and two powerful streams of water escaped his hands. The water collided with the fire with an earsplitting hiss, filling the air with smoldering swirls of steam. For a brief moment, a shimmering white veil separated Damian from his foe, and he used the opportunity to pull back slightly.

"Damian, hang in there!" Jamie's magically magnified voice rolled across the chasm.

The wind picked up, clearing the screen of steam. Lightning flared over his head, and thunder exploded, deafening him for a split second. Suddenly, the Aspid roared again, its terrible voice filled with pain and annoyance beyond measure. It thrashed so violently, the giant oak shook with it, a downpour of leaves showering the ground beneath it. Looking down, the blood ran cold in Damian's veins. Jamie was on one knee, his dagger protruding from the tip of the Aspid's tail.

"Jamie, run!" Damian shouted and touched his bracelet, turning it into the whip.

As Jamie pulled his dagger out, ducking to the side to get away from the vigorously beating tail of the serpent, Damian swung the whip with all the strength he could gather. The silver thong whistled through the air, its sound melting into the howling of the wind. Before the Aspid could unwind its massive body enough to strike the wizard, the thong wrapped around it right under its head. Damian yanked the whip back, the muscles on his arms and chest bulging from strain.

"*Illucious!*" he shouted at the same time, and the silver knives attached to the end of the whip lit up with the purifying energy of Creation, cutting through the serpent's thick scales. Dark, flaming blood gushed down from the terrible wound, and the Aspid screamed, its partially decapitated head swinging from side to side.

"*Commander, go! Take care of the nestlings!*" Zhulik's voice sounded in Damian's mind, and the gargoyle materialized next to him.

Gone were the wagging tail, sad eyes, and doggish grin. Supported by wide wings, in his true form, Zhulik looked intimidating. His massive lion-like body was a solid piece of rock, yet thick ropes of muscles rippled under his rocky hide. His large round eyes shone with a blinding blue light, and his paws ending in massive claws cut through the air. He opened his large mouth filled with sharp fangs and emitted a terrible roar. For a moment, all sounds ceased. Even the wind stopped blowing. The Aspid froze, staring at Zhulik. A fearsome leer stretched the gargoyle's mouth as he met the Aspid's burning gaze.

"You can't turn stone into stone, dumbass," growled the gargoyle and zoomed toward the Aspid.

As the powerful beast smashed into the vicious monster, an ear-splitting hiss entwined with deafening roars filled the air. Damian didn't wait to see the outcome of the battle between the deadly serpent and the gargoyle. He wrapped his whip around his wrist, turning it back into a bracelet, and then flew up, landing softly on the thick branch to which the nest was attached. Folding his wings, he walked toward the nest, carefully measuring his every step.

The powerful gust of wind kept ravaging the tree, and he had to check his balance a few times, nearly falling. As he reached the nest, he grabbed the top and pulled himself up, vaulting over the edge. He landed on the soft bottom of the nest and ended up facing three birds who were no more than two weeks old, judging by the development level of their feathers. Their round eyes were the size of dessert plates, and they stared at Damian without blinking.

When Zhulik said they were as large as a small pony, he wasn't kidding, but Damian hoped that at least they were lighter than they looked. Carefully approaching the baby birds, he raised his arms in a placating manner. The nestlings opened their beaks, and the screeching chirps and peeps escaped their wide-open mouths. To Damian's dismay, their hungry call was a lot louder than he expected, sounding clear over the noise of the ravaging winds and mighty booms of the thunderstorm. He clasped his hands to his ears, cringing.

The thunderstorm intensified. The wind turned into a violent storm, and a sudden torrential downpour of rain nearly threw him off his feet. The constant flashing of lightning became a blinding nightmare, and the blaring rumbling of thunder morphed into an endless echo, reverberating in the chasm and the forest.

Damian raised his arm to shield his face from the slashing streams of water, but to no avail. Fighting the winds and the rain, it took him longer than he expected to make it to the birds, but just as he was about to touch a nestling in front of him, he detected a new spike in the magical energy field in the area. The energy was dark—he had no doubts about that—but it didn't belong to the Aspid either. He looked up but could see nothing through the terrifying storm unfolding over the clearing.

"*Commander, the Aspid is coming!*" He heard Zhulik's strained voice in his mind. "*I can't hold him any longer!*"

Like in some mind-bending nightmare, Damian watched the black outline of a large serpent rise above him. For a brief second, the flares of the thunderstorms ceased, and he could clearly see the flaming eyes of the Aspid and its wide-open mouth with ghastly fangs dripping thick, green poison mixed in with streams of rain.

The serpent gave off a dissonant hiss and dove down, aiming at the birds. With no time to run, Damian opened his giant wings, covering the nestlings, and braced for the impact.

CHAPTER 23

~ DAMIAN BLAKE ~

Time slowed down as Damian held his breath, bracing for the serpent's attack. Whispering a quick protection spell, he was positive it wouldn't hold the Aspid's magically empowered assault for longer than a few seconds, but he was hoping it would soften the bone-crushing impact. He closed his eyes and dropped his head. With the next boom of thunder, the first strike came with a devastating force. Damian screamed, struggling to hold on to his magic, but the Aspid's fangs ripped through his shield, shredding it to pieces, as if it were nothing more than a flimsy piece of paper.

The monster's fangs tore his shirt, grazing his bare back, and he cried out in pain, his skin burning and blistering from the touch of Aspid's poison. The birds screeched, cowering closer to Damian, as though they could understand that he was trying to save them.

Glancing over his shoulder, Damian watched the Aspid raise its head, getting ready for the second attack. As if observing from above, he saw himself kneeling at the bottom of a giant nest with his wings spread over the nestlings. A lightning bolt flared through the sky, and for a split second, a giant dark shadow obscured the lightshow from Hell. Whatever it was, it came and melted into the darkness, fast and soundless, and the next thing Damian saw were the flaming eyes of the giant serpent and its terrifying fangs as the monster struck again.

"*Commander, incoming!*" Damian heard Zhulik's desperate cry in his mind, but he could do nothing. The nest rattled beneath him as the gargoyle pushed off its edge, throwing himself in the Aspid's way.

Damian didn't think it was possible, but somehow, it became even darker than it had been before. The storm intensified tenfold, the wind nearly ripping the heavy nest off the swaying tree. The gargoyle and the Aspid collided again with a mighty boom that rolled across the clearing, disappearing into the chasm. Then a new sound—a shrill call like that of a raven but a hundred times louder—broke through the cacophony of the raging elements, ear-splitting hisses of the Aspid and guttural growls of the gargoyle. The nestlings replied to the call with high-pitched, eager peeps but didn't try to escape from under the cover of Damian's wings.

The Aspid hissed furiously, its deafening call turning into a terrifying wail the likes of which Damian had never heard coming from a serpent before.

And suddenly, everything went quiet—no hisses of the angry snake or growls of the gargoyle. The storm ceased, and the winds dwindled into complete calmness.

"*Zhulik?*" Damian called in his mind, but the gargoyle remained silent.

He felt cold air brush over his hot, blistered skin, and a wave of dark magical energy assailed his senses, its signature bearing a dire resemblance to the energy of the Dark Nav. Afraid of what he would find next, Damian glanced over his shoulder, his entire body shaking from strain and pain.

A giant bird, the size of an African elephant, perched itself on the edge of the nest. With its head cocked, it observed

Damian with blunt curiosity. The stormy clouds were gone, and the bird's dark ultramarine plumage gleamed with the reflected light of the moon, its iron beak and talons shining with a metallic, silvery light.

Zhulik sat next to her, looking tiny and insignificant in his puppy form, a wide grin playing on his muzzle. Straightening his body with a labored groan, Damian rose to his feet and folded his wings, quickly checking the nestlings to make sure they were okay. His back responded with a debilitating ache, jolts of pain rushing through his body from the welts left by the Aspid's fangs. Even though the cuts weren't deep, the Aspid's poison circulating through his system was making him weaker by the moment. Turning around, Damian swayed, nearly losing his balance, and he could swear the enormous bird frowned, watching him.

"Your master is gravely injured, gargoyle," the bird said to Zhulik, her voice unexpectedly soft and melodious for a raven. *"I am truly sorry, but saving my children will cost him his life. The serpent's poison will kill him in no time."*

"The poison is not going to kill me," objected Damian, with shock realizing how weak his voice sounded. "I just need to go down to the ground and heal myself."

"You can hear me? You can understand—" The bird cocked its head, observing him with deep attention. *"Oh... You're a Child of Earth, aren't you?"*

"Yes..." Damian inclined his head slightly, the nausea rising to his throat followed by an overwhelming wave of weakness.

Without saying anything else, the bird spread its giant wings and rose in the air. Making a circle around the nest, she scooped Damian up, holding him in her iron talons, and flew down, gently lowering him to the ground in front of Jamie. The wizard stood with his back pressed against the oak, staring at the oversized raven with fear in his wide eyes, his hand squeezing the grip of his dagger so hard, his knuckles turned white. The body of the Aspid torn into three pieces lay at his feet, slowly turning into chunks of rock.

"Damian." He made a move toward him, but halted, staring at the enormous raven indecisively.

"Have no fear, young wizard," the raven said out loud. Humorous twinkles ignited in her attentive eyes as she took in Jamie's flabbergasted look. "I'm not going to harm you, and yes, I can speak."

"Jamie," Damian called and swallowed, closing his eyes. "Don't be afraid. This is a bird Mogol. Even though she is born of the Dark Nav, she's not evil… I recognized whose nest it was as soon as I saw the nestlings… ahh…" He exhaled, suppressing a moan, and closed his eyes. "I'm sorry, but I need a few minutes to heal. The Aspid's poison is a bitch…"

He connected with his element, allowing it to take him over. As the healing energy of Earth surged through him, taking care of his injuries and clearing his system from the deadly poison, his body arched, his fingers grasping at the grass. A few seconds later, he let go of the healing magic and relaxed, a tortured moan escaping his tightly pressed lips.

"Damian? Are you okay?" Jamie's voice sounded somewhere above him, and Damian forced himself to open his eyes.

"I'll be fine. I just need a few minutes to rest." He pushed himself into an upright position and carefully spread his shoulders. "Between the fight with the Aspid and performing self-healing, I'm a little drained. Healing magic, you know how it is… But don't worry, I'll recover much faster here, in the nexus."

"Yeah, I figured," muttered Jamie, lowering himself to the ground next to Damian, his eyes darting to the giant raven.

The bird took a step forward and touched Damian's shoulder with her large wing.

"My gratitude, Child of Earth," she said in her musical voice. "You and your friends saved my children, even though you didn't have to risk your life to do so. I will never forget your kindness." The bird looked around and tilted her head, her round, black eyes fogging with sadness for a moment as she gazed at him. "If I may ask… What is a Child of Earth doing next to the backdoor into the Dark Nav? The Slavic realm of spirits and demons is not a good place for the likes of you."

Supporting himself on Jamie's shoulder, Damian got up with a strenuous groan and took a deep breath, dealing with crippling weakness. Moving slowly, he headed toward the chasm and halted at the very edge, staring down in awe.

An enormous gorge spread in both directions as far as he could see. It was so wide that the other side of it was barely visible, partially obscured by the veil of dirty, swirling smoke. A fast river flowed at the bottom of the chasm, and even though its bright orange-red waves carried an eerie resemblance to smoldering flames, it emitted neither warmth nor the elemental energy of Fire. On the contrary, it seemed to feed on any energy —magical or elemental—suppressing and destroying it.

"River *Smorodina*," Damian exhaled, taking a step back involuntarily. Standing in such close proximity to the river of torment, his weakness seemed to increase, making him dizzy and nauseous.

"Yes, it is," the Mogol agreed flatly, halting by his side. "Neither you nor your human friend should be anywhere next to it. It'll destroy your humanity. You should leave this place and never return here again."

Damian smiled mirthlessly. "I wish I could," he said, staring across the chasm at the invisible shores of the Sacred Isle. "This is where we need to be." He jerked his chin toward the other side of the gorge.

The bird Mogol shook her head, kicking a stone off the cliff with her iron talons. As the rock flew down, Damian held his breath, counting the seconds, but the sound of it landing never came.

"Please enlighten me, Child of Earth," Mogol said, her voice filled with sarcasm. "How were you planning to cross the river? On your wings?" She chuckled. "As soon as you rise above the river, it'll drain your magic and your elemental energy, making you weaker than you are right now. Your wings will give in, and you'll plummet down, feeble and helpless like a newborn hatchling. I know you're immortal, but you'll be dying and getting resurrected in a never-ending cycle, and the river *Smorodina* will never release its hold on you. And even if you find a way to break free, what comes out after won't be you."

She fell silent and took in a deep breath, her electric-ultramarine feathers puffing out on her chest.

"I see your friend is protected by Veles," Mogol continued, nodding at Jamie. "But even this powerful amulet can't save his soul if he falls into the flaming waters."

"I know all that," Damian replied, averting his gaze. "I wasn't going to travel on my wings. Besides, as a Child of Earth, flying is not my strongest suit."

"Very true." Mogol inclined her head, sparkles of good-natured humor shining in her eyes. "Children of Earth don't appreciate the beauty of air."

"I hate flying," murmured Damian and then added louder, "I knew that Veles' amulet would protect Jamie as long as he didn't touch the flames of the river. My plan was to summon Chernobog and ask for his help and protection. He's the only god of the Slavic pantheon who can grant safe passage to a human soul across the river *Smorodina*. Not even the god of the Three Realms, Veles, can do it."

"Ask Chernobog?" The Mogol laughed, the sound of her laughter resembling the guttural call of a raven. "Chernobog doesn't do favors, and one doesn't just ask the King of the Dark Nav for help. You beg him on your knees. And even if he agrees to help you, you'll be forever in his debt. Is that what you wanted to do, Child of Earth? Become a slave of one of the most powerful dark deities?" The Mogol looked away before continuing. "Since you're not an angel, judging by your wings, you're a Commander of the Destiny Enforcers. Am I right?"

"Yes," replied Damian, knowing ahead of time what the Mogol was going to say next.

"Chernobog hates the Destiny Council," the bird continued. "What do you think he would do to you? I understand he can't kill you, but trust me…" The Mogol's voice trailed off as she touched Damian's shoulder with her giant wing. "There are things he can do to you that are a lot worse than death."

"Everything you said is true. I know that," agreed Damian, "and I'm still going to do it. This is the only way I can complete my mission."

"Your mission? Fire and Ice, Child of Earth!" The bird threw her wings up, desperation in her voice. "I know that when it comes to the Destiny Enforcers, once orders are given, they have no choice but to obey. Is that what drives you to sacrifice yourself?"

"No." He glanced at Jamie and then at his gargoyle, an ache settling in his tightly pressed jaw. "My back can attest that I questioned and disobeyed direct orders from the Destiny Council more than once. I have to do it because even though a lot depends on my success, this mission is also personal to me."

"How so?"

"My brother's life depends on it." Damian ran his hand through his dirty, wet hair, his heart contracting painfully at the thought of Cole. "I never beg, Mogol… I rather die than live on my knees, but I will do anything for my brother."

"Your brother?" asked the Mogol, suddenly alert. "You're a Child of Earth, so most likely you're quite old. The only way your brother can still be alive is if he is also a being of magic. What is he?"

"A vampire."

The Mogol folded her wings behind her back, her beak opening slightly. "A vampire?" she echoed him, her eyes staring somewhere over Damian's head. "Two brothers—the Darkness and the Light..." Her voice trailed off, and she shook her head. "No, it can't be."

"What are you talking about?" asked Damian, goosebumps rising on his arms.

"Nothing," the Mogol cut him off abruptly and lowered herself to the ground, spreading her wings. "Climb on my back, Child of Earth. You saved my children from a terrible death, and I'm glad I can repay your kindness." She glanced at Jamie, expectation in her eyes. "You too, young wizard. I will carry you all across the river. Besides Veles, I'm the only being of magic who can travel between all three realms, and I'm the only child of the Dark Nav who can safely fly over the river of torment."

The bird Mogol made it clear that she wasn't going to say more on the subject of his brother and asking more questions was pointless.

"Thank you," said Damian, his stomach twisting with dread. He ran his fingers over his tattoo, staring pointedly at the gargoyle. *"Zhulik, time to go, my friend."*

"Oh, ma-a-an," Zhulik whined, getting up. *"I was so hoping to see the river* Smorodina *from a bird's-eye view..."* He glanced at the bird Mogol and grinned, wagging his tail. *"Literally."* He winked at Damian and vanished with a light pop, morphing into his tattoo.

Damian carefully stepped on the Mogol's wing, her feathers slippery under his feet as he made his way up. He settled on her back between her wings, wondering if the giant bird even felt his weight. As soon as Jamie joined him, the Mogol got up and was high in the air with one flap of her powerful wings.

"Are you ready?" she asked, slowly picking up some height. "I'm going to fly high over the river to make sure its magic won't feed on your souls as much. But for you, Child of Earth, it's not going to be easy. So, brace yourself and hold on tight, so you don't fall."

"I'm as ready as I can be," muttered Damian, grasping at the slippery feathers.

"Giddy-up!" Zhulik snickered in his mind.

The Mogol rose higher in the air, her powerful muscles working hard under her feathers. Damian closed his eyes and lay flat on her back, holding on for dear life. He heard Jamie's gasp of awe but didn't care to look down at the view, praying that Veles' *Triglav* was powerful enough to keep his friend safe.

The sickening reek of sulfur assailed his senses, and he buried his face into the Mogol's rich plumage. Despite the height, he could still feel the deadly presence of the river *Smorodina*. The icy tendrils of darkness reached up and wrapped around his heart, making it beat desperately against his ribcage like a scared little bird in a cage. His mind, obscured by a strange fog, was drifting on and off while everything inside him ached with despair, grief, and fear.

It seemed as though all his happy memories—as few as he had—were gone now, and all he could see in his future was pain and loss. The most horrifying moments of his entire existence flashed before his eyes in a never-ending merry-go-round of nightmares, and the only desire he had left in his tormented soul was to let go and fall to his death. The river's deadly magic overpowered his mind, extinguishing the need to live and fight. His fingers unlocked of their own accord, and his tense muscles relaxed.

"Commander, you must fight!" Damian heard Zhulik's voice in his mind but had a hard time comprehending the meaning of his words. *"It's the pull of the Dark Nav. Find something to hold on to and fight it, dammit! It's going to be over soon."*

Damian groaned, trying to find any scraps of anything that could help him hold on to reality. As the last resort, he reached to his brother but found only a terrifying void in the place where their connection had been.

"Commander, listen to my voice!" Zhulik boomed in his mind,

painfully ripping him out of the emptiness and despair. *"Try to remember!"*

A new chain of images started to move before his eyes, dispelling the horrific nightmares the Dark Nav was inflicting on him. They were flashing fast, as if someone were shuffling a deck of cards in his mind, but strangely, he remembered every single moment Zhulik was showing him. A young blond boy standing next to him, his dirty, skinny arms wrapped around his waist, his shaking body pressed against his, searching for warmth and protection. A cliff over the river under the endless blue sky. A young man with blond curls framing his handsome face, gazing at him with affection and trust. He saw himself lying in tall grass, a pair of velvety, brown eyes shining above him like two stars. And finally, an image of a woman with flaming red hair appeared in his mind. She stretched her hand to him, love in her cerulean gaze, her lips forming three words over and over—*return to me...*

Gradually, the influence of the river of torment on him started dwindling. His mind cleared, and he gasped as he realized how close he had come to slipping into the flaming inferno. He pulled himself up, his arms wrapping tighter around the Mogol's back, his fingers squeezing her shining feathers.

"Zhulik..." he whispered, his voice hoarse. *"Thank you."*

"No problem," the gargoyle grumbled. *"Just remind me to never go through your memories again. A terrifying place, I must say... I don't think I'm going to sleep tonight."*

An image of a trembling little puppy with overly large, round eyes manifested in Damian's mind, and he couldn't help it when his lips stretched into a grin.

A few endless minutes passed before the bird made a wide circle and started to drop height. She landed softly and spread her wings, waiting for them to go down. Following Jamie, Damian slipped to the ground and exhaled with relief. He moved forward, halting in front of the Mogol and bowed, pressing his fist to his chest.

"My gratitude," he said, straightening.

The giant raven inclined her head, gently touching his shoulder with her iron beak. "Go, save your brother, Child of Earth," she said. Then, without a warning, she spread her wings and rose in the air, quickly disappearing from view.

Damian followed her with his eyes until she was gone and then turned to Jamie. "Let's put some distance between us and the river, and then we'll take a short break if you don't mind."

He turned his back toward the chasm, ready to start walking when a soft touch to his mind made him halt and sharpen his senses. It wasn't the deadly pull of the Dark Nav, and it wasn't the call of his gargoyle. It felt safe and familiar, and a tiny spark of hope ignited in his heart. He took a deep breath and closed his eyes, opening his mind.

"Dima, where are you?" His brother's voice, distant and breaking, sounded through their blood bond.

"Cole?" he asked, still unable to believe it wasn't some kind of twisted illusion conjured by the Dark Nav. *"Nikolai!"*

Cole didn't reply right away, and in a matter of a few heartbeats, thousands of worst-case scenarios flashed through Damian's mind. When his brother spoke again, a wave of relief spread through Damian, adding to his overall weakened state.

"Dima... Thank God," said Cole, speaking so fast that Damian had a hard time making out his words. *"I found one place in the bunker where our connection is not completely blocked, but I don't want to use it for too long. Who knows... Amaris may notice, and right now, I'm just trying to stay on his good side."*

"Cole, are you okay?" asked Damian. *"Did he keep his word?"*

"Yes, he was true to his word," Cole replied calmly, but a barely noticeable vibe of anger touched Damian's senses through their blood bond. *"He treats me and Ruslan well... um... mostly. Doesn't matter. Let me tell you what's going on, and we need to disconnect."*

"*Go on.*" Damian swallowed, anger and dread spiking through him. *Mostly well? What the hell is that supposed to mean?*

"*I found Sylvana. Amaris has abducted her and keeps her under his control, using necromancy,*" Cole continued, speaking a touch faster than before. "*She was the one who trained his fake slayers and gave them the poison. She had no choice.*"

"*Dammit,*" muttered Damian, shaking his head. "*Even if we save her from Amaris, the Sisterhood will have her head for that...*"

"*Agreed.*" The vibe of anger emanating from his brother intensified. "*We'll have to figure something out to protect her. But one step at a time.*" He fell silent for a heartbeat and then continued, "*You and Zabava were right. Amaris collects the magical energy of witches.*"

"*Did you see it with your own eyes?*"

"*No,*" replied Cole, "*but I hope to find my way into the room where he does it soon. I'll have the proof, brother. Trust me.*"

"*I trust you, Cole,*" murmured Damian. "*I don't trust Amaris. Especially because we still don't know his supernatural identity.*"

"*I believe he's a demon,*" said Cole. "*Even though I haven't seen his face—he always wears a mask—I came close enough to him to have a taste of his blood. He has traces of demonic essence in his bloodstream. Don't get me wrong, I've tasted demonic blood before—that of pure demons and human bodies possessed by demonic essence. His blood is different from both, but I'm pretty sure he's some kind of demonic entity.*"

Damian frowned. He expected Amaris to be anything, but not a demon. Too smart, too elegant in his manners, too cunning.

"*Cole, be careful,*" he said. "*Make sure he doesn't find out about your*"—he took a deep breath—"*magical abilities. Demons are sensitive to fluctuations of the magical energy field, so keep yours under control.*"

"*I have no idea how to do that, but I'll do my best...*" Cole's voice wavered and disappeared for a moment. *"Dima, when are you coming back? How much time do I have?"*

"I don't know," replied Damian, staring into the dark. *"I found the place. Now I need to find the magical entity, and I have no idea what to expect."*

"Understand... Be careful..." Sadness washed over Damian through their unsteady connection. *"We should disconnect now, but I'll try to speak with you again when I learn something new."*

"Watch your back, brother mine..."

"Always..."

CHAPTER 24

~ DAMIAN BLAKE ~

The magical ball of yarn moved through the tall grass, running slowly up and down endless rolling hills. Unlike before, it was moving a lot slower, and Damian and Jamie didn't have to run to follow it. Even though it was a relief, Damian couldn't help but wonder why the pace of the yarn had changed so drastically but couldn't find a reasonable explanation.

The sun rose over the Sacred Isle, showering the everlasting planes with its warmth and light. They walked for quite some time, but the scenery never changed. Every time they made it to the top of the next hill, Damian hoped to see something different, yet he saw only more hills and the infinite ocean of green grass speckled with white and yellow wildflowers.

The air was filled with the freshness of morning dew, the delicate fragrance of flowers and the scent of damp earth. Surrounded by his element, Damian felt stronger and more powerful than ever, and for a while, he let go of his worries and just enjoyed nature in its virginal state.

"Damian, can I ask you a question?" Jamie's voice sounded somewhere on the outskirts of his mind.

"You just did." Damian threw a sideways glance at his

companion. Jamie's jaw dropped, and Damian laughed, tapping him on his shoulder. "What do you want to know?"

"I understand that your daggers are bound to you by the Destiny Council," he started, his gaze darting to Damian's wrist, wrapped in the leather of his bracelet. "But how about your whip? I've never seen a weapon like that before, and I've seen quite a few unusual weapons in the Guardians Order's arsenal."

Damian winced and kept walking, staring straight ahead, his fingers automatically reaching for his bracelet. "It's a long story," he replied at length.

Jamie glanced at him, understanding changing his features. "Sorry if I brought back some hard memories. I shouldn't have asked."

Damian cleared his throat, raking his fingers through his hair to cover the left side of his face. "It's okay," he said. "The whip was a gift from the Romani people."

"Romani people?" parroted Jamie, confusion written all over his face.

"Gypsies." Damian chuckled, shaking his head. "You probably don't know, but gypsy magic is extremely powerful and one of a kind. They crafted this whip for me, tailoring it to my magical energy signature. So, when I use it, it feels like an extension of my arm, a part of my body, you know? Just like my daggers respond to my mental command, my whip responds to my magic, my every move and thought. Except for me, no one can use it to its full potential."

"Fascinating." Jamie's eyes darted to Damian's bracelet, regarding it with extra attention.

"It happened over five hundred years ago in the Carpathian Mountains..." Damian sighed, his mind slowly unraveling old memories he considered both happy and painful. "At the time, I was still one of the Commanders of the Destiny Enforcers. Before I assumed the *'no one'* status, that is." He frowned, rubbing his forehead. "I had a team and a friend whom I trusted with my life. My friend Cossack and I were sent to investigate some dangerous activities of an old *Hutsuls* covenant."

"Evil witches?" Jamie's eyes ignited with curiosity.

"As evil as they come." Damian smiled at his friend's youthful excitement. Things like these had stopped being interesting or exciting to him centuries ago. Just another day at the office. "To make a long story short—"

"Please don't make it short. Keep it very-very long," Jamie exhaled. "I want all the details." He waved at the endless fields and hills of the Sacred Isle. "Besides, we do have a long walk to I-don't-know-where, as it seems."

"The covenant discovered our presence... I still believe someone betrayed us," Damian continued with a shake of his head. "The witches were more powerful than we expected, and they managed to sever our connection with the Destiny Council realm. We couldn't teleport or open a portal. We couldn't even call for help." Catching Jamie's bewildered gaze, he stifled a sigh. "They isolated a large area and... er... siphoned all magical energy out of it, for the lack of a better word." He scratched the back of his head and shrugged. "It's hard to explain. In a way, their enchantment worked like a God's snare, but I'm sure it was something else. It's impossible to sustain a God's snare spell over such a large territory. It would take an unprecedented amount of magical energy. Anyway, just take my word for it—all we could do was run."

For a moment, his vision fogged, and he saw himself running through the thickets of the Carpathian Mountains, chased by a pack of volkolaks. He felt the coolness of the midnight wind brush his hot skin, throwing his long hair off his face. He heard the dull thumps of his own steps as his feet hit the ground covered in a rug of long pine needles, the sound of his blood pumping too loud in his ears. Damian shuddered at the clarity of his memory, small hairs rising on the back of his neck.

"The lack of magical energy made us weaker physically, but despite that, we ran, hoping that we could get out of the affected area before the witches would catch up with us. Somehow, Cossack and I got separated, and I lost him in the dark of the forest. In hindsight, I'm glad he wasn't with me."

"Why?"

"Because I didn't make it out of the enchanted territory. The witches caught up with me," Damian explained. "In the end, I managed to escape, but not before they cursed me..." His voice trailed away, and for a few long seconds he walked in silence, images of his past flashing before his eyes. "I think they knew they couldn't kill me, so they just let their magic do the job. It took a short while for the curse to take hold of me, but once it did, it completely disabled me, blocking my access not only to my magic, but also to my elemental power, of which I still have no idea how that was possible. I tumbled down off the top of a tall hill, hitting every rock and crushing probably every bone in my body on the way down, unable to break the fall..."

He stopped talking, pain coiling in the pit of his stomach as he relived that time. Jamie glanced at him but didn't ask anything, sympathy reflected in his eyes.

"Anyway, when the Romani people found me, I was hurt and helpless like a newborn baby. I couldn't move. I couldn't speak. I couldn't heal myself. But worst of all—I couldn't remember anything," said Damian quietly. "It took them a few months to break the curse and take care of my injuries, but they managed to do it. They saved me, in more ways than one, and I lived with them for quite a few years, refusing to return to the Destiny Council realm. I don't know why the High Council didn't pull me back by force, because they had the power to do it, but for the first time in over five hundred years, I was truly free, and I couldn't care less..."

He sighed, unable to speak for a few seconds. "The gypsies taught me their magic, traditions and their fighting style. I'm not sure why, but their *shuvani*—a witch—believed that a whip was the best weapon for me. So, their blacksmith forged this whip especially for me, and the old *shuvani* bound it to my magical energy signature, making it uniquely mine." He touched the bracelet, rubbing its edge in a habitual gesture. "And that's the story of my whip."

"Why did you leave?" asked Jamie.

Damian glanced at him, feeling the blood draining from his face, and switched his attention to the ball of yarn climbing up a tall hill.

"I don't want to talk about that," he said. His chest locked with a nagging pain, and he massaged his left shoulder and arm absentmindedly. "You already made me say more than I wanted to share."

He ran up to the top of the hill and stilled, staring down. Far on the horizon, separated from the valley by the dark line of a forest, proud cupolas of a large palace reached toward the blue sky, the rays of the morning sun throwing bright flares at their golden surface. It was positioned on the crest of a tall hill and surrounded by a wall, a dark, narrow serpentine of a road slithering down the hillside.

"I guess this is where we need to be," said Damian, pointing at the palace. From that distance, the palace looked peaceful, but it was impossible to say if it truly was.

Jamie nodded, starting on his way down. "At this pace, we should be there by nightfall."

* * *

THEIR PASSAGE through the forest was uneventful. Trying to speed up the process, Damian used his power over nature to make sure their path was unobstructed by thickets, making their walk a lot faster and easier. By the time the sun crawled its way down to the horizon, they reached the edge of the woods and halted, observing the palace towering over the small valley at the foot of the hill.

The road, Damian had noticed before, cut abruptly at the border with the forest. Paved with light cobblestones, it was easily visible even in the dimming light of the early dusk. The red ball of yarn rolled onto the road and halted, moving back and forth slightly, as if expecting Damian and Jamie to follow it.

Jamie separated the bushes, ready to walk out, but Damian seized his shoulder, pulling him back. A barely noticeable spike in the magical energy field touched his senses, causing him to hold his breath. It was so faint that Damian wasn't sure he didn't imagine it, but it was enough for his intuition to raise a red flag.

"Isn't it where we're supposed to go?" asked Jamie, giving him an arched stare. "Everything seems to be quiet and peaceful."

"Yes, but try to remember where we are. You're not in Arizona anymore. The Land of Dreams is not a place where you can trust your human eyes. Nothing here is what it appears to be," Damian whispered.

Taking a deep breath, he channeled his power toward his eyes to reinforce his second sight. As he surveyed the castle, chills ran down his back. A veil of dark magical energy swayed with the breeze, circling around the tall walls built of solid white rocks. From where they stood, Damian could see the tall gates into the palace. They were locked, but he couldn't see any guards either by the entrance or on top of the wall.

"Dammit…" he exhaled, massaging the back of his neck. "Nothing is ever easy."

"What is it?"

"I don't know," replied Damian, "but since we have no choice but to go up there, I'm sure we're about to find out." He glanced at Jamie, fighting the desire to ask him to stay behind. Knowing full well that Jamie would never agree to that, he tapped the young man's shoulder, jerking his chin toward the road. "Get your dagger ready, my friend. I think we're about to have some fun Slavic style."

"Slavic style?" Jamie unsheathed his dagger, squeezing its grip tightly in his hand. "What's that supposed to mean?"

"It means…" murmured Damian, carefully separating the bushes and stepping on the road. He glanced at Jamie, and the corners of his mouth lifted into a mirthless smile. "It means that when you think that things can't get any worse, they most certainly will."

Keeping his senses attuned to the fluctuations of the magical energy field around the palace, he took a few careful steps up the hill and halted, holding his hand up to stop Jamie. The energy spiked again, and a piercing scream shattered the silence of the evening. The sound echoed through the forest, bouncing from tree to tree, but instead of dwindling, with every next reverberation, it became louder and rose higher until it turned into a bone-chilling, high-pitched, continuous shrill.

A pain, harsh and unyielding, took hold of him, blinding him for a moment. Damian cried out and wrapped his arms around his head, his knees bending of their own accord. A new scream rang above the palace. Dark and malignant, it was followed by a sharp increase in the dark magical energy. The screams kept changing, resembling first the cry of a child, then the meow of a cat, and finally, the bleat of a goat. It became darker as if the moon were swallowed by some horrendous invisible monster.

One grating shriek followed the other. They fused into a choir from Hell, echoing between the trees, bouncing against the hills, rising high into the black sky. Struggling to stand on his feet, Damian raised his face, drops of sweat slipping down his forehead. His vision was blurry, but he wasn't sure if it was his imagination fueled by the non-stop, blinding pain in his head playing tricks on him.

Like a giant tidal wave, something dark and eerie rose from behind the palace. It reached higher and higher, and soon the dismal veil was taller than the tallest tower of the palace. It didn't appear to be solid but rather misty, its large particles moving and shifting as they bounced up and down. The reek of demonic essence invaded Damian's nostrils, making him choke as he struggled for breath. While it felt familiar, there was something different about it, and Damian was positive this energy signature didn't belong to a run-of-the-mill demon.

As a sudden realization flashed through Damian's frazzled mind, he forced himself to tear his eyes off of the quickly approaching horror and turned toward Jamie. The young man was on his knees, his hands pressed to his ears. His face was contorted with pain, blood dripping between his fingers and from his nose. Taking an unsteady step toward him, Damian seized his shoulder and hauled him to his feet.

"Jamie, I'm going to do something to stop this ruckus," he shouted, leaning down to Jamie's ear. "Unfortunately, it will kill all sound. I won't be able to communicate with you." He glanced at his friend, worry gnawing at his insides. "Do you understand me?"

Jamie nodded, bloody tears slipping from his blue eyes. "Do you know what it is?"

Damian couldn't hear his friend's words, but he read his lips and nodded. "I suspect it's the Drekavac. Many of them… too many to be natural. The Drekavac is a demonic entity similar to the phantoms of the Dark Nav, but a lot worse and more dangerous."

"Awesome…"

Ignoring the pain, Damian channeled his magic and whispered, *"Silenties..."*

As soon as the word of the silencing spell escaped his lips, all sound ceased. The change was so abrupt that after the non-stop cacophony of the demonic shrieks, the silence was so thick and heavy, it felt almost painful. Gesturing for Jamie to follow,

Damian summoned his daggers and ran toward the approaching tidal surge of darkness.

"Zhulik," he reached out to his gargoyle in his mind. *"I need you to protect Jamie."*

"But Commander—," the gargoyle started, but Damian interrupted him.

"I have no time to argue with you," he snapped. *"Do as I say."*

"Dictator!"

"Yeah, you got that right," muttered Damian, ignoring the light zing of electricity Zhulik sent through his arm.

He managed to reach the walls of the palace before the demonic cloud swallowed him, wrapping its icy tendrils around him. He had been right—it wasn't solid. Thousands of semi-transparent creatures spun around him in a dizzying, continuous whirl. They had weird thin bodies and heads that were twice as big as their torsos. Dirty, leathery wings sprouted out of their deformed backs, and all four of their limbs ended in terrifying talons.

Their mouths, filled with small, sharp teeth, were opened in silent screams, but no sound came out, and their eyes, shining with a malignant purple light, stared at Damian without blinking. Icy fear the likes of which he had never experienced before squeezed his heart, sending his mind into a wild frenzy, and for a moment, all he wanted to do was run.

Realizing it was the demonic influence on his mind, he took a deep breath, channeling his magic toward his daggers.

"Illucious," he thought the spell, and his blades ignited with a blinding white light, the purifying magic of Creation surging through them.

The Drekavacs' eyes flashed with a boiling fury, and their round mouths stretched wider, covering more than half of their deformed faces. Damian squeezed the grips of his daggers tighter, a rush of anger catalyzing his power. He spun in place, and every strike of his deadly weapons found a target. At the touch of the purifying magical energy, emitted by his blades, the demons twitched and convulsed, their ugly bodies turning into black smoke of pure demonic essence before getting absorbed by the ground.

As the Drekavacs pulled away from him, Damian glanced back and saw the gargoyle in the shape of a giant dog standing with his wings open in front of Jamie. The demons didn't attack them, visibly terrified of Zhulik, and that was enough for Damian to know that his friend was well protected. He channeled his power of the Destiny Enforcer, and his giant black wings opened behind his back. Rising a few feet off the ground, he moved forward at full speed, destroying as many demons as he could on his way. His progress was fast and forceful, but there were so many monsters around him that it was impossible to block all their attacks, their talons ripping his arms and shoulders.

He glanced up, noticing that the thick cloud of demons started to get thinner, and he doubled his effort, blocking the stinging pain in his wounds. Suddenly, a powerful blast of magical energy rushed through the area. It was so strong that the demons froze in midair, and their wide mouths snapped shut. The second wave followed soon after, melting the Drekavacs' ugly bodies into dirty swirls of black smoke. Those that survived the second blast came out of their stupor. They huddled closer together and started to swirl. Moving faster, their bodies assembled into a disgusting tornado which kept rising higher and higher until every single Drekavac was gone, disappearing into the dark sky.

Damian landed on the ground and folded his wings, his chest rising and falling with laborious breaths. He saw Jamie and Zhulik standing a few feet behind him, pointing at the gates of the palace. Damian walked up to his friends, quickly assessing Jamie's state to make sure he wasn't wounded. Then his eyes darted to the entrance, and his jaw dropped. A group of people walked out of the gates and halted, staring at them with curiosity.

An older man, dressed in a white linen shirt that resembled a tunic and wide, black pants, stepped in front of the crowd. He wasn't tall, his short, gray hair in disarray, but the light of white magical energy surrounded him as he wasn't trying to hide or suppress it. He pointed at his ears, gesturing for Damian to remove his silencing spell.

"Incanto Comlium," Damian commanded in his mind, and all sound came rushing into the area.

The man approached Damian and lowered to one knee, pressing his fist to his chest.

"My lord," he said, inclining his head. "I'm yours to command."

CHAPTER 25

~ COLE ADAMS ~

Ruslan pulled a small stool closer to the couch where Cole sat with his head bowed down, deep in contemplation. He lowered himself onto the stool and gently touched Cole's knee, causing him to lift his head. Cole glanced at his maker's face and warmth spread through his chest, dispelling his heavy thoughts for a moment.

"I'm fine," he said, pulling a small throw pillow to his side to lean on it.

"You're not. You're tired, my boy," Ruslan objected, his voice sounding below a whisper.

Cole chuckled mirthlessly. "We're vampires. The word 'tired' has no meaning to us."

"You're right. I don't think I remember how it feels to be physically tired." Ruslan got up and headed toward the electric fireplace where he halted, turning his back to Cole. He braced his hands against the wall, dropping his head, and stood like this for a few seconds. "But I wasn't talking about the exhaustion of your body. I was talking about your soul, my child." He turned around and rested his back against the wall, folding his arms over his chest.

"This too shall pass," Cole whispered, but a nagging feeling of dread spread through him.

"I have a bad feeling about all this," said Ruslan, echoing Cole's thoughts, which only added to Cole's feeling of unease.

A soft knock on the door interrupted their quiet conversation, but before Cole could answer, Ruslan was by his side, his hand lying firmly on Cole's shoulder.

"Jeff, probably," Cole whispered and added aloud, "Please, come in."

The door opened up slowly and soundlessly, but no one walked in. The light in the room flickered, and it seemed as though darkness emerged through the entrance, lingering there like a stormy cloud for a heartbeat. The light flickered again, igniting brighter, and the shadow was gone, ephemeral like some freakish illusion.

The Head of the Arizona House stood in the doorway, his left hand in the pocket of his suit pants. His face was partially covered by a black leather mask, his eyes glowing with a deep purple light through the slits. The corners of his mouth lifted a little, his eyes darting from Ruslan to Cole. Ruslan's fingers dug deeper into Cole's shoulder, nearly tearing through his black dress shirt, and his teeth squeaked as he clenched his jaw.

"Good evening," Amaris said, remaining in place.

"Mr. Amaris," Ruslan growled instead of a greeting, his entire body stiff with suppressed rage.

Cole tapped Ruslan's hand and got up, appearing relaxed and at ease. "Good evening, Erick. I was expecting Jeff to notify me when you were ready."

"Why? We don't need a middleman between us, do we?" Amaris' smile grew wider as he switched his attention to Ruslan. "Ruslan, do you mind if I borrow your multi-talented son for a few hours?"

"Not at all," replied Ruslan, returning a smile, but his was so dark and ferocious that if Amaris were human, the blood would've run cold in his veins from the mere looks of it.

With a tiny nod in Ruslan's direction, Cole left the room, following the Head of the Arizona House. Amaris closed the door and turned to Cole.

"Let's talk some business, my friend," he said, motioning for him to follow. Suddenly, his easy, leisurely demeanor was gone, and now he looked so nervous and tense that Cole had to do a double take.

Without waiting for Cole's reply, Amaris turned left and picked up the pace, marching along the same hallway Cole and Sylvana had walked recently. For a moment, everything inside Cole somersaulted as he expected Amaris to take him to the locked room surrounded by magical energy. But at the cross point of the two hallways, the Head of the Arizona House threw a curious stare at him and turned right.

As they passed the room where he spent the night with Sylvana, Amaris' lips twitched a little, but he didn't say anything and just kept moving forward until the hallway came to a dead-end. Cole glanced around but couldn't see anything resembling a door.

"Do you feel it?" Amaris breathed out and moved his hand over the wall, leaving a purple swoosh of light behind.

"No," Cole lied as smoothly as he could muster while his skin prickled with the amount of magical energy this area emanated. "I'm a vampire. Sure, I can detect the presence of vampires, werewolves, demons"—he peered at Amaris, expecting a reaction, but the man didn't even blink—"and a few other supernatural types, but that's as far as it goes. My brother always talks about magical and elemental energy, and sometimes I wish I could feel it too… but oh, well."

"Uh-huh," Amaris hummed, tilting his head slightly, his eyes drilling into Cole as if he were trying to read his soul. Rising on his tiptoes, he drew a glowing rectangle in the air, whispering a spell in Dragon tongue. The rectangle ignited brighter, and when the light dwindled, a tall door materialized on the wall in front of them.

With a condescending sneer, Amaris pushed the door open and bowed ceremoniously. "After you, my lord."

Cole crossed the threshold and halted, staring around in awe. The giant space with a high ceiling and steel reinforced beams looked like an industrial warehouse, and it was filled with floor-to-ceiling shelves, glass cases, and locked safes. Dimly illuminated by the shimmering, bluish light of magical orbs, the far end of the room was concealed by darkness, shadows gathering behind every shelf and in every corner.

Ancient weapons, strange objects, vials with shimmering liquids inside and thick books in leather covers filled all of the available holding space. Some of the shelves were crisscrossed by iron and silver chains in addition to other security measures. A light smell of dust mixed with a barely noticeable odor of sulfur and some other smells Cole didn't recognize lingered in the air, and the magical energy that flowed around the shelves was so thick, it could have been cut with an ax.

Cole dropped his shoulders, lead-like heaviness settling in his limbs—this wasn't what he had expected to find.

"So, what do you think?" Amaris' voice sounded next to him, causing Cole to flinch and snap toward him.

"I think I've seen this show before," Cole muttered, a thin layer of sarcasm in his voice. "A warehouse built to keep dangerous magical artifacts from the reach of humans?" Cole motioned at the shelves. "I assume all these… um… items have magical properties?"

"Right you are, my friend." Amaris put his hand on the small of Cole's back, pushing him forward slightly. "Don't feel shy. Come closer, take a look. Just don't touch anything without asking me first. Some of these things are quite powerful, and I don't know how they would react to the touch of a vampire."

Cole moved forward, walking slowly between the shelves. He pretended to look around, but with his mind working on overdrive, he barely paid any attention to the magical artifacts before him.

"This is the business I wanted to talk to you about," continued Amaris. "I collect these magical objects and then auction them off to the highest bidder. However, my lifestyle and my other enterprises keep me tied up to this facility, and I need someone on the outside, in the realm of humans, to run this business."

Cole halted and turned around, understanding dawning on him. "Ricardo's collection," he whispered, a deep shudder running through him. "You created it. You're the supplier."

"Clever little vampire," Amaris muttered, patting his cheek affectionately. "Yes, I am. Originally, I thought Ricardo could take the role I'm offering to you, but soon, I realized he was too weak and too human to deal with my type of buyers." He ran his finger over the edge of the shelf as he promenaded along the aisle. "Nevertheless, with time, Ricardo proved to be a great provider of captive fighters for my House, so I decided to keep him around." He shrugged. "Besides, you probably noticed that living in this bunker day in and day out can be quite boring, and his beautiful sister is a great source of entertainment to me."

He giggled, shaking his head, and halted, turning around. Cole came to a sharp stop and surveyed the area. While nothing particular attracted his attention, the magical energy in this place of the warehouse throbbed and pulsated, wrapping around him, caressing his skin as if inviting him to find it, touch it, own it. He groaned and closed his eyes as they ignited with a bright scarlet light.

A sharp breath that sounded more like a gasp brushed Cole's hearing, and he felt a light touch to his chest. He opened his eyes and looked at Amaris' hand moving down his stomach. But as his fingers reached the waistband of Cole's pants, Cole grabbed the shirt on Amaris' chest, and in one swift motion, swung him around, pressing his back against the shelf.

Then he lowered his face and froze, his lips less than an inch away from Amaris'. "Is that what you truly want from me, Erick?" he hissed, his hand seizing the hair on the back of Amaris' head, forcing him to look up. "You want me in your bed?"

Amaris raised his eyes, and his lips parted, his chest shuddering with short breaths.

"Yes," he breathed. "That and a lot more." The purple glow vanished, and for a heartbeat, Cole could see the true color of his eyes through the openings in his mask. They were light and foggy, drunk even. "Heaven and Earth, Cole... You have no idea how long I've been waiting to meet you in person. Ever since I captured your maker—" He closed his eyes and swallowed with effort, turning away. "I've been watching you for years, and I wish I could have it all with you, but not in this—" He cut himself off, his gaze traveling down his own body. Then he sighed and grabbed something from the shelf behind him. "For now, I just want you to hold this for me."

Before Cole could back away, Amaris thrust something into his hands. A sharp ping of magical energy rushed through him, and he recognized its energy signature. It was the same magic that he'd sensed earlier in this area, the one that called to him, fogging his mind.

With fear clawing through him, he glanced down and saw a short sword, sheathed in a beautifully crafted leather scabbard. It resembled an ancient Roman gladius, but what shocked him the most was that it looked almost the same as his own sword except for the stone embedded in the pommel. His sword had a red stone that looked like a large ruby, but this stone was a dark blue like sapphire, and it shone with a dim ultramarine light. Without giving it a second thought, he unsheathed the blade and raised it a little. A wave of warmth traveled through his arm, and he moaned, his lips parting like in ecstasy.

"I'll be damned," exhaled Amaris, taking a step to the side to put some distance between himself and the glowing blade in Cole's hands. "The sword responded to you. It's *you*... and your righteous brother... Two brothers—the Light, marked by the Darkness, and the Darkness, touched by the Light." He pressed his hand to his mouth, his eyes igniting brighter than ever. "Dammit! I was so hoping it wasn't the case..."

"What are you talking about?" asked Cole, feeling chills going through him. He sheathed the sword and offered it to Amaris, but he shook his head, raising his arm.

"Hold on to it, but don't get any bright ideas—you can't kill me with a sword. It's time we had a serious conversation, my friend," said Amaris, grabbing Cole's wrist. He turned around and headed out of the warehouse, pulling Cole with him.

* * *

Amaris didn't return to his office but ushered Cole into the same room where he spent the night with Sylvana. Not sure what to expect, Cole froze by the entrance, his fingers squeezing the scabbard of the sword. Amaris sat down on the edge of the bed and leaned forward, resting his elbows atop his knees. He covered his face with his hands and there was something so despondent in his pose that Cole's stomach twisted with dread.

Without taking his eyes off Amaris, Cole made his way to the armchair and lowered himself onto it, hoping that the weak connection with his brother in this place was still intact. He placed the sword across his lap, his fingers tracing the design on the scabbard absentmindedly.

"Mr. Amaris," he called after a while. "I would appreciate an explanation."

Amaris raised his head, his hand reaching up to readjust his mask, but then a bitter laugh escaped his lips, and he dropped his hands on his lap.

"Well, my dear, I really don't know what to tell you," he started, shaking his head, "but your position in my House has changed."

"I don't understand—," Cole started, but Amaris snapped his fingers, and invisible ropes of his magic wrapped around Cole's arms and legs, tying him to the chair. Cole gasped and pushed against the restraints, but to no avail.

"Don't struggle, Cole. It's pointless. You can't fight my magic." Amaris got up and halted in front of him, his lips pressed into a bitter straight line. "I know it's hard for you to believe, but I'm truly, sincerely sorry it has to be this way."

"If that's the way you *truly* feel, wouldn't it be easier for you to just let me go then?" Cole raised his face, meeting Amaris' eyes without blinking. "My brother will deliver on his promise. Damian is always true to his word."

"I do need your brother to come through. After all, I asked him to deliver what's rightfully mine, anyway." Amaris sighed, biting his lip. "But that is not the problem. I can't release you because I've been searching for that one very special vampire for quite some time. Unfortunately, it happened to be you." He fell silent, rubbing the stubble on his chin. "Well, not me personally, per se. I have..." He turned away, staring at the door, and when he continued, his voice sounded hoarse. "You're old enough to know that in the World of Magic, there's always someone who has power over you. I also have a master, my friend, and by capturing you, I'm just doing his bidding." He exhaled a ragged breath, his hands forming tight fists. "It pains me more than you know, but I have no choice."

"There is always a choice," replied Cole.

"You're right," Amaris agreed. "In this case, it's either your freedom or mine, and I hope you can understand why I choose my freedom over yours."

"Oh, I understand that. What else could have I expected from a low-life slaver such as yourself?" Cole tilted his head, forcing down a sick feeling. "It's everything else that I need you to explain."

Amaris nodded, a pained expression settling in his glowing eyes. Taking a step closer, he seized Cole's chin, lifting his face gently. "There is an ancient prophecy. At least, I think it's a prophecy. Something about two brothers who are destined to —" He let go of Cole's chin and twirled his wrist dismissively. "Sorry, but I didn't bother memorizing the text. All I know, is that the brothers must be immortal to fit the description. One is the Light, marked by the Darkness. The second one is the Darkness, touched by the Light. That is all I know."

"Go on," said Cole through gritted teeth.

"My master decided that it would be easier to find the second brother—the one who's the Darkness," Amaris continued with a sigh. "After years of research and exploration, he came to the conclusion that the second brother must be an ancient vampire, and this was when the real search began. We searched all over the human realm, testing every ancient male vampire we could find. I abducted Sylvana, hoping to entrap her maker, Santiago del Castillo, but he was too smart to fall for something like this, I guess. Instead, he kept sending his people. I kept catching and enslaving them, using that special Sisterhood necromancy rune, but he kept sending more until your brother captured the last one. Anyway, I had to send my people after him. I couldn't let him go back to Vegas and warn Santiago…"

Amaris paused, shoving his hands into the pockets of his pants. He stood like this for a few seconds, but since Cole said nothing, he continued, "This is why I needed powerful fighters trained to deal with vampires as easily as the Sisterhood slayers, and the main reason I wanted their infamous poison. I had to have a way to fight and subdue all these old vamps, if push came to shove. Ancient vampires are smart and insidious. You have no idea what kind of hoops I had to jump through to capture and test them."

"My heart is breaking for you," muttered Cole, narrowing his eyes.

"For three years, I held your maker captive because I was positive it was him, but I couldn't test him." Amaris chuckled, shaking his head. "Little did I know..."

"Ruslan doesn't have a brother," snapped Cole, struggling to contain the rising wave of anger.

"I had no way of knowing that," replied Amaris, "and he seemed to be righteous enough to fit the *'touched by the Light'* part."

"Why couldn't you test him?" asked Cole. "What is the test, anyway?"

"The sword you're holding is the test," replied Amaris, bending forward to touch the stone. "My master came into possession of this blade centuries ago, before we started the search. According to some old lore, this sword has a twin brother. Both used to belong to some powerful ancient deity whose name has been forgotten and who is no longer worshipped by humans. We've been looking for the second sword for ages with nothing to show.

"I don't know all their magical properties, but there is something unusual in the way these swords are forged—they react to anything unnatural in the supernatural world. You're a vampire who can wield magic—it doesn't get more unnatural than that, does it? So, the sword reacted to your magical energy." He fell silent, his purple eyes exploring Cole with fascination. "Ruslan wasn't willing to comply with my request, and you know how magic works. It's all about free will."

Cole peered down at the weapon, a disarray of thoughts

crowding his mind. "Erick," he said at length, raising his eyes. "Before you deliver me to your master, can you do me a favor and satisfy my curiosity?"

Amaris' mouth opened a little, and he took a step closer, moving like in a trance. "Cole, I'm sorry, but if you want to know who my master is, I can't tell you that. Besides, I have no idea what his true identity is. He always deals from the shadows."

"Just like you—always in that goddamn mask," Cole said bitterly, jerking his chin at Amaris. "No, that wasn't what I was going to ask you."

"What do you want to know?"

"Ricardo told us he made some kind of mistake that allowed you to learn about his plan," said Cole, relaxing his tense shoulders. "He had no idea what that was, and it's been bugging me ever since. Can you tell me what he did wrong? How did you find out?"

A shadow of sadness flew across Amaris' eyes. "I knew about your little plan quite a while before the day I entrapped Ricardo, demanding him to deliver you and your brother to me. Ricardo didn't do anything wrong. He didn't lie to you and your terrifying brute of a brother," he said. "Actually, it was your brother who made the mistake."

"I don't understand… How so?"

"To be completely honest, he didn't do anything wrong either," replied Amaris. "He stayed true to what he is, doing exactly what he's supposed to do. He couldn't have known that I have connections in all the right places."

Dammit, Dima... Who did you tell... Oh, fuck...

"Cole." Amaris' voice ripped through the veil of frenzied thoughts in Cole's mind.

"Yes?"

"I have to do something to prepare you for the meeting with my master," said Amaris, his voice trembling slightly. "I'm sorry, but it'll hurt—"

Cole laughed mirthlessly. "Wait. Don't tell me. It'll hurt you a lot more than it'll hurt me."

He could see only the bottom part of Amaris' face, but whatever skin was exposed turned ashen gray. Amaris didn't say anything but took one knee in front of Cole and started to unbutton the shirt on his chest. Cole averted his gaze, praying to all the gods he knew that Yakov's magic would hold against Amaris and his demonic powers.

Amaris pulled the shirt open, exposing Cole's chest, and placed his hand over his heart. He didn't channel his magic. Instead, he leaned closer and caressed his icy skin gently, his finger trembling.

"I'm truly sorry, *meu amigo*," he whispered into Cole's chest. "I had no idea it was going to be so hard…"

"Just spare me the drama, Amaris," growled Cole, jerking within the restraints of demonic magic. "As if I don't know what you're going to do. Go ahead, use your necromancy. You have my fucking blessing." *A demon with feelings… Someone, please stake me before I throw up…*

Amaris pulled back and placed his palm flat against his chest. The magical energy around him spiked, and the reek of pure demonic essence assailed Cole's senses. Amaris' hand grew hotter, and the pain—pure liquid torment—surged through Cole's body. He clenched his teeth, struggling not to scream, but as the potency of Amaris' spell intensified, he could hold the screams no more.

His body arched within the restraints of the dark magic like from an electric shock, and he threw his head back, a terrible howl of pain erupting from his lips. Suddenly, something inside him twitched, and a wave of different magic spread through him, repelling the darkness of necromancy. Amaris gasped and jerked away, falling on his back. He scrambled into a kneeling position, nursing his right hand as if it were burned.

Staring at Cole in awe, he started, "You are—"

"Stain-resistant, like your carpet," Cole growled, his body still shaking with strain. "You can't use necromancy on me, you evil bastard. I told you, it'll hurt you a lot more than it'll hurt me. I wasn't being sarcastic, you know?" A sardonic grin stretched his lips, and he touched the tips of his fangs with his tongue. "So, if you want to deliver me to your master, lover, you'll have to do it as is—in all my unnatural vampiric glory."

Amaris got up to his feet, his arms hanging along his sides, his fingers locking and unlocking.

"You…" he whispered, panting. "You have no idea what you're talking about! Don't judge! You know nothing about me."

"Are you kidding me?" Cole hissed, his voice getting softer. "You're a low-life demon! What else do I need to know?"

"And you're a vampire!" yelled Amaris, his voice rising to a high-pitched shrill. "An undead leech without a heartbeat, incapable of love or affection or any true feelings. All you know is thirst and lust!"

Cole growled, fighting against his restraints. Amaris dropped on the bed, as if he suddenly ran out of steam.

"Cole, I'm sorry. I'm a little upset," he said, his voice a hoarse whisper. "You wanted to see me without this mask?" He reached up and placed his hand over his face. "Except for one person, no one has seen my true form for centuries, and I'm tired of living like this. For the first time in so many years, I've met a man who…" He shook his head, and there was so much pain and bitterness in his move that Cole stiffened with his lips parted. "I hate myself and this illusion I'm forced to keep up day in and day out to hide who I truly am. I just want you to know that… I want you to see the real me before I have to…" His voice trembled and broke, and he turned away. "So, here I am…"

He pulled the mask off, and the air around him shimmered, a thick veil of dark, purple mist wrapping around him. When the mist dissipated, Cole lifted his face and gasped, his eyes widening.

"Oh... my... God..." he whispered, reaching through his blood bond to Damian.

CHAPTER 26

~ DAMIAN BLAKE ~

"Are you…" Damian stared at the man, flabbergasted. "Are you a Destiny Enforcer?"

"Yes, Commander," the man replied, rising. "My name is Petrukha, and I'm the Shadow Enforcer to Lord Ulric Aramir."

"To Lord Aramir?" echoed Damian in disbelief, scratching the back of his head. "When did you have your last communication with your master?"

The man glanced around, and a shadow of doubt crossed his face. "Commander, I'm sorry, but it's getting late, and we should get back into the palace. In the last few days, the Isle has been attacked by all sorts of demonic entities, and I can't figure out what's going on. The Sacred Isle is supposed to be the safest place in the Land of Dreams." He furrowed his brow, raking his fingers through the mess of his gray hair, and then gestured at the gates. "Please, follow me. We can continue our conversation inside the safety of these walls."

Damian followed Petrukha and his men through the gates and halted, observing his surroundings with interest. Steep-roofed houses built in the early Muscovite architectural style encircled a large city square. A single road, paved with light cobblestones, led toward the large palace, its white walls and five golden domes prominent even in the darkness of the evening.

Petrukha motioned for Damian and Jamie to follow and headed toward the palace, walking briskly with his left hand resting on the hilt of his sword. He didn't slow down until he reached the stone steps leading toward the tall, double door of the palace. Giving quick orders to his men, he pushed the door open and bowed, pressing his fist to his chest.

"Lord Commander," he said, straightening. "Welcome to my domain."

"Are you the Lord of the Isle?" asked Damian, confused. "How can a Destiny Enforcer, let alone a Shadow Enforcer, become the Lord of the Sacred Isle?"

"Patience, Lord Commander." Petrukha smiled, his smile accentuating deep wrinkles around his eyes. "I promise to explain everything as soon as we sit down and relax."

"I have plenty of patience," muttered Damian, following Petrukha through a large hall with walls decorated by ancient frescos. "It's time that I don't have. Please, help us find what we came for, and we'll be out of your hair."

Petrukha ran up the stairs and marched through a wide but poorly illuminated hallway, which opened into another spacious hall. He halted in front of a white door, decorated with gold-plated ornaments. Placing his hand on the golden door handle, he pushed it open and stepped aside, allowing Damian and Jamie to walk through first.

The room wasn't large, and unlike the rest of the palace, it was decorated with the modesty and laconism of a warrior. A narrow bed stood by the wall, and a large table surrounded by four chairs took the center of the room. A single half-burned candle sat on the table, illuminating the space with its unsteady, orange light, and the light scent of melted wax and smoke permeated the air. A thick book, opened in the middle, lay next to the candle.

"Take a seat," offered Petrukha, pulling one of the chairs out. "Can I get you anything to eat or drink?" His eyes darted from Damian to Jamie, and he raised his sandy eyebrows, expecting their answer.

Damian exchanged a quick look with Jamie and shook his head. "No, thank you. We truly are in a rush."

He headed toward the table and placed his hand on the back of a chair, ready to pull it out, when the world tilted and spun around him. A wave of urgency, followed by happiness and then deep despair flooded his mind through the blood bond with Cole. Damian groaned and leaned forward, bracing his arms against the table.

"Cole?" He carefully probed their bond and immediately received another overpowering wave of emotions—this time of shock and fear. *"Brother, are you okay?"*

"No." The response came right away, but Cole's voice was coming through with strange interferences. *"I'm in trouble, Dima. You need to come back as soon as you can."*

Damian's heart halted in his chest, cold sweat beading his forehead. Cole would never ask him to come if he wasn't in a truly dangerous situation he couldn't resolve on his own.

"What's going on?" he asked, barely able to breathe.

"Amaris is not who we think he is," said Cole, speaking so fast that his words blended together. *"He is not even... a m—"* Cole's voice broke and disappeared just to reappear a couple of seconds later. *"Dima, besides River, Jamie and me, who did you speak with about your agreement with Ricardo?"*

"Why?"

"Figure out—these people are—you can't trust them," Cole continued, his voice breaking and disappearing. *"—works for Amaris—knew a few months before..."*

Dammit... Damian cursed in his mind and projected to his

brother, *"I should be back shortly. I found the place, and I just need to find the item. Hang in there, little bro."*

"Dima, Amaris said—the item he asked—to deliv—belongs to him, anyway..." Cole's voice wavered and vanished.

"Cole?"

There was no answer. Damian probed the blood bond again, but it was gone.

"Dammit!" He slammed his hand against the table, making the candle jump up a little.

"Damian, what's going on?" asked Jamie, staring at him with concern.

"I just spoke with Cole. He's in trouble. We don't have time, Jamie. I have to go back as soon as possible." Damian pulled the chair out and sat down heavily. Switching his attention to Petrukha he said, "I need your help, Lord of the Isle."

Petrukha frowned, regarding Damian with blunt curiosity. "Fine," he said, folding his arms atop the table. "Let's start by you telling me who the both of you are and why you are here."

"This is Jamie Coldwell, a wizard," said Damian with a light wave of his hand in Jamie's direction. "I'm Commander Damian Blake, the Shadow Enforcer to Lord Magnus."

"Whoa… Hold on a second. Lord Magnus?" Petrukha asked, his eyebrows rising. "When I visited the Destiny Council realm the last time, Magnus was just the Master Commander in charge of the Destiny Enforcers."

"I guess you've been here for a while," muttered Damian, pursing his lips into a firm line. "Let me give you a quick overview. Lord Ulric Aramir is no longer in charge. He's been convicted of manipulating the Board of Destiny. Magnus is the Head of the Destiny Council now, one of the top three."

Petrukha pressed his hand to his mouth, and his eyes widened. "I understand you're running out of time, so tell me the details later," he exhaled after a moment. "In the meantime, tell me why you are here, Commander Blake."

"I was ordered to go there—I don't know where, and find that—I don't know what," said Damian, cringing at how habitual saying this strange riddle had become to him. "My quest brought me to the Sacred Isle, and I hope you can tell what this *'I don't know what'* is."

Petrukha rose slowly, the blood draining off his round face. "Who sent you?"

"It's complicated—"

"Then uncomplicate it, Commander," snapped Petrukha, suddenly tense, his fingers squeezing the edge of the table until his knuckles turned white, "or you will leave my domain empty-handed."

Damian frowned, swallowing with effort. Cole's voice—unsteady and troubled—surfaced in his memory, and he bit his lip, pinching the bridge of his nose. Making a split-second decision, he told Petrukha everything that happened since he met the Head of the Arizona House.

"You had to leave your brother behind with that monster…" Petrukha shook his head. "I thought with time the Destiny Council would grow more humane."

Damian chuckled mirthlessly. "No, you didn't."

"No, I did not," Petrukha echoed his words airily, his eyes going foggy like that of a person deep in his thoughts. Then he grunted and asked, "Do you know who this Head of the Arizona House is?"

"No," replied Damian, "but apparently my brother does, and whoever Amaris is, he is not what he appears to be. Also, Cole said that the item I was supposed to retrieve from the Sacred Isle was something that used to belong to Amaris. Any ideas?"

Petrukha got up heavily, his face a sickly green. Moving his chair back with a loud screech, he slowly made his way to the only window. He halted there and pushed a curtain aside, staring at the dark street.

"Petrukha?" called Damian. "I'm sorry, but I have no time for intermissions. If you know something, you need to tell me now."

"My karma finally caught up with me," he whispered, turning around. "Everything that is happening to you and your brother is my fault."

"Please explain," said Damian, leaning back in his chair.

"The name Amaris. Do you know what it means?" asked Petrukha, clenching his hands.

"No." Damian glanced at Jamie, but the wizard just shook his head with a bewildered shrug.

"There are two meanings to this name. One of them is *a child of the moon*," whispered Petrukha. "Her choice of the name and your brother's message about the item belonging to her, made it all clear."

"Her? Amaris is a man," objected Damian, his chest constricted with the expectation of the next troubling news. "I haven't seen him close enough or without his mask, but I'm positive he's a man."

Petrukha exhaled, shaking his head. "She was always the best master of illusions," he whispered, returning to the table. He sat down, placing his clenched hands on the table. "I assure you, Commander, the dark entity you're dealing with is a woman, and I'm the one who made the mistake that brought all of us here."

CHAPTER 27

~ DAMIAN BLAKE ~

For a moment, Damian stared at Petrukha, unable to speak as a wave of fear and frustration bubbled up in him. "You made a mistake?" he finally managed to say. "When Destiny Enforcers make mistakes, people die. What kind of mistake did you make?"

"I've been punished plenty for it, Commander." Petrukha sighed, rubbing his forehead, his shoulders slumped. "But trust me, no one can punish me worse than I punish myself every single goddamn day since the moment I learned the truth."

"I'm sorry." Damian swallowed, looking away. "Those who live in glass houses shouldn't throw stones. Please, continue."

"It was the year sixteen eighty-nine," Petrukha started, his voice so raspy it was barely audible. "I was stationed in Selo Preobrazhenskoye, shadowing my charge, Tsar Peter the Great. I was posing as the constantly drunk jester, but people thought me to be the Holy Fool—*yurodivy*—which made it easier for me to get close to the young Tsar.

"He was just a teenage boy at the time, but his future had been written all over the Board of Destiny from the moment he was born. His sister, Tsarevna Sophia Alekseyevna, was a smart and educated woman of her time, but she fell under the influence of a beautiful Portuguese actress, Donna Luna. The first time I laid my eyes on this actress, I knew she had dark magic, but no matter what I tried, I couldn't break her influence on the Tsarevna.

"At first, I thought she was just another dark witch, but soon I realized it wasn't the case. Careful and cunning, it was practically impossible for me to get close to her. Besides, even though she didn't recognize the Destiny Enforcer in me, I was positive she knew I was a wizard, and she made sure to conceal her energy signature any time I was around."

He stopped talking, as if every word caused him physical pain, and frowned, two deep wrinkles appearing between his eyebrows.

"Skip the details. Get to the point," said Damian through gritted teeth.

"Anyway, after a few months of trying to uncover her supernatural identity, I came to the conclusion that she was a Master of the Dark Arts, but I could also sense some demonic powers in her, which at the time, I couldn't explain." Petrukha shook his head, pressing his hand to his eyes. "I couldn't have been more wrong..."

He got up and walked toward the bed where he lay down on the floor and reached under it. When he got up again, he held a small silver box, its former shine tarnished by the years.

"As Donna Luna moved forward with her plan, I had to do whatever it took to protect my charge and enforce the proper course of Destiny," he continued, lowering the box on the table between himself and Damian. "The problem was, I was acting under the wrong assumption. When the sorceress made her next move, I confronted her. While I managed to stop some parts of her plan from being executed, saving the lives of quite a few people in the process, I couldn't have predicted..."

His voice trailed off, and he touched the box, sending a burst of his magic through it. The lid cracked opened, and he reached inside, pulling out two pieces of a broken mask that were bedazzled with shards of a mirror. Damian sucked in a sharp breath as a wave of powerful magic emanating from the mask touched his senses. Even without opening his other sight, he could detect the darkness in its energy signature.

"What is it?" Jamie reached for the mask, but Damian grabbed his hand, stopping him.

Petrukha laughed softly, kindness shining in his light eyes. "Yeah, don't touch it, young one," he said, glancing at Jamie. "I don't think it can hurt you, but it's better to be safe than sorry."

"What is it?" Damian repeated Jamie's question. "I sense its magical energy signature. It's dark."

"It's dark because it was enchanted to keep the Darkness under control," explained Petrukha, pointing at the mask. "You see all these pieces of mirror? Some of them are shards of the long-lost Hyperborean mirror."

"Are you kidding me?" Jamie exhaled breathlessly, his eyes shining with wonderment. "Are you saying Hyperborea is real?"

Petrukha glanced at Damian, a corner of his mouth lifting into a lopsided smile. "He truly is as young as he looks." He jerked his thumb at Jamie.

"Even younger than that," muttered Damian, switching his attention to Jamie. "Everything is real, my friend."

"Yes, Hyperborea exists," confirmed Petrukha. "Ancient Greek philosophers disagreed about the location of this mystical place, naming a few different areas. What they didn't know was that Hyperborea never stays in one place for a prolonged period of time. It moves, not unlike my Sacred Isle, and just like my domain, it harbors great and dangerous magical powers. The shards of Hyperborean mirror hold some of that power in them."

Petrukha averted his gaze, his fingers tracing the shape of the ornaments decorating the silver box absentmindedly.

"Anyway," he continued at length, "when I detected the traces of Hyperborean magic, I realized that as a Master of the Dark Arts, she was skilled in evocation, necromancy and other forbidden branches of dark magic. I was positive she used the magic of the mirror to channel demonic powers. So, logically, I thought that if I destroyed the mask, I would sever her connection with the demon, and that would allow me to kill her, using the purifying light of Creation."

"I would have probably assumed the same thing," Damian murmured with a light shrug.

"Yes, seemed logical to me at the time," Petrukha said. "So, in the heat of the fight, I managed to rip the mask off her face and break it, severing her connection with the demon—or so I thought. When she tried to run, I saw the visage of the demon hovering over her, and it was terrifying… Nevertheless, I caught up with her and set her ablaze, catalyzing the fire with the purifying light of Creation. As I expected, unable to channel the demonic powers, she burned, but before she perished, she shouted that I won the battle, but I lost the war, and her words stuck with me."

"What did you do next?" asked Jamie, shifting closer.

"I did what any Destiny Enforcer would do," replied Petrukha. "After I made sure my charge was alive and well, I took the box with the mask to the Destiny Council realm and reported everything that happened to my master and the High Council. I also told them about the sorceress' last words and asked them to launch a full investigation into her affiliations and magical background. At first, Lord Aramir dismissed my concerns, but since the other two members of the High Council wanted to investigate, he had no choice but to agree.

"The investigation took a while. The best wizards of the Wardens Order explored the mask and when they finally announced the results of their research, I wished I were dead…" His voice morphed into a pregnant pause, and he pressed the heels of his hands to his eyes. Exhaling a ragged breath, he continued, "To make a long story short, most of my assumptions were wrong, and instead of fixing the situation, I made everything a lot worse."

"What did the Wardens find out?" asked Damian, shivering as if the temperature in the room had dropped by a few degrees.

"As I suspected, Donna Luna was an ancient sorceress. Channeling her magic from the moon, she was a gifted Master of the Dark Arts with quite a few unusual powers in her arsenal," continued Petrukha. "I was wrong, however, when I thought she was just channeling demonic powers. She wasn't. She made a deal with a demon, a Guard of Hell most likely. What I also didn't know was that her deal backfired. She overestimated her abilities, and her power alone wasn't enough to keep that high-level abomination of Hell under control. When she realized her mistake, she used the Hyperborean magic to stop the monster from ascending to its full power in the human realm. Basically, she locked the demonic entity inside her body, binding it with the magic of the Hyperborean mirror."

"Oh, dammit…" Damian muttered under his breath as understanding dawned on him. "So, you broke the mask and released the demonic entity she summoned from some twisted demonic realm into the world of humans."

"Yeah, that's exactly what happened." Petrukha nodded slowly, visibly struggling with his relentless guilt.

"But what happened to that… whatchamacallit… Donna Luna?" asked Jamie. "Did she actually die in the fire?"

"No, she didn't die," replied Petrukha at length. "I believe the contract with that monster made her immortal. As long as the demon is alive, she can't die. As long as she's alive, the demon won't stop searching for her. The Destiny Council sent a few teams to search for the demon I had released, but they couldn't find it anywhere, neither could they find Donna Luna herself. So they hoped that both had left the realm of humans."

"Nice," muttered Damian, shaking his head. "Some high-level demon is rampaging all over the world, searching for her, while she's hiding in some underground bunker." He rubbed his forehead, feeling a throbbing pain manifesting in his temples. His thoughts returned to Cole, and he closed his eyes, thinking of his brother's desperate situation. "So, why are you here, Petrukha? How did you become the Lord of the Isle?"

He averted his eyes, his fingers clasped together so tightly, his knuckles turned white. "I was punished, Commander. It was time to replace the old Lord of the Isle, and the High Council sent me here to take over the position. I've been here ever since. You're the first person from the Destiny Council realm who's spoken with me since that time. Being here… all alone… thinking about what I did and unable to do anything about it… That's the worst kind of punishment."

Damian grunted, clenching his teeth. "So, what does the second part of the riddle mean? *'Bring me that—I don't know what'*," he asked, changing the subject. "What exactly does she want me to bring to her?"

Petrukha chuckled. "Me," he said with a half-shrug, as if it were the most obvious thing in the world. "She wants her Hyperborean mirror and me, so she can bind that demon and harness its powers again. But to do that, she needs her mask and the blood of the person who broke it." He took the broken mask and put it back into the silver box, sealing it. "As far as the weird riddle, I can explain the meaning of it. Since the location of this Isle is constantly changing, Slavic lore calls it *'I don't know where'*. The same principle applies to the entity who protects the Isle—the Lord of the Isle. This position is never filled by a human. It could be any being of magic, not necessarily a person—hence *'you don't know what'*."

"Well, Petrukha," said Damian, rising, "you're coming with me. I'm not leaving my brother in the hands of an evil Master of the Dark Arts with demonic tendencies. Besides, it's about time you had a chance to fix that mistake and move on with your life."

"You're not going to—," Petrukha started, but Damian shook his head, a dark smile on his lips.

"Of course not," he replied calmly. "But I need your help. Donna Luna sent me here to find you and her mask, holding my brother's life as a bargaining chip. On the other hand, I have orders from the Destiny Council to find out what she wants, retrieve it and deliver it to any of their holding facilities." He paused, staring out the window. "If I do that, Donna Luna will kill my brother and a few other people who deserve better. So, if you agree to help me, I will deliver her what she wants, but not in the way she wants me to do it." He peered down at Petrukha, raising his eyebrows. "So, what is it going to be, Enforcer?"

"I wish I could go with you, Commander." Petrukha got up, his mouth set in a hard, angry line. "I wish I could finally put it all behind me, but I can't leave the Isle. As long as I'm the Lord, I'm bound to it."

"Oh, God damn it all…" Damian pressed his hands to his eyes and then ran them up, through his hair.

"Can you transfer your… um… Lordship?" asked Jamie, his eyes darting from Damian to Petrukha.

"To whom? I have a few men here, but they're all humans exposed to the World of Magic." Petrukha shrugged. "Unless the Destiny Council sends a replacement, I have no one to transfer my power to."

Jamie raised his eyes at Damian, and Damian's heart skipped a beat as he realized what the young man was about to propose. With a shake of his head, he took a step closer to him, but Jamie raised his hand, stopping him.

"To me," he said, his voice calm and firm. "Transfer your position to me and go with Damian. I'm not going to let this evil bitch kill Cole or endanger any of my friends. Once you're done, we can switch back, right?" A heavy silence enveloped the room. Jamie moved closer to Petrukha, placing his hand on his shoulder. "Can we switch back later?"

Petrukha nodded, a muscle twitching in his jaw. "Yes, we can," he replied, his voice raspier than before. "I'll have to prepare you for the transfer of power. It's not going to take long." He threw a veiled glance at Damian. "Once you receive the power, you will also receive some secret knowledge, so I need you to swear that anything you learn here, you will never repeat anywhere else. Swear to me." He pointed at the dagger sheathed at Jamie's belt. "Swear on your power, young wizard." He switched his attention to Damian, giving him a puzzled stare. "Did you teach him how to swear properly?"

Damian nodded, his throat too tight to speak. Like in a slow, feverish nightmare, he watched Jamie unsheathe his dagger and lower to one knee, placing the tip of the blade on the floor.

"I swear on my power that anything I learn here, I will keep a secret, protecting the sacred knowledge with my life," said Jamie, clearly pronouncing every word. Then he got up slowly and turned toward Damian, furrowing his brow. "Damian, tell Cole—"

"You tell him whatever you want to say yourself, Jamie. I *will* come back for you. Now that I know what I need to do, it's not going to take long." Damian took a step closer to the young man and pulled him into a quick hug, giving him a light tap on his back. "Thank you, my friend. I owe you one."

CHAPTER 28

~ DAMIAN BLAKE ~

The transition didn't take long, and as Damian watched Jamie assume the position as the Lord of the Sacred Isle, his chest tightened, numbness spreading through his arms. More than half of his long life, he had spent alone, but in the last few years, he had found his brother, and he had been surrounded by people who actually sincerely cared about him. Despite the Destiny Enforcers' rules, he had gotten attached to them, loving them in the way only a deeply lonely soul could love those who showed him true kindness.

Even though he knew he wasn't leaving Jamie in this strange Isle forever, he couldn't get rid of the feeling that he was losing all the people he cared about, one by one, and there was nothing he could do to stop it. He wasn't afraid to face Donna Luna. A Master of the Dark Arts or a demoness—he didn't care what she was and what kind of powers she had in her possession. He had gotten used to fighting evil in all sorts of shapes and forms every day of his life. He had lost battles before. He had made plenty of mistakes. But this was a battle he couldn't afford to lose.

No doubts.

No fear.

No hesitation.

Today, he couldn't afford any of that.

"I'm ready, Commander." Petrukha's voice brought him back from his heavy thoughts, and Damian flinched, raising his head.

"Give me that damn box," said Damian through clenched teeth, barely recognizing the icy, hoarse sound in his voice. Petrukha hesitated for a moment, but then took the box and gave it to Damian, throwing a shocked gaze at Jamie.

Damian touched the box with his fingers, whispering a short spell. It lit up with the bright, white light of his magic. The light spread through his arm, slowly dwindling, and when it was gone so was the box. Damian grunted and braced his hands against the table, leaning heavily on it until the last traces of pain inflicted by his magic vanished.

Then he put his hand on Petrukha's shoulder and gave Jamie a short nod. "I'll see you soon, Jamie."

He snapped his fingers and vanished from the Sacred Isle, taking Petrukha with him.

* * *

It was past midnight when Damian materialized on the steps of Paradise Manor. He glanced around, taking a deep breath. The familiar scents of the desert and the loud shrills of cicadas and crickets invaded his senses, and despite the severity of the situation, a tiny smile tugged at his lips. This place was his home, and he loved everything about it, but right now, he had no time to relax and enjoy it. If Donna Luna truly had someone in his circle who worked for her, he needed to be fast, executing his plan before she could find out that he was back.

Cole said she had known about his and Ricardo's plan a few months before they were forced to meet with the Head of the Arizona House for the first time. Damian frowned, nibbling on his lip. There were only a few people he could trust unconditionally, and all of them lived in this house.

He ran up the steps, gesturing for Petrukha to follow him, and unlocked the door, stepping into the cool darkness of the foyer. The antique silver mirror lit up with a soft white light, and he approached it, gently brushing his fingers over the frame. Petrukha's reflection materialized next to his, and Damian felt some relief, confirming what he thought originally—he could trust the old Enforcer.

"Thank you." He nodded at his own reflection, and for a brief moment, the shadow of a beautiful young woman with braided, blonde hair manifested in front of him. The Zerkalitsa nodded to him, sending him an air kiss, and vanished.

"You have your own Zerkalitsa?" asked Petrukha, but as his voice bounced from wall to wall in a continuous, whispering echo, he winced. "What the hell?"

"Welcome to Paradise Manor," Damian murmured and headed toward the hallway on his right, waving for Petrukha to follow.

The kitchen was dark and empty. He found the light switch on his right and flipped it on. To his surprise, Gypsy was sleeping on the counter by the coffee machine, her long, bushy tail covering her nose. She lifted her head, blinking at him sleepily, and a wide feline grin appeared on her face.

"Well, hello, stranger," she purred, stretching her paws toward him lazily. *"How convenient. I was just thinking that I needed some entertainment."*

"Is River asleep?" Damian asked, holding his breath while expecting Gypsy's answer.

"No, she's not home. They called her to work about an hour ago," she replied, rolling her green eyes. *"What is it with you humans and work? You are doing it all wrong. As far as I am concerned, working one day a week is more than enough. The rest of the week should be considered a weekend."* She rose to her feet and arched

her back with a large yawn. *"Just make sure, it's not a Monday. I hate the Monday blues."*

"I assume you're talking to this cat?" asked Petrukha, staring at him with curiosity.

"No, you village simpleton," replied Gypsy, jumping off the counter. *"The cat is talking to him. Peasants don't speak to us Queens unless they're spoken to. Where do you find your friends, Sasquatch?"*

"I'm a Child of Earth," Damian said, suppressing a burst of laughter which came out in a loud snort. "I'd love to show you around, but we don't have time, Petrukha. Let's get straight to business."

"Sorry," he mumbled, spreading his arms. "It's been years since I was locked up on that cursed Isle. I'm just enjoying the freedom, as short-lived as it may be."

Damian nodded and channeled his magic, directing it to his hands. Then he drew a rune in the air and whispered a summoning spell, calling to Zabava. A heartbeat later, the rune was replaced by the vortex of a portal, and Zabava stepped out of it, her unnaturally green eyes halting on Damian and then darting to Petrukha.

"I see you found what you've been looking for, Commander," she said. She pulled a chair out and sat down, leaning back with her legs spread wide in a man-like manner.

"Oh, my God!" squealed Gypsy. *"The Goddess of all Kitchens is here!"* She hopped on Zabava's lap, and she couldn't help but smile, her fingers threading through Gypsy's long fur with affection.

Damian pressed his hand to his mouth, trying not to laugh. He leaned against the counter, folding his arms.

"Zabava, I need your help," he said, all mirth gone. He briefed her in on all the latest events and some details of his plan. "I need to block the entire Downtown Phoenix. I want this whole area to be a magicless void. Can you help me get it done?"

"The entire Downtown Phoenix," muttered Zabava, shaking

her head. "I knew you were a crazy SOB, but I didn't realize how truly crazy you were. What you want to do hasn't been done in centuries. What makes you think something like this is even possible?"

"I know it's possible because I've experienced this kind of magic on my own self," he replied, telling her the same story he had told Jamie on his way across the Sacred Isle. "If some Carpathian witches could do something like this, I'm sure we can recreate the spell."

"Wait... what?" Zabava stared at him for a moment and then burst out laughing. "On yourself?" She slapped her hands on her thighs, shaking her head.

Damian glowered at her, feeling the heat rising to his cheeks. "Zabava," he growled, but she just waved her hand, wiping tears of laughter off her eyes.

"Oh, come on, Damian," she sang once she could speak again. "I had no idea you were one of those two unfortunate Destiny Enforcers who got disabled by a *Hutsuls* covenant. You have to admit, they had you by the balls. I have no idea how you managed to get away, magicless and all."

Damian threw his arms up. "I have no time for entertainment, Zabava. Can you do it or not?"

"He never has time for anything good, Zabava. Just ignore him," purred Gypsy, stretching under Zabava's fingers. *"Once a Sasquatch, always a Sasquatch."*

Zabava sobered up and frowned, her fingers drumming on the table absentmindedly. "I've heard this story," she said, now completely serious. "Those witches still brag about it. The problem is, they summoned and trapped two high-level demons for a short time, just enough to power that spell. Not just any demons—the Guards of Hell, I believe." She shook her head, nibbling on her lip. "Besides, using the demonic essence was the only way they could have cursed you in a territory void of magical energy."

"I can't summon demons. That is out of the question," Damian snapped, but then raised his hands apologetically. "Any other ideas?"

"The power of two Guards of Hell would be close enough to the power of two gods, at least..." mused Zabava. "Well, I'm a goddess. Do you know any other gods who'd be willing to work for you?"

"All gods hate Destiny Enforcers," muttered Petrukha, pulling a chair out to sit down.

"Tell me something new. No one is comfortable around Destiny Enforcers." Zabava shrugged her shoulders nonchalantly. "Present company not excluded."

"Oh, come on, Zabava." Gypsy slipped to the floor, liquid and soundless like all felines, and circled Damian's legs, settling by his feet. *"Maybe he is a Destiny Enforcer, but he is my Enforcer, and I love him. You know how it is... We get used to our pets, and they become like members of the family... sor-r-r-ta..."*

Damian stared at the cat, flabbergasted, thousands of thoughts rushing through his mind at once. Then he raked his hand through his hair, covering his face, and got up.

"I think I know someone who can help. But get ready, Zabava. It may come as a shock," he said, channeling his power.

Whispering a summoning spell, he drew a glowing orange rune using his elemental power and pressed his hand over it, completing the summons. Before he finished the last word of the spell, a woman, short and slender, materialized next to him in swirls of dark mist. Her large, black eyes halted on Damian, and a slow, alluring smile stretched her full lips. Approaching him, she placed her hand on his chest and tilted her head back as if she was looking at a high-rise.

"Well, hello, lover," she purred, long strands of her black hair moving in soft waves around her. "You summoned me. I'm stunned."

"Not as much as I am," Zabava snapped, jolting to her feet. "Damian, are you out of your fucking mind? She's a dark deity. A goddess of Nightmares! What the fuck were you thinking, man?"

Damian raised his hands, asking Zabava to calm down, and looked at the goddess of Nightmares. "Mara, I need your help," he said flatly.

"Hmm, wouldn't be the first time." She chuckled softly, her long fingernail, covered in something resembling black nail polish, drawing circles on his chest. "What can I do for you?"

"Before I tell you what I need," said Damian, removing her hand off his chest, "I wanted to mention that I spoke with Veles about your situation, and he told me exactly what I need to do to get you home."

"You are not lying, Damian?" she exhaled, her pale complexion turning almost blue. "You wouldn't lie about something like that, would you?"

He took one knee before her and placed her hand on his forehead. "Read my mind, Mara. I know you can see my thoughts if I let you in," he offered. "I'd never use something like this just to get you to do my bidding." She removed her hand, and he got up. "The reason I'm telling you this, is so in case you agree to help me, you won't play any games and do exactly what I need you to do."

"You got yourself a deal, Enforcer," replied Mara. "Tell me what you need."

Damian turned to Zabava, motioning for her to explain. With a shake of her head and a deep sigh, Zabava told Mara what needed to be done. The dark goddesses' face lit up with mischief, and she hopped in place, clapping her hands like a little girl.

"Aw, sounds like so much fun." She turned to Damian, cocking her head. "But darling, to complete this incantation, you need five people. They don't need to be gods, but they must have powerful magic. Do you have anyone who's crazy enough to do something like this?"

Damian stifled a sigh. Normally, he would summon Luc de la Crosse or Cossack, but in the given situation, he couldn't trust anyone who knew about his plans. As much as he hated to think that Luc or Adrian could betray him, he couldn't take the chance. He couldn't use Yakov Bruce either for the same reason—the old eagle was involved with the Wardens. He needed someone who knew nothing about his plans for infiltrating the Arizona underground fighting House, going back a few months.

"Zabava, summon Grand Master Elony," he said quietly. "She's a powerful mage. Her magic should be enough."

"She hates your guts, Damian," Zabava objected.

"Maybe so, but if she helps me break into the underground bunker, she'll find her fake slayers and the missing witches. Isn't that what she wants?" asked Damian.

"You know your brother is a vamp, and it's—," Zabava started.

"And please make sure Grand Master Elony knows that if she so much as looks at Cole the wrong way, she'll die a slow and painful death," replied Damian dryly, his mouth set in a grim line.

Mara cackled, dancing in place. "That's my boy. I've yet to make a Dark Enforcer out of you."

"Dream on," grumbled Damian at Mara, eliciting a downpour of giggles out of her. He glanced at her reproachfully and switched his attention to Zabava. "Please, Zabava. I don't have time to argue with you."

"Fine." Zabava turned away and drew a rune in the air, using her magic.

Damian didn't wait for her to complete her summons and channeled his magic again, conjuring another rune. He pressed his hand over it and whispered, "Archmage Allerton, I summon thee."

He didn't expect it to happen so fast, but a swirling portal opened up almost immediately, and a man in glasses with a thick mop of graying hair stepped out of it. He readjusted his glasses, his attentive eyes slipping from one face to the next. As his gaze reached Mara, his jaw dropped. Switching his attention to Damian, he waved his hand in Mara's direction.

"I do hope you have a reasonable explanation for all this"—he waved his hand around—"including the presence of the dark Slavic deity in this room," he said, pursing his lips.

"Thank you for answering my call, Archmage." Damian inclined his head in a respectful bow. "Give me a moment, please, sir. I just need to summon one more person. I do have an explanation, and I promise to make everything clear."

"It better be a good one, Enforcer," growled Grand Master Elony, approaching them. She placed her hands on her hips, tapping her foot, her gray eyes sparkling with annoyance.

"Ma'am." Damian raked her with an icy stare and turned away, channeling his elemental power. Despite his effort to control it, his suppressed aggravation fueled by concern for the entire situation took over, and the floor trembled slightly, making the dishes in the cabinets jingle.

He drew a rune in the air and pressed his hand over it, infusing it with the elemental energy of Earth. "Oleg Svetlov," he whispered, "I summon thee."

He expected a communication window to open, and it did flicker on and off before disappearing. A heartbeat later, Oleg materialized next to him with a light pop. He glanced around without showing any surprise and inclined his head, greeting everyone. Then he turned to Damian, and his face relaxed.

"You called?" he asked, raising his eyebrows. Damian nodded. He didn't expect Oleg to travel from Kendral with no questions asked, but Oleg just shrugged, as if reading his thoughts, and added, sounding all business, "I thought you wouldn't call me because you had nothing better to do. So, here I am. What can I do for you?"

"Oh, Heaven, Earth and all the stars," mumbled Mara, making a slow circle around Oleg, her fingers brushing his backside. Once she completed the circle, she turned toward Damian. "Damian, are all Children of Earth this tall? You with your giant friend by your side make an unforgettable view."

"No," replied Oleg, not without sarcasm. "Most of us are actually dwarfs."

Damian sent a pointed stare at Mara, and she raised her hands in a placating manner, giggling.

"Okay, now that we're all here, I can explain what's going on, and why I summoned you," started Damian. He explained the situation and his plan, carefully gauging the reaction of all present in the room to every word he said. Once he finished, for a short while no one said a word, an identical expression of bewilderment on all faces.

Grand Master Elony spoke up first.

"It's crazy dangerous," she said, her unnatural light eyes dimming slightly. "Commander Blake, I understand that blocking magic in the Downtown area is the only way you can bring down the defensive spells and wards placed on the underground bunker and teleport directly inside. But come on!" She threw her hands up. "As soon as you and your Enforcer cross into the enchanted territory, you will lose your magic and your elemental power. You'll be human. Even less than human because without your connection with your element, you'll be as weak as a child."

"I know," replied Damian calmly, "but so will Donna Luna."

"You don't know that," objected Archmage Allerton. "If she retained any demonic powers in her after the mask was broken —which I believe she did—she will still have some of the demonic essence in her. She will lose her magical abilities, but not the demonic ones."

"Very true," agreed Damian calmly. "But my brother, his maker and Sylvana are powerful ancient vampires, and they're not going to lose what comes with their nature. I also count on their help."

"Wait, Commander. You have a hole the size of the Grand Canyon in your plan. How are you going to get there?" asked the Archmage. "I understand that you don't know the location of the underground bunker, and you're planning to teleport almost blindly, aiming at the location of your brother, which you sense through your blood bond. Once you lose your magic, you can't teleport, and opening a portal into an unknown location is impossible."

"I think I have a solution." Zabava got up, observing everyone in the room. "Both Damian and Petrukha will lose their magic, which will make them weaker, but if Damian keeps his elemental energy, he can use his other sight and teleport. He won't need a potion to open a portal. All we have to do is modify the original spell just a little to allow him to keep his elemental power."

Zabava walked to the counter and grabbed the notepad and pen River always kept there. She scribbled something quickly and ripped the page off, offering it to Archmage Allerton. His eyes darted from side to side as he read every word, nodding with approval.

"Brilliant." He bowed to Zabava, returning the page to her. "You're just as wise as your parents, my lady."

"I'm brilliant," she whispered into Damian's ear as she passed by him, returning to the counter. She tore four more pages and wrote the modified spell on each of them. Then she made a circle around the room, giving one of the pages to each person present.

Once done, she halted by the table and muttered something under her breath, her green eyes igniting with the magical energy she was wielding. The surface of the table rippled, waves spreading through it as if it were liquid, and then turned into a large map of Downtown Phoenix and some of the surrounding areas. She touched the five points of the map, and bright red flags materialized in each place she touched.

"To complete this spell, we have to create a ginormous pentagram." She moved her hand over the map and thin, glowing lines connected the five flags, creating a large pentagram that encapsulated the entire Downtown. She glanced at Mara, her lips curling in distaste. "Mara, you'll need to be here, and I will take this point." She touched two flags on the map. "This position will allow our godly powers to spread evenly over the area."

"Agreed," replied Mara without her usual snideness.

"Grand Master Elony, Archmage Allerton and Oleg will take these points," continued Zabava, pointing at the three flags on the map. She looked around the room, thinking. "We need some kind of signal… We must start chanting at the same time, but we'll be separated by miles."

"I'll give you a signal," said Damian. He exchanged a look with Oleg, and he gave him a short nod, understanding what Damian wanted to do without any explanation.

"Okay," said Zabava, her natural exuberance gone. "We are ready to go. Damian?" She gave him an arched stare.

Damian looked down, feeling a strange emptiness inside. "Give me a minute," he said, glancing at Petrukha apologetically. "I just need to pick up something before I go."

He turned on his heels and walked out the door. He marched through the dark hallway, his steps echoing through the entire building. A small, dark shadow darted past him, and he saw Gypsy trotting ahead of him with her bushy tail up, its white tip almost glowing in the dark. He halted by River's room and pushed the door open. He knew she wasn't there, and he wasn't sure why he did that. Taking a deep breath, the slight fragrance of her perfume touched his nostrils, and his jaw tightened, a strange ache gripping at his chest.

Stifling a sigh, Damian closed the door and headed toward Cole's room. He walked inside, trying not to think about his brother, and made his way into the closet. Opening Cole's trench coat, he took the leather scabbard with his sword in it, and put it on, slightly readjusting the straps to his size.

"Hey, Sasquatch." Gypsy's voice sounded in his head, and he snapped around to see the cat sitting on the bed, her eyes glowing with a phosphoric light in the darkness of the room. *"I need you to come back. You will return, won't you?"*

"Most likely," replied Damian flatly. He lowered himself on the bed next to the cat, scratching her behind the ears. "I'm immortal, but there is always—"

"Don't say that." Gypsy shifted closer to him, nibbling on his arm lightly. *"You're the best belly-rubber in the world, and no one can scratch a cat behind her ear the way you do. It's not going to be easy to find a replacement, you know?"*

"I hear yah," he replied softly. "Sorry."

"And River... she needs you, you know?" Gypsy continued, her bushy tail jerking from side to side nervously. *"She's not going to admit it, but ma-a-an, she has no idea how to fix that old dryer or knock a nail into a wall. She definitely needs you for that."*

Damian snorted, shaking his head. "Well, thank you for letting me know. I'll keep it in mind, and I'll do my best to come back here after everything is over."

"Let me help you with that, Child of Earth."

A soft, musical voice sounded on his right, and Damian jolted to his feet, turning toward the sound. Mara stood in the doorway, almost invisible against the darkness of the hallway. She sauntered toward Damian and waved her hand, gesturing for him to sit down. As he lowered himself on the bed, Gypsy hissed, her long claws coming out, and shifted closer to Damian, pressing her side to his.

"Don't be upset, pretty kitty," purred Mara, her eyes strangely foggy and dazed. "I'm not going to hurt your boyfriend… After all, I still need him, so it's in my interest to keep him alive and well…"

"*Boyfriend!*" Gypsy hissed indignantly, flashing sharp fangs. "*He can dream about that. Still, I claimed him a long time ago, and he's under my protection, so you better don't hurt him or else.*"

"I hear you, kitty-cat… no worries, he's all yours…" Mara placed her hand on Damian's forehead. "Sit still, Child of Earth."

"Mara, what are—," Damian started, but magic spiked around the goddess of Nightmares, and he sucked in a short breath, unable to speak.

A wave of cold spread through him, settling somewhere in the pit of his stomach, but as soon as Mara removed her hand, the knot was gone.

"What did you do?" he asked, panting, struggling to fill his lungs with oxygen.

"You'll find out soon enough." A mysterious light ignited at the bottom of her eyes. She moved closer to him and whispered into his ear, her cold lips brushing his skin. "Sometimes, the only way to fight the darkness is to become the darkness…"

She patted Damian on his cheek gently and made her way toward the exit. Halting in the doorway, she looked back at him. "But you have to rush, my little darling, because my spell has a Cinderella-type expiration date. It'll be gone as soon as the first rays of the rising sun will touch the ground…" She wagged her eyebrows at him and walked away.

"Jeez, I hope I'm not going to turn into a pumpkin," muttered Damian, shaking his head.

He picked up Gypsy and let her settle on his shoulder before heading back to the kitchen. As soon as he walked in, everyone turned to him. He halted between Oleg and Petrukha and lowered Gypsy to the floor.

Zabava got up and touched the table, making the map of

Phoenix vanish. "Everyone ready? Does everyone remember where they need to be?" Except for Oleg, everyone nodded.

"Oleg is new to Arizona, and he doesn't know the Phoenix area," explained Damian. "I'll take him to his location, and Petrukha and I will go from there."

"Let's get moving then," muttered Grand Master Elony. She glanced at Damian, and he didn't find the usual frosty animosity in her gaze. "Be careful, Enforcer. I'll have my best team of slayers on standby in case you need a backup."

"My gratitude, Grand Master." Damian inclined his head.

Archmage Allerton stepped forward, his eyes gliding up and down Damian's body, halting on the sword sheathed behind his back. A shadow of astonishment crossed his face, but it was gone right away.

"While you were out, I directed a few of my mages to shadow the magic we'll be wielding around Downtown." He tapped Damian's shoulder, and while he tried to sound confident and calm, his tense shoulders betrayed his true state of mind. "Godspeed, Commander."

Then he snapped his fingers and disappeared from the room. Zabava, Mara and Grand Master Elony followed him.

"Let's get it over with," muttered Damian. He placed his hand on Oleg's shoulder, and Petrukha seized his elbow. With a snap of his fingers, all three of them vanished from Paradise Manor.

CHAPTER 29

~ DAMIAN BLAKE ~

Damian materialized in a dark alley at the edge of Downtown, and a deep shudder rushed down his spine at the sight of the high-rises towering over him. Something fell with a clatter too loud for a midnight street, and a small shadow darted behind a dumpster.

"For fuck's sake! What are these humans doing here? It's midnight! Goddammit! If you're lucky enough to have a bed, go, make use of it... No, they're skulking around dark alleys."

"A foulmouthed alley cat," murmured Damian, turning to Oleg and Petrukha. "Let's go." He pointed at the street at the end of the alley. "Oleg, your position is at the intersection, just a few feet to the left."

They walked in silence until they reached their final destination. The streets were unusually empty, and the stoplights on the intersection were blinking red in all four directions, throwing crimson flares of light on the asphalt. Damian inhaled the night air tinted by the ever-present odor of dust and exhaust. He opened his other sight and turned in place, craning his neck to look up. A barely noticeable glow of magical energy spread around and over the tall buildings as far as he could see.

"The Guardian mages are doing their job," Oleg said matter-of-factly, confirming his observation. "Are you guys ready?" His light hazel eyes moved from Petrukha to Damian.

"No," whispered Petrukha, a short sword materializing in his hand. "I'll be honest with you. I'm scared... I'll be powerless and useless, and all the hard work will fall on Damian's shoulders. I'm terrified of what could happen if Damian's plan fails... But I've been waiting for this moment way too long, so I guess I'm as ready as I can be."

"Always ready," replied Damian, observing Oleg with interest. He was always calm and collected, and it seemed like there was nothing in this world or any other world that could faze this man.

"The team is waiting for our signal. Let's do it, then." Oleg held out his hands, palms up, and connected with his element. Damian joined him, and soon, a large orb made of the pure elemental energy of Earth materialized between their hands. It rotated slowly, tiny bolts of electricity crackling around it. A scent of ozone and damp earth permeated the air, and the corners of Oleg's mouth lifted slightly, his eyes foggy and drunk.

Carefully, Damian moved his right arm away from the energy orb and placed his hand under it. As he started to chant in Dragon tongue, the orb began to rise, moving higher and higher, until it was hovering high in the air, shining like a mini sun in the star-spangled sky. Oleg lowered his hands and looked at Damian, a soft smile dancing on his lips. He reached up with his hand and whispered one word. The orb exploded soundlessly, thousands of small, orange stars floating toward the ground, gradually dissipating.

For a moment, all three of them stood illuminated by the dwindling orange glow of their magic and the red shades of blinking stoplights. Then Oleg offered his hand first to Petrukha and then to Damian.

"Godspeed," he said, squeezing Damian's hand in his, and then repeated it in Russian, a fleeting shadow of concern crossing his features. "*Udachi*, brother in element. Watch your back."

Without pulling the page with the enchantment out of his pocket, Oleg turned toward Downtown and spread his arms wide. He channeled his power and started to chant, clearly pronouncing the words in Dragon tongue. The air around him shimmered, and glittering mist surrounded him like a sheer veil.

Damian opened his other sight and held his breath. Two thin lines of pure magical energy separated from Oleg's hands, entwining into a single line above his head. It ran up and forward, and as Damian followed it with his eyes, he saw the other four lines rising, crisscrossing, creating an enormous dome of light over Phoenix.

He reached to his brother through their blood bond, noticing with relief that his connection with Cole was loud and clear now. So far, his plan worked exactly as he expected. Draining all magical energy out of the area where the bunker was located deactivated all its magical defenses, including the spells that blocked their blood bond.

A moment later, Oleg glanced at him over his shoulder, his eyes glowing a bright orange.

"Go, Commander," he mouthed and continued his chant.

"Brace yourself, Petrukha. The initial effect will be jarring." Damian jerked his thumb at the dome of magical energy, gesturing for him to follow, and stepped forward.

As soon as he crossed inside, he felt as if someone punched him in the gut. He leaned forward, bracing his hands against his knees, gasping for air. Just as Zabava had promised, his connection with his element was as strong as ever, so he knew that the crippling effect of magical energy deprivation would dwindle as soon as he adapted to the magicless environment. Even though he realized it would drain some of his strength, and he wouldn't be able to cast even a basic spell, the debilitating weakness and nausea would be gone soon. Petrukha, however, looked like he was ready to faint, his face a sickening green, his mouth opened.

Damian placed his hand on Petrukha's shoulder, sending some of the healing energy of Earth through him. The old Enforcer moaned and straightened, his face slowly gaining some color. Still holding his hand on Petrukha's shoulder, Damian nodded at him and focused on his brother's presence.

"Here goes nothing," he muttered and snapped his fingers.

* * *

TELEPORTING without knowing exactly where he was going was never a sure thing, prone to all sorts of mishaps, and Damian hated doing it. In his entire life, he had to teleport blindly only twice, and both times he had regretted doing it.

Even though he could feel his brother's presence clearly, he materialized in a dark hallway, hitting his head against the wall. He rubbed his bruised forehead, cursing under his breath. On his left, he heard Petrukha's strangled gasp, but it was immediately swallowed by a blood-chilling shriek—a sound filled with so much horror and blinding fury that the small hairs on the back of Damian's neck stood on end.

Connecting with his elemental power, Damian summoned his daggers and jetted toward the sound. A tall door was the only entrance he could see, and the sound as well as the vampiric energy signature of his brother was coming from behind it. Without thinking twice, he applied a powerful push kick. The door flew off its hinges, sliding across the carpeted floor with a dull bang.

Damian crossed inside a dimly illuminated room and halted with his jaw dropped. The contents of the room could easily put to shame any adult store, and its furnishing left no doubt as to what the purpose of this chamber was. Cole sat on a soft leather chair, his shirt unbuttoned on his chest, and a woman stood over him, screaming, her face contorted by fear and fuming anger. Holding a short sword with a dark ultramarine stone in its pommel, she raised her hand over Cole as if ready to plummet it down.

"Donna Luna!" shouted Damian, and the walls of the bunker shook as his elemental power took him over. "Amaris! I'm here. I did what you ordered me to do. I brought you *'that—I don't know what'.*" He stepped forward, and the floor quaked under his feet. A few items rolled off the shelves, falling to the floor with soft thuds. "Amaris!"

He grabbed Petrukha's shoulder, pushing him forward slightly. The woman snapped toward him, pointing her sword at him.

"What did you do?" she hissed at Damian, her entire body locked with rage. "I lost my magic! All magic is gone. Everywhere!" She spun in place, dismay and horror twisting her otherwise beautiful features. "You have no idea what you've done, idiot! All my wards and cloaking spells are gone!" She stopped shouting and looked around, blackness filling her dark eyes to the brim as she listened to something only she could hear. "It's coming... I can feel it already... There is no way out now—"

"Release my brother and the rest of my friends, and we'll help you fight the demon you made a deal with centuries ago," offered Damian.

She cackled, her hysterical laughter cutting through Damian's hearing like a microphone feedback. "You and this joke of a wizard are just as powerless as I am," she screeched, waving her sword at them. "As far as I can detect, the entire Downtown Phoenix has a magical energy outage." She stepped closer to Damian, rising on her tiptoes. "How did you do it, Blake? It's impossible to do something like this alone!"

"Who said I was alone?" Damian arched his eyebrow, raising

his dagger glowing with the orange light of his elemental power. "And what makes you think I'm powerless?" He channeled more of his elemental power, making the floor quake for added affect, and laughed, throwing his head back. "So, what is it going to be, Donna Luna?"

"You're an imbecile!" she squealed at Damian. Then she turned to Cole, lowering her sword. "Cole, are you sure you and this village simpleton have the same parentage?" She approached him, her chest rising and falling with heavy breaths, a strange glimmer of longing appearing in her black eyes for a heartbeat. "It's been a long while since I actually enjoyed the company of a man, and I wish we could have had more time together, but it is what it is. You're free to go, Cole."

She brushed his cheek with her fingers.

What the hell? A thought flashed through Damian's mind as he watched the obvious signs of affection slowly vanish from Donna Luna's face.

"You can take your maker and anyone else you wish to safety. The bunker is no longer locked. The hidden exit door is located in the central room." She ripped a delicate necklace off her neck and threw it into Cole's hands. "Give it to Jeff, and he'll let all of you out."

Cole got up but hesitated, his troubled gaze lingering on Damian.

"Go! Now!" growled Damian, pointing at the exit, and then projected using their blood bond. *"Save everyone you can, brother. I'll see you soon."*

Suddenly the walls shook so violently that a few fractures materialized in the ceiling. Donna Luna screamed in fear, bending her knees. She dropped her sword, wrapping her arms around her head, and closed her eyes.

"Now!" Damian shouted. Crossing the distance between himself and his brother in a few long strides, he seized his arm and dragged him all the way to the exit. Quickly taking the scabbard with the sword off, he shoved it into Cole's hands and pushed him out the door.

"Damian, the abducted witches... I believe I found them. Follow this hallway all the way to the end. There is only one room there. The amount of magical energy I can sense there is enough to turn Downtown Phoenix into ground zero," Cole projected through their connection and took off running. "Watch your back, brat moi... I'll come back for you!"

"No! Stay out of this," yelled Damian, tones of desperation clear in his voice even through their blood bond. "For once, Cole, do as I say!" As his brother disappeared from view, he turned to Donna Luna.

"I honored my side of the deal," she said, holding out her hand. "Give me my mask and"—she jerked her chin toward Petrukha—"this holy fool before the demon breaks inside."

The bunker quaked again, eliciting another scream of fear out of Donna Luna.

Damian channeled his elemental power, and his daggers vanished. Then he moved his hand over his left arm, and an old silver box materialized in his palm. He grunted, cold sweat dripping down his back. Without magic, he had to use his elemental energy for everything, and it was taking a lot of strength and concentration. He touched the box with the tip of his index finger, and the lid cracked open. Donna Luna sucked in a sharp breath that sounded like a gasp and pressed her hand to her chest.

"Give it to me, quickly!" she hissed, stretching her trembling hand toward the box, her fingers slowly morphing into demonic claws.

Damian grabbed both pieces of the broken mask out of the box and threw them into her hands, disgust making his skin crawl. She caught them and dropped to her knees, realigning the pieces on the floor. The dark smoke of demonic essence swirled around her as she touched the mask, whispering something. The pieces snapped together, but a tiny, thin line still remained in the place where it was broken.

"Dammit! I have a bad feeling... Without magic, the demonic essence is not enough to evoke the power of this mask," she hissed, stretching her deformed, clawed fingers toward Petrukha. "Still, worth trying. I need his blood next." She noticed that the old Enforcer threw a desperate gaze at Damian, and added in an angry growl, "Not all of your blood. Unfortunately, you'll survive, old, drunken fool."

"Do it," ordered Damian, giving Petrukha a short nod.

Swallowing hard, Petrukha took one knee next to Donna Luna and extended his arm, pulling the sleeve of his shirt up. She cackled, shaking her head.

"You miserable halfwit. You cost me hundreds of years in hiding and..." Her voice trailed away, her eyes burning with hatred. "I wish I could slice your chest and rip your beating heart out of it," she hissed through clenched teeth, so much malice in her voice that Petrukha flinched, involuntarily yanking his arm back. She cackled with icy contempt. "Don't worry, old fool. You have a guard, who at the moment is more powerful than I am, and I don't start fights I can't win."

With one sharp move of her claws, she sliced Petrukha's arm above his wrist and seized the hair on the back of his head to keep him steady. The metallic odor of blood permeated the air, and Petrukha clenched his jaw, his eyes glued to the shining shards of mirror that were bedazzling the mask.

As the first drops of blood came in contact with the mask, they boiled, and dirty, gray swirls of smoke rose in the air above it. Donna Luna allowed the blood to flow, holding Petrukha in place. A few seconds later, she waved her hand to dispel the smoke and squealed in delight. Pushing Petrukha out of the way, she grabbed the mask and hopped to her feet, a wild glee igniting her eyes with a dark purple glow. Placing the mask over her face, she reached back, trying to secure it on the back of her head.

Petrukha fell, hitting his head hard against the floor. His eyes rolled back, and he blacked out. Damian grabbed his shoulders, pulling him away from Donna Luna. Then he placed his hand over his tattoo, summoning his gargoyle.

"Zhulik, I need you to take Petrukha outside the circle and find Archmage Allerton," he said, speaking in a quick whisper. "Tell him that his mages need to increase the potency of their spell to the maximum."

"No, Commander. I can't leave you here alone to face this abomination," Zhulik's voice sounded in his mind, and the gargoyle in his natural state materialized next to him, his large eyes glowing a bright blue.

"Alone is what I do best, Zhulik," said Damian, spreading his shoulders. "A powerful demon is coming, and I can't let it back out into the world. I'll do whatever I have to do to make this bunker its final grave. Go. Now! It's important that you deliver my message to the Archmage."

"Fine. I'll be back in a jiffy. Don't start all the fun without me." Zhulik grabbed Petrukha, throwing him on his back as if the fully grown man weighed nothing, and with a light pop, they both vanished.

The bunker shook harder than before, sending a shower of dust and debris down. Damian looked up at the ceiling covered in a web of cracks, and an uneven smirk distorted his lips.

"Your demon is coming, Donna Luna or Amaris, whatever you want to call yourself these days," he said calmly. "What are you going to do now?" Anger swirled within him, and a bright glimmer of elemental energy emitted by his body illuminated the room. A glowing pair of handcuffs materialized in his hands, and Donna Luna hissed, taking a step away from him. "Come with me, and I'll make you invisible to the Guard of Hell you brought into this world."

"A Guard of Hell?" Donna Luna laughed, her face slowly changing its form, morphing into something dark and unnatural. Her already black eyes tilted at a sharp angle. Her mouth became wider, displaying a set of terrifying fangs, and her skin turned a shade of greenish blue. All her features sharpened, bones protruding through her thin, scaled hide. "You wish it were a Guard of Hell, Enforcer. That would be a mercy."

"What kind of evil did you bring into this world? If it's more powerful than a Guard of Hell, what is it?" Damian shouted, taking a step closer to her.

"You thought you could outsmart me, asshole? Wait, and you will find out quite soon." Donna Luna turned away from him, and swirls of demonic essence spiked around her. "But I'm not sticking around to see the expression on your face when you meet him."

Using her demonic essence, she drew a black rune in the air and pressed her deformed, shaking palm over it, whispering the words of summons. She waited for a few long seconds, but as nothing happened, she stomped her foot and screamed, digging her claws into her own scalp in helpless fury and desperation. With one aggravated wave of her hand, Donna Luna got rid of the rune and repeated the same procedure.

Damian folded his arms, the shiny handcuffs dangling over the crook of his elbow. "You're wasting your time, Amaris… Donna Luna," he said icily. "If you think your master will come to your rescue, you'll be disappointed."

"You know nothing about my master," she snapped back angrily. "He'll come. He won't leave me."

"You're right," agreed Damian. "I know nothing about your master. A second ago, I didn't even know he existed. Thank you for confirming my suspicions."

Donna Luna screeched something incoherent, and two weak, leathery wings sprouted behind her back. She flapped them, but without magic, she couldn't fully use her demonic powers either. She bent down and grabbed the sword from the floor, charging Damian with full force. The handcuffs vanished from his hands, replaced by his daggers, and he blocked her strike with ease. Pushing her away, he laughed, infuriating her even more.

She squealed, raising her sword again, but before she could make another move, the bunker shook with such a violent power that she fell on her back, dropping the sword. An earsplitting bang of a powerful impact rolled through the empty hallways, and the entire building trembled again. The first impact was followed by a second one, and soon the bangs turned into a continuously rumbling clamor.

The amount of demonic energy rose to overwhelming proportions, taking Damian's breath away. He staggered backward until his back hit the wall and looked up. The cracks on the ceiling became wider and suddenly, it caved in, giant pieces of metal and concrete falling inside the room.

A huge, gaping hole remained in the place where the ceiling had once been. A long, wide vertical shaft ran up through the ground all the way to the surface, parts of concrete reinforcing blocks, bent and broken steel rods, pipes, and pieces of wood protruding from its walls. A cloud of dust and debris rose in the air, making it unsuitable for breathing. Hiding his face in the crook of his elbow, Damian raised his eyes, afraid to find out what kind of monster could've created something like this.

As the dust settled down, he saw a piece of the midnight sky at the end of the tunnel, partially obscured by an enormous, winged silhouette, darkness, darker than night, slithering around it like a bunch of snakes. Cold sweat covered Damian's forehead, his arms dangling at his sides, his daggers gone.

Oh, God damn it all... I wasn't ready for that...

CHAPTER 30

~ COLE ADAMS ~

Cole zoomed through the dark hallways at full speed and burst through the entrance into his room. Just as he crossed the threshold, the bunker shook again, nearly sending him flying. He staggered forward a few steps but caught himself and straightened, fastening his back scabbard and readjusting the straps.

At first, Ruslan jumped to his feet, but then froze in place, ready to spring into action at any moment, his unblinking eyes on Cole. Sylvana stood behind him, her face a stone mask.

"Cole, what's going on?" Ruslan glanced up as another tremor ran through the floor.

"We're leaving. I'll explain everything later," snapped Cole, waving toward the exit. "Now!"

Turning on his heels, he stormed out the door. He didn't look back, his vampiric senses detecting the presence of his maker and Sylvana right behind him. Glancing up, he noticed that every single piece of anti-magic tech was down. He didn't think Amaris had turned his security off voluntarily, but he had neither the time nor the desire to find out what happened.

Like a bodiless shadow in the depth of the night, he zoomed

across the central area, moving at such speed that no one even noticed him. He rushed through the familiar hallway and turned the corner toward Ricardo's room without dropping speed. He came to a screeching halt in front of a door and kicked it open without knocking. The door swung, hitting the wall with a loud bang, and at the same time, the bunker shook again, deep tremors running through the floor.

He walked inside and stilled, his muscles turning into iron as he took in the situation. Ricardo was on his knees, his hands bound behind his back. His sister stood behind him, holding a knife under his chin. As his dark eyes halted on Cole, his lips parted, but he said nothing, disbelief still reflected on his face.

Two women, armed to the teeth, stood between him and Ricardo, their swords at the ready. A movement of air behind him told him that Ruslan and Sylvana were with him, and a frosty smile touched Cole's lips.

"Give me Ricardo and Camila, and I'll let you leave with your lives," he growled, pointing at the women.

"The Sisterhood of the Sun is coming for you, vamp," hissed the woman on his left, taking a step closer to him.

Cole laughed, his laughter so cold and menacing that the women exchanged a terrified look, and their hands, holding swords, trembled slightly.

"You don't belong to the Sisterhood. You're nothing but worthless imposters," Cole growled, unsheathing his sword in one fluid motion.

The red stone embedded into the pommel reacted to his touch, and a weak wave of magical energy spread through him, raising goosebumps on his arms.

How is it possible? Damian blocked the magic... A thought flashed through his mind, but he had no time to dwell on it.

He turned his head slowly from left to right and touched the tips of his fangs with his tongue, a soft hiss escaping his mouth.

"I have already killed four of Amaris' impostors. Do you

seriously think I can't take care of the two of you?" He moved his sword, drawing a figure eight, the steel whistling through the air. "I think I'll enjoy it."

The women exchanged another look and charged at him at the same time, shouting profanities at the top of their lungs. Cole moved forward, closing the distance between himself and the woman on his left in a moment shorter than a heartbeat. Before she realized what was happening, Cole seized her throat with his left hand and thrust his blade through her heart. She gasped, her wide eyes filled with horror never leaving his. He yanked his sword back, a spurt of bright, red blood splattering his half-opened shirt. As her pupils dilated, and the motionless void of death settled in her gaze, he unlocked his fingers, letting her lifeless body fall to the floor with a soft thud.

Cole snapped to the right, but before he could make a move, a dark shadow darted past him, and the second woman fell dead, her headless corpse lying on the floor next to her fallen teammate. Ruslan stood next to her, his blood-coated fingers still holding her head. A crooked, carnivorous smile lifted a corner of his mouth, his dangerous fangs fully expanded. As the odor of blood infused the air, touching his senses, his eyes lit up brighter, and he grunted, forcing his thirst under control.

"You talk too much, my son," Ruslan growled, dropping the head. As it rolled across the floor, he shrugged and wiped his hands on his pants. "One day, your love for social conversation will kill you."

"Still alive," muttered Cole, winking at his maker. He stepped over the dead body and headed toward Camila and Ricardo.

"Sisterhood slayers they are not," grumbled Sylvana, her upper lip curling in disdain as she kicked one of the dead women.

She lowered to one knee next to the corpses and grabbed the sword lying on the floor by her feet. With one sharp move, she cut the right arm of the dead woman closest to her, severing her hand and the part of her arms with the tattoo. Then she repeated the procedure with the other fake slayer. Rising to her feet, she stuffed the still bleeding hands into the pockets of her robe, ignoring the fact that the sheer fabric got soaked through in a matter of seconds.

As the next tremor rushed through the bunker, Cole approached Camila and Ricardo. He sheathed his sword and raised his hands in a peaceful gesture.

"Camila," he said softly, hoping he sounded friendly enough to convince her. "It's over. Please, lower your knife. You and your brother are finally free. You both can go and live your life in peace."

"Free?" she squealed, pressing her knife tighter under Ricardo's chin. A few drops of blood escaped from under the blade, and Ricardo groaned, his face strained. "Who said that I wasn't free before? Who told you I wanted to leave Donna Luna?" She stared around, a maniacal glimmer in her wide-open eyes. "I'm happy with her. She's my only friend, you bloodsucking leech. Unlike my brother, she treated me like a queen, my every tiniest desire met immediately. Why would I want to leave her for this good-for-nothing loser?"

"Camila, what are you saying?" Ricardo moaned, his voice weak and trembling, a pained expression never leaving his dazed eyes. "I gave up my life, my freedom... everything... What I had to do for you..."

"He is your brother." Cole took a step forward, his throat tight. "Your flesh and blood. The only family you have. How can you betray him like this?

"Come one more step closer, and I'll cut his throat!" she screeched at Cole, yanking her brother's head back.

"Go for it. I had enough of this human soap opera," muttered Ruslan through clenched teeth. Before Cole could stop him, he thrust his arm forward. For him, it was a light jab, but Camila dropped back unconscious, her knife falling to the floor with a loud clatter. The ancient vampire walked around Ricardo and picked her up, throwing her over his shoulder carelessly. Then he turned to Cole, humor sparkling in his dark eyes. "Like I said, you talk too much. Let's get moving before this rattrap collapses on top of us."

Cole hauled Ricardo to his feet and spun him around. Seizing his handcuffs, he yanked them apart, breaking the chain connecting them.

"Let's go," he said, tapping Ricardo's shoulder. The man looked like a shadow of his former self, but he nodded and followed Cole out the door.

They ran through the empty hallways as tremors kept rattling the floor under their feet. Cole zoomed through the central area but instead of stopping there, he kept navigating the maze of hallways until they reached the locked room where he had sensed the accumulation of magical energy before. Now, he could detect nothing, but he was positive he was in the right place.

He kicked the door, but it didn't budge. He exchanged an annoyed look with Ruslan and stepped aside, giving his maker some space by his side. They kicked the door at the same time, putting all their strength into a single kick. It broke with a thunderous bang, shattering into slivers of wood and strips of warped silver and iron.

As Cole crossed into a spacious room, everything inside him twisted. The sweet, nauseating odor of decay overwhelmed his sharp sense of smell, and he pressed his hand over his nose and mouth. Five dead bodies—all women—in different stages of decomposition lay on the cold, concrete floor.

There was no furniture in this large, empty room, but at the far end, three giant cylindrical contraptions stood, taking the entire space from the ceiling to the floor. All three were filled with a strange, shimmering substance. Moving in a bizarre, phantasmal way, it glowed from the inside, its blue glimmer illuminating the dark space, throwing wide cerulean circles of light on the gray floor. Transfixed, Cole stared at the magical energy in its purest form, unable to make a move. Since all magic had been suppressed in the entire area, he had to wonder if the glass-like cylinders were protecting the collected energy from vanishing.

A mighty impact rattled the entire building, breaking Cole's trance, and the powerful bang that followed cut painfully through his heightened senses. One bang followed the next, and soon they fused into a continuous, deafening ruckus. Cole backed away from the bodies of the dead witches and the strange vessels holding the magical energy. Then he took off running at human speed and didn't slow down until he reached the central area.

The guards stood in a tight formation. Stupefied, they stared up at the cracked ceiling in horror, as if expecting it to collapse on their heads at any moment. Cole found Jeff among them and seized the shirt on his chest, giving him a good shake.

"Snap out of it, jackass!" he shouted, shoving the necklace Donna Luna had given him into his hands. "Mr. Amaris wants us all to leave the bunker immediately. Open the door."

Jeff nodded. "Yes, Mr. Adams," he stammered, barely regarding the jewelry in his hand, and pointed at the wall on their right. Unhooking a chain with a set of keys attached to it from his belt, he made his way to the small, well-hidden door and unlocked it. "It will lead you into a tunnel that exits on the outskirts of Downtown."

Cole let Sylvana, Ricardo and Ruslan with the unconscious Camila on his shoulder pass through the door first. With a shake of his head, he turned to the mortified guard.

"Jeff, unlock all your holding cells, and let your captive fighters go." He glanced up and bit his lip, trying not to think of his brother. "Something terrible is coming, and no one deserves this kind of death. Take your people and the fighters and leave."

Jeff nodded again, the Adam's apple in his throat working as if he was trying to say something but couldn't.

"Wake up," Cole growled and slapped the stupefied man across his face. Jeff gasped, pressing his hand to his cheek involuntarily, but at least now he seemed to be more aware of the situation. "Do it now, if you want to live."

Then he turned around and walked through the door into the coolness of the underground tunnel, quickly catching up with his friends.

* * *

AFTER A FEW MINUTES of running at the fastest pace Ricardo could manage, the tunnel came to an abrupt dead-end, and Cole halted, staring up the long, vertical shaft with a metal stair attached to its concrete wall. He climbed up and carefully moved a heavy, cast iron manhole cover to the side. Once on the surface, he surveyed the area, making sure there was no one watching, and then took Camila from Ruslan, stepping out of the way.

It was still early in the morning, and the narrow alley was dark and empty. Once everyone was out of the tunnel, he headed toward the main street, moving stealthily in the shadows of the night. As soon as he stepped out of the alley, he saw a man standing with his arms spread wide. His head was upturned, and he was chanting, monotonously repeating the same set of words in Dragon tongue over and over.

"Archmage Allerton," Cole whispered, recognizing the man. *This is how my brother blocked the magic... He didn't lie to Amaris. For once, he didn't try to do everything on his own.*

A loud boom rolled through the empty streets of Phoenix, the echo amplifying the terrible sound as it bounced between high-rises. Cole spun in the direction of the noise and froze in place, unable to move, small hairs rising on the back of his neck.

Right on the very edge of Downtown, no more than a couple of blocks away from where he stood, a colossal, winged silhouette rose above one of the tall buildings, its wide, webbed wings obscuring a big part of the sky. The darkness became thicker, almost tangible around it, sucking up all the scraps of light in the area. The monster raised his enormous arm, bulging with grotesque muscles, and then lowered it on something only it could see. A bloodcurdling growl rumbled in its wide chest as it kept punching, tearing, and breaking everything in its way.

Without fully realizing what he was doing, Cole let Camila's body slip to the ground, and he pressed his hand to his throat as if he needed air to breathe but couldn't inhale. Fear the likes of which he hadn't felt in years enveloped him, and his motionless heart jolted in his chest. As the next fountain of dust and debris rose in the air, surrounding the beast like a dirty veil, the ground shook under his feet, and the beast roared—the unmistakable sound of triumph.

With his senses stretched to the limit, Cole turned on his heels and jetted back into the dark alley. He was about to dive into the manhole when a strong hand seized his arm above the elbow, halting him in midair.

"Where are you going, son?" Ruslan's fingers squeezed his arm in an iron grip.

"I'm not leaving my brother to fight this monstrosity alone!" Cole growled, struggling against his maker's hold. "Please, Father... Don't you understand? I must go..."

Ruslan's fingers unlocked, and he dropped his arm powerlessly. "Cole, my boy, you have no idea what this thing is and—"

"You're right, I have no idea what that is," Cole interrupted him calmly, "and I don't give a damn. My brother is there, and I will kill anything that stands in my way."

Without waiting for Ruslan's response, Cole turned around and jumped into the shaft.

CHAPTER 31

~ DAMIAN BLAKE ~

"What have you done, Damian Blake?" Donna Luna whispered, scrambling to her feet. Pure torment replaced burning rage, and she looked tired and a little lost. She glanced up and around, shaking her head in resignation. Leaving her sword on the floor, she rushed toward Damian and grabbed his arm with both hands, her eyes almost pleading with him. "Damian, you have no idea what you've done, and now it's too late to fix it."

Donna Luna spoke fast, her teeth chattering, and he had a hard time understanding her words. She looked scared and miserable, but at this point all he cared about was the monster that was about to break in, destroying everything and killing everyone on its way down. The bunker kept rattling, tremors running through the heavy concrete walls as if they were made of paper, and a cloud of dust obscured the tunnel, concealing the monster from his view. He had to let it into the bunker so he could trap it inside, but for now, all he could do was wait for it to happen and deal with the situation the best he could.

Leaning down just a little, he seized her hands, prying her fingers off his wrist.

"I've done nothing," he growled, squeezing her wrists tighter until she yelped. "You brought this monster into the realm of humans. Not me. But I'm the one stuck cleaning up your mess."

"Yes, yes, you're right." She nodded, a feverish glimmer igniting in her eyes. "That's true. But with my magic, I locked him within my body, and I was in complete control until that drunken fool broke my mask. The demon served my every command, unable to break the prison I created for him. All I had to do to keep the beast tamed was channel the magic of the moon through my mask once a month during the full moon…" She moaned in despair, rocking back and forth on her feet slightly. "Ever since I lost my mask, all I wanted was to have it back, so I could stop hiding and restore my power over the demon."

She glanced up at the broken ceiling, but except for the canopy of dust and the outline of the black hole beneath it, there was nothing there.

"Do you think my captive fighters are slaves?" She cackled and yanked her arms out of Damian's grip. "I'm the only true slave here." She hit her chest with her index finger, angry tears brimming her eyes. "Without my mask, I was doomed to spend my life here, in this God-forsaken bunker my master built to hide me from the demon." She grabbed her hair with both hands, her sharp claws digging into her scalp. "All I wanted was my freedom! Don't you get it?"

"Oh, I get it, alright." Damian stepped away from her, his skin crawling from being so close to her. "My heart is breaking for you. You're a poor, sweet damsel in distress. All you wished for was your freedom… and to harness the otherworldly power that has the potential of destroying this world. All you wanted was to be equal to the gods. Really, nothing big."

"Yes, but I wasn't going to—"

A furious growl rumbled in Damian's chest as he exhaled and held out his hand. "Strike number one—attempt to change the path of the Board of Destiny by dethroning Peter the Great." He extended an index finger, showing it to her. "Strike number two—summoning a high-level demonic entity from the unknown realm of spirits and demons." He extended his second finger. "Slave trade and gladiatorial fights, and only God knows what else. In my books, that's strike number three." He showed three fingers, barely containing his anger. "Three strikes—you're out."

"Agh…" She stomped her foot. "Do you seriously think I was trying to kill young Tsar Peter because I wanted to?" She threw her hands up, slipping worrisome glances at the broken ceiling. "I also have someone above me. I was just doing what I'd been ordered, you giant moron. Do you think I care about who sat on the Russian throne, or the trivialities of everyday life of the human realm, or about gathering magical energy from witches, for that matter? I don't give a damn about any of that. My master is the one who wanted all that! I don't even know why he needed it. But he promised to take care of the demon situation, and I needed his protection—"

Her feverish speech was interrupted by a deafening noise coming from above. Clouds of dust and debris fell through the hole in the ceiling, and the building shook as something large and heavy made its way down the shaft.

Donna Luna gasped and threw herself at Damian's chest, wrapping her arm around his waist, her entire body trembling.

"Please, please, please," she begged, tears running down her pale face. "I'll agree to anything you want. Use your cuffs, please! Take me to the Destiny Council. Anything… Just please, don't let it—"

"Too late for that," Damian whispered.

Suddenly, the tremors stopped, and an invisible force seized Donna Luna, ripping her away from Damian. She screamed, a grimace of pain and terror twisting her face. The entire room flooded with absolute darkness, and Damian staggered backward until his back hit the wall, his chest shuddering with shallow breaths as he struggled to inhale. A strange weakness enveloped him, and he knew it had nothing to do with the lack of magic. This weakness, all-consuming and gloomy, felt familiar. He had experienced it before, just recently as a matter of fact.

The Dark Nav.

It felt as if he were crossing river *Smorodina* once again, losing all his hopes and dreams, the desire to live and the need to survive. He wanted to lie down and close his eyes, never to open them again.

The demonic entity emitted the energy of the Dark Nav in its purest form. It wasn't just oozing the presence of the Slavic realm of demons and spirits—it was the Dark Nav in all its deadly splendor.

Perun almighty, a terrifying thought rushed through his frazzled mind, and he swallowed with effort. *She managed to summon and control a Navij, a high-level demon of the Dark Nav... How the hell...*

"Finally..." A voice filled with hatred and carnivorous gloating rolled through the room. While Damian was aware that the monster was communicating telepathically, it seemed as if the voice was coming from every direction at once, consuming all available space. *"You dared break our deal, puny witch? You dare try controlling me?"* The demon gave a loud guffaw, but cut it off abruptly, turning it into a menacing roar. *"Now, I'm planning to return the favor."*

Damian tried to push away from the wall he was pressed against, but he couldn't make a move, his body numb, his muscles refusing to obey the commands of his fogged mind. The surrounding blackness became so heavy that he wasn't sure his eyes were still open.

"No! NOOO!"

Donna Luna's scream, filled with dismay and anguish

beyond that of a regular human, ripped through Damian's mind, clearing it for a brief moment. He groaned, fighting the debilitating embrace of the Dark Nav, and reached for his element. It didn't respond to his call right away, but soon he felt a tiny touch of the energy flowing through him, accumulating somewhere around his heart. He dropped his head and closed his eyes, obsolete in the surrounding dark.

Focusing on its weak flow, he redirected it toward his hands, calling to his daggers. For a heartbeat, he thought what he had wasn't enough to summon his weapons, but as the familiar coolness of the hilts touched his palms, his lips quirked up despite the danger of the situation. He wrapped his fingers tighter, sending all the energy he could gather through the blades.

The weapons in his hands lit up with an orange glow of elemental energy, their light breaking through the wall of gloom and despair. The heaviness lifted off his chest, and he inhaled deeply, filling his lungs with oxygen. With a furious groan, he pushed away from the wall and stepped forward, raising one of his glowing daggers above his head.

Dark shadows shifted, cowering from the light. He spun around, searching for Donna Luna, but couldn't find her anywhere.

"Looking for someone, Child of Earth?" a soft whisper sounded somewhere above him.

Damian raised his face, squinting his blazing eyes into the darkness. Something swished through the air with a soft hiss, and an excruciating pain spiked through him. He cried out, staggering back a step. Pressing his fist to his chest, he felt a slippery wetness, and for a moment, the room spun around him. Something hissed through the air again, cutting him across his chest, too close to his throat.

Either the monster moved too fast for him to notice the motion, or the light of his daggers wasn't enough for him to see it. Damian held his breath and opened his other sight while sharpening all his senses. At first, he could hear nothing except for the loud beating of his heart and the rhythmical pumping of blood in his ears. But as he forced himself to calm down, he heard it.

He didn't really hear or see the monster. He detected it with all his senses at once, including his magical sight, his brain completing the image. No more than a foot away from him, the monster stood with its ghastly fangs exposed, its wide bat-like wings folded behind its back. As the demon raised his hand, ready to strike him again, Damian rolled over his shoulder, slipping under the demon's arm, and came to his feet on the other side of the monster. He thrust his dagger forward, wishing he could cast a spell to call to the light of Creation, but it was impossible without his magical energy.

The demon howled and spun toward him, cutting the air with its talons. Damian kept backing away from it, using every opportunity he had to inflict an injury on his opponent. But even though his every strike reached the target, he had no doubt —he wouldn't be able to hold the Navij for long. For a short while, he danced around the monster, trying to deliver as much damage as he could. But the energy of the Dark Nav it emanated was feeding on his life-force and elemental energy, and every next move he made came with more effort than the previous one.

"*Stop fighting, Child of Earth,*" the deep, grinding voice boomed in his mind as the Navij spoke again, sounding as though it was trying to reason with him. "*You're old and smart enough to know you can't fight me. Now, that I have a human body to anchor myself to the realm of humans, I'm unstoppable. Even Chernobog himself no longer has power over me.*"

The Navij cackled, and for a brief moment, the darkness retreated, giving Damian a glimpse of the demon's new appearance. A ghastly version of Donna Luna hovered a few feet above the floor, supported by the dirty, leathery wings. She was at least eight feet tall, and her sharply angled demonic eyes with the vertical pupils of a serpent shone with a deep purple light. While her features still kept some semblance to her former self, there was nothing human about her looks. Her talons were smeared with blood—his blood—and a predatory snarl stretched her black lips, showing off a set of sharp fangs. Her long tail resembling that of a dragon swiped angrily from side to side, wrapping around her legs.

"I'm the Dark Nav, and the Children of Elements can't survive my embrace," continued the monster. *"Give up, boy. You have no chance against me. You're too weak, and the closer I'm to you, the weaker you become. You're too slow, and once I touch you... ohhh..."* The monster's voice faded into a nearly ecstatic, harsh breath as it reached forward with its bloody talon. *"Drop your weapons, and I may take mercy on you. I'll let you die fast. You know I'm right."*

Damian lowered his daggers, his chest rising and falling with heavy breaths, sweat dripping down his flushed face and back, plastering the remains of his shirt to his body.

"I know," he replied calmly. "You're right. I can't kill you. Supposedly, it's impossible to kill a Navij, but I'll be damned if I don't try." He raised his daggers again, assuming a fighting stance. "Yeah, I'm slow and weak compared to you, but—"

"But I'm not!"

Ringing with suppressed fury, a familiar voice boomed behind Damian, causing him to spin around. His brother stood in a partially destroyed doorway with his sword in his hand. Damian had seen Cole angry on more than one occasion. He had seen him fight with his full vampiric force more than once, but never had he seen his brother like this.

With his shirt partially unbuttoned and ripped on his chest, he was covered in splatters of dried blood, and his entire body was producing a soft red glow of magical energy. The sword in his hand was glowing as brightly as his scarlet eyes, and

Damian couldn't understand how Cole could channel magic when he knew for a fact that the magical energy was still blocked. A massive gargoyle in its natural form stood by his side, the low rumble of a continuous growl vibrating in his solid-rock chest, and Cole's fingers were stroking Zhulik's back automatically.

"I believe this belongs to me." Giving Damian a curt nod, Cole held out his hand, pointing at the second sword that Donna Luna had dropped on the floor earlier. The weapon started to vibrate, igniting with a deep ultramarine light, and then vanished, reappearing immediately in Cole's hand. He squeezed its grip, raising both swords, and as he did that, a brilliant white light flooded the room.

The Navij hissed, pulling away from the light, and Cole laughed in response, switching into a full-force attack.

"How dare you threaten my brother?" he roared, crashing his swords at the demon. "Maybe he's slower and weaker than you, but as God is my witness, I am not! And I will take pleasure in taking you down, part by goddamn part, you fuckin demonic scumbag."

Fighting with two swords in the best style of Roman *dimachaeri*, Cole moved at his full vampire speed, and the Navij had no choice but to respond in kind. Soon, both turned into blur barely perceptible by a human eye, and only by using his other sight could Damian see at least some bits of the blood-curdling fight unfolding in the destroyed room.

"*Stay out of the way, Commander. Let the big dogs do the talking,*" Zhulik growled and joined the confrontation, assailing the demon from its other side to give Cole a few seconds' reprieve.

Damian pressed his back to the wall and shifted to the side, inching his way toward the exit. He wasn't going to leave his brother alone, but he also knew it was impossible to kill a Navij. The only thing Cole could do was to keep it busy long enough for him to figure out how to block the exit out of the bunker and then send this malevolent creature of the Dark Nav back into the hellhole it had been summoned from.

He stepped through the threshold into the hallway littered with pieces of concrete and assorted debris and glanced up. Now that the Navij was preoccupied with Cole and Zhulik, the darkness wasn't as thick as before, and he could see the giant hole in the ceiling with a shaft leading to the outside world. He had to close it. No matter what would happen next, he couldn't let the Navij escape back into the realm of humans.

Damian put his daggers on the floor by the wall and took a deep breath, focusing on the task at hand. Gathering all his strength, he channeled the elemental energy of Earth. The floor quaked, responding to his power, and the muscles of his arms and shoulders strained as if he were trying to lift something heavy.

He raised his arms and redirected the flow of energy toward the shaft. A loud, grinding noise filled the room, overwhelming the cacophony of the fight, rising over the shrills of the demon and growls of the gargoyle. A shower of small pieces of rocks, slivers of wood, and warped rods fell through the hole, and a murky curtain of dust veiled the fighters.

The walls started to close gradually, the patch of the sky high above the surface no longer visible. Damian screamed and brought his arms together, placing his remaining strength into the last push, and the hole closed up, cutting the Navij's only way out. The demon jerked back, putting some distance between himself and Cole, and raised its ugly head, staring at the blocked hole with an expression that could have been described only as a mix of annoyance and apprehension.

"What did you do, Child of Earth?" it hissed, saliva dripping from its fangs. "*You locked yourself, your brother and this annoying pest of yours here, underground, with me. I thought you loved your brother.*" The demon cackled, spreading his arms wide. "Or is that a form of... um... what do you humans call it? A murder-suicide?"

Breathing heavily, Damian couldn't say anything, barely keeping the upright position. Instead, Cole stepped forward.

"No, asshole," the vampire replied calmly. "It's not a murder-suicide. It's just me killing you."

With his arms spread wide, he leaped in the air, and Damian could swear for a few endless seconds, his brother levitated there, his swords blazing with an eye-watering light. He watched Cole swing his swords in a cross motion, the blades cutting through the demon's thick neck like it was a flabby pudding. A blood-chilling shrill of pain and shock erupted from the Navij's deformed mouth. Cole dropped to the floor softly like a giant cat, landing on one knee, and brought his terrifying weapons down.

The Navij's form started to shrink until it reached a normal human size. Its wings and tail turned to dust, and for a moment, Donna Luna stood there, gazing at Cole with wide-open eyes, death already imprinted in the blackness of her expanding pupils. A horrendous visage of the demon, composed of slowly evaporating demonic essence, appeared over her like a dark, menacing shadow, spreading its wings to their full extent. She lifted her hand, reaching toward Cole, her lips moving like in a last prayer. Then her appearance changed again into that of a demon.

For a heartbeat, Damian couldn't breathe. Killing a Navij wasn't possible. It could've only been compared to killing a god, yet he was watching the demon's head roll off its shoulders, falling to the floor. Its body followed less than a second later. The demonic essence of the Navij twisted over it, spinning into a mini-tornado, and Damian couldn't help but stare at it in disbelief.

His brother had managed to do the impossible—he had destroyed an indestructible monster, but Damian knew better. In the case of creatures of the Dark Nav, nothing stayed dead for long. Before his eyes, the body of the monster started to disintegrate with a light hissing noise, turning into a pile of disgusting, gray flakes. The flakes lifted a few inches off the floor, starting to rotate counterclockwise slowly, and with desperate clarity, Damian realized what was coming next.

He dropped to his knees, gathering every scrap of elemental energy he still had in his drained body, and then tapped into his internal resources. A strained scream broke from his lips, and his entire body arched as he spread his arms wide. A large dome of pure elemental energy encapsulated the quickly transforming remains of the Navij, his brother and the gargoyle. The rotation came to a full halt, and time itself seemed to slow down.

Cole lowered to his knees next to him, the scarlet glow vanishing from his eyes. "Dima, what are you doing?"

"Cole," said Damian, his voice hoarse with strain. "Please, listen to me, and for once, do as I say."

Cole moved to say something, but Damian gave him a barely visible shake no.

"Don't interrupt. We don't have time. You killed a Navij… don't know how… But the monsters of the Dark Nav don't vanish after death. They transform… I can see the transformation has already started. Its body will morph into hundreds, if not thousands, of phantoms. Don't get me wrong—it's better to deal with phantoms than with a Navij, but…" He took a short breath, channeling more of his energy into the giant dome he was holding. "I can't leave phantoms in the bunker because sooner or later they will find their way to the surface through the vents or some other way… Can't have it… thousands of people will die if I fail…"

"I'm sorry… I had no idea…" Cole frowned, clutching his swords.

"Not your fault… Mine… I wasn't ready to deal with a Navij," whispered Damian. "I didn't know either."

"What do you need me to do?" asked Cole quietly.

"The shield I'm holding is slowing down the flow of time a

little, and it takes all my energy and strength. I can't hold it for much longer, but I know what I need to do to deal with these phantoms," replied Damian, speaking as fast as he could. "I need you to take Zhulik and go to the surface. Zhulik can teleport both of you out of here. I have two gods, two high-level mages and a Child of Earth blocking all the magical energy in Downtown Phoenix."

He took a short breath as the room started to spin around him in a slow and nauseating motion, his vision going in and out of focus.

"Cole, I need you to find all five of them as fast as you can," he continued. "Zhulik knows the points… Tell them to restore the flow of magic as soon as possible and block the area above the bunker—the most powerful shield they can conjure… If I'm to survive, I need all the magic I can get."

"Dima, what are you talking about? You're an immortal Child of Earth," Cole whispered, his hands shaking slightly. "You can't—"

"You just killed an immortal, god-like demon, Cole. There is no such thing as unconditional immortality," Damian replied, sweat dripping down his face.

"No… please…" Cole whispered—a barely audible sound filled with anguish and despair.

Damian sighed, gazing at his brother with warmth. "Please, listen to me. I love you, little bro. I always have, and I always will. You're strong… so much stronger than I am… and smarter, too…" A faint smile touched his lips. "You can do it. The future of the human realm depends on you now. So, please go and let me do my duty as a Destiny Enforcer…"

"Dima, I can't—"

"Yes, you can, Nikolai… The faster you move, the bigger the chance I'll survive. Restore the flow of magic in Downtown—save the world." He switched his attention to his gargoyle. "Zhulik, you and Cole are leaving now. Go. It's an order!"

"I'll see you on the surface, Commander," said Zhulik, inclining his head.

Cole placed his hand on the gargoyle's back, and both vanished with a light pop.

* * *

Damian dropped the shield of elemental energy and nearly collapsed. With sheer effort of will, he pulled himself to his feet. The flakes resumed their rotation, moving faster and faster, quickly transforming into hundreds of semi-transparent phantoms.

All of a sudden, the rotation ceased, and for a moment shorter than a heartbeat, the flock of phantoms imploded in on itself, disappearing from view. Then the floor shook, rocks falling from the barricade Damian had created to block the tunnel in the ceiling, and hundreds of fully formed phantoms manifested in midair. Looking like giant black birds with iron beaks and semi-transparent bodies, they screeched all at once and then stilled, their menacing, black eyes glaring at Damian without blinking.

"Good little birdies," muttered Damian. "Now, try to follow me."

He pivoted on his heels and ran along the partially demolished hallway as fast as his drained body would allow. He wasn't certain where he was going, but according to Cole, there was only one more room in this entire hallway, so he couldn't miss it. Every next step he took required more effort, and he wasn't sure he could reach the room before the phantoms caught up with him.

Cole, please, faster, brother mine... I need my magic...

Far ahead, in the darkness of the hallway, he noticed the black rectangle of a broken door and doubled his effort, his feet hitting the floor with heavy thumps, each step resonating through his worn-out body. Abruptly, a sharp pain pierced his chest, and he felt like his heart was about to explode. He slowed down and came to a halt. Pressing his hand to his chest, he glanced back, trying to understand what had just happened.

He was just a few steps away from the door, but the dark cloud of phantoms had caught up with him. He was out of strength, out of elemental energy, and the flow of magic was still blocked. The bird-like monsters of the Dark Nav swooped down at him, tearing his flesh with their iron beaks and talons, aiming at his eyes. But as one of the phantoms flew through his chest, phasing out on the other side, the same spike of pain twisted his insides, sending his heart into overdrive. He cried out and dropped to his knees. The phantoms kept attacking him, phasing in and out of his convulsing body. He fell to his side and curled into a tight ball, covering his head with his arms.

Cole... please...

The change came so suddenly that he didn't recognize what had happened right away. The phantoms froze in mid-air, their beaks open in mute shrieks. For a split second, absolute silence engulfed the bunker. A powerful gust of wind rushed through the hallway, and something impacted Damian on his chest with a mighty force. His arms unlocked as he turned to his back, and his body arched like a tightly stretched bow. He screamed, but it wasn't in pain.

It was pure joy.

The flow of magical energy was restored, and it filled his drained body, partially reviving his strength and charging him like an adrenaline shot. He got up to his feet and spread his arms, his daggers manifesting in his hands.

"*Illucious*," he yelled, swinging his blades at the cloud of phantoms.

At the touch of the purifying light of Creation, the phantoms hissed and disintegrated into cold flakes of ash, soundlessly floating to the floor. But there were just too many of them, and fighting them with his daggers wasn't an option. The door he needed was within his reach, so he turned around and bolted toward it. He rushed through the threshold into the dark room.

The nauseating reek of decay hit him like a sledgehammer, but he ignored it and headed toward the three massive cylindrical contraptions filled with the pure energy of magic. He came to a screeching halt in front of the cylinder in the middle and snapped around, waiting for the phantoms to catch up with him.

As the phantoms filled the room, Damian turned back toward the cylinders.

"Exitius!" he shouted, pointing at the glass, but his spell hit the shining surface of the cylinders without doing any damage. He channeled as much magical energy as his drained and injured body could hold and tried again, increasing the potency of his spell. *"Exitius Amplio!"*

Dammit!

The cylinders deflected his magic and elemental power, and there was nothing he could do. The phantoms swooshed down, assailing him from all directions, phasing in and out of his body. He groaned, struggling to keep his mind clear despite the continuous torment the phantoms inflicted on him.

I failed... An agonizing thought flashed through his mind. *Again.*

He squeezed his head with his hands, his fingers digging into the mass of his matted hair. In a last-ditch effort, he channeled his magic again and connected with the energy within, praying to all the gods he knew to help him. Something twitched in his chest, and an unusual cold wave spread through his body, freezing him from the inside.

His wings opened up of their own accord, and before he knew it, he was levitating a few feet above the ground. The pain was gone. There were no more fears or worries, and just now he noticed that the phantoms ceased their relentless assaults and cowered away. They surrounded him in a tight circle, glowering at him in complete silence.

Strangely, he couldn't care less about their peculiar behavior. He turned toward the cylinders and raised his hands, but instead of the familiar orange or white glow of his magic, his entire body emitted a deep purple light. It wasn't his magical energy signature. It was dark and evil, but for some reason that didn't bother him either.

Thank you, Mara... He laughed, barely recognizing his voice, and exhaled a single word, *"Exitius..."*

Two rays of magical energy—a white one and a purple one—erupted from his hands. Entwining with each other, they impacted the glass cylinders with a tremendous force. The magically reinforced glass blew up, and a thunderous bang echoed through the bunker. The shards of glass flew in every direction, biting into Damian's arms, chest and face.

Time slowed down.

The concentrated magical energy exploded outward, consuming everything in its way, burning the skin and flesh off his face and chest. As an unbearable pain assailed him, he dropped to his knees, and then collapsed to his side. The phantoms hissed and twisted in place, their deformed bodies evaporating like from an atomic blast, leaving nothing behind.

The ceiling caved in, and the floor under him cracked. Time resumed its motion, and the magical storm consumed him. His body was taken apart cell by cell, and for a brief moment, he ceased to exist, hovering in his astral form high above the raving inferno he created. But then something dark and imperceptible wrapped around him, pulling him back together, restoring his broken body. With that came pain. He wanted to fight it, but he couldn't. His mouth opened, but no sound came out from his constricted throat.

The bunker collapsed with a deafening noise, burying him under giant chunks of concrete and debris, crushing his battered body. Long, steel rods pierced his chest and stomach, ripping through his heart, and he knew it was the end.

With the last spark of his dwindling consciousness, he reached to his brother through their blood bond.

"Cole, I'm sorry... *live well,* brat moi..."

CHAPTER 32

~ COLE ADAMS ~

Teleporting with the gargoyle, Cole made a full circle around Downtown and finally stopped by Archmage Allerton's side where Ruslan, Sylvana and Ricardo with his sister sat on the sidewalk, waiting for him. Petrukha was pacing by the wall, clenching his hands nervously. No more than a couple of city blocks away, a half-demolished building stood out against the dark sky like a sore thumb, and Cole couldn't take his eyes off of it.

An enormous dome of protective magic encapsulated what was left of the building. Glowing with a dim, white light, it was prominent against the ultramarine sky slightly shaded by the first colors of early dawn, and the only reason human authorities hadn't arrived yet was that the Archmage and the Guardians mages had shadowed the entire area, concealing all disturbances —mundane and magical—from human eyes.

The flow of magic had been restored, and Cole could feel the presence of magical energy sharper than he had ever felt it before. Both swords in his hands were glowing, emitting a soft red and blue light, and his entire body buzzed and vibrated on the inside, responding to the call of these strange weapons.

"Mr. Adams, can you explain why Commander Blake requested such a powerful shield over that area? It was never a part of his original plan," Archmage Allerton asked, waving in the direction of the half-demolished building.

Cole didn't react. He didn't ignore the question. He was afraid of what he would have to say if he needed to explain everything.

"Cole, what's going on? What's your brother planning to do?" Ruslan approached him and placed his hand on his shoulder, giving it a gentle squeeze. Cole raised his eyes at his maker, his chest tight with the expectation of something terrible—something he could neither prevent nor fix.

"Father, please, don't ask. Not now—"

A loud grinding noise echoed through the empty streets, interrupting him, and slow tremors spread through the ground, originating somewhere in the area of the underground bunker. The magical energy field over it spiked with such a ferocious force that the Archmage gasped, his eyes igniting with a blinding white light.

Trying not to think of what this could mean, Cole sheathed one of his swords and approached Allerton, pointing at the building. "Is that the strongest shield you and your mages can conjure?"

"Yes, it is," replied the Archmage, deep wrinkles crossing his forehead. "Besides me and the high-level Guardians mages, Captain Svetlov, Grand Master Elony and her slayers, as well as two goddesses have joined the effort. This shield is as strong as they come."

Cole nibbled on his lip, trying to deal with the unusual for him trepidation but to no avail. He didn't breathe, and his heart wasn't beating, yet he felt lightheaded and slightly dizzy, the tips of his fingers tingling. A gentle touch to his mind made him halt with his eyes wide open. His brother's voice filled their connection with endless warmth and sadness. For some reason, the connection wasn't clear, and he couldn't make out what Damian was saying, but the emotional message was enough for him to understand him without any words.

"Oh, God," Cole moaned, taking a step toward the building involuntarily. "Please, Dima... don't do it..."

"Cole, what is he doing?" Ruslan asked.

"Saving us all," whispered Cole. "He—"

A powerful explosion rattled the area, and a column of blinding white light burst out from the place where the building had been just a moment ago. The ray of concentrated magical energy impacted the protective dome, expanding within it. Allerton roared, leaning back with his arms spread as he struggled to hold the shield. A thick, pulsing vein crossed his forehead, and a deep shade of magenta colored his strained face, but he didn't let go.

Cole raised his arm, shielding his eyes from the brilliant glow, but no matter how hard he tried, he could see nothing. A strong gust of wind rushed through the street, carrying sand and dust, and suddenly, everything went silent. The light dwindled, and Cole lowered his arm, blinking to readjust his vision.

The building was gone, a tall pile of debris remaining in its place. He reached to Damian through their blood bond but didn't find a connection. His experience told him it could mean only one thing—his brother was no longer among the living, but his mind refused to believe it.

"Dima?" he called tentatively. There was no answer. No connection. No sign of life. He stilled, turning into an unmoving statue in that eerie way only vampires could. The light in his eyes vanished, and a deep ache settled in his soul while his mind still refused to believe. "Dima, no..."

With a low groan, Archmage Allerton let go of his magic and dropped his arms, sweat running down his face. As the shield slowly dissipated, he turned around to face Cole, an expression of remorse etched on his features. Cole took in his appearance, and a wave of defiance surged through him.

"Mr. Adams," started the Archmage. "Cole, I'm sorry… The amount of concentrated magical energy would have been deadly even for—"

"Don't say it," Cole hissed, backing away from him. "I don't want to hear it. Not from you, not from anyone else." He glanced back at his maker, but Ruslan averted his gaze, a muscle twitching in his tightly pressed jaw.

With a light pop, Grand Master Elony appeared next to them, and then Zabava followed with her hand on Oleg's shoulder. Lowering himself down next to Ruslan, Zhulik dropped his head with a soft whine-like howl, and now, he truly looked like a sad little puppy.

Cole regarded all the people surrounding him, the sympathetic expressions on their faces making his stomach heave, and he took another step back. Even though most of them meant well, he just couldn't take it. He needed a moment for himself to process, to understand, and he couldn't do it with everyone looking at him, as if expecting for him to say something.

"I'm sorry," he muttered to the Archmage, his vocal cords too sore to function properly. "Please, give me a moment to... I need to…" He desperately searched for the right words, but his mind was painfully blank. "I'll be right back."

Without waiting for anyone's response, he pivoted on his heels and headed into the dark alley. He made sure no one could see him and halted in the shadow of a building, resting his back against the wall. He squeezed his head with his hands and bent forward, his mouth open in a silent scream, both denial and anger ripping his soul apart.

"It's gonna be all right, little vamp," a soft female voice sounded in his mind, and Cole sprang up, searching for the source of the whispers. *"It's Mara, your dream goddess."* The voice giggled. *"We need to have a word, and the sooner we do it, the better for you."*

"Mara?" he whispered tentatively, surveying the alley.

"I'm here." The goddess of Nightmares stepped out of the shadows, her long black hair moving in soft waves around her even though there wasn't even the slightest breeze. She halted before Cole and tilted her head, staring at the sword with the blue stone in his hand with unconcealed curiosity. Then her eyes darted to the pommel of his other sword sheathed behind his back, and she chuckled, shaking her head.

"What did you want to talk about?" asked Cole, barely finding the strength to produce coherent words. "I'm not in the mood for your—"

"You, little vamp. I wanted to talk about you." She reached for his sword, moving the tips of her fingers over the cold steel. "I should have figured it out earlier. But even gods can get blindsided."

"What are you talking about?" asked Cole, pulling away.

"The Darkness touched by the Light," she whispered breathlessly.

"No," Cole objected quietly, staring to the side so she couldn't see the haunted look in his eyes. "Impossible. This prophecy cannot be about me. My brother is—"

"Alive," Mara breathed out, a strange longing crossing her face. "Well, technically he's very much dead… but he won't be for much longer. So, trust me, you don't want anyone else to know your little secret." She giggled. "Give me this sword, and I'll hide it until you're ready to claim it back. No one should know that you can wield the…" Her voice trailed away, and her lips quirked up. "I don't think you should know it either. You're not ready."

"Mara," Cole growled. He seized her arm and pulled her closer. She didn't resist, leaning into his chest willingly. "Stop speaking in riddles. Tell me the truth."

She giggled again, covering her mouth with her free hand in

such a girly manner that Cole had to force himself not to roll his eyes.

"I would, but can you handle the truth?" She arched her brow. "This is the reason we gods speak in riddles, work in mysterious ways, and avoid direct communication with humans. You people can't take the gospel truth, too delicate for the brutal reality."

Cole threw his hands up and turned away, starting on his way out of the alley.

"Wait, Cole, fine!" Mara yelled, and he halted, waiting for her to catch up. "Cole, these two swords chose you, otherwise you wouldn't be able to wield them, and I saw them respond to your magic—the magic, which you as a vampire shouldn't have had in the first place."

She pressed her hand to her chest, her eyes growing darker. "Hello, Godslayer. So nice to make your acquaintance…" She reached up, brushing her cold fingertips over his cheek.

"I have no idea what you're talking about," Cole growled, waving her hand off as if she were nothing more than an annoying mosquito.

"As far as I recall, these two swords are the only weapons that can kill gods or any of their equals. Like an indestructible Navij, for example…" A playful smile touched her lips. "They were created by one of the ancient ones millennia ago and forged in the breath of the first dragon, and until today, no one else could invoke their power. This makes you the new Godslayer, the killer of gods. And if anyone finds out—both you and your brother will be in more danger than you can handle. No one should know these swords have been reunited. No one should know what you have become… Let me hide one of these swords until you and Damian are ready to deal with this situation."

"Why are you doing it, Mara?" Cole asked, narrowing his

eyes. "You're a dark deity. You don't do charitable deeds. It's not in your nature."

"You're right," she agreed with a half-shrug. "The idea of helping someone without getting anything back hurts me more than I can say." She looked away for a moment. "The truth is, I'm doing it for your brother. Tell Damian this has nothing to do with our deal. This is personal, and he owes me one." Then she pressed her fist to her chest and kneeled before Cole, inclining her head. "Here goes... Cole Adams, I swear on my power that I'll keep your secret safe, and that I will return this sword to you or Damian at your first request." She rose to her feet, gazing up at him. "Now, give it to me because the show is about to get started, and you don't want to miss it." She took her long, black veil off and placed it around Cole's neck. "Don't ask any questions. You'll thank me later."

A feeling of unease twisted his gut, but Cole pushed it to the back of his mind and gave the sword to the goddess of Nightmares. Mara was right. Until he knew more about the prophecy and how to handle the situation, he needed to keep the sword hidden. Donna Luna's mysterious master was actively searching for the brothers who fit the prophecy, and that alone was a serious reason for concern.

He opened his mouth to ask Mara if she knew anything about this person, but before he could say anything, she snapped her fingers and vanished. With a heavy heart, he started on his way back when a deep tremor rumbled through the ground. He halted, surveying the area.

Even without a second sight, he could feel some strange disturbances in the area. The tremors rushed through the asphalt again, and a flock of birds took off from the roofs and wires, rising high into the sky with piercing screeches. The wind picked up, too cold for this time of the year, scattering pieces of newspapers and litter all over the road. The tremors increased, morphing into a continuous earthquake, and it seemed like nature was responding to whatever was happening out there.

"Dima," Cole whispered, hope igniting in his soul. He zoomed through the alley and halted sharply next to the Archmage, making him flinch and hop back.

"Allerton, please tell me you're still shadowing the area around the bunker," he said through clenched teeth, pointing at the demolished building.

"No," the Archmage whispered, sweat beading his forehead. "I didn't think I had a need since—"

"My brother is an immortal Child of Earth!" Cole yelled. "Of course, you had a need!"

"Mr. Adams, you're grieving. So, I'll forgive you for your ignorance and disrespectful behavior. Even an immortal god couldn't have survived the direct impact of such an enormous amount of concentrated magical energy. It's like a magical atomic bomb," Grand Master Elony said coldly, placing her hands on her hips. "Your brother, as powerful as he was, had a human body, and it would have been obliterated at the first blast. He couldn't have survived it, and the elemental energy of Earth wouldn't be able to bring him back because there wouldn't be anything to bring back. I hate to say it, but your brother is gone."

"Keep hating to say it," Cole snapped at her and turned to the Archmage. "Please, my lord, shadow the bunker now, before it is too late."

"It's too late," the Archmage echoed, staring in the direction of the demolished building, transfixed.

"I've never felt so much elemental energy of Earth even in Kendral… Oh, God…" Oleg threw his head back, opening his arms. He was breathing hard, his chest shuddering with short, uneven breaths, and his body lit up with a bright glow, responding to the massive elemental storm raging around them.

A dome, shining with dazzling orange light, encapsulated

the area above the bunker. It was growing brighter and brighter, quickly spreading around, its movement accompanied by tremors, loud grinding noise and powerful gusts of wind. Its radiance became so bright that it was unbearable to look at. The tremors grew stronger, and a few cars responded with shrilling howls of security alarms, adding to the clamor of the earthquake.

"Heaven and Earth! We're exposing the World of Magic!" shouted the Archmage, his face distorted by fear. With a shaking hand, he drew a glowing rune in the air, whispering a summoning call.

As the light slowly decreased, Cole saw a man levitating above the ruins, his giant black wings stark against the morning sky. His long black hair fell in a disarray of strands to his shoulders and back, partially covering his face, and the first rays of the rising sun colored his absolutely unobstructed body in soft reddish and yellow shades.

"Dima?" Cole searched for the blood bond with his brother, but it was gone. "Damian," he whispered.

Damian turned in midair, and Cole could swear his glowing eyes settled on his. His brother raised his hand and snapped his fingers. As soon as he manifested next to Cole, he dropped to his knees, wrapping his arms and his wings around himself in an attempt to cover his state of undress. His entire body was shaking either from cold or from whatever he had gone through, and he kept his head bowed down.

Cole took one knee in front of him and gently moved his long hair off his face, realizing with shock that his brother looked the way he did when he was still human, before he died the first human death. The only difference was that he still had the ugly scar disfiguring the left side of his face, and even without checking, Cole was sure the scars on Damian's back were still intact as well.

Just now he remembered about the veil Mara had given him

and couldn't help but shake his head. The goddess knew what was coming, but of course, she wouldn't tell him straight. He took the veil, offering it to his brother.

"Dima, are you okay?" he asked gently.

"No..." Damian whispered, his hands tightening into fists, his every muscle tense. He took the veil and got up, quickly wrapping it around his hips. Then he rolled his shoulders, moving his head slowly from left to right, and his wings disappeared.

"What happened, Commander?" asked Archmage Allerton, approaching him from behind, and Damian spun around, his glowing eyes igniting brighter. "Did you kill the demon?"

"Yes, sir," Damian replied, the tension slowly draining off his face. "Donna Luna is gone forever. Unfortunately, the monster she summoned wasn't your regular demon. She had bound herself to a Navij, an abomination of the Dark Nav. It's a long story"—he threw a warning glance at Cole—"but to make it short, I had to use the concentrated magical energy Donna Luna had been collecting for a while to destroy it. The Navij possessed her body, anchoring himself to the human realm through whatever contract she had made with him. I couldn't let him escape the bunker, and that was the only way I could kill it."

He turned toward Grand Master Elony, his face void of emotions. "I'm sorry, ma'am," he continued calmly. "When I got there, all the witches were dead already. I was too late to save them. I did everything I could—"

A slow clapping interrupted him, echoing through the morning street.

"And what a marvelous job you did today, Commander Blake. Just as per usual," a deep male voice sounded behind him, and Cole turned around, his hand reaching for his sword.

A tall man in a black uniform stood behind him, staring at Damian with unconcealed hostility. He held out his hand, and a pair of glowing handcuffs materialized in his palm. Recognizing the Destiny cuffs, Cole hissed and jumped between the man and his brother, his sword in his hand.

"Stay out of it, vamp, if you know what's good for you," the man said icily, his upper lip curling in a snarl. Then he switched his attention to Damian, showing him the cuffs. "In the name of the Destiny Council, Commander Blake, you're under arrest. On your knees, hands behind your head."

"Hold on just a second." Archmage Allerton approached them, holding his hands up in a peaceful gesture. "Commander Moore, what's going on? I was here all the time. I assure you, Commander Blake didn't do anything wrong. If I have to, I'll speak with the High Council on his behalf."

"That won't be necessary, my lord," Moore replied, a wild, euphoric glimmer in his eyes. "I'm positive Commander Blake is well aware of what he did wrong, but to make it clear to everyone present—he disregarded his obligations as a Destiny Enforcer, and he must be punished in accordance with the law."

"How so?" asked the Archmage, a deep frown shadowing his features.

Moore all but rolled his eyes, annoyance lingering over him. "He was ordered to find whatever Amaris wanted him to retrieve and deliver it directly to the Destiny Council. Instead, he chose to come back here and save the life of this disgusting vamp." He jerked his chin in Cole's direction, eliciting a furious hiss out of him. "Now, he has to pay for his crimes. He's charged with disregarding direct orders, exposing the World of Magic, and endangering human lives." He waved his hand around with an exaggerated look of horror on his face. "A giant building exploded in the middle of Downtown. Earthquake in Arizona. A blinding light visible for miles around. Why do you think the local authorities are not here, sirens blazing, huh? Because Ivor and I had to clean up his mess. Again!" He pointed at Damian, his jaw clenched.

A fit of blazing anger rushed through Cole, and the sword in his hand lit up with a deep, red light. "You touch a hair on my brother's head, and I'll rip you apart with my bare hands," he hissed, his fangs expanding.

"I second that." Ruslan halted by Cole's side, looking dark and ferocious.

"Commander Moore," said Oleg, stepping next to Cole. "There is some kind of misunderstanding here. Can we just—"

"Go back to Kendral, Child of Earth," Moore hissed. He tongued his cheek and spat on the ground. "Run back home. You have no place in all this, and I don't need the Master of Kendral sticking his nose into the Destiny Enforcers' business. This is an internal affair, and none of you have any say so in it." He glanced at Petrukha, and his lips twitched in distaste. "Another low-life asshole who loves to break the rules…"

Petrukha blanched and cowered away from him until he ran into Sylvana. With a deep sigh, Damian stepped forward, placing his hand on Cole's arm.

"Sheathe your sword, brother," he said calmly. "It's going to be all right. Not the first time for me." Then he turned to Moore, regarding him with cold indifference. "I'm coming with you willingly, Commander Moore. There is no need for the cuffs."

"Are you kidding me?" Moore gave a deep guffaw, spinning the cuffs on his index finger. "I've been wanting to see you wearing these for centuries. I think they will perfectly match the fashion statement you're sporting." He moved his arm up and down, gesturing at the black veil wrapped around Damian's hips. "I'm not going to deprive myself of the pleasure. On your knees, Blake. Your hands."

"Fine," Damian replied calmly. Completely disregarding Moore, he turned to Cole. He brushed his arm lightly, and Cole crumbled inside. "I need you to keep your cool, little bro. The Destiny cuffs will make me weak… extremely weak. I don't want you to react when you see me fall." He leaned down, whispering into his ear so quietly, only the vampires could hear. "Don't give this jackass the satisfaction of seeing you hurt. I'm going to be all right. I promise. Go home. River is probably going crazy not knowing where we are. Take care of Ruslan. I'll be back soon."

Damian's eyes darted around as if he were searching for something. Cole followed the direction of his gaze, realizing that his brother was looking for his gargoyle, but Zhulik was nowhere to be found, and Zabava was gone as well.

Giving Cole an encouraging nod, Damian turned to face Moore. He held out his hands but didn't kneel.

"Oh, yeah, I forgot." Moore snickered, sarcasm dripping from his every word. "You kneel before no one." He seized Damian's arm, pulling him closer, and locked the Destiny Cuffs on his wrists. "We'll see about that."

As soon as the cuffs touched Damian's skin, they lit up brighter. Damian moaned and dropped first to his knees and then to his back, his chest shuddering with arduous breaths as if he couldn't inhale. Then his eyes closed, and his head lolled to the side. Cole didn't move, but everything inside him was stretched to the limit, and he knew if Moore said one wrong word to him, he wouldn't be able to control his anger.

Moore bent down and lifted Damian with a low groan, throwing him over his shoulder carelessly. Then he gestured for Petrukha to approach. "You're coming with me, too," he said flatly. "The Destiny Council wants to have a word with you."

Placing his hand on Petrukha's shoulder, he snapped his fingers and vanished, taking Damian with him.

* * *

MOVING TORTUROUSLY SLOW, Cole patted the pockets of his pants just to remember that he didn't have a phone. Turning toward the Archmage, he lifted his shoulders in an apologetic shrug.

"Can I borrow your cellphone, my lord?" he asked flatly. "I need to get back to Paradise Manor, and for whatever reason, I feel drained." He chuckled mirthlessly. "I know. I'm a vampire. I'm not supposed to feel exhaustion, but I don't think I can take another step right now." He massaged his shoulder absentmindedly. "Also, I need to call Santiago del Castillo. I'm sure Sylvana wants to speak with him."

"Hold your horses, Mr. Adams," said Grand Master Elony with a commanding look of a person who got used to her orders being obeyed with no questions asked. "Sylvana Erickson goes with me. She broke the sacred oath, and I can no longer trust her with the secrets of the Sisterhood. End of story."

She snapped her fingers, and two of her slayers materialized next to her, dark and silent like shadows. They stepped on either side of Sylvana, seizing her arms. Sylvana winced and sent a veiled gaze to Cole, silently pleading for help.

Dammit... That's something I didn't need to deal with right now. Cole stifled a sigh. "Grand Master Elony, all the impostors are dead. I killed them all with my own hands, and Sylvana has proof if you want to see it. I swear the secrets of the Sisterhood are still safe."

"And I should trust a vamp why?" Elony asked, cocking her head.

Cole closed his eyes, cursing under his breath. "I'm sorry, Syl," he muttered, feeling dead on the inside. He eased her robe off her shoulder, exposing the dark rune on her chest. Then he turned to Grand Master Elony, meeting her scrutinizing gaze. "Sylvana didn't break her oath. She would never betray you. She had no choice."

"And that just proves my point." Elony folded her arms, raking Cole with frosty contempt. "One can never trust a vamp. What's dead must stay dead. You have no place in the world of the living. But that's beside the point." She waved her hand as if dismissing the issue. "Now that she has this rune, any necromancer can turn her into their willing puppet."

Cole shook his head, a corner of his mouth lifting in a sardonic grin. "I have no desire to argue with you, Grand Master." He turned to Allerton and ripped his torn shirt open. "My lord, do me a favor. Check my body for the presence of any runes. Tell her what you see."

"Are you sure?" Archmage Allerton raised his eyebrows. "This kind of check can be a little unpleasant."

"Yeah, I know. I am sure," replied Cole.

"As you wish." The Archmage placed his hand on Cole's chest and whispered a few words.

Cole groaned as a burning pain ripped him from the inside, forcing himself to remain still. His chest lit up with a shimmering white glimmer, and the runes that Yakov Bruce embedded into his ribs ignited brighter, glowing over his skin.

"I'll be damned," whispered Allerton, staring at him in awe. "Who cast this spell? Quite old and powerful." He lifted his hand, and the glowing runes vanished. Turning toward Grand Master Elony, he continued, "Elony, Cole Adams is fully protected against necromancy. I guess this is what he wanted me to confirm. If he can do the same for Sylvana Erickson, it'll solve the problem."

"That's right," replied Cole. "A powerful wizard of the Wardens Order cast this spell to protect me. He can remove the rune from Sylvana's chest and do the same for her." He paused, carefully observing Elony's reaction, but since her face showed no emotions, he continued, "Would that be enough for you to let Sylvana get back to her life in peace?"

Elony huffed, pursing her lips, her steel eyes blazing with displeasure. "Who is this Warden? I want to know who his Master is so I can confirm your statement and make sure he takes care of Sylvana's situation."

"His name is Yakov Bruce, my lady," Cole replied, and a thin layer of sarcasm snaked into his voice despite his effort to sound even. "He serves under Master Luc de la Crosse. You are welcome to contact Master de la Crosse to confirm my statement."

He heard a constrained gasp and glanced in the direction of the sound. Camila, Ricardo's sister, sat by the wall, finally awake. Her arms were wrapped tightly around her bent knees, and a haunted expression seemed to be permanently etched on her tender face. Cole narrowed his eyes, a few crazy thoughts zooming through his mind, but he said nothing to her, returning his attention to Elony.

"Fine," she snapped. "If you don't deliver on your promise, Mr. Adams, it's your head."

"Whatever," Cole muttered, turning toward the Archmage. "Can I please use your cellphone, my lord?"

As Allerton reached into his pocket, Oleg approached them, his face gray with exhaustion. "You do not need to call a taxi, my friend," he said to Cole calmly. "I can give you a lift to Paradise Manor." He glanced around and added, "And to whoever comes with you."

"Thank you," replied Cole, truly grateful that he didn't have to wait for a ride. "Can you teleport with three passengers?"

Oleg chuckled. "It is going to be tricky, but I think I can manage it. No problem."

"I guess the problem's solved," muttered the Archmage. He gave Cole a quick once-over and sighed. "Cole, if I may suggest… Don't do anything rash. Just sit tight and wait. The best thing you can do for your brother is do nothing. As soon as I get back to the Guardian's HQ, I'll contact Lord Magnus and explain everything to him. I promise it's going to be all right."

"Thank you," said Cole, and as the Archmage snapped his fingers, vanishing from the street, he turned to Ricardo. "Are you gonna be okay?" he asked.

While he did feel bad for Ricardo after his sister's betrayal, he still wasn't comfortable in the company of a man who sold hundreds of people into slavery, no matter what his reasons were. His eyes darted to Camila, but she shied away from his gaze, hiding in the shadows.

"Yeah, she has a phone," Ricardo replied, barely meeting his eyes. "We'll call a cab." He got up, rubbing the back of his neck, discomfort prominent in his every move. "Cole, listen... I am—"

"Go home, Ricardo," Cole interrupted him. "Whatever you want to say can wait. I'm sure we'll speak again at some point."

Cole turned to Oleg. "I look like a serial killer on the run, and River is going to have something to say about that," he mumbled, staring down at his torn clothes covered in brown stains of blood. "I'm so going to time-out."

"I'm looking forward to meeting this River," muttered Ruslan. "In a short period of time, she managed to do what I couldn't in centuries."

"What is that?" asked Oleg with curiosity, placing his hands on Cole's and Ruslan's shoulders.

"Keep this troublemaker in line." Ruslan's dark eyes crinkled at the corners, his gaze settling on Cole.

"Home, finally..." Cole whispered, pulling Sylvana closer. Oleg snapped his fingers, leaving Downtown behind in a swirl of colors and sounds.

CHAPTER 33

~ DAMIAN BLAKE ~

A touch of cold air to his exposed back ripped Damian out of unconsciousness. He groaned and opened his eyes but could see nothing, everything too bright and blurry. Feeling a painful numbness in his shoulders, he tried to move his arms just to realize that he couldn't. As his vision cleared, he found himself on his knees in a small, empty room, his arms stretched wide apart and shackled to the walls with long, thick chains.

At the opposite end of the room, he saw Petrukha. He sat on a chair, securely tied to it with iron chains. His head was bowed down low, and the mop of his gray hair fell over his eyes, so Damian couldn't say if he was conscious. However, the dark purple blemishes on the visible areas of his arms and chest suggested that he had taken quite a beating. Weakened by the previous events and drained by the Destiny cuffs, he knew fighting the restraints was pointless, so he dropped his head and let go, trying not to think about anything.

He wasn't sure how long he had been waiting, but to him it seemed like forever, his frazzled mind drifting on and off. When the door on his right opened with a soft squeak, and Commander Moore walked inside accompanied by Miranda, one of the three Destiny Council representatives, he wasn't sure it wasn't an illusion. She sauntered her way to him, her long robe flowing around her in soft waves. Halting no more than a foot away from him, she observed him with cold superiority. Damian groaned, averting his gaze as her shameless eyes explored every inch of his unclad body. Moore snickered, gloating over his helplessness.

"Look at you now," Miranda whispered, closing the distance between them. "Not so high and mighty anymore, are you, Commander Blake?"

Damian raised his eyes but didn't say anything. She seized his hair, yanking his head back, and moved her finger over the scar on his face, pressing her fingernail deeper to inflict as much pain as she could.

"So strange," she whispered, and Damian was positive she was talking neither to him nor Moore, but rather thought out loud. "Magnus is right, you are extremely powerful..." She let go of his hair and probed his bicep, her fingers quickly exploring the muscles of his arms and shoulders, raising goosebumps on his skin in their wake. "You're also quite capable as a man. But look at you now." She waved at the chains holding Damian's arm. "Simple iron chains, and you're absolutely helpless, on your knees before me. All your physical strength and magical abilities can't help you now. I can do with you whatever my heart desires." She fell silent, a strange glimmer in her gaze. "How does it feel to be at someone else's mercy? How do you feel about that, Commander Blake?"

"What do you want?" asked Damian through gritted teeth, too drained to be angry.

She laughed softly, slapping his cheek. "Still as rude of a peasant as you have always been." She arched her eyebrow at Moore. "Let's see if Commander Moore's whip can teach you some manners and how to respect the chain of command." She cackled, but as Moore made a move to come closer, she raised her hand, stopping him. "But before we jump into that, I would like to know why Magnus values you so much."

"You should ask him then," Damian suggested, pulling at his restraints slightly to readjust his position.

"Nuh," she sang, derision gleaming in her eyes. "Why should I, if I can just look under the hood myself?"

She placed her hand on his chest, and he stiffened, knowing full well what was coming next. As she channeled her power and proceeded with the soul-reading, he groaned, realizing with shock that he couldn't control the pain. He couldn't resist her invasive magic. He couldn't do anything to protect his soul or his mind. Feeling as if she was turning him inside out, he clenched his teeth, wrestling the need to scream.

A few seconds later, Miranda let go and folded her arms over her chest, a troubled look on her face. He dropped his head and hung in his restraints, his chest shuddering with laborious breaths.

"Hmm," she hummed, pursing her lips. "There is something very peculiar about you, Commander Blake. I can read anyone's soul. It's one of my specialties. But yours seems to be partially obscured, and whatever keeps me from fully reading it is more powerful than I am. Just like your path on the Board of Destiny... For whatever reason, I can never get a clear reading on anything to do with you or that undead brother of yours. Why is that?"

Damian looked up at her from under the overgrown mane of his hair, and a dark grin split his face before he could contain it.

"I. Have. No. Idea," he muttered, spitting one word at the time.

"Okay, fine. Then one more question before we proceed." She approached him, raking her fingers through the wild mass of his hair to expose the scar on his face. "I remember the first time I saw you," she said, her eyes getting foggy as she looked back in time. "A giant, handsome barbarian, clad in that strange Russian armor and covered in blood from head to toe. You had long, black hair—just the way you have it now—but your face was unscarred, and so was your back. I believe you received these marks somewhere around the time when you accepted the *'no one'* status. Is that correct?"

"Yes. Why is it of any importance?" he replied, wondering where she was going with it.

"You see, Commander Blake, you're a Child of Earth," she mused softly. "It means you possess great healing power. You should have no scars on your body whatsoever." She ran her finger across his face, and he jerked his head to the side, pulling away from her touch. "From what I understood, just a few hours ago, you died, and the elemental Earth brought you back." She tugged at his hair. "Your long hair is proof of that. Every time you die a human death, you're restored to the way you looked at the moment of your original ascension—the wild Russian barbarian. So why do you still have these scars—the marks you acquired about five hundred years after your ascension?"

"No idea," muttered Damian.

"Let's see if we can find out." She cackled, giving a nod to Moore. "Did you notice you couldn't control the pain, Blake?" Damian lifted his shoulders in a shrug as much as his restraints would allow him, and she continued, a carnivorous glee in her eyes. "Imagine how you will feel once Moore starts working? Trust me. He is not going to take it easy on you, and you'll feel every single lash."

"Do your worst." Damian lowered his head and braced for pain as Moore walked around him, positioning himself behind his back.

The whip hissed through the air, biting deep into his flesh, ripping his skin on its way down. Hot, blinding pain assailed him, and his hands clenched into tight fists of their own accord. Damian jerked within his restraints but didn't scream.

Miranda raised her hand with a wintry smile, stopping Moore, and waved at Petrukha. "Commander Moore, I almost forgot…"

Damian raised his head, tension building up in him as he waited to hear what this cruel woman was about to say. She probably noticed his reaction, because her smile grew wider.

"This one." Miranda touched Petrukha's forehead, whispering something, and he jerked awake, staring around wildly. "I don't need him anymore. Get one of your people to escort him to any of our holding facilities. He's done."

Petrukha's eyes flew wide open, and he pushed with his chest against the chains binding him to his chair.

"My lady, please," he yelled. "I beg your mercy, but not for myself. Please do what you wish with me but spare the young wizard who took my place as the Lord of the Sacred Isle, so I could assist Commander Blake. Please! Have mercy on his soul. It's not his destiny to spend his life as a prisoner of the Isle. He's young and innocent in all that. All he's guilty of is being loyal to his mentor and friends."

She halted and turned back to Petrukha, a thoughtful expression on her face. Then she glanced back at Damian, raising her eyebrows.

"Maybe you're right, old Enforcer," she murmured, staring down at Petrukha. "I'm willing to send you back to the Isle and free James Coldwell if—and only if—Commander Blake cooperates with me."

Damian shook his head, gazing heavenwards. "How am I supposed to cooperate with you if I truly don't know the answers to your questions?"

"I guess your answer settles that." Miranda wiped her hands on her long robe and headed toward the exit. She halted there and nodded to Moore. "Fifty lashes, Commander Moore, and don't hold back. If he faints, revive him and continue." Then she jerked her chin at Petrukha. "Once you're done, make sure

Petrukha is locked in one of the holding facilities for the remainder of his life. Effective immediately, James Coldwell is the permanent Lord of the Sacred Isle." She waved her hand at Moore. "You have your orders, Commander. Please proceed."

The whip hissed through the air again and again, and Damian lost count, endless anguish tormenting his body, setting his mind on fire. At first, he tried not to scream, but soon he stopped caring, strangled screams ripping his tortured vocal cords. Miranda stood by the door, an expression of sick delight on her face as she watched Moore doing his job.

Suddenly, the door flew off its hinges, sliding across the floor with a loud bang, and Miranda jumped aside with a shriek of fear. Thunder rumbled, and multiple lightning bolts forked through the air inside the room. The floor quaked, and Magnus walked inside accompanied by a gargoyle in his natural state.

Zhulik zoomed across the room and positioned himself between Damian and Moore, a dangerous growl rumbling in his stone chest. Magnus turned to Miranda, and his entire body lit up with such a brilliant light that she staggered back, raising her arm to protect her vision. The air around him crackled with electrical discharges, and the lightning storm increased as he assessed the situation.

"The next person who dares put their hand on my Shadow Enforcer will die screaming," he growled through his clenched teeth. "Am I clear, Commander Moore?"

Damian heard a soft thud as Moore dropped the whip, and his lips twitched.

"Yes, my lord," Moore replied, anxiety clear in his voice. "I was just doing what I was told by Lady Miranda."

Another man dressed in the long robes of a high member of the Destiny Council walked inside the room and stopped next to Magnus.

"Lady Miranda," he said softly, but his rigid posture showed just how furious he was, "you had no right to do what you did.

Commander Blake is Lord Magnus' Shadow Enforcer, and everything he did was done on his orders. And even if it wasn't so, it's Magnus' job to deal with his indiscretions and reprimand him if needed. As far as James Coldwell, we both know it's not his destiny to be the Lord of the Sacred Isle." He sent a veiled gaze at Damian, and his eyebrows lowered over his eyes. Then he turned to Magnus and added, "Magnus, these two are all yours. I trust you to make the right decision, my lord." He inclined his head in a respectful bow and turned to Miranda, his features growing harder. "Lady Miranda, let's have a friendly chat while Lord Magnus takes care of the situation." He pointed at the exit. "After you."

Throwing an angry scowl at Magnus, Miranda turned on her heels and stormed out the door, followed by the third member of the Destiny Council. As soon as they were gone, Magnus looked around and threw his hands up.

"Commander Moore, you are free to go," Magnus ordered and made his way to Petrukha.

He touched his chains, and they fell to the floor with a loud clatter. Then he reached into the pocket of his pants, pushing the side of his robe out of the way, his moves sharp with frustration. He produced a small vial with shimmering blue liquid inside and gave it to Petrukha.

"I'm going to send you back to the Sacred Isle where you are going to resume your duty as the Lord and Protector," he said, sounding harsher than normal. "This potion is to send Jamie back home. It'll lead him to Paradise Manor. Are you clear on what you need to do, Enforcer?"

"Yes, my lord." Petrukha got up with a low groan and bowed, pressing his fist to his chest. "I'm yours to command."

"Off you go." Magnus touched Petrukha's shoulder, muttering something under his breath, and the old Enforcer vanished from the room.

Moving slowly and heavily, he walked around Damian and

stopped behind him. "Goddammit," he cursed quietly. He came back and squatted in front of him, moving his hair off his face. "I'm so sorry, my boy," he whispered, watching Zhulik settle next to Damian, pressing his hard side to his knee. "When your gargoyle showed up at my door, I knew something was wrong, but it took me forever to find you and get the support I needed. This b—Lady Miranda cloaked your location..."

He got up and touched the restraints holding Damian in place. As the chains dropped to the floor, Damian cried out and would've fallen if Magnus hadn't caught him. The Head of the Destiny Council turned him to his stomach and lowered him to the ground, resting his head on his lap. Then he moved his hand over Damian's back, and a wave of warmth spread through him, relieving the pain in his injured back.

"I'm sorry, my child," Magnus said, gently probing the partially healed welts on Damian's back. "Healing magic was never my strength, and it always takes such an ungodly amount of energy, I can barely stay awake after I'm done with it. Let me take you to our healers."

"No." Damian pushed off the floor and sat up. The room around him spun, and he swallowed, suppressing the rising nausea. "I'll survive. I can always heal myself later. We need to talk."

"You're right," Magnus agreed. He petted Zhulik's head as if he weren't a giant stone monster but a tiny puppy. "Thank you for your help, Zhulik. Your master is absolutely safe with me, but I need to have a private conversation with him. You can go home now."

"*Says you*," muttered Zhulik defiantly and switched his attention to Damian. "*When it comes to you, I trust no one.*"

"I'll be all right, Zhulik." Damian couldn't help but smile. "Go to Paradise Manor and wait for me there, my friend. I'll see you soon."

The gargoyle gave a warning stare to Magnus and vanished

with a soft pop. Magnus put his arm around Damian's shoulders and snapped his fingers. As the room twirled around him, Damian held his breath, grateful for Magnus' support.

* * *

THE SKY WAS BLACK—NOT dark, but infinitely black. The hard, rocky ground was also black, and as far as Damian could see, there was nothing around. The light, silvery mist spread over the ground, weaving and moving silently in a continuous flow.

"We're nowhere?" asked Damian, leaning forward to wrap his arms around his bent legs.

"The safest place for us to speak," replied Magnus. "Can you sit without my support?"

Damian nodded, and Magnus changed his position to face him. He snapped his fingers, and a weak flame ignited in the palm of his hand. His eyes were glinting in the firelight, but he looked tired, his face nearly gray despite the bright, orange-red flares lighting it up. He lowered the flame to the ground and reached up, his hand barely grazing Damian's cheek before he dropped it into his lap.

"What happened, my boy?" he asked gently. "Archmage Allerton spoke to me right before your gargoyle showed up, but I want to hear the full story from you."

Damian rubbed his forehead, numbness spreading through his arms. Making an effort to remain calm, he told Magnus everything that transpired from the moment he spoke with him the last time. When he finished, Magnus didn't ask or say anything, but dropped his head, hunching his back, and for a split second, he looked like he had aged twenty years.

"Magnus," Damian called, touching his knee. "I have a question, and I need you to be honest with me. If you can't answer it straight, just tell me that. Don't try to speak riddles or wiggle your way out."

Magnus met his eyes, giving him a slow nod. "What is it, my child?"

"When I spoke with Yaginya, she told me I was marked by the beast," said Damian, shuddering at the memory of that day. "I think she was talking about my scars, but I have no idea what it means. She also said you knew the truth, but you lied to protect me."

Magnus flinched, and a deep wrinkle appeared between his eyebrows as he bit his lip. "Dmitri, I prefer not to—"

"When Miranda spoke with me just a few minutes ago," he continued, interrupting him, "she was also interested in my scars." He ran his fingers over the disfigured side of his face, not realizing he was doing it. "Please, Magnus, whatever it is, I have to know the truth."

For a while, Magnus didn't reply, and Damian didn't rush him, giving him some space to make up his mind. Then he sighed and pressed his hand to his eyes.

"It's not going to be easy for me to explain because unfortunately, I don't know everything myself," he started from afar. "But I'll do my best, and even though some things may shock you, I implore you to be patient and let me finish."

"Go on."

"I had been watching you and your brother since the moment you were born, Dmitri," he started and raised his hand to stop Damian from interrupting him. "I know it sounds creepy, but I promise, it wasn't an empty curiosity. From the moment you were born, I knew there was something special about you, just like there was something just as special about Nikolai. And on the day you both died the human death, I started to suspect what that so-called *'special'* could be."

"I don't understand—"

"Neither do I." Magnus chuckled. "There is an ancient prophecy about two brothers—one is the Light, marked by the

Darkness, and the second one is the Darkness, touched by the Light. A paradox, if you think about it…"

"I've never heard of it."

"I'm not surprised," replied Magnus. "The full text of the prophecy has been lost, and no one truly knows its full context. It's something about two brothers who are destined to bring the end to"—Magnus sucked in a short breath, opening his arms in a slight shrug—"something. I have no idea what that is."

"Wonderful," muttered Damian, staring into the darkness above Magnus' head. "Why do you think it's about Cole and me? There are more than enough mortal and immortal brothers out there."

"Yes, you would think so." Magnus chuckled again, a vibe of discomfort emanating from him. "As I watched Ruslan turn your brother, a wild suspicion rushed through my mind. Vampires—they're supposed to be pure darkness, yet I followed Ruslan's adventures long enough to realize that it wasn't the case. Don't get me wrong—as an ancient vamp, Ruslan has enough blood on his hands, especially in his early days as an undead. So has your brother. But I'm sure you will agree with me—Cole is not evil."

"I don't know much about Ruslan, but you're right about Cole," said Damian.

"Anyway, as I observed you and your brother for centuries, my suspicion grew stronger. That night, when you lost Vita, you were marked by the Darkness, my child, and that confirmed my hunch about you both. The mark of the beast, the way Yaginya put it, is powerful dark magic, and this is the reason your scars cannot be healed. Scars left by magic never disappear."

"But who marked me and why?" Damian leaned forward, his heart picking up the pace. "Who sent those monsters and killed Vita? Who was the man Mara showed me in the vision? Who is the Beast Master?"

Magnus shook his head, his warm gaze never leaving

Damian. "I'm sorry, my boy, but I have no idea who he is. I searched all the remaining records and came up empty."

"Fine. Let's assume you're right about me being marked by the Darkness," said Damian, chills running down his spine. "But how is Cole touched by the Light? I understand he's not evil, but there are other vampires who live the same lifestyle as he does. Just to give you a few names… Santiago del Castillo and Sylvana, Akira Ida and Yaroslav Potemkin. There are quite a few other old vampires who don't want to kill if they can help it."

Magnus looked down, his fingers twisting the ring on the middle finger of his right hand. "Have you ever seen your brother fight with two swords?" he asked after a while. "Roman *dimachaeri* style?"

Damian froze, unable to take his eyes off Magnus as if he saw him for the first time. "Yes," he whispered inaudibly. "When he fought the Navij, he used two swords. He killed the Navij, and I still can't wrap my mind around it… Killing a Navij is equivalent to killing a dark deity. It's supposed to be impossible. Sorry, I left it out of my report, but I was just—"

"Trying to protect your brother," Magnus finished for him, sadness shadowing his features. "You never have to protect your brother from me, my boy. His secret is safe with me." He tapped Damian's arm lightly. "Besides, I already knew it. Cole is ambidextrous, and I watched Ruslan train him in this ancient fighting style for years. Something tells me he knew Cole would need it sooner or later."

"Are you saying Ruslan knew about the prophecy?" asked Damian.

"I have no idea," replied Magnus. "Perhaps he knew, or maybe he suspected Cole had magic." Damian stiffened, and Magnus rolled his eyes at him. "I've been observing both of you since the moment of your birth. I knew it before either of you found out. You did the right thing by keeping it to yourselves.

No one should know. Do you understand me, Dmitri? No one should know about the prophecy either."

"Yes, sir," mumbled Damian, trying to process all the information.

"I suggest at some point you sit down with Cole and Ruslan and find out everything Ruslan knows or suspects about your brother," continued Magnus. "Do it gently. Ruslan loves your brother, but he's also an extremely old vampire. Old school, you know what I mean? Don't test his fatherly devotion and don't insult his intelligence by trying to manipulate him. You can trust him, so find the right moment for this conversation and ask all the questions straight."

"I will," said Damian. "Is there anything else I need to know related to Cole or the prophecy?"

"Quite a bit," murmured Magnus, his eyes going out off focus for a moment. "You and Cole will have to learn it on your own when the time comes. I believe he learned a lot already. He'll share with you when you see him again."

Damian nodded, realizing that this part of the conversation was over, and as always, Magnus wasn't going to say more than he could without exposing some obscured reading of the Board of Destiny.

"Just one more question before we move on, sir," he said tentatively.

"Huh?" Magnus frowned, tapping his fingers against his knee.

"Miranda said she couldn't read my soul," said Damian. "But both Yaginya and Veles had no problem doing it. Why is that?"

"Oh, that? This is one thing you don't have to worry about." Magnus tittered as if a heavy weight was lifted off his shoulders, and Damian couldn't help but wonder what question the Head of the Destiny Council had expected from him. "When I restored you as my Shadow Enforcer, I also conjured a protective barrier around your soul so other members of the Council couldn't read it. Everyone else is free to do it if you allow them, but not the High Council." He wagged his finger warningly. "And don't you dare ask me why. Just say, thank you, my lord, and leave it at that."

"Thank you, my lord." The corners of Damian's mouth quirked up, and for the first time since he had been brought to the Destiny Council realm by Commander Moore, he allowed himself to relax.

Magnus got up and started to pace, the silvery mist wrapping around his ankles like shimmering ribbons.

"Riddle me this, Dmitri," he said, sounding as if he spoke to himself. "You said Donna Luna acted on the orders from an unknown man, her master. He was the one who needed magical energy. But why did he need it? And how does the overthrowing of Peter the Great fit in all that?"

"As far as the situation with Peter the Great, I have no idea, but magical energy is a hard-to-get commodity," replied Damian, following Magnus' progress with his eyes. "The amount of magical energy she had stored in her underground bunker could have bought her master a world in the supernatural circles."

Magnus came to an abrupt halt and turned to him, tension in his narrowed eyes. "You're right," he whispered, his voice as dry as the grass in the Sanora Desert. "It could have bought him a world or a ticket out of a world. What if he needed all this magical energy to break out of one of the locked realms of death, like Hell, or the Celtic Otherworld, or the Dark Nav?"

"Could be," Damian agreed. "But it could also be anything else."

"You're absolutely right, my boy." Magnus started to pace again, nervously clutching his hands behind his back. "It's all connected. It must be. This Donna Luna's master, the rise of Koschei the Deathless, the absurd amount of magical energy. There must be something that connects it all."

Magnus kept pacing, quickly muttering something under his breath, but Damian couldn't make out anything he was saying. After a while, he scrambled to his feet, wincing from the sharp pain in his injured back. His energy drained by the Destiny cuffs still wasn't restored and suppressing the pain as well as self-healing was out of the question.

He stepped forward, blocking Magnus' path. "Magnus, stop," he said softly. "I've never seen you so troubled and… lost. We'll figure it out."

Magnus' gaze focused on Damian's face. "Do you remember what Ace said before she died?" he asked, his deep voice raspy.

"Of course," replied Damian. "She said someone gave her orders to put a rift between me and my brother. She also started to say something about you, but she's never finished her statement."

"Damian, be careful… you must help… Magnus is—those were her words," whispered Magnus. "I believe she was trying to warn you about some kind of danger. If my word is not enough, I can swear on my power that I didn't give her the orders to break you and your brother apart, and I would never hurt you. At least not willingly. So, I believe the complete statement is 'You must help. Magnus is in danger'…" His voice trailed off as he pressed his lips into a firm line. Then he shook his head, furrowing his brow. "It must all be connected somehow."

"Magnus," said Damian, and his words broke Magnus out of his stupor. "We'll figure it out. We always do. We just need a little time to think things through."

"I'm afraid time is the one thing we don't have," mumbled Magnus. "Go home, Dmitri. Heal yourself and get some rest before you start your investigation. Speak with Cole and Ruslan, but don't bring anyone else into it. Trust no one else. Do you understand me, my child?"

"Yes, sir, but—"

Magnus stepped back and pulled the sides of his robe apart,

shoving his hands into the pockets of his pants. "Commander Blake, I expect your reports daily."

"Yes, sir."

"Ugh…" Magnus rolled his eyes exaggeratedly. "Dmitri!"

Damian suppressed a smile as he lowered to one knee, pressing his fist to his chest. "I'm yours to command, my lord."

Magnus approached him and grabbed a handful of his hair. "Dammit, boy," he said softly. "Go home and get a haircut. And for God's sake, don't do it with your daggers. There are barbershops for that in the human realm, I believe."

He placed two fingers on Damian's forehead and stilled, his eyes searching his face. Then he twirled his wrist, and a thick cloak of darkness took Damian in its cold embrace.

CHAPTER 34

~ COLE ADAMS ~

Cole sat on a lounge chair under the cover of a flat porch roof and watched Ruslan swim endless laps in the Olympic-size swimming pool he had installed after he purchased the Brown's estate. After three years in restraints, Ruslan just wanted to feel free, and swimming seemed to satisfy the need for now. Ignoring the discomfort brought by the blazing Arizona sun, he kept at it, his muscled arms breaking the surface of the water in even, powerful strokes.

It had been close to twenty-four hours since Damian had been taken, and Cole had a hard time complying with Archmage Allerton's suggestion to stay put. On the other hand, he had no idea what to do. Damian had never spoken of this part of his life, and except for Luc de la Crosse and Quinn Allerton, Cole didn't know anyone else who could help him find his brother. Allerton had made it clear that Cole needed to stand down, and Luc de la Crosse was on his list of possible suspects in connection with Amaris.

Deep inside, Cole knew Luc couldn't have been the traitor, but in a situation like this, he had to remain vigilant no matter how much he trusted a person. He had some suspicions, but he needed solid proof.

The loud shrill of his new cellphone broke him out of his thoughts. He leaned to the side, reaching for the device, and swiped across the screen, answering the call.

"Cole," Jamie's voice sounded on the other side of the line. "I'm so glad to hear your voice, my friend."

"Jamie, you're back." Cole got up, his spirits rising. "Is Damian with you?"

A pause of hesitation filled the line, and Cole leaned his shoulder against the wall, getting ready for the bad news.

"No, Damian is not back yet. He's still in the Destiny Council realm, wherever that might be," said Jamie, his voice coming through dull. "Petrukha returned to the Sacred Isle and sent me home, to Paradise Manor. He told me that Damian was..." His voice morphed into a heavy silence, but Cole could hear his angry breaths.

"They punished him?" he asked, trying to help Jamie form the words. "Did they flog him?"

"Yes," Jamie replied at length. "I'm sorry, Cole. From what Petrukha explained, he had it bad until Magnus showed up and stopped that medieval cruelty." He cleared his throat and added quickly, "Damian is with Magnus now, so he should be all right."

'That's good. Magnus treats him well, more or less," Cole whispered, staring at the cracks in the tiles of the patio. "Listen, Jamie, I know you just came back and probably didn't even have a moment to get any rest, but I was wondering if you could help me with something." He thought for a moment and added, "It's not really your help I need, per se, but I think what I'm about to do will benefit you as well."

"Of course," the young man replied right away. "I'll go with you."

"I'm at home, at the Brown's estate. Can you come over now?" asked Cole, gesturing for Ruslan to come out of the pool.

"See you soon," Jamie replied and hung up the phone.

* * *

AN HOUR LATER, Cole parked his car in front of the gatehouse of Ricardo's house. Ruslan and Jamie sat in the back, conversing quietly. Jamie had never met a vampire as old as Ruslan, and unsurprisingly, he had hundreds of questions. What surprised Cole, however, was that his normally reserved and antisocial maker had taken a liking to the young man and didn't mind answering all his questions.

He reached for his phone and dialed Ricardo's phone number, counting the beeps. Ricardo answered almost immediately, his voice coming through too tense for Cole's comfort.

"Ricardo, we do everything as we discussed earlier, and remember, you must keep your cool and let me and Ruslan do all the talking," said Cole, staring out the window at the gate. "I'm parked outside the gates, waiting for you and your sister."

He hung up the phone and got out of the vehicle. Soon, the gate opened, and a golf cart driven by Ricardo parked next to the gatehouse. Ricardo stepped out of the cart and helped his sister out. She brushed her hands over her skirt, readjusting wrinkles visible only to her, and turned to her brother, tapping her foot.

Cole approached them, flashing a wide grin. "Please, my lady, have a seat," he said with an elegant bow as he directed her toward his car and opened the door for her. "Since I've met your brother, I've heard so much about you. Sometimes when meeting under extreme circumstances, the first impression could be wrong, so I begged Ricardo for the opportunity to get to know you better. He picked the venue since he knows your preferences so much better."

"At least something he did right," she grumbled, but as her eyes fell on Cole's beautiful blue *Maserati*, the expression on her face changed from annoyance to lustful hunger. She halted by the open door, gracing Cole with a long glance, and several emotions chased each other across her face. Displeasure and open disgust were replaced by surprise, and finally, a playful smile lit up her face.

"Thank you, Mr. Adams," she breathed, taking his hand to lower herself onto the seat.

He returned her smile, battling the desire to be as far away from this woman as he could. Thinking about how great it would feel to sink his fangs into her neck, he marched around the car and slid into the driver's seat.

As they took the freeway toward Scottsdale, she kept talking, asking him about his business, his life among humans as well as vampires, wondering what it took to be the King of a Vampire Court. He answered her questions in his usual lighthearted manner, pretending to respond to her flirtatious advances. Glancing into the rearview mirror, he caught sight of Ricardo's face and cursed inwardly. The man looked like he was about to be sick, his sun-tanned skin so pale it appeared to be yellow.

Cole's phone rang, interrupting the conversation, and he reached into his pocket, knowing ahead of time it was Jamie calling. He answered the call, pressing the device to his ear, and even though Jamie remained silent, he pretended to have an ongoing conversation.

"Cole Adams…" he said, pausing. "Yes, but do we need it today?" He paused again. "Sure, I'm not too far away. I'll pick it up."

Putting his phone back in his pocket, Cole took an exit from the freeway and then turned into a small plaza, parking it in front of a small bookshop. He glanced into the rearview mirror, giving a pointed stare to Ruslan. Then he stepped out of the car and walked around it to open the passenger door. Offering his hand to Camila, he smiled and turned his vampire charm on, forcing her to relax and drop her guard.

"Camila, darling, I'm sorry, but I need to make an unplanned stop. I hope you don't mind accompanying me. It won't take long," he purred, watching her eyes widened and pupils dilate as his glamor fogged her mind.

"But of course." She took his hand, turning in her seat to place both feet on the asphalt.

As they walked toward the store, Cole did his best to keep her occupied, so she realized where they were only when Cole halted in front of the door. Her eyes darted up at the name of the bookshop, and all color drained from her face.

"On second thought, I think I'll wait for you in the car," she mumbled, staggering back just to run into her brother.

"I think not," muttered Ricardo.

He opened the door and pushed Camila inside. Then he followed her into the store and quickly checked for silver traps before allowing Ruslan and Cole to pass inside. Jamie came in last and closed the door behind them with a loud thud to attract the attention of the store owner.

Aaron Cooper walked out from the back room to greet them. As his gaze halted on Camila, his eyes widened for less than a tenth of a second, but it was enough for Cole's sharp vampiric vision to register the change. The Warden regarded Cole and Ruslan with an icy stare, and his lip curled up in aversion. Nevertheless, he forced a dutiful smile and inclined his head.

"Mr. Adams," he said frostily, folding his arm over his skinny chest. "To what do I owe the pleasure this time?"

"Good afternoon, Mr. Cooper." Cole smiled brightly. "Just as usual, I need to speak with Master Luc de la Crosse. It's urgent."

"But of course, it is," grumbled Aaron, shuffling toward the counter. "When it comes to you, it's always urgent, and now you've dragged in more of your repulsive kind."

He reached behind the counter and fished out his cellphone. Then he dialed Luc's number and pressed the device to his ear.

"Master de la Crosse," he said once Luc answered the call. "Mr. Cole Adams is here to see you. What should I tell him?" He took a quick pause. "Oh, you're on your way? Yes, fine."

A portal, rotating with a shimmering blue light, opened in the middle room, and a young man in the black attire of a priest walked out of it, halting in front of Cole. His attentive hazel eyes took in every person in the room, and his features hardened, a shadow of concern crossing his face.

"Master de la Crosse, allow me to introduce my father," said Cole, gesturing at Ruslan.

"Ruslan," said Luc, offering Ruslan his hand for a handshake before Cole had the opportunity to say his name. "I've heard a lot about you, and not only from Cole. I'm glad to see you well after the terrible ordeal you've been through."

"Thank you, my lord," replied Ruslan, carefully squeezing his hand. "It's not every day a vampire gets to meet a Master of the Wardens Order and lives to tell the tale."

"You and your son are absolutely safe here," replied Luc. He turned toward Camila and Ricardo, and as Cole introduced them, he was positive Luc had never met either of them before.

"Cole," said Luc, gesturing for them to proceed into the small back room they used for private audiences. "I noticed Commander Blake is not with you. After the latest events, I hope he's okay. I don't know all the details, but the disturbance in the magical and elemental energy fields could be detected from miles away. Would you mind telling me what's going on?"

Cole made his way to the small table in the center of the room and pulled a chair out, helping Camila to sit down. Then he pulled the chair next to her and lowered himself onto it. With a shudder, he recalled the last time he was in this room—covered in the blood of his best friend whom he had no choice but to kill. Lowering his eyes, he waited until everyone found a place.

"I don't know if he'll be all right, Luc," he said quietly. "I don't think so. I know he disregarded orders of his superiors to save Ruslan, Sylvana and me, and the Destiny Council doesn't take these kinds of offenses lightly."

"As well they shouldn't," snapped Aaron. He didn't sit down but stood tense and erect with his hands clenched into fists at his sides. "Not only did he disobey orders, but he also made quite a light show from what I've heard, exposing the World of Magic and all. And all that just to save a few worthless vamps? He deserves everything that's coming to him."

"Aaron, what's wrong with you?" asked Luc, turning toward his human Warden. "Cole is Damian's brother, and Commander Blake would never leave anyone behind, let alone his brother. Besides, I thought we had this conversation already, and you agreed with me—not every supernatural being is evil. Your hate toward vampires and werewolves is clouding your judgment."

Camila laughed, her laughter sounding like the soft jingle of a silver bell. *"Monsieur de la Crosse, s'il vous plaît,"* she said with an elegant twirl of her wrist. "You can't be serious about that, can you?" She pointed at Ruslan, a look of superiority turning her tender face into an ugly grimace. "Look at him. From what I've learned over the last three years, this monster is at least a few thousand years old. Are you telling me there is no innocent human blood on his fangs?"

Ruslan's lips stretched into a wide, carnivorous smile, his fangs fully expanded. "My deepest apologies, my lady," he purred as softly as Cole, but the sound of his voice was a lot deeper, spreading around the room in soft, velvety waves. "I don't mean to offend your delicate senses, but I do brush my fangs at least twice a day. Rest assured, when I sink them into your deliciously elegant neck, there will be no other blood on them."

Camila snorted very unladylike and threw her hands up. "I don't understand how you, *Monsieur* de la Crosse, can tolerate something like this. You're a Master of the Wardens Order. I thought it was your duty to protect humanity against all the supernatural freaks."

"It is my duty, *mademoiselle*," Luc replied calmly, but Cole detected tones of irritation in his even voice, "and I assure you, I do my duty well."

"I beg to differ," she huffed, leaning forward, her hands gripping the edge of the table. "If that were true, we wouldn't have an old vampire named Arizona's most desirable bachelor, and the entire Vampire Court lurking in the shadows, hiding behind their King." She pointed at Cole, anger coloring her cheeks in a bright shade of pink.

"You don't think I'm desirable?" Cole leaned closer to her, whispering into her ear, and for a brief moment, her eyes became foggy with lust. "I'm wounded..."

"That's not the point." She pushed Cole away, rising sharply.

"We have hundreds of vampires, werewolves, shifters and other supernatural beings walking the streets of Phoenix among humans, leading normal lives, Camila," Luc said peacefully, but his French accent became heavier—a sure sign of his turmoiled emotions. "They are not hunting and killing humans, and I don't see a reason to prosecute them. The Destiny Council supports peaceful co-existence. So, vampires like Cole Adams and Ruslan, who are trying to move the Arizona Vampire Court in this direction, have our full support and cooperation."

"This is a preposterous statement and coming from a figure of authority like you, Master de la Crosse, it's unacceptable." She slammed her fist on the table, blinding fury taking hold of her. "This is the main reason humanity can't count on the Destiny Council and their affiliates to keep us safe. As far as I am concerned, the underground supernatural fighting Houses are doing a much better job by cleaning our streets and keeping them supernatural-free and safe."

Luc stared at her, slack-jawed. Slowly rising, he braced his fists against the table. "You can't be seriously condoning modern-day slavery, gladiatorial fights, and the violation of human rights, Camila? Because this was what Amaris had been doing for years until Commander Blake put the end to this atrocity by destroying his evil kingdom and killing him."

"Human rights?" she squealed, stomping her foot.

Turning toward Ruslan, she pointed at him with a shaking hand. Ruslan's smile stretched wider as he allowed his true nature to take him over fully, and now, he looked positively terrifying, and that just added oil to the blazing fire of her righteous wrath.

"Does this monster look like a human to you, with his red eyes and shark-like fangs? Just look at his hands!" Ruslan lifted his hand with elongated fingers, ending in sharp claws, and waved at her, and she squealed furiously, all but hopping in place. "Wake up, Luc!" she shrilled. "What human rights violation are you talking about? They are not HUMANS!" She slammed her fist on the table again, fury radiating around her in thick waves. "And your Commander Blake is a rude, barbaric beast. I hope the Destiny Council flogs him to death for what he did. Amaris was the only person in Arizona who kept us all safe. She was the only one who kept all these supernatural animals under control."

She spoke fast, barely taking a breath between words. Ricardo pressed his hand over his mouth, an expression of horror permanently etched into his features. Aaron shifted closer to her, his hands rising of their own volition. Shaking his head, he was trying to put a word in, but the floodgate had been opened, and Camila wasn't paying attention to anything around her, her eyes, filled to the brim with hatred, drilling through Ruslan.

"Are you going to attack and kill Animal Control Officers for keeping dogs with rabies off the streets?" she continued passionately. "No! So, what's so different here? None of these creatures are human, and I am proud to say that Mr. Cooper and I did everything in our power to help Amaris do her honorable job!"

A heavy silence enveloped the room. No one moved or said a word. Ruslan glanced at Cole and gave him a nod of approval, assuming his normal human look. Cole closed his eyes, dropping his tensed shoulders.

"*Oh... mon... Dieu...*" whispered Luc de la Crosse, staring at his human Warden with an appalled look in his wide-open eyes. "Aaron, why? You've been a Warden for most of your life. We accepted you as one of our own even though you didn't have magic. I trusted you! The Destiny Council trusted you... What did you do?"

Aaron narrowed his eyes, lifting his chin.

"What do you think?" he asked, his high-pitched voice flat and even, as if he were reading a phone book. "I was just a boy when I joined the Wardens Order. I had nothing but my idealistic beliefs and the need for revenge, and I was sure by joining your Order, I would get everything I was looking for. As years passed, I realized just how wrong I had been, believing in you." He shook his head and folded his arms, judgment reflected in his scornful stare. "And when you forced me to assist a vampire, running fucking errands for him, I had enough."

"What exactly did you do, Aaron?" asked Luc, his soft voice barely audible. "Tell me the truth, and maybe I can ask for some kind of leniency when it's time for you to face the Grand Master of the Wardens Order and the brotherhood."

"What did I do?" He snickered, a maniacal grimace twisting his face. He took a deep breath, his caved-in chest expanding. "Everything. I did everything Amaris told me to do. Every word that I heard here, I delivered to her. I didn't want to compromise my position by meeting with the Head of the Arizona House in person, so Camila was our close liaison." He scratched his chin thoughtfully, but then shrugged defiantly and continued, "When Commander Blake reported to you about his plan to infiltrate the Arizona House with Ricardo's help, I contacted Camila right away, and that's how Amaris was able to entrap your Commander and this undead leech."

His eyes darted to Cole, and unconcealed hatred darkened his features. Before Cole realized what Aaron was up to, he moved his hand behind his back and pulled out a wooden stake. With a wild shrill that didn't resemble any sound produced by human vocal cords, Aaron launched at Cole.

"Aaron, no!" Luc shouted, reaching for the human Warden, but he was a moment too late to stop him.

Camila cackled, clapping her hands.

A dagger appeared in Jamie's hand as he threw himself in Aaron's way.

Cole burst out laughing.

Aaron's holler of anger turned into a strangled wheeze.

"Are you serious, dude?" Ruslan stood with his left hand on his hip, holding Aaron by the scruff of his neck with his right hand, dangling him at least a foot above the ground. He turned Aaron slightly so he could see his face. "Did you seriously think you could be faster than two ancient vampires? The audacity!" He pursed his lips, wild twinkles of laughter dancing in his black eyes.

"Father," Cole managed to say through bursts of laughter. "Dude? Where the hell did you learn to speak like that? You used to chastise me for polluting my language with modern-day slang."

"Amaris' guards called me that for three years. I think they beat it into me," murmured Ruslan. He slammed Aaron flat on the floor, ignoring his groan of pain, and twisted his arms behind his back, holding him down. "What do you want me to do with him, Master de la Crosse?"

"I have to take him to the Wardens' HQ in Paris," replied Luc. He produced a pair of standard human handcuffs and restrained Aaron.

"Take her, too." Ricardo, who sat silently through the entire conversation, got up and took his sister's arm, ignoring her resistance and screams of protest. "I'm done. There is nothing I can do to make things right, but maybe your people still have a chance to fix whatever is broken in her head."

"As you wish," Luc replied with a sharp wave of his hand, and a portal opened in front of him. He seized Aaron and Camila's arms, pushing them toward the rotating vortex, but halted there, glancing back at Cole. "It's not going to take me long. Can you please wait for me here?" His eyes halted on Jamie, and a faint smile touched his lips. "You too, Jamie."

As soon as Luc walked through the portal, taking his prisoners with him, Ricardo inhaled as if he had been holding his breath for a long time. His eyes darted from Cole to Ruslan, and he dropped his head, clenching his hands in front of him.

"I should apologize to you and Ruslan for everything I've done," he said quietly, "but there are no words that can make any of it right." He bit his lip and looked somewhere above Cole's shoulder, unable to meet his eyes. "Ruslan, three years of pain and suffering... three years of your life..."

Ruslan smiled, barely lifting his shoulders in a shrug. "What is three years compared to thousands?"

Ricardo nodded, but the deep remorse never left his dark eyes. "Cole, I'm leaving Arizona," he continued. "Your brother kept his word, and now, I'm finally free. It didn't happen the way I expected, but I'll take my freedom in any shape and form. I want to move on with my life, and to do so, I need to step away from all this supernatural crap." He reached into his pocket and produced a set of keys, offering them to Cole. "My house has never belonged to me. It was owned by Amaris and his evil corporation. But now that he... she's dead, I want you and Damian to have the collection of magical artifacts and weapons. You can do with it as you wish. Your SUV is parked in my garage. You can come over and get everything at any time."

"Ricardo—," Cole started, but Ricardo just smiled with a half-hearted shrug.

"It's my final decision," he said softly. "I spent most of my life worrying about my sister's wellbeing, doing things for her that made me disgusted with myself. And now…" His voice trailed off, and he took a deep breath. "Now, I'm going to start my life anew—a clean slate. I just hope I'll find a way to atone for my sins." His eyes slipped from Jamie to Ruslan and then halted on Cole. "I hope Damian is all right. I truly wish I could see him before I leave, but if I don't… just tell him thank you. He saved me in more ways than one."

He walked out of the room, and soon, a soft thud of the main door announced that he had left the shop.

"Poor bastard," muttered Ruslan, lowering himself onto one of the chairs. "His sister, his own flesh and blood…" He shook his head and fell silent.

* * *

Luc came back sooner than Cole expected. He walked out of his portal, carrying a small leather bag over his shoulder. Even if he noticed that Ricardo was gone, he didn't ask anything and halted in front of Jamie. The young wizard looked up at him and rose to his feet slowly, a question in his eyes. Luc smiled, warmth suffusing his features, wiping out the remains of tiredness.

"Jamie," he said, taking the bag off his shoulder. "Yakov Bruce and I worked with you for a while, and we both agreed you have what it takes to be a valuable member of the Order." He opened the bag and reached inside, his eyes never leaving Jamie's. "With the blessing of the Grand Master of the Wardens Order, and in the presence of these two honorable witnesses, I would like to offer you the mantle of a Warden. Would you accept our humble offer, my young friend?"

Jamie threw a desperate and slightly lost glance at Cole, and he gave him an encouraging nod.

"Master de la Crosse," he said. "I would love that, but Damian—"

"I know, you chose Commander Blake as your mentor, and I have nothing against it," said Luc, interrupting him. "You can continue practicing combat magic with Damian whenever he has time. Becoming a Warden doesn't stop you from doing that. As you're well aware, Wardens are not only scholars but also trained warriors and powerful wizards."

"Do it, Jamie," said Cole. "I'm sure Damian will support your choice, too."

Jamie turned to Luc and smiled his shy smile that turned his eyes into two narrow arches. "I guess it's a yes then."

Luc exhaled with relief and pulled a folded piece of white linen out of the bag. He unfolded and placed a long white cloak with the red insignia of the Wardens Order embroidered on it over Jamie's shoulders.

"The official initiation ceremony is in five days in Paris," he said, readjusting the folds of the cloak. "The Grand Master would like to welcome you himself. In the meantime, this store and all the local Wardens affairs are yours. If you stay behind for a few hours, I can walk you through some of your responsibilities." He reached into his pocket and produced a set of keys, offering them to Jamie. "Effective immediately, you're on the Wardens payroll."

Cole exchanged a quick look with Ruslan, and both got up. "I guess it's our cue to leave." He inclined his head in a light bow, ready to walk out, but Luc stopped him.

"Cole, the Grand Master of the Wardens Order tried to get in touch with Lord Magnus to ask about Damian's situation, but he couldn't find him anywhere. I'm sorry, *mon ami*," he said, stifling a sigh. "I'm sure Damian will be back soon. You know how it is—the time in the Destiny Council realm moves differently."

"Thank you, Luc," Cole replied softly. "I know he's coming home. In a day or a year, but my brother will return. He always does."

He bowed to the Master Warden and walked out the door.

CHAPTER 35

~ DAMIAN BLAKE ~

Damian manifested next to the entrance into Paradise Manor and pushed the door, but it was locked. Lowering on the cold steps, he cursed his bad luck under his breath. He didn't have the key and his phone was gone, too. As his eyes traveled across the front yard, an old memory sprung up to life in his mind—River always kept a spare key hidden among the desert landscape of her front yard.

He scrambled to his feet with a pained groan and headed toward the only saguaro cactus that stood tall on her land. Counting three pebbles away from the cactus, he pulled out a small stone with a plastic container attached to it. A silvery key was locked inside the container. With a winning grin on his face, he pulled the key out, covered the container and shoved it back into the ground next to the cactus.

Barely moving his feet, Damian made it back and unlocked the door. As the cool air enveloped him, he swayed and closed his eyes, enjoying the silence and peacefulness of the empty house. He halted in front of the antique silver mirror in the foyer and gave himself a quick once-over, shuddering at the look of his reflection.

"Dammit," he muttered, brushing dust and dirt off his hair, face and shoulders. As his eyes halted on the black veil wrapped around his hips, he threw his hands up. "I look like a friggin' Roman gladiator after a full day in the arena."

Then he turned his back to the mirror, twisting his body slightly to explore the extent of the damage. The Zerkalitsa readjusted the angle of the surface so he could see better, and he gasped.

"Oh, fuck... Scratch that," he muttered, exploring partially healed welts, cuts and tears on his blood-covered back. "I don't look like a gladiator... I look like a runaway Roman slave. And this hair..." He tugged at the long strands falling down his shoulders. "Perun almighty. I'm glad River is not home to see me like this."

"Personally, I think you look like a victim of the Spanish Inquisition," a high-pitched voice offered, sounding in his mind, and Damian snapped around to see Gypsy strolling into the foyer, accompanied by Zhulik in his puppy form. *"As far as your hair... wait... let me stop laughing..."* She pressed her paw to her mouth as if she was giggling. *"Whatchamacallit the Barbarian, Russian style. Finally, your inside matches your outside."*

"Ha-ha, very funny," murmured Damian, heading toward the kitchen.

"That's the best you can do, Commander. Are you losing your wit?" asked Zhulik, trotting by his side. *"Oh, wait. I know it's the Destiny cuffs, right? Power deprivation affects your brain."*

"I'm surrounded by furry comedians," grumbled Damian, walking into the kitchen. "Is River still at work?"

"No, she went out with Zabava a while ago," replied Gypsy, jumping on top of the counter and settling there by the coffeemaker. *"Zabava has been hanging around a lot since you've been gone. Last night, she even stayed here overnight, which is good. Zabava plus kitchen equals good food."* She licked her paw, narrowing her eyes at Damian.

Thanking all the gods he knew for Zabava sticking around to keep an eye on River, he dropped onto a chair and pulled closer a round table mirror River always kept here. Channeling his magic, he noticed how truly drained he still was. Even the simple act of summoning one of his daggers came with serious effort. Pursing his lips, he grabbed a handful of his hair and placed the dagger above his fist, ready to slice.

"Sir, put down your weapon and step away from the mirror! Hands behind your head!" River's voice, choking on laughter, sounded in front of him, and he dropped his dagger, raising his hands as he looked up over the mirror.

River and Zabava stood in the doorway, their eyes sparkling with laughter. He got up sharply, forgetting to hold on to his improvised loincloth, and it would've slipped off if he hadn't caught it in the last moment.

"My eyes, my eyes!" squealed Gypsy, arching her back, her tail thicker than her body.

"Well, Commander," said Zabava, tears of laughter glistening in her eyes, "I must say, resurrection becomes you. You look at least nine hundred years younger, and your attire..." She exhaled, waving her hand. "Anyway, now that you're home, I'll leave you two kids alone."

Before either River or Damian could stop her, she snapped her fingers and vanished. River approached him and touched his dagger, tracing the design on its hilt with her finger. Then she reached up and took a strand of his hair, moving her fingers through it.

"Despite the layer of dirt, you have gorgeous hair," she said calmly. "I'm not going to bother asking how it grew to this length so quickly, though." With soft laughter, she opened one of the drawers and shuffled there for a while until she found a set of scissors. "Are you sure you want to cut it?"

"Yes. I want it just the way it was. But it can wait," he

objected, realizing belatedly what she would see if she looked at his back. "Let's wait until tomorrow."

She grabbed the scissors and walked around him, disregarding his protests. As she halted there, a gasp escaped her lips, and Damian dropped onto the chair, hiding his face in his palms.

"What the hell is that?" she whispered hoarsely, and then added, nearly screaming. "Damian, what the fuck is that? Who did this to you?"

He turned to face her, the shocked expression on her face sending waves of shivers down his back.

"River, it's okay. I wish you didn't have to see that, but my magic is drained, and I can't heal myself," he said, looking up at her. "I just need a few hours, and all this mess is going to be over."

She bit her lip, shaking her head. "Your world is barbaric and cruel," she whispered, gently caressing his cheek. "I'm not sure I want any part of it."

"The World of Magic brings nothing but pain and suffering," Damian echoed her, his thoughts far away. He rose to his feet slowly and touched his dagger, making it vanish. "Let's leave the haircut for tomorrow. I need to take a shower and get some sleep. I'm exhausted."

"Dima, are you in pain? Do you need me to help you clean up your wounds?" she asked, her voice trembling slightly.

"Just give his back a few good licks, and he'll be as good as new," suggested Gypsy, snickering.

Damian almost choked, sending Gypsy a veiled gaze. "No, River, thank you. A shower will do the trick. As far as the pain, I'm used to that. I'll survive." Turning toward the gargoyle, he smiled faintly. "Zhulik, will you stay guard tonight?"

"While you and River—," the gargoyle started, wagging his eyebrows suggestively, a wide grin on his muzzle.

"While I am going to be dead to the world," muttered Damian. "Until I wake up in the morning, I don't want to hear from either of you." He pointed at Gypsy and then at Zhulik. "Or else. Am I clear?"

"I assume you weren't addressing me, soldier?" asked River, chuckling.

"No, ma'am," replied Damian, slowly making his way around the kitchen table.

He walked through the hallway barely moving his feet, supporting himself with his hand against the wall. When he finally made it to his room and closed the door, he sighed with relief, dropping the dirty veil on the floor. Then he grabbed clean pajama pants and headed to the bathroom.

Leaving the pants on the counter, he stepped into the shower stall and opened the faucet without waiting for the water to warm up. As the cool jets enveloped him, the welts on his back responded with a tingling pain, but he ignored it. For a while, he just stood there, watching dirty streams of water run down the drain, his mind blissfully blank. Then he took a deep breath and started to wash his hair and body, careful not to disturb the half-closed wounds.

A while later, Damian shut down the water and took a towel, gently patting the water off his skin. After the shower, the weakness took hold of him with full force, and a task as simple as putting his pants on came with effort. He pushed the door open, wishing for nothing but to fall onto his bed and close his eyes. But as he stepped into the room, he froze, his eyebrows rising.

Dressed in a light, silky robe, River sat on the edge of his bed, her copper hair spilling over her chest and shoulders. She raised her blue eyes, bright against her pale complexion, and a shy smile tugged at the corners of her lips. At the look of her, everything inside Damian expanded with warmth, and all the terrible events he had survived in the last few weeks seemed to fade into the depth of his memory.

"Damian," she whispered his name, her fingers fumbling with the edge of her short robe. "I just wanted to make sure…" Her voice trailed off, but she didn't lower her eyes, gazing at him with so much affection, his breath hitched.

He wasn't sure why he did that—it was driven by a pure need rather than a conscious thought—but he crossed the distance between them and lowered to his knees, wrapping his arms around her waist. Then he placed his head on her lap and closed his eyes, inhaling the delicate scent of her body—a fragrance of midnight desert mixed in with the aroma of wildflowers. Her fingers threaded gently through his hair, and he didn't want to move, afraid to take a breath.

"Dima," she called, gently tugging at his wet hair.

He raised his face, meeting the azure gaze of her eyes, and got up, spreading his shoulders.

"At my worst moment—and there were a few of them while I was away—all I could think of was coming back to you." He sat down by her side and leaned forward, propping his elbows on his lap. "When the world went dark before my eyes, and I thought that was the end, I saw your face… River…" He turned to her and took her hand into his. Raising it to his lips, he kissed one finger at the time. "I just want…" His voice broke, and he shook his head, realizing that he shouldn't voice what he truly wanted. "Nothing. What I want is impossible, and it's not fair to you."

"I don't understand. How so?" she asked, genuine surprise and confusion in her voice.

"Destiny Enforcers can't have personal attachments for a reason," he started, stifling a sigh. "Personal attachments make us vulnerable, but I'm not worried about me. If word gets out that I have a woman in my life, it will put a giant bullseye on your back. Every supernatural creep out there who holds a grudge against me will do their best to hurt you."

"And how is that any different from me being a cop?" She

shrugged indifferently. "Every criminal asshole I've ever put behind bars sleeps and dreams about putting their hands on me."

"Most of your criminal assholes, as bad as they are, don't have magical powers that can destroy the world," Damian objected quietly. "Anyway, you need a man who can protect you and take care of you. A man who makes you happy, who is there for you whenever you need him, no matter what." He dropped his head, rubbing the edge of his bracelet. "My job can take me to the end of the world and back at any moment of night or day, and I have no choice but to go. I can't quit. I can't say no. I must obey or suffer the consequences." He glanced at the black veil on the floor, biting his lip. "You deserve better than that."

"Now, you really sound your age, Damian Blake." River smiled, rolling her eyes. "It's not the twelfth century, and I don't need a man to protect and take care of me. I can do all that perfectly well on my own, thank you very much." She huffed, looking at him with reproach. "Cole told me you were old school, but I had no idea how old." She sighed and took his hand, caressing his knuckles with her thumb. "I don't need you to do anything for me, Damian. I just want to have you in my life... All I need to know is that when you're summoned in the middle of the night to do your crazy job, sooner or later, you will return to me. Not because I asked you to or you think I need your protection, but because you want to be here, with me. Because"—she waved her hand—"Paradise Manor is as much your home as it is mine."

Damian opened his mouth to object, but catching the tense expression on her face, he snapped his mouth shut.

"Forget about your crazy job, vindictive monsters, and your code of honor worthy of any medieval knight. It's a simple question, Damian. Do you want me in your life?" she asked, getting off the bed. "Yes or no?"

"Yes…" The word rolled off his tongue before he could stop it, and he cursed himself inwardly.

River exhaled with relief, and her tense features softened. She lifted the blanket and pointed at the bed. "I'm sorry. I shouldn't have started this conversation when you were tired and in pain. Get some sleep."

"Yeah, the timing could have been better." Damian chuckled softly and lay down, rolling to his side.

She grabbed an extra pillow, placing it into his hands, and then covered him with the blanket.

"I know how you like to sleep," she murmured, planting a soft kiss on his cheek. "I'll see you when you wake up."

As she tiptoed toward the exit, he called her, halting her by the door.

"River, can you please call my brother and let him know I am back?" he asked, his mind fogged by exhaustion. "I don't even know where my phone is… and I am…"

"Cole is taking care of his… um… Ruslan, so he stays with him at the Brown's estate, but he's called me during the day a few times, asking about you. I'll let him know, don't worry," replied River. "I'll buy you a new cellphone first thing in the morning."

"Thank you," he mumbled and was fast asleep before River left the room.

A BRIGHT RAY of sunlight touched his face, and Damian groaned, turning to his other side. His back responded with a sharp pain, and he moaned, carefully lowering himself on his stomach. For some reason, today his wounds seemed to be more sore than yesterday.

"Zhulik, are you here?" he reached out to his gargoyle.

"Kitchen." The answer came right away. *"River is cooking."*

"River is cooking?" asked Damian, flabbergasted. "That's a first." He chuckled and sucked in a sharp breath as pain spiked through him again. "Zhulik, I need to heal myself. Can I count on you to guard the house a little longer? The healing will take about fifteen minutes, but you know how exhausting the healing magic is. I'll need some time to recover after it."

"Heal-away, Commander," the gargoyle replied, "and come join us while the kitchen is still in one piece."

Damian smiled and closed his eyes, surrendering himself to the healing energy of Earth. As it circulated through his system, with every passing moment, the nagging pain in his wounds subsided, and a few minutes later, it was gone completely, leaving behind the lightheadedness and debilitating weakness. He took a deep breath and closed his eyes.

He didn't notice when he fell asleep again, but when he woke up, the sun was inching its way down to the horizon, coloring the purple rock formation with its last pink shades. Damian sat up and stretched his arms and shoulders, noticing with satisfaction that nothing hurt, and he felt strong and energized.

He noticed a box with a new cellphone on the bedstand and smiled, wondering when River had time to take care of everything and go to work. He took the phone out of the box and turned it on. She already set it up for him and entered the very short list of contacts he had. The only thing that was missing was the photo of Cole and River he loved and used to use as his lock screen image.

He put the phone on the stand and grabbed a fresh set of clothes out of the closet on his way to the bathroom. A brief examination in front of the mirror showed him that all the welts were healed, and except for the usual scars disfiguring his back, his skin looked perfectly normal.

Damian cleaned up, got dressed and made his way to the kitchen, enjoying the cool touch of the carpet to his bare feet. Zhulik lay on the floor by the entrance, his nose in his paws, and Gypsy had enthroned herself on her favorite spot, guarding the coffeemaker. Everything looked quiet and peaceful. As if answering his thought, Zhulik lifted his head and yawned, his long pink tongue curling.

"Everything is quiet, Commander," he murmured and put his head back down, closing his eyes.

Noticing a yellow piece of paper covered in River's even writing on the table, he sat down and picked it up.

"Dima,

I hope you feel better. You looked like hell yesterday, so I didn't want to wake you up. Cole called earlier and said that he'll stop by in a few. I think I should be back at about the same time. If you are hungry, I left some takeout from that little restaurant you like in the refrigerator. I'll see you soon.

River."

A takeout. Damian smiled. *So much for River cooking.*

He got up and stilled, listening intently. It wasn't as if he heard anything out of the ordinary, yet something attracted his attention, sending chills down his spine. A low growl rumbled in Zhulik's chest as he morphed into his natural state.

"Commander, something's coming," he growled, staring toward the main entrance.

Damian opened his other sight but still didn't detect anything unusual. The Guardians magic flowed through the left wing of the house in soft, even waves, and the wards remained silent. Nevertheless, he decided to check it out. Stepping soundlessly on the carpet, he ran through the dark hallway and halted in the foyer.

Sharpening all his senses, he checked the area as far as he could reach but detected nothing. Yet something was bothering him, and not only him. Zhulik stood by his side, pressing his giant stone side to his leg, and if he had fur, it would've been standing up on his back.

"Something is coming, Commander, and it's up to no good," the gargoyle growled.

Dammit... The daggers materialized in Damian's hands as he closed his eyes, relying on his other sight.

When the door opened with a light squeak, he spun to his left, his blades igniting with a blinding light.

"Damian, what's going on?" River asked, entering the foyer. "Why do you—"

"River, run!" he yelled desperately, but it was too late.

The entrance door snapped shut with a loud bang which echoed through the hallways. The wards howled all at once, filling the house with an ear-splitting noise. Zhulik spread his wings and went up to the tall ceiling, his eyes glowing a bright blue. The entire house shook violently, and the energy of powerful dark magic assailed Damian's senses with such force that he could barely take a breath. Darkness descended on the house, swallowing all the remaining light, and he could no longer see River in the quickly changing surroundings.

Damian raised one of his daggers and shouted, *"Illucious."*

The shadows slithered away from him, but it wasn't enough to illuminate the entire foyer. He ran in the direction where he thought River was, his movements slow and heavy like in a nightmare, and for a split second, he thought Mara was playing her games with him again. But the dark energy signature he detected was different, so he abandoned that thought. While it felt familiar, he couldn't quite place it.

"River!" he yelled desperately, but his voice disappeared in the cacophony of the wards. As the entire building vibrated and trembled, he knew it was only a matter of time before the wards failed, and he still had no idea who was attacking him and why.

A strong wave of tremors spread under his feet, and suddenly, a wide fracture ran across the floor and up the wall, quickly increasing in size. Dropping his daggers, Damian connected with his element, but no matter what he tried, he couldn't stop the process. On his left, he heard River's constrained scream and darted in the direction of the sound, cutting his bare feet on the small rocks and debris. The concrete tiles kept breaking away under his steps, falling into the endless, growing hole in the floor. A waterfall of rocks fell from the ceiling, but he couldn't see anything up above. He zoomed toward the wall and finally found River, pulling her to his chest. She wrapped her arms around his waist just in time as the remaining tiles vanished, sending them flying into the void.

He tried to open his wings but couldn't, feeling as if some invisible ties locked parts of his Destiny Enforcer's magic within his body. At the last moment, he touched his bracelet, and it turned into the whip. He swung it, aiming blindly for the area where the chandelier should have been, but Zhulik swooped down and caught the chain, stopping their fall.

"Commander, I see no way out," he growled, making Damian's blood run cold.

The storm of dark magical energy intensified, suffocating him, and he opened his other sight again, scanning for anything that could help him identify the perpetrator. Right above him, the darkness seemed to be thicker, forming a malignant, black mass. He couldn't say who was there or what it was, but that was all he had.

"River, hold on tight," he yelled, hoping she could hear him. As she wrapped her arms tighter around him, he channeled all the magic he could gather and pointed in the direction of the dark mass. *"Exitius!"*

As the blinding white light of his spell impacted the mass, it hissed and twirled in place, revealing the silhouette of a tall, skinny man wrapped in a black cloak. The man cackled, the sound of his laughter cutting through the racket of the ward. Before Damian could react, he zoomed through the air and seized River, ripping her away. She yelped, fighting his hold, but to no avail.

Damian screamed as if his heart was ripped out of his chest, but since the monster held River in front of him, using her as a shield, there was nothing he could do. He connected with his element, calling to the power of nature. Thick wines erupted from the hole in the floor. They broke through the walls and the doorway. Entwining together, they created a sturdy canopy beneath him.

"Zhulik, let go of the whip," he commanded, and as the gargoyle let go, he dropped to the canopy, landing softly on one knee. Looking up, he saw the man holding River right above him, and he growled, *"Now, attack!"*

Without waiting for a second invitation, Zhulik zoomed toward the man. He flew around him at an incredible speed, using every opportunity to hurt him without injuring River. The man twirled in the air, waving his hands at the gargoyle as if he were an annoying fly.

River screamed as she started to fall.

Distracted by the gargoyle, the man's attention wavered, and Damian was able to open his wings to their full extend. He flew up, catching River in midair, and lowered her to the net of vines. Conjuring one high-voltage energy ball after another, he propelled them through the air, assailing the monster with full force. The man howled—a cry of blazing fury—and extended both hands toward Damian.

Damian didn't recognize the spell he used, but he had no time to wonder about it. As the stream of purple light exploded out of the man's hands, he pulled River closer to his chest and covered her with his body, wrapping his arms and wings around her.

"Procedia Amnia," he shouted, erecting the shield of the basic protective spell around them.

The purple light of the dark magic wrapped around the dome of his spell, eating at it, corroding it with its malignant power.

"Commander Damian Blake!" the man shouted. "I'm Koschei the Deathless, and I'm here to make you a promise." He fell silent for a moment, as if giving Damian a chance to process his words. "You imprisoned and killed my loyal servants. You destroyed the magical energy I've been collecting. So, here is my promise to you, boy. What happened today is just the beginning. I will not rest until every person and everything you hold dear to your heart is either dead or destroyed. Today, consider yourself lucky."

Koschei snapped his fingers and vanished. The darkness dissipated, and the wards stopped buzzing. The light flooded the foyer, deadly silence enveloping them. Damian let go of River and folded his wings behind his back. Helping her to her feet, he quickly checked her for any visible injuries, but she seemed to be completely unharmed. Feeling a heavy numbness spreading through his chest, he backed away from her.

"Damian, I'm okay," she said, taking a step toward him, but he raised his hands, shaking his head.

"River, I'm sorry," he whispered, unable to speak louder than a hoarse whisper. "This is the reason Destiny Enforcers can't fall in love, have a family, have any kind of life."

"Damian, wait, please," she begged, tears brimming her eyes. "Let's talk about it—"

"No. This conversation is over." He wrapped his whip over his wrist, turning it into the bracelet, and then ran his fingers over his tattoo, summoning his gargoyle. As Zhulik merged into it, he bowed to her, pressing his fist to his chest. "As long as you're around me, you are in danger. I need time to think and decide—"

"Dima, what the fuck is going on here?"

Damian heard his brother's voice coming from behind him and spun toward him. His eyes took in Cole's appearance, and a deep sadness suffused his numb chest. He stepped closer to him and pulled him into a quick embrace, his heart stopping for a brief moment.

"I love you, little bro," he whispered so quietly that only Cole could hear him. "I'm glad Ruslan is back with you, because I..." His voice shook and he paused, searching for a better word. "Protect River... and don't look for me."

Before Cole could stop him, Damian snapped his fingers and vanished.

EPILOGUE

* * *

~ Damian Blake ~
Coral Springs, Florida.
Twenty-four hours later.

Despite the late hour, the air was heavy with heat and humidity, the scent of ocean reaching far inland. The last rays of the setting sun reflected in the polished surface of the gravestones, the light breeze rustling the palm tree leaves, playing with flowers left by the graves.

Sitting on the ground with his back rested against a tree, Damian took a deep breath and closed his eyes, trying to stop the endless rush of chaotic thoughts in his mind. All he wanted was a few minutes of peace so he could assess the situation calmly and come up with a rational decision, but his brain refused to comply. He spent the night and most of the day here, alone, but no matter what he tried, he couldn't find a way to keep River out of harm's way now that Koschei knew about their relationship. He blamed himself for everything that had happened and all that could happen in the future.

He wasn't sure how long he sat like that when a slight fluctuation of the elemental energy field touched his senses, followed by a cold wave of vampiric essence. He exhaled with a shake of his head, recognizing the energy signature of the vampire. He didn't react, however, keeping his eyes closed, but just to be on the safe side, he added extra effort into concealing his own magic.

"Commander Blake." The rolling R's and the low timbre of the voice were as familiar as the elemental energy of Earth emanating from the person who spoke.

With a deep sigh, Damian cracked his eyes open and raised his head. Three men stood in front of him—two of them observing him with interest and concern while Cole stared at him with a mix of irritation and relief. His brother threw his hands up, shaking his head.

"Florida? Really?" he grumbled. "You made me travel all the way across the country to find you."

"I told you not to look for me," Damian replied flatly.

"Yeah, I know." Cole rolled his eyes, annoyance prominent in his every move. "You love to boss people around, and if I've listened to all your orders…" Cole's voice trailed away, and he shoved his hands into the pockets of his pants.

"How did you find me, anyway?" asked Damian, rising.

His eyes halted on a short man standing behind Oleg. He was positive they weren't personally acquainted, yet he knew he had seen him before. The man didn't bother concealing his energy signature, and Damian suspected he wanted him to know that he was a Child of Fire.

"I couldn't. After your resurrection, our blood bond was gone," muttered Cole. "But Luc knew what to do, and luckily, a few things came together nicely. He told me it's impossible to find a Destiny Enforcer who doesn't want to be found, but another Child of Earth could sense you. So, he contacted Oleg, who happened to be visiting his friend here, in Coral Springs at the time. To make a long story short, when you teleported to this cemetery, you created such a splash that Oleg couldn't help but detect the spike in the elemental energy of Earth in the area. The rest was a matter of Luc talking to him and putting two and two together."

Damian huffed. "Sorry, but I'm not the only Child of Earth in this realm. It could have been anybody."

"No, you are not," Oleg agreed. "But you are the only Child of Earth who has Destiny Enforcer magic, and when you materialized here, you forgot to conceal it."

"Dammit," muttered Damian, staring at the darkening sky over his brother's head.

"Damian, you're not going to do something as stupid as disappearing for a few centuries again, are you?" asked Cole, and the amount of sadness in his voice made Damian cringe inwardly.

"No, Cole. I needed to be alone for a while," he said quietly, unable to hide the reproach in his voice. "I needed to think, and this place gives me a sense of peace and clarity."

The short man stepped forward, offering his hand to Damian. "I'm Zane Burns," he introduced himself, a lopsided grin bringing a single dimple on his left cheek. "We had a brief… um… interaction a while ago in this cemetery, Commander."

"I remember." Damian shook his hand, looking down at him with curiosity. "You're a Fire Salamander."

"Guilty as charged," Zane replied and turned to Oleg and Cole. "Guys, I'm sorry, but can you please give me a few minutes alone with Commander Blake."

Oleg and Cole exchanged a quick look and walked away, halting by the fence. Zane squatted next to the gravestone and dusted its cracked surface with his fingers. The stone was old, and the name was erased by time and weather, if it had ever been there in the first place. He looked back at Damian, his face calm and a little sad.

"Whose grave is it, Commander?" he asked, getting up to his feet.

"I don't know," Damian replied absentmindedly. "I needed some kind of closure. A place to—" He cut himself off, looking away.

Zane nodded. "Walk with me," he offered, gesturing for Damian to follow.

They walked between graves until Zane halted in front of a polished, marble gravestone. He kneeled next to it, carefully removing all traces of dust and sand, and readjusted the fresh flowers in the stand in front of it. He didn't say anything, but Damian could see the reflection of deep heartache in his steel eyes.

The inscription on the stone read: *"Angelique. You saved the World from Chaos... Forever in my heart."*

"Zane—," Damian started, but the Fire Salamander straightened and raised his hand, stopping him.

"She's not here either. Her body just ceased to exist when she fused her spirit with that of the Lord of Chaos..." He bit his lip, his chest shuddering with short breaths. "I loved her more than life itself, but with all my power and magic, I couldn't save her," he said quietly, clutching his throat, his voice raspy. "You can still save your love."

"What did Cole tell you?" asked Damian, rubbing the back of his neck.

"Nothing," replied Zane, lifting his shoulders in a half-shrug. "Your brother is loyal to you through and through. I think even if I tortured him, he wouldn't say a word." He chuckled, shaking his head. "If you hadn't noticed, Oleg is quite observant and perceptive. So, except for what he told me, I know nothing about you." The corners of his mouth quirked up a little, giving him a slightly guilty look. "I've been around the World of Magic long enough to take a pretty accurate guess."

Damian didn't say anything, heaviness settling in the pit of his stomach.

"You're a Destiny Enforcer, so it won't be a stretch if I say you have more supernatural enemies than you can count," he continued, his calm, gray eyes searching Damian's face. "One of them, or maybe a group of them, tried to get you off their case, holding the lives of those you love over your head." A lopsided smile touched his full lips. "How am I doing so far?"

Damian nodded, unable to speak.

"Now you're about to make the same mistake I made." Zane glanced at the gravestone, and a painful wrinkle materialized between his dark eyebrows. "I wish I hadn't been so ignorant in the ways of magic back then…"

His voice trembled, and he bit his lip again. Damian didn't say anything, sensing his internal torment.

"Anyway," Zane continued as he quickly composed himself. "I know you're a lot older than me, so please don't be offended by me trying to give advice. Putting a physical distance between yourself and the people you love won't stop the supernatural bastards from coming after them. If anything, it will make things a lot worse. Distance means nothing. The only thing that matters is what you keep here." He placed his hand over his heart, flames igniting on the bottom of his eyes. "Even though your brother is not a damsel in distress himself, by distancing yourself from him and the woman you love, you're putting them in danger, my friend. Since they have already been marked by your enemies, they are a lot safer with you by their side than without you."

"Thank you, Zane, but I know that," Damian whispered, everything inside him twisting in agony. "I was a little shocked, to be honest, and I needed time to process. I don't know how much you know about the Destiny Enforcers, but I'm not a free man."

Zane looked up at him with an expression of sympathy in his eyes. "I experienced the pleasures of Commander Moore's Bootcamp myself, and I must tell you…" He shuddered, his expression hardening. "No mercy, no remorse, no regrets, no choice… Isn't that how the Destiny Enforcers operate?"

"Yes, that sums it up nicely," agreed Damian. "I have to figure out how to balance my subserviency to the Destiny Council with what I need to do to protect my brother, River and my friends without getting my skin flogged off my back." He chuckled bitterly, rubbing his brow. "I wasn't going to run."

"You could have fooled me." Cole's voice sounded behind him, and Damian turned around to face him. "What happened, big bro? River was so upset by your sudden departure that she couldn't explain anything. Between us, that evil asshole didn't scare her even a tiny bit, but you running away pissed her off." He snickered. "She'll have something to say when you come back home, and like a real lady, she is not going to be gentle with the choice of words."

"Dammit…" Damian exhaled weakly, raking his hand through his overgrown hair.

"So, who is the monster in question?" asked Oleg.

Taking a deep breath, Damian told them what happened at Paradise Manor and the promise Koschei made before leaving.

"Fucking pervert," muttered Oleg. "He always goes after women." He glanced at the Fire Salamander, regret in his glowing, orange light. "Sorry, Zane, but I think my vacation is over. I must go back to Kendral and let Master Alliandr know that Koschei finally surfaced and is on the path of war."

"Understood. We all have our hands full." Zane gave his friend a light tap on his arm, and then turned to Damian. "So, what's the plan, Commander?"

"At the moment, I have no plan," replied Damian. "But I'll

figure it out. One thing is for sure though—I'm not going to bend my knee just because Koschei tried to blackmail me."

"We'll do what we always do." Cole flashed him a smile that exposed his long fangs. "We'll find this undernourished, evil bastard, and we'll fight him until he meets his true death." He placed his hand on Damian's shoulder, squeezing it lightly. "I'm with you all the way, no matter what your crazy plan is going to be, *brat moi.*"

"I know." Damian glanced at his brother, a sad smile touching his lips. *Brother mine...*

EXCERPT

*Read on for an excerpt from
N.M. Thorn's new book
The Shadow Enforcer Book 4:*

*~ Damian Blake ~
Blue Creek, Arizona*

The sharp edge of a sword cut through the air above Damian's head with a soft whistle. He ducked down and rolled on his shoulder, coming up to his feet right away. Without slowing down, he snapped toward his opponent just to receive a bone-crushing punch to his jaw. As a burst of white light exploded in his head, he staggered backward but managed to remain standing. He shook his head, endeavoring to dispel the dizziness, and spat the blood that quickly filled his mouth.

With his vision still slightly out of focus, Damian swung his whip, aiming at the silhouette of a man with glowing, scarlet eyes. The silver thong whooshed through the air, but his opponent was faster. He took a quick step back and raised his arm, allowing the whip to wrap around it. As silver came in contact

EXCERPT

with his skin, a hiss of pain broke from his lips, but he didn't let go. Instead, he yanked his arm across his chest and pulled back with all his strength.

Before Damian could release the grip of his weapon, he was dragged across the hard desert floor, unable to control his fall. Fast and fluid, his opponent closed the distance between them and seized his throat, raising him off the ground. Barely pulling his free hand back, he punched him in the face, but to Damian it felt as if a demolition ball struck him at full force.

His nose broke with a loud crunch, and blood gushed down his chin. His fingers unlocked, and his whip fell with a soft thud, raising a small cloud of dust. He squeezed his opponent's wrist with both hands but couldn't break his vice-like grip. For a moment, everything went black before his eyes, and he groaned, dropping his arms powerlessly.

"Father, stop!" Cole's desperate voice broke through the cotton wall in Damian's frazzled mind, and he cracked his eyelids open but could see nothing—everything still blurry. "It's enough. You're killing him!"

"If I don't kill him in training, someone else will in real combat," Ruslan muttered, but lightened his grip, carefully lowering Damian to the ground.

A sharp breath that sounded almost like a moan escaped Damian's lips as he pressed his hands to his face, feeling the wetness of blood under his fingers.

"I thought we agreed on light contact sparring," Damian growled, glowering at Ruslan over his hands. "I didn't use my daggers, and I removed the silver blades from my whip—"

"It *was* light contact," replied Ruslan reproachfully, accentuating the word *was*. "Neither Cole nor I used our full strength or speed. You're off your game, Commander." He shook his head, his lips pressed in a firm line. "Before, even an ancient vampire couldn't get the best of you. Now, any baby-vamp…" He didn't finish his statement and whistled, throwing a troubled gaze at

Cole. "You need to figure out what's wrong with you and restore your strength before it's too late."

"I know what's wrong with him." Cole moved behind Damian and hauled him up into a sitting position, resting his back against his chest. "It's called sleep deprivation."

The coolness of his brother's body against his overheated skin felt calming, and Damian closed his eyes, focusing on suppressing the pain in his broken nose and bruised jaw.

"How long has it been since Koschei's attack, Damian?" continued Cole. "Five months? Six? Should I remind you that you have a human body? You need to sleep, eat and lead a normal lifestyle."

"Define normal," mumbled Damian, his mind drifting on and off.

"Normal means you sleep at night and work in the daytime," snapped Cole. "From dusk till dawn, you guard Paradise Manor, lurking in the shadows like a thief just so River won't catch you doing it. Then you return home to get two-three hours of sleep before you receive a call from Luc or Allerton or anyone else who needs a Destiny Enforcer on duty in Arizona."

"Uh-huh…" Damian looked up, a weary smile tugging at his lips. "Should I tell all of them to fuck off because I need my beauty sleep?"

"Goddammit, Dima!" Cole yelled. "At least you can let Ruslan and me take shifts guarding Paradise Manor at night, so you can get some rest."

"If Koschei attacks again, neither you nor Ruslan have what it takes to fight him," Damian whispered, heaviness settling in his heart. "He'll kill River and both of you… I can't have it."

Ruslan shifted closer, crossing his legs.

"I hate to point out the obvious, Damian, but if I could beat the living hell out of you in five minutes, Koschei will destroy you in one second." Ruslan grabbed a small stone and propelled it into the desert, aggravation visible in his sharp moves. "You don't sleep. You barely eat, and when you get hurt on your job, you don't use your healing magic because it supposedly takes too much out of you." He threw his hands up. "I know you're not my son, Commander, and I can't tell you what to do, but this needs to stop."

Since Damian didn't react, Ruslan muttered something in his native Pecheneg tongue under his breath. Given that it was an extinct Turkic language, Damian couldn't understand a single word he said, but the expression on Ruslan's face clearly indicated that it couldn't have been anything other than profanity.

"Just heal him, son, would you?" Ruslan waved his hand at Cole in resignation. "And for God's sake, reestablish your blood bond with your dimwitted brother if you still want to have him around."

Cole chucked, shaking his head at his maker, but tapped Damian's shoulder and asked, "Just healing or the blood bond?" He raised his wrist to his mouth, ready to bite, but stilled, waiting for his brother's decision.

"Let's do it," said Damian quietly. "As much as I hate to admit it, Ruslan is right." His eyes darted up from Ruslan to Cole, and he added, "You are both right."

"Finally, some spark of an intelligent thought." Ruslan got up and headed to a large boulder where he sat down, crossing his legs at the knee.

It had been six months since Koschei the Deathless attacked Paradise Manor, trying to abduct River. Following the attack, Damian had made the decision to move to Cole's estate located within walking distance from Paradise Manor, but since then, he had spent every single night patrolling the area, expecting either Koschei himself or one of his flunkies to pay a visit.

The situation in Arizona also wasn't the calmest. Every day, either Hawk, Jamie or Luc de la Crosse reported strange unrest in different supernatural communities, but none of them could point out the source of turmoil. With rogue vampires crawling out of the woodwork, Cole had a hard time controlling his Court, and Ruslan was positive a dangerous opposition was forming in the shadows.

Between trying to maintain peace in his state and keeping River safe, Damian felt at the end of his rope, the extensive use of his magic and sleep deprivation taking a toll on his body. But today, while sparring with Cole and Ruslan, for the first time, he truly realized the extent of his exhaustion, and how it affected him physically and magically.

A soft hissing noise told Damian that Cole expanded his fangs ready to bite, and he grabbed his arm.

"Make it hurt, Cole," he muttered warningly.

"I think you had enough pain for one day," replied Cole as he tilted Damian's head to the side and sunk his fangs into his neck.

A short ping of pain spiked through Damian, and the metallic scent of blood touched his nostrils. But before he could react, a wave of sticky, mushy weakness spread through him, and he moaned, leaning heavier against his brother's chest. He wasn't sure if it was the effect of the vampire bite or his general condition, but all he wanted was to close his eyes and forget about everything. All he needed was a few minutes of peace and oblivion. When Cole let go, he didn't move, refusing to open his eyes and return to his painful reality.

"Dima, are you ready?" asked Cole, gently slapping his cheek.

"Not at all, but let's do it anyway," he whispered.

Cole bit his wrist, pressing it to Damian's lips. Damian grimaced at the sweet taste of the vampire's blood but forced himself to drink until his brother stopped him. As the fog in his mind started to clear, taking away the aches and pains of his worn-out body, he unlocked Cole's arms and lay down flat on his back, allowing his element to take him over. The earth trembled slightly beneath him, and small stones rose a few inches off the ground. Damian smiled a drunk smile and lifted his hand, making a circular motion. The pebbles danced around him, responding to his command.

"I never get tired of watching a Child of Earth in his element," murmured Ruslan, his eyes following the movement of the stones.

The shrill ring of Cole's cellphone made Damian jolt upright, dropping all the pebbles. Cole pulled out his phone and swiped his finger across the screen, answering the call. Then he showed the screen with River's name on it to Damian and put the call on speaker.

"Cole?" River's voice sounded strangely distant. "I hope I'm not interrupting anything."

"Hey, River," Cole replied lightly. "What's up?"

River sighed and fell silent for a moment. "Is your brother with you, by any chance?"

"He's here," replied Cole, giving Damian a pointed stare. "Do you want to speak with him?"

"Not really," she replied, her voice turning dull. "But I seem to have no choice in the matter. We received a call from Flagstaff PD. They have a strange case on their hands…" Something fell with a loud thud and after a moment River continued, "Anyway, I have no idea why or how they found out about his existence in the first place, but they demand Damian on this case. Since your brother is registered with Blue Creek PD as my consultant, the captain is sending both of us to Flagstaff to assist with the investigation."

Listening to River's flat, emotionless voice, Damian dropped his head, rubbing the back of his neck.

"Let me put him on the phone," offered Cole, ready to give the device to Damian.

"No, it's okay," objected River. "Frankly, I wish I could work with you instead. You know, with someone who has more brains and balls… Someone I can trust not to vanish at the first sign of trouble… But it is what it is." She sighed audibly. "Just tell him to be in Paradise Manor in thirty minutes and to keep it magic-free. I have a new partner, and I'm sure Commander Blake doesn't want to get flogged again for exposing the World of Magic to an unsuspecting human."

"I'm coming with Damian," said Cole in a tone of voice that left no place for objections.

"Good idea," replied River. "I'll see you soon."

Cole hung up and shoved the phone in his pocket, offering his hand to Damian. As he got to his feet, Ruslan approached him, a sly grin on his face.

"Your big chance to fix the situation, boy," he said, tapping him on his shoulder.

"Or, knowing my brother, he'll destroy any hope for reconciliation," interjected Cole, snickering. "That's why I'm going with him."

Damian threw a menacing glare at Cole and grabbed a handful of hair on the back of his head, giving it a good yank. Then he placed his hand on Ruslan's shoulder, teleporting all of them back to the Brown's Estate.

* * *

Thirty minutes later, Cole drove through the gates of Paradise Manor and parked his car on the driveway in front of the main entrance. River was already outside, waiting for them. She stood next to her Charger, speaking to a young woman in a business suit. She was slightly shorter and a lot curvier than River, her dark, brown hair falling to her shoulders in soft strands. As Cole and Damian stepped out of the vehicle, she took in their appearance, and her brown eyes rounded for a split second. But then a wide, friendly grin split her round face, and she waved her hand at them.

"You're Cole Adams, aren't yah?" she asked with a barely noticeable southern drawl, curiosity twinkling in her eyes.

EXCERPT

"Rich entrepreneur, Arizona's most eligible bachelor, yadda yadda yadda. I remember seeing your photo in some newspaper a while ago."

"Yes, I am," replied Cole, returning her smile. "This is my brother, Damian Blake."

"Nice to meet you, ma'am," said Damian, making sure that his eyes didn't light up with the energy of his magic as he carefully scanned her with his other sight. As far as he could see, she was human—not an ounce of magic in her. Nevertheless, he decided to err on the side of caution until he was sure. There were enough supernatural beings who knew how to suppress their magical energy signature to the point where it wasn't detectible at all.

"Oh," she mumbled, narrowing her eyes at Damian. "You two are biological brothers?"

"I know. It's hard to believe, but these two are in fact siblings," chimed in River. Her eyes halted on Damian, and his heart skipped a beat. But she quickly switched her attention to Cole and proceeded with the introduction. "This is my new partner, Detective Alison Twain."

She walked around Damian and opened the back door of her car, gesturing at it. "Get in. We have a slightly over two-hour drive, and I want to get on the road as soon as possible."

Damian swallowed, thinking about spending two hours in a tiny, cramped car with three more people inside, and cold sweat beaded his forehead. But he clenched his teeth and slipped inside, following Cole. As soon as River and her partner got in and shut the doors, his claustrophobia made its presence known, and he leaned back, closing his eyes, taking a few deep breaths to keep it under control.

River punched the address into the car's GPS and drove out of Paradise Manor. As soon as she merged into the traffic on I-17, she glanced back in the rearview mirror. Her gaze landed on Damian, and she frowned.

"Damian, we have two more hours of driving," she said flatly. "You look a little… um… uncomfortable. Are you going to be all right?"

"I'm fine," he replied, but before he could say anything else, she switched the subject.

"The case we're going to be working on involves theft," she said, staring at the road ahead.

"What is so mysterious about a theft that the local police department can't solve it?" asked Cole, throwing a sideways glance at Damian.

"Good question," River murmured, switching lanes to pass a truck. "As far as I can see—absolutely nothing. The house in question is located a few miles north of Flagstaff, literally in the middle of nowhere. The owners—husband and wife—are rich collectors who travel worldwide, collecting rare ethnic artifacts of different cultures. Once in a while, they appear on archeological summits and conferences and lecture in universities all over the world. Since both have a Ph.D. in Archeology, they know exactly how rare and valuable every item in their collection is."

"Aw, River, come on, girl." Alison gave River a light push on her shoulder as if they were two schoolgirls, gossiping about boys during one of their sleepovers. Then she twisted in her seat so she could see Damian and Cole and continued, her eyes twinkling with excitement. "Everything River said is true, but so bo-o-o-ring! Here is the fun part, boys. Someone has gone through every corner of their house, obviously searching for something. Everything was thrown on the floor, all drawers were opened, and furniture moved. Besides ethnic artifacts, the owners have a lot of modern valuables in their home. Yet"—she paused, raising her index finger with a mysterious look—"the husband is positive nothing was taken. He said every item is accounted for."

"So…" Cole mused, his eyebrows rising. "If nothing was stolen, why are we going there?"

"Because," Alison continued eagerly, ignoring River's stifled sigh, "the wife disagreed with her husband. She said one item is indeed missing—" She cut herself off and rolled her eyes. "Well, not exactly. The item is still in the house, but she's positive it has been replaced with a replica."

"This is where it gets really confusing," River took over, glancing at Cole in the rearview mirror. "The local specialist in archeology and their insurance company appraiser checked it, and both said it's an absolutely authentic, original item." She chewed on her lip, her eyebrows drawing together. "They're rich and influential people. You know how it is, Cole. Money talks, right?"

Cole nodded with a nonchalant smile, but the stiffness of his shoulders told Damian how uneasy his brother felt about this story.

"Anyway, I don't know what kind of generous donation they've made to the local PD, but when the wife demanded Damian's assistance, they called my precinct right away, and here we are—searching for an artifact that hasn't been stolen," River continued, tones of annoyance in her voice.

"They requested Damian's assistance," repeated Cole, flabbergasted. "They actually said his name."

"Exactamundo!" Alison sang, throwing a curious glance at Damian. "She said the only person who can find the missing artifact is Damian Blake and refused to deal with anyone else or give any details."

"Dammit," Damian cursed, projecting his thoughts to Cole. *"Are you thinking what I'm thinking?"*

"Unfortunately, yes," replied Cole. *"Whoever these collectors are, they know your supernatural identity."*

"I have no idea why they would want me," said Damian aloud, glancing from Alison to River. "I know absolutely nothing about historical artifacts or their value. My area of expertise has nothing to do—"

"Yeah, I know. Long-distance running is *your* area of expertise," River interrupted him, the pained tones in her quiet voice making Damian do a double-take. But then she shrugged as if nothing happened and switched her attention back to the road ahead of her. "I guess we'll find out soon."

Already on edge, Damian clenched his teeth to stop himself from saying something he would most certainly regret later and looked out the window. With Koschei's threat hanging over him like the sword of Damocles, and the situation in his state thickening by the day, he already had more problems than he could handle. The idea of some rich archeologist knowing his supernatural identity just added to his overall feeling of unease, sending chills down his spine.

Dammit... When it rains, it pours...

TEASER: THE BURNS FIRE
(THE FIRE SALAMANDER CHRONICLES BOOK 1)

~Zane Burns, a.k.a. Gunz~
Modern Day, South Florida

The restaurant was nothing special, just another tiny hole-in-the-wall located on one of the countless South Florida canals. There wasn't anything noteworthy about its limited menu either. The only thing special about this place was its relaxed atmosphere. The restaurant had an open porch with three tables facing the canal. But the regulars were never sitting on the porch. They preferred to stay inside, leaving the romantic view to tourists and lovey-dovey couples.

Gunz had discovered this place shortly after he moved to South Florida, and since then he had become one of the regulars, visiting the restaurant at least a couple of times a week. He liked the laid-back atmosphere and easy-going crowd. It was a place where he allowed himself to relax and drop his guard. To a degree.

The inside room of the restaurant wasn't big, just a few tables and a bar. A big screen TV was hanging on the wall behind the bar, next to a few shelves with liquor. The air was infused with the smell of alcohol and fried food, and a heavy curtain of cigarette smoke was hanging under the ceiling. The room was relatively dark. Out of six wall lights only three were on, but no one ever asked to turn up the light.

Gunz walked through the room, quickly surveying every corner, and sat down at the bar. Tonight, besides a few regulars, there was no one new. A pretty young woman in her mid-twenties approached him right away. Here, she was everything—the owner of the restaurant, a bartender, a waitress—all-in-one, cross-functional queen of *Missi's Kitchen*.

"Usual, Mr. Burns?" she asked, smiling at him. Her skin, the color of dark chocolate, was smooth like silk and her large gray eyes framed with thick black eyelashes looked unnaturally bright on her face. Her long black hair was braided into countless thin braids and pulled into a ponytail on the back of her head, calling attention to her elegant neck.

"Yes, Missi, thank you," said Gunz.

She put three small shot glasses on the bar table in front of him and filled them with vodka. "I'll be back with your food in a moment," she told him, heading toward the kitchen door.

"Take your time, Missi," muttered Gunz, picking up the first shot glass. "I'm not in any rush tonight." He took a deep breath and downed the vodka without flinching. Placing the empty shot glass on the table, he exhaled and closed his eyes, enjoying the feeling of the harsh burning liquid rushing down his throat.

For a few minutes, he sat quietly staring at the TV. It was set to the local news channel, but he didn't listen to the news, his thoughts far away. Then he sighed and picked up the second shot glass. He gulped the vodka and put the empty glass next to the first one.

"Hard day, Mr. Burns?" asked Missi, placing a plate with a burger and steaming pile of french fries in front of him. "You seem to look broodier than usual."

Gunz smirked. He picked up a hot french fry with his fingers and nibbled on it. "You could say so," he said finally. "Just one of those days... This day a couple of years ago, I lost... someone."

"Your friend?" asked Missi, gazing at him with sympathy in her bright eyes.

"Yeah... friend. Vladislav Kirilenko," he replied absentmindedly, taking the next burning-hot fry from his plate. "I lost him to the world of magic. He's never coming back."

"*The World of Magic*," she repeated in disbelief, her eyebrows rising. "What is that? A fantasy novel? There is no such thing as magic. You're making fun of me, Mr. Burns." She shook her head, a soft smile tugging at her full lips.

Gunz smiled tiredly and picked up the last shot glass, squeezing it in his fist. "Third one for the fallen," he murmured and drank it quickly, returning the empty glass to Missi. "You know, Missi, I've been coming to your restaurant for over a year. Don't you think it's time you stop calling me *Mr. Burns*? I don't think I'm that much older than you. You know that you can call me Zane, or even Gunz, if you prefer to use my nickname."

"I know. I don't like nicknames. You're a man, not a pet," she said lightly, taking away the empty shot glasses and wiping the tabletop with a white towel. "Zane Burns..." She pronounced his name slowly, like she was sizing it up. "Sounds good, but I prefer to call you Mr. Burns. For some reason, it seems to fit you better."

Gunz felt someone's hand on his elbow and a hardly noticeable wave of magical energy swept through him. He snapped his head to the right and found a fake blond sitting next to him. She was devouring him with her eyes, her lipstick-enhanced lips stretched in a sensual smile. Her hand unceremoniously traveled up his arm, following the shape of his biceps, and stopped at his shoulder.

"Yum," she said, gently probing him with her magic. "I'll call you anything you want, hon."

Gunz gave her a frosty once-over, turning his senses up. He had no doubt that she was something other than human. Her fingers softly massaged his shoulder, sending a stronger wave of magical energy through him. For a moment, his mind became clouded with desire and his body responded to her salacious magic with more eagerness than he expected.

Succubus, concluded Gunz, channeling the Fire, burning the poison of her magic out of his body. Her hand traveled down his arm, landing on his inner thigh. He seized her wrist, prying it off his leg and sent some fire toward his hand. Her skin blistered like from the touch of a hot stove and she yelped in pain.

"Who are you? What are you?" she whimpered, trying to free herself from his smoldering grip, but he didn't let her go.

Gunz glanced around, making sure that no one, including Missi, was watching. "I'm a man who is not looking for company," he growled, sending some fire toward his eyes. The bright flames went up in the depths of his eyes, and she gasped. "Especially not the company of your kind." He released her wrist, observing red spots of burns and blisters on her skin. "Leave this place and forget about its existence. You understand?"

She nodded, fear making her every move jerky, and rushed out of the restaurant, nursing her burnt wrist. Gunz sighed, releasing the Fire, and turned back to the bar.

"Hey, Missi," he called and waited a moment as she appeared from the kitchen. "Can I have everything to go, please? And one more before I leave." He pointed at the bottle of Russian vodka that he usually ordered.

She put a shot glass on the bar table and filled it with vodka. "That's unusual," she murmured, her hands quickly packaging the burger and fries into a take-out box. "You never drink more than three shots."

A lopsided smile crossed his face, making a single dimple

appear on one of his cheeks. "I know. Usually three shots are my limit, but today I felt like I needed more." He downed the vodka and got up, grabbing the take-out box.

Missi shook her head, checking him with concern. "Do you want me to call you a cab?"

"Thank you, Missi. I'll walk. Take care." He nodded to her and walked out of the restaurant.

* * *

Gunz walked away from the restaurant and turned into a dark alley. He stopped and rubbed his forehead tiredly. *Maybe Missi was right. I didn't need that fourth shot,* he thought, smirking. It had been a while since he felt drunk and right now the world around him seemed to be unsteady. Possibly it was a combination of vodka with the residuals of the succubus magic. He surveyed the alley carefully to make sure that no one could see him and once satisfied, he waved his hand, unfolding the fire curtain of a portal.

He walked through the fire and ended up in the backyard of his house in Coral Springs. The house wasn't really his. It belonged to his friend, but she was away and wasn't planning to come back any time soon. In the meantime, Gunz had the full use of her house. Dizziness assailed him as he took a step forward. He chuckled and sat down heavily on the steps in front of the back door.

He closed his eyes and leaned his back against the door of the house, still feeling a little buzzed. He was about to get up when he felt a soft touch to his leg. Gunz looked down and noticed a small kitten. It couldn't have been more than a month old. The kitten was trying to climb on his lap, its tiny sharp claws catching the hard fabric of his jeans.

"Oh, hello, little buddy. What are you doing here?" said Gunz. He put the take-out box on the steps and gently picked up the kitten, holding it in his hands. The kitten turned on his engine, purring loudly, and licked his hand. Gunz laughed, gently stroking the kitten's thick gray fur with his fingers. "You found the wrong man, little buddy. I'm a dog person—give me a giant German Shepherd any day. Well, occasionally, I don't mind dealing with lizards. But cats…"

The kitten ignored his statement and climbed up his shirt, settling on his shoulder. He meowed into his ear and poked his cheek with his wet nose. Gunz petted the kitten, leaving him sitting on his shoulder, and picked up the take-out box. "Well, you're taking your life in your own paws, buddy… but if you're sure that you want to adopt a man like me then let's get going." He unlocked the door and walked into the kitchen.

Inside, Gunz put the kitten on the floor and opened the refrigerator. He poured some milk in a small bowl and placed it in front of him.

"Sorry, little buddy, I don't have any cat food or litter for you"—he quickly glanced at the wall clock that was showing past one in the morning—"and it's too late for shopping. I'll buy everything you need first thing in the morning."

The kitten ignored him, preoccupied with his milk. Gunz squatted next to him and softly stroked his back. The kitten moved closer to his bowl and growled defensively. Gunz laughed, rising. "I think I'll call you Mishka in honor of my good friend. You sure remind me of him."

He left the kitten in the kitchen and walked to the living room. His body was buzzing with the exhaustion of this endless day and the incident with the succubus didn't sit well with him. Missi's restaurant was normally free of supernatural visitors. He was probably the only one. And the succubus' behavior seemed a bit odd too. Until he used his power, she didn't sense the creature of magic in him. Something didn't feel right.

His cell phone rang, making him flinch. He pulled it out and looked at the display. Jim. *One o'clock in the morning? That can't be good.* He clicked the green button, answering the call.

"Hello, Jim," he said and fell silent for a few seconds, listening to Jim. "You want me to come over now? Can it wait till morning?"

He lowered the phone down for a moment and sighed, bringing the shouting device back to his ear.

"No, I'm not drunk. Just a little—," Jim interrupted him urgently, obviously not pleased and Gunz fell silent again, listening to his boss. "Yes, sir, I know the consequences of losing control of my power and I assure you, I'm in complete control."

Gunz lowered himself on the couch, rubbing the stubble on his chin tiredly.

"Yes, sir, I know that my job doesn't have weekends and days off," he said, hoping to calm Jim down. "I'm sorry, sir, I needed to unwind a little… I'm not drunk…"

He had been working with Agent Andrews for over a year and he had never heard him talking like this to him. Something serious was going on.

"Yes, sir, I know what Code Shadow means… I understand the urgency of the situation… No, sir. You don't need to summon me."

Jim didn't have magic and he couldn't use summoning spells, but his partner, Angelique, could. She was a witch and a seer. Gunz hated when they used summoning spells to call him. The persistent pull of the summoning spell on his mind was driving him crazy, giving him a pounding headache afterwards.

"I prefer not to drive right now, so I'll open my portal to your office right away, if you don't mind… Yes, sir, to Angelique's office… I'll see you both in a few minutes."

Gunz hung up the phone and shook his head, biting his lip. Code Shadow. It meant an abnormally high level of supernatural activity, endangering civilian lives. Since he started to work with the secret division of the FBI, dealing with supernatural occurrences, it was the first time that Code Shadow was officially issued.

"Fire Salamander—go," he muttered to himself and waved his hand, opening the fire portal into Angelique's office.

* * *

Get your copy of The Burns Fire Online Today!

DEAR READER

Thank you so much for reading The Shadow Paradox. I hope you enjoyed the book and will join Damian Blake's next adventure in the fourth book of the series.

If you would like to stay up-to-date on the latest information about new releases, special offers, and more, sign up for my mailing list and get a FREE novella—www.nmthorn.com.

For more information follow me on
Facebook (www.facebook.com/nmthornauthor)
Instagram (www.instagram.com/nmthornauthor)
Or visit my website www.nmthorn.com
Join N.M Thorn's readers group to meet other readers, discuss the novels and the characters, get updates and do anything else related to the series.
www.facebook.com/groups/authornmthorn

BEFORE YOU GO...

Your reviews mean the world to me and are greatly appreciated. If you enjoyed the Shadow Deception, please take a few minutes to leave a review. It doesn't have to be long. It can be just a few words or stars rating.

Please help spread the word by taking this small extra step and leave your review on Amazon and/or Goodreads.

ALSO BY N. M. THORN

The Fire Salamander Chronicles
The Burns Path (Prequel Novella Book 0 - for my subscribers)
The Burns Fire - Book 1
The Burns War - Book 2
The Burns Defiance - Book 3
The Burns Codex - Book 4
The Burns Enigma - Book 5
The Burns Destiny - Book 6

The Shadow Enforcer Series
The Shadow Enforcer - Book 1
The Shadow Deception - Book 2
The Shadow Paradox - Book 3

ABOUT THE AUTHOR

N.M. Thorn currently lives in South Florida with her husband and son. Owner of a digital marketing agency by day and a writer by night, she loves spending her times creating new worlds, paranormal planes of existence and anything that could be described as supernatural.

When she is not busy working with everything digital or exploring fantasy worlds, she enjoys spending time with her family, reading, painting and practicing martial arts.

If you would like to share your thoughts, ideas or just send N.M. Thorn a message about the Fire Salamander world, feel free to contact her at: nmthornauthor@gmail.com

- facebook.com/nmthornauthor
- instagram.com/nmthornauthor
- amazon.com/N-M-Thorn/e/B07MY9JZMB
- bookbub.com/authors/n-m-thorn

Printed in Great Britain
by Amazon